KI'TI's STORY, 75,000 BC

BONNYE MATTHEWS

For Dee and George

KI'TI'S STORY, 75,000 BC

BOOK ONE OF WINDS OF CHANGE, A PREHISTORIC FICTION SERIES ON THE PEOPLING OF THE AMERICAS

BONNYE MATTHEWS

Bonnye Matthews

PO Box 221974 Anchorage, Alaska 99522-1974
books@publicationconsultants.com—www.publicationconsultants.com

ISBN 978-1-59433-312-5
Library of Congress Catalog Card Number: 2012946067

Manufactured in the United States of America.

Dedication

For Katy

Acknowledgements

Without the assistance of several people, this book would never have seen life. Those people are: first, my brother, Randy Matthews, and then Karen Hunt, Sally Sutherland, Skip (Lorene) Henderson, Patricia Gilmore, Robert Arthur, John Morris. Each contributed far in excess of what could be expected or hoped for on the basis of family or friendship. I also thank my publisher, Evan Swensen, who had the courage to take on this project.

INTRODUCTION

Ki'ti's Story, 75,000 BC, launches a new novel series that takes an alternative view of the peopling of the Americas. What is currently taught is that the First Americans, called Clovis people, arrived in the Americas via a "land bridge" from Russia to Alaska some 12,000 years ago. They travelled through an "ice-free corridor" in Canada to what is now the United States. Once here they covered the Americas from North through South in about 500 years, exterminating the megafauna (large animals such as mammoth, mastodon, and giant bison) evidenced by "kill sites" where bones were piled together and where, sometimes, spear points were found. The idea of a land bridge was put forward in 1589 by Fray José de Acosta, who had never been to the site. The ice-free corridor was not derived from evidence but rather from a conjecture of W. A. Johnson at the Geological Survey of Canada in 1933. The term "ice-free corridor" was coined by Ernst Antevs in 1935.

There are problems with that view. First, geneticists have shown that the land bridge was not a necessity because the arrival of people from Asia began earlier than 30,000 BC when there was no glaciation. That view is substantiated by scores of sites of human Pleistocene evidence throughout the Americas. Second, Dr. Lionel E. Jackson, Jr., of the Geological Survey of Canada, along with Canadian archaeologists, searched carefully to establish the presence of the ice-free corridor in Canada in the 1990s. They concluded, after the application of science, that there had been no ice-free passage from 21,000 to 12,000 years before the present. Third, there is another explanation of what are viewed as kill sites of megafauna. Since numbers of large animals were found together in bone beds, it makes as much—if not more—

sense to speculate that the animals may have died in groups from floods that would have been prevalent with the ending of glaciation. Just because human tools were found in the bone beds does not provide evidence that humans killed the large animals. Humans could have been at the bone beds scavenging meat from a flood kill or gathering bone and ivory to extend the life of hearth fires, for carving tools, or for carving various items, including art. Fourth, the Clovis spear points that are found at the "kill sites" have no connection with any tools made in Asia, where Clovis people supposedly originated. Instead, the Clovis spear points share characteristics with spear points made by European Solutreans. Finally, changing climate altered the vegetation available to mastodons, mammoths, and the giant bison. Extinction of megafauna did not require human intervention.

There is additional evidence that humans have been living in the Americas long before what is even being brought to light today. Some fossil data show humans present in the Americas in the hundreds of thousands of geologic years ago. There is potential for an enormous prehistory of humans in the Americas.

Ki'ti's Story begins in time with the eruption of Mt. Toba, a real supervolcano that exploded somewhere between 69,000 and 77,000 BC. The major part of the story takes place in what is today China.

For more information, see www.booksbybonnye.com

Ki'ti's Story, 75,000 BC: Book One of Winds of Change, a Prehistoric Fiction Series on the Peopling of the Americas

The Neanderthals

The People (Group 2)

Emaea

Gruid-na + Veymun

Mootmu-na + Amey   Flayk + Ermol-na

Kai + Mitrak   Ermi + Shmyukuk
   Ketra   Trokug

Ekuktu + Wamumal
   Ekoy and Smig
Lamul
Blanagah
Olintak
Lamk
Seenaha

The People (Group 1)

Wamumur

Chamul-na   Pechki + Neamu-na   Nanichak-na

Grypchon-na + Likichi   Enut +   Hahami-na

Manak   Reemast
Minagle   Slamika
Ki'ti   Domur
   Yomuk
   Elemaea
Frakja

Homo erectus   The Mol

Chief Gnomuth + Yukich

Lifu + Beway
Gukmor + Elaha
Ghoman
Mungum
Putan
Alme
Wau
Tongip
May
Untuk

Cro-Magnon   Others (The Minguat)

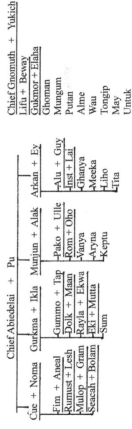

Chief Abiedelai + Pu

Cue + Noma   Gurkma + Ikla   Munjun + Alak   Arkan + Ey

Fim + Aneal   Gummo + Tap   Pako + Ulle   Alu + Guy
Rumust + Lesh   Dolk + Maan   Rom + Oho   Inst + Lai
Mulop + Gram   Rayla + Ekwa   Vanya   Ghanya
Seacah + Bolam   Eki + Mutta   Aryna   Meeka
         Sum   Keptu   Liho
                         Tita

Chapter 1

"Why? Wisdom, why?" The old man was shouting while tears of frustration rolled down his wrinkled cheeks to become lost in his beard. "We're having enough trouble just keeping the People alive without this quick, forced move to only you-know-where! Why are you letting this evil befall us? You could have forestalled this eruption or prevented it altogether. You have the power! There is nothing that justifies the time this is taking! Nothing! Do you no longer care for your People? Why are you cursing us? Ah! Who can understand you?" Wamumur shouted, shaking his fists in the air above his head. His stocky body was filled with tension. White curly hairs on his shoulders and arms glistened in the daylight. He was old at sixty, but he shouldered a backpack as heavy as any man. He was at the end of the line of refugees, with his back toward them. He would never have said those words if anyone could have heard him. It was blasphemy. Wisdom was not to be questioned. He stood there not expecting an answer, lowered his head, and then turned with a shrug and a sigh, wiped his face, and rejoined the line, taking longer strides to catch up.

Ki'ti had looked back and observed the old man shaking his fists. She was seven years old. Her blue eyes burned with fire in her small face that was framed with slightly tangled light brown hair. She knew that Wamumur, the Wise One, was talking with Wisdom, but the Wise One looked angry. She also knew that anger toward Wisdom was not right. She turned and faced the other way so he would not catch her watching. She guessed she'd seen something she shouldn't have seen. Small lines of perspiration in the dirt on her body and beads of sweat on her scalp showed her exertion in the heat.

She plodded in line with the People as they moved slowly northward. She was tired but did not complain. She wondered briefly what caused the Wise One to shake his fists. The smell of rotten eggs assailed her nostrils. There was an irritation in her lungs when she inhaled. She watched her brother, Manak, move just ahead of her. He walked almost casually, seeming never to tire, but then he was fifteen years old. Unlike the Wise One, Manak seemed to be enjoying the trip. His brown hair was cut shoulder length and secured with leather across the forehead to the back in the fashion of the young male. He carried a large load. Ki'ti had to lead dogs that were burdened with tools for the hearth and other necessities. The dogs seemed pleased to carry or drag their loads. They held their tails high and kept their heads up.

Behind them, Baambas had spewed out another plume that rose higher in the sky than any they had seen. The mountain had been puffing reddish-looking smoke for months. Finally, the People had decided they must leave their homeland. Wamumur, the Wise One, had insisted after he talked to Wisdom and fell to the ground, shaking. The Winds of Change had been exhaled from the nostrils of Wisdom. There was no alternative but to follow the lead of Wisdom. Often, so the stories told, those who didn't follow Wisdom perished. The sun was beginning to sink in the west. Soon, they would have to stop to rest and eat. Ki'ti felt the ground move again. She was more curious than frightened. Ki'ti wondered if the earth might be as hungry as her belly, which also rumbled.

Ki'ti could hear Nanichak-na from the front of the line calling a halt. She allowed herself to feel a great sense of hope that the day's march had finally concluded. She squatted on the ground to rest. The old man stood high on the hill, his white hair blowing in the wind. His bushy, stiff eyebrows stuck out beyond his eyes at odd angles. His eyebrows made her think of the large bird called the brown-eared pheasant, which had showy white feathers that stuck out of the back of its head below the chin. The back of Nanichak-na's head where the bone formed a protrusion was prominent as the breeze parted his hair at the back. Nanichak-na had a flowing beard and it, too, was moving. His sturdy body was amazing for his age. He was not called the leader, but everyone in the group looked to him for leadership. They didn't have a named leader like the Minguat people, or Others, as they were known. Nanichak-na's leather tunic was stained from the trek. The lacing in the arm strap was worn very thin and needed repair. He had a gash on his leg from a rock on the trail, but it had healed over quickly because Totamu had put herbs and honey on it. The wrap had recently been removed but blood still stained his leg in broad lines. Other older men stood near Nanichak-na. Chamul-na, her paternal grandfather, was talking to Nanichak-na. Neamu-na, her maternal grandfather, seemed to disagree with Chamul-na. She knew the language of their bodies even though she could not hear their words.

Ki'ti looked off to the west. A large group of flowers bloomed just beyond the path they followed. The flowers were almost as tall as she was. There were brilliant blues, yellows, reds, and oranges. They were flat with petals radiating from the center. Ki'ti loved to examine flowers and spent much time thinking on their different constructions. She would draw images of them in the dirt to get the differences caught in her mind web. She also compared the scents of the flowers. She knew their ecological needs and some of their medicinal uses. Leaves were just turning yellow and red on the flowers and the trees beyond. The season of colorful leaves had begun. There was a thick woodland where large animals lived in the distance. Ki'ti was not at home in the deep woods where hardwoods predominated. That was a place for the hunters. The margins were hers.

Ki'ti noticed one of the pole dog's straps had loosened; she jumped up to tighten it. She took her responsibility seriously. Some dogs carried backpacks; some dragged poles with another dog. Skins fixed to the poles held items too heavy for a single dog. Crosspieces of lighter weight branches held the poles apart. They were green wood so that they would be less likely to snap.

"I think we are going to eat and rest and then continue on," she heard Manak tell her mother, Likichi, who looked at him without expression. Manak had beautiful dark blue eyes with long eyelashes. He smiled at his mother. Likichi was tired. Her brownish gray hair was long and was held back by a piece of leather. Her face was marked with wrinkles and it showed that, normally, she smiled often. She had been carrying a heavy load as well as a two-year-old, Frakja. She busied herself getting ready to prepare trek food, but she was not pleased to be continuing on into the night, even though she suspected the need for it. She knew the mountain was rumbling and they had to flee, but flight could be very tiring. She placed Frakja's carrier to the side and whistled to two of the dogs for her hearth tools. The other women were joining her to prepare the food.

Nanichak-na had seated himself and the other men joined in a circle. Nanichak-na pointed to the ash plume high in the sky. The tip of the plume seemed to have changed direction and was headed toward them. The faces of the men did not reveal their concern, which showed only in the raised hairs on the backs of their necks.

15

"We can outrun the danger only if we can get to the caves quickly. Cave Kwa has a very large underground and that should protect us. It has water," Nanichak-na reasoned.

"Safe from what?" Manak asked.

"Safe from what is to come," the Wise One muttered. His white hair pulled back from the sides and top with a piece of leather at the back, framed his face. There was one section of hair on his left temple that refused to whiten and the brown streak gave him a look of being physically off balance at first glance, until you looked into his piercing blue eyes. Anyone knew then that if one of the People was well balanced both physically and mentally, it was he.

"Wise One," Manak asked with deference and a bowed head, "what is to come?"

Wamumur dropped his head slowly to his chest in sadness, not deference. He scratched the back of his neck and said, "The sky will become dark and filled with particles like the ones in the air now, some larger. But there will be too much of it to breathe and it will choke the life from all who are left out in the open. The particles will get larger and it will pile up on the ground."

"Have you seen this?" Chamul-na asked, scratching his head.

"No. It's in the history. The stories of Maknu-na and Rimlad tell of this. We tell this story every season of cold days. Remember how they fled from the giant Notempa?"

Manak looked up. "You mean Notempa is not a giant person?"

Nanichak-na and Grypchon-na, Manak's father, looked at each other in surprise and gently laughed. "No, Manak, Notempa was a mountain that exploded. Don't you remember how it rained down on the People for five days?" Wamumur said.

"I thought that was an expression of anger," Manak responded.

"Manak," Chamul-na, his grandfather, said gently, "the stories are what they are. They aren't trying to represent something other than what they tell. See that tall cloud? The mountain far to the southwest is clearing its throat to get ready to cough up terrible gray material from under the earth. What you see right now is just a hint of what is to come. The whole sky will cloud over and there will be little sun. It will be a time of great difficulty. That's why we have the stories in the season of cold days. It's a way we tell all the People our history and provide lessons on how to survive together through the Winds of Change."

Manak hadn't heard Chamul-na say that many words together for a long time. He listened carefully. The words had a profound effect on Manak. He had listened to the stories in the past and let his mind wander as they gathered around the fire and listened to the stories late into the night. Manak had accepted the stories more as entertainment than critical guidelines for living. His view of the stories made a dramatic shift. He knew that although Wamumur told the stories, both his father and Hahami-na, his uncle, were learning the stories verbatim from the older man. Sometimes, they were asked to tell a story around the fire. If they missed a word, the Wise One said so. Nobody realized that Ki'ti was also learning the stories word for word and she had no idea that such a thing might be unusual.

"So we call Notempa a giant because it was a big mountain?" Finally, Manak reached understanding.

"Yes. That's what Notempa means, tall mountain. You didn't know what Notempa meant?"

"I don't think anyone ever told me. I just thought it was a name."

Hahami-na leaned toward Manak. "And whose name means nothing?" he asked in his deep voice.

Manak was put on the spot. All names meant something. How could he have concluded that a name of a mountain meant nothing? Manak meant Strong Rock. He felt foolish. He crossed his arms, holding his shoulders by his fingers. His shoulders curved forward. He thought. His belly hurt.

"Uncle, my mind web must have become ensnared in daydream. I can give no reason for my lack of understanding."

"Manak," the Wise One said as he put his hand gently on Manak's back, "You learn well because you examine your own mind web and fix it when it tears. Like a good spider, you are going to be successful because you tend to what is yours. I know now that you will listen more carefully to the stories."

"Yes, Wise One." Manak glowed in the words of approval from the wise man. Manak loosened his grip on his shoulders, and let his hands rest beside him in a return to relaxation.

"We have to walk through the night because the cloud is blowing our way." Nanichak-na said.

"But Nanichak-na, the People are tired," Grypchon-na said quietly. "I don't know if all can continue at this pace."

Nanichak-na looked at the People circled around. "We do it, or the People die." He hit his left palm with his right fist. He knew the truth of his words and feared that even with the continued walk, they might not make it to the cave. Nanichak-na ran his fingers over the twelve tiny holes he'd punched in the side of his tunic. One hole was for his deceased wife and the other eleven were for his children who had died either at birth or later.

Hunting accidents killed two of his sons. Two sons died in combat. There was a drowning and one daughter had died of a fever. Four daughters died in childbirth, like the last, which took the life of his wife. Only Hahami-na had lived. For Nanichak-na, holes in his tunic represented holes in his life.

Grypchon-na looked up. "What of Totamu?" Totamu was his wife's mother's mother. She was the eldest of any of the People. At age sixty-three, she was older than Wamumur by three years. She was fine walking flat terrain, but they faced some hills between their present location and the caves.

"Totamu will have to keep up," Nanichak-na said with finality. He took his right fist and hit the palm of his left hand with it, signifying forceful finality of his words. Grypchon-na slightly raised his eyebrows but otherwise made no facial move. He, too, knew it was necessary for survival. Neamu-na seemed to have expected the sign. He was staring at the light colored earth on which he sat and didn't jump at the sound. Manak had kept his composure despite his deep love for Totamu. He had learned much in the last few moments. Life was sometimes hard. The men looked at each other and nodded agreement. At the same time, they sealed the agreement with a palm strike.

When the men rose from the circle, Reemast hit Manak on his upper arm. "So the good spider will be successful," Reemast said under his breath with a sneer.

"I hope so. I sincerely hope so," Manak replied aloud, intentionally ignoring the bait Reemast had offered in mockery.

The women had dinner prepared and the men came to be served. Those whose names carried the superior hunter "-na" suffix were served first. This was a trek meal. There was jerky and some boiled grain with some peas and beans that had been picked with haste as they left the homeland. As soon as the men were seated, the women and children were served. Ki'ti had to be wakened. She had gone to sleep beside her baby brother. Everyone ate quickly and cleaned up the tools, repacked them, and prepared to continue the trek.

The People trekked by moonlight, and, with the cooler temperature, travel was easier. The ground continued to tremble and, occasionally, there was noise with it. Ki'ti walked beside Totamu, still behind Manak. Totamu's white hair was pulled into two separate parts and held just below her ears with leather bands. She carried a light load and used a walking stick that was polished from many years of use. Her long tunic had been made recently by Pechki, her daughter. Pechki had made it of one piece of skin with a hole to put the head through and side seams instead of the single shoulder band of most of the clothing made by the People. She made it long because often, her mother chilled. The tunic fell between Totamu's knees and ankles, longer than most of the women's attire, which rarely came below the knee. Pechki had carefully drilled treasured shells with an old bone awl and tied them to the front of the tunic near the neck. A decorated garment was a novelty. The long garment was to have been a way to honor Totamu, and she wore it on the trek with pleasure. In the back of her mind, it might be her last trek, and it was a special occasion to her.

"Izumo," Ki'ti said quietly, using the term for grandmother or elder woman, "Are you well?"

"I am quite well, my child," the older woman replied automatically.

"Did you see the bear over there at the edge of the woods?" Ki'ti was frightened. She'd seen the bear clearly among the willows. Bears weren't normally that willing to show themselves when humans were present. It was the strange behavior that alarmed Ki'ti.

"Yes, my little one, I saw the bear. It won't bother us."

"How do you know?" Ki'ti asked, twisting her hair. Her eyes were open wide, searching the face of Totamu.

"It is doing the same thing we are doing, finding a safe place. It knows the earth is troubled."

"You can tell that?"

"Ki'ti, did you see how it kept stopping and anxiously looking about and sniffing?"

"Yes."

"The signs of anxiety are the clues. It's more worried about the place where it is than what's happening with other living things."

"You don't seem worried, Izumo."

"I am not worried. I have had a good life." Izumo stopped for a moment and hit her palm with her right fist, though it was awkward with the walking stick she carried. She continued, "This will either be an introduction to more life or an end. Whichever way it is, I will not be troubled."

"Izumo, you cannot die now. I need you."

"Little one, what is—is. But I will tell you, I have more ability to make this trek than some of those who are a lot younger than I am. I fully expect to make it to the cave and live with the People more years." Again, she hit her right fist into the palm of her left hand.

"There's a falling star, Izumo." Ki'ti yawned.

"They have been falling this night. You have not been looking up. They were falling last night also."

"Well, it's hard to see the path when Wisdom sucks the color from the land," she offered as an excuse for not seeing the falling stars. "Is that part of the mountain and the shaking earth?" Ki'ti looked at the dogs to be sure all was well with them. They were fine. She yawned again and again, yawn tears falling from her eyes.

Totamu walked in silence a bit. She reached into her neck bag and got a tiny piece of a leaf to put in her mouth and she began to chew. She slipped the neck bag back inside her tunic. She knew Ki'ti was bright, but she was often unprepared for the connections she made. She walked through her mind web to see whether she could make the connection that Ki'ti questioned. Finally, she said, "No. They are not connected. One is of the Underground; the other is of the Sky." Totamu reached out her hand for Ki'ti's hand. The child quickly gave it to her. Totamu was her rock. She was calmed by the touch of a hand and small talk that all would be well with her world, even though the Winds of Change were blowing.

As night wore on, Ki'ti stumbled. She was terribly tired. She was the youngest of the trekkers. Her younger brother was carried.

"Manak," Wamumur called from the rear.

Manak turned around and faced the Wise One.

"Get your sister and put her on my backpack."

Manak replied, "But I . . . ." Wamumur's stern glare silenced Manak's intended offer to carry her. He picked up Ki'ti and placed her on her belly across Wamumur's already heavy backpack where she quickly fell to sleep. The trek continued. Manak made a mental note to carry tired, small children in the future so elders didn't find the need to do it.

Behind Totamu in line were Minagle and Domur. Minagle was Ki'ti's twelve-year-old sister and Domur was Hahami-na and Enut's thirteen-year-old daughter. Minagle and Domur were close friends. Each carried a pack just a little lighter than Manak, Slamika, and Reemast carried. Slamika and Reemast were Domur's brothers. Slamika was sixteen and Reemast was eighteen. The girls struggled but tried hard not to let their struggling show. Each was proud of her own strength, despite the fact that the People discouraged pride.

"Which of my brothers will be your husband, Minagle?" Domur asked as they climbed a tough hill.

"I don't know." In fact, Minagle didn't care for either one of them. Minagle was concerned about the subject. She was very slender, unlike the rest of the People who were stocky. Her hair was jet black, straight, and thick, framing a face that was different from the People. Her forehead didn't take the gentle slope at the brow but rose vertically instead. The hair of the People was fine and brown to reddish. She also had brown eyes, while most of the People had blue, hazel, or greenish eyes. Minagle didn't care for Slamika because he was unattractive to her and rarely talked. She disliked Reemast because he kept creeping up on her when she was gathering. She didn't like their reddish hair. Reemast would pin her down and grope her under her tunic while he laughed. So far, he hadn't forced her to copulate, but he was threatening, and she was uncomfortable around him. Maybe he knew she wasn't woman yet. She often wondered what he would do when she became woman.

"You like my brother?" Minagle asked, shifting the perspective, already knowing the answer.

Domur looked at Minagle and smiled. "I cannot wait to become woman. Manak is special and I really want him for my husband."

"I am sure that he wants you also, my friend. Sometimes, he has asked me questions about you." Minagle smiled.

"Like what?"

"What your meat preference is," Minagle responded and paused, "and whether you like him."

"What did you tell him?"

"I told him that you liked aurochs and him."

"You didn't!" Domur knew that the meat preference was often what the prospective husband had to exchange for a wife. Aurochs was more than what would be appropriate. "If he had to get one of those for me, he'd get to be Manak-na at an early age—or we'd have to wait a long time." Her last comment ended with a drop in voice.

"The way he feels about you, he'd find a way to get it as soon as you become woman." Minagle did a palm strike.

Behind the girls, Enut had heard snatches of the girls' conversation. She was having serious trouble breathing but her hearing was sharp. She knew that Minagle didn't care for her sons, and that bothered her. *Her sons were fairly good hunters and should be a good match for any girl of the People, but then Minagle didn't look like the People. Sons needed wives. Reemast should be Minagle's choice,* Enut thought, *because he had a great sense of humor and had good vitality. Slamika didn't talk much so nobody knew what he thought. He didn't seem very interested in Minagle, and she was the only girl available for a long time. Ki'ti was only seven and it would be years before she was ready. Of course, whichever brother got Minagle, he could share his wife with his brother. That might be the best. At least, until Ki'ti became woman. Minagle was, perhaps, too high-minded to be such a strange-looking female. She needed a husband to straighten her out.* Enut's thoughts shifted to her breathing. The girls had stopped talking. The headband to help ease her load was cutting into Enut's forehead. She was sweating and was very tired. Her breathing whistled when she exhaled through pursed lips. She coughed frequently. She was aware that her health was failing but had discussed it with no one. All that mattered to her was reaching the cave. She had a spell of dizziness but kept her footing and continued on.

Just before daybreak, Nanichak-na shouted a long O sound three times and the column came to a halt. The whistle came from Nanichak-na to the end of the line, and was answered with another whistle. The whistling told Wamumur at the end of the line that Nanichak-na had spotted Cave Kwa. It seemed they would be safe. The line began to move again. Suddenly, the earth moved with a great jarring and then a rolling. Wamumur and Nanichak-na looked back. There were multiple plumes from Baambas, and those didn't seem to subtract from the smoky output, since all were equally large. Their eyes squinted and their lips thinned. This was something for which they had not been prepared. Without a word, all adults knew that this was unprecedented and they moved along at a faster pace. Even though Enut was struggling, she tried to keep up, but her breathing was worsening and she was lagging. Her cough was increasing in frequency. Wamumur whistled. Nanichak-na halted the line. Wamumur sent a message to Nanichak-na that Enut was failing. Nanichak-na told Slamika and Reemast to put their arms around their mother and help her along. The column began to move again.

When they neared the cave, they had hardly reached the entrance when they saw light. It was not necessarily a good sign to see light from a cave they expected would be empty, but something was beginning to rain down and they entered, wondering what would happen. They were met by another group of the People they already knew. Greetings were extended. Each of the newcomers laid down their burdens and stopped to wash their feet using water from the bowls provided for them. Then the men circled and sat or kneeled to talk. The women were shown areas where it would be good for them to set up residence, out of the way of the entrance.

Wamumur looked around. His eyes sought Emaea, his love from youth, whom he had not been able to marry. Was Thrullut-na still living? Thrullut-na wasn't at the circle of men. He thought he saw Emaea over with the women, but he couldn't be sure and he had to attend to the male conversation. Instead of feeling the overwhelming exhaustion of brief moments before, Wamumur felt the giddiness of energy and youth and hope.

"We saw the Minguat as we crossed the toothed mountains. There were many of them," Gruid-na said.

"How many of the Others?" Nanichak-na asked. A piece of facial hair got caught in his mouth and he pulled it out.

Gruid-na showed ten fingers four times. His brown eyes reflected concern.

"How many hunters?" Nanichak-na persisted.

Gruid-na showed ten fingers twice. "No more than that."

"How far away?"

"Less than a day from here now."

"Were they heading this way or toward Cave Sumbrel?"

"How can one say?" Gruid-na asked. "The path they trekked headed toward Cave Sumbrel but there is a path near the creek that leads here."

Nanichak-na looked toward Manak. "Go to the cave entrance, study the falling particles, and return to report to us of it."

Manak got to his feet quickly and sprinted to the cave entrance. He returned, reseated himself, and said, "You can see nothing. It is very thick and it's entering the cave. It's this deep," he said showing the first digit of his forefinger.

"You can stand on it without mashing it flat," Manak added, holding out his hand to Gruid-na and showed him the material. Gruid-na held his hand palm upwards and Manak emptied his hand into Gruid-na's.

Gruid-na said, "Thank you, Manak," slightly lowering his head.

Manak lowered his head in respect.

Gruid-na examined it. It was gritty gray powder with a few very tiny granules. He sniffed it very lightly noting the sulfurous odor. He passed the handful to the others. Each examined it carefully. It was caustic.

"If they are still trekking, they will die," Nanichak-na said, voicing what others suspected. "Let's call this ash," he said quietly.

Wamumur cleared his throat. "We must plan. There will be a food scarcity when this ash stops falling. We will need to hunt for the animals that we can find and prepare the meat so that we can survive until the land heals itself and living animals are available. We have to see that neither we nor our people starve. We will need hunters to hunt and the younger males can gather firewood. Is there coal nearby?"

Gruid-na shook his head. "I know of no coal."

Ermol-na, Gruid-na's thirty-eight-year-old son-in-law cleared his throat. He was late to have white hair. At thirty-eight, he should have some white, but his hair was solid black. Against the black hair and olive complexion, his pale brown eyes were startling. They looked like wolf eyes, flecked as they were with gold. "There's a place. It's not far from here. We used to go there to gather coal when I was a child. It's between here and Cave Sumbrel."

"When the ash stops falling, you could take several people and begin to stockpile coal in the cave," Gruid-na said, glad for once that his daughter had married this slender fellow with the light brown eyes.

Ermol-na lowered his head to Gruid-na. Ermol-na smiled. His life was special for once. He couldn't wait to share with Flayk. He listened as the other assignments were made for the time when the ash ceased to fall.

The women automatically began to store the foodstuffs they had brought to the common area. Food was always something the People owned together. Even when two groups joined, all food was combined for the use of all. There was no differentiation according to group. There was very little personal ownership of anything. It seemed fortuitous that there was a good complementary mix of food that had been brought. The women busied themselves with the evening meal.

Each person had roles in their original groups. When the two groups gathered, nobody needed to tell other People what to do. There was a unified understanding. Even the young knew what was expected. The People were not by nature rebellious but worked together in harmony as they had for hundreds of thousands of geologic years. Voices were low as they spoke what was needed and little that wasn't as they worked. It never occurred to the People that not working might be an option. For far longer than anyone living could remember, this was the way to live successfully. They must preserve the group at all costs or the People would perish. It was the way of Wisdom.

Totamu hugged her friend, Emaea. "How is it with your People?" she asked.

"The good news is that Mootmu-na and Amey have" she showed seven fingers "living children. There is only"—she showed one finger—"other child born to Ermi and Shmyukuk. Each generation shrinks, and I have remained barren. And you?"

"Of this latest generation, one pair has"—she showed four fingers—"and the other"—she showed three fingers. "We, too, shrink. I was a child of"—she showed ten fingers and then five. "If I remember right, you were a child of more than that. What is happening?"

"I don't know. I worry. So many children cannot be born because their heads won't pass. To save the mothers, we've had to pull them out and damage their heads so they don't live. Two of Neamu-na's daughters died when their babies wouldn't pass. The girls were so young. It's horrible. To lose mothers and babies is double loss." Emaea looked sickened.

"We've had the same problem with babies not being able to pass," Totamu admitted. "Some others are born dead for no reason we can see. I worry about our long term survival."

Emaea nodded solemnly.

Ki'ti and her sister, Minagle, saw to the dogs that were placed near the cave entrance. They unburdened, fed, and watered each dog. Unsure what to do, the dogs relieved themselves just outside the opening of the cave beyond where the People had walked. Later, the men would sweep a large area for the dogs. The girls wondered why they were the only ones with dogs.

Ki'ti looked around. She noticed that Enut was sitting on her sleeping mat. She looked very tired, and she was sitting with her arms around her legs and her shoulders pulled far forward. Ki'ti walked over to her and said, "My aunt, are you well?"

"I struggle to get a breath," Enut answered honestly with no trace of self pity, almost too bland. Enut was not fully alert. Few thoughts crossed her mind. She was mesmerized by the sounds of her own breathing. She experienced neither fear nor sadness once she realized she was dying.

Ki'ti walked over to Totamu. When Totamu recognized her, she said, "Izumo, Enut is struggling to breathe. Can you help her?"

Totamu put her hand on Ki'ti's shoulder. "I will go."

Ki'ti lowered her head. She watched Totamu go to Enut and take out the bag she wore around her neck. She saw her give Enut a leaf to chew. She took another leaf and broke off a piece of it. She put it into a gourd and carried it to the clay pot that held heating water. She spooned hot water into the gourd and took it to Enut. Ki'ti could hear her say, "Drink all of this and do it while it's hot. It doesn't taste good, but drink it anyway. I'm suffering with the same problem. These leaves help a lot." Making eye contact, Totamu put her hand on the side of Enut's face. She stared into her granddaughter's eyes. Enut put her hand on the side of Totamu's face. They spoke in silence with their eyes. Then Totamu returned to her work. Both women knew that Enut's condition was grave. Totamu was irritated with herself for failing to recognize the severity of Enut's condition during the trek, but even if she had, she admitted, she could have done little.

Ki'ti settled down on her sleeping mat, waiting for her time to be served food. She looked at the cooking pot and wondered why fire made black above where it warmed things. A great jarring of earth occurred. It knocked Manak off his feet and the sight of it caused her to chuckle, because he was always so strong and athletic. For just a second, he looked like a dead bug lying on his back. She caught sight of Minagle and Domur who had heard her chuckle, and she expected their expressions to be unfavorable, but instead they too shared a smile at Manak's expense, but they tried to hide it behind their hands. Ki'ti learned. From then on, she would remember to cover her mouth when she smiled at other people when it might be inappropriate.

Meanwhile, Wamumur had found that Thrullut-na had died in a hunt when he fell over a cliff. On hearing the news, he tried very hard not to show the excitement he felt. After they ate and things calmed down, he would search for a chance to be alone with Emaea. The men were called and they lined up, -na hunters first, to be served dinner.

Later that day after the evening meal, Blanagah, the fourteen-year-old grand-daughter of Gruid-na, noticed Manak and Reemast. Blanagah had brown hair that she could sit on when it wasn't braided down the back. She had large wide set blue eyes. She was particularly drawn to Reemast because of his apparent status in the People. She found his reddish hair fascinating. His self esteem appeared very high and it appealed to her. He was to her like a male bird, showy to attract a mate. He seemed to have a sense of humor. She noticed that he seemed interested in Minagle and that Manak had eyes only for Domur. Blanagah was eager to find a husband. She and her sister, Olintak, who was a year younger, would have to find husbands outside their group. Blanagah would have had Kumut for her husband and Olintak was to have been the wife of Lamon, but both men were killed while hunting. Blanagah would like to have Reemast for herself and for her sister to take Slamika. Both brothers looked alike, but she observed that Slamika was too quiet for her taste. For them to join these brothers would settle both of them. She was justifiably shocked when she saw Reemast grab Minagle around the waist and head off toward the entry to the cave. Minagle was struggling but Reemast had his hand over her mouth. She could not hear Reemast threaten her, but she thought it was a game because he was laughing. How she longed to be in Minagle's position and be part of the game. She had found out that Minagle was not woman yet, so Blanagah had hope.

At the cave entrance, which was not visible to the cave because there was a curve in the entryway, Reemast held Minagle's head securely. He told her to hold her tongue or he would hurt her badly. She believed him and was silent. The falling ash frightened her but not as much as when he lifted her tunic and ran his rough hands over her breasts, squeezing and pinching. His hands cupped her buttocks, and he found her private parts and felt them, rubbing against her flesh with his fingers, but not penetrating. She tried to push him away, but her strength was nothing compared to his. Her fury grew. She had no idea how to handle such an outrage. The dogs noticed, and one growled so quietly that nobody in the cave would have paid any attention. The dogs had been trained to be silent unless a stranger approached.

Reemast told her, "As soon as you become woman, I will be your husband."

"You will not!" she responded immediately, trying unsuccessfully to jerk herself free from his grasp.

"You are wrong. What is your favorite meat?"

Minagle stared at him hard, "Rhinoceros."

Reemast laughed. "Then I shall have to threaten to hurt you very badly until you say mouse."

"Then you will have to hurt me," she scowled.

That seemed to make Reemast think. He had never considered her consenting to being hurt. The People would notice an injury and that could bring disfavor upon him. They had come to a deadlock. Without consideration, however, he walked nearer the cave entrance and while he held her arm tight, he punched her in the solar plexus. She slumped but he held her in his arms while she tried to recover breathing.

While she struggled, he laughed out loud. He told her, "Think of that any time you think of the word 'rhinoceros'." He touched her again and she did not resist. Silently, tears rolled down the dirt on her face. Reemast stood there with her, savoring his victory. He wiped her tears away with his fingers so that her crying would be less evident. "There will come a day when you beg me to touch you," Reemast said as he turned away and left her at the cave entrance. She remained there for a few minutes and then turned and went to her sleeping mat and buried herself beneath the skin covering. Her silent tears and anguish went unnoticed. She felt utterly helpless and alone in the midst of many People.

The People were preparing for sleep. The men were discussing who would watch the cave entrance and how to divide up the watch. Surely, nobody would be outside during the falling ash, but it was always wise to be prepared. Mootmu-na, Gruid-na's son, and Neamu-na would take the first watch. After the wick in the oil lamp burned down, they would awaken Hahami-na and Ermol-na for the second watch.

Several days into the ashfall, Blanagah made her intentions clear to Reemast. He considered the idea of becoming husband to Blanagah and realized it would be to his benefit. They could copulate and he could still harass Minagle and keep her silent about it. Reemast and Blanagah went to the men's council and asked for permission to be joined. Bringing the meat exchange for a wife was impossible in the ashfall, so they asked for what would be considered a waiver of the requirement. When the thought of joining Olintak to Slamika was not met with any disfavor from those two, the People rejoiced. There were two joinings, and that would be good for the People. A celebration was set up for the evening of the fourth day of ashfall. Gruid-na would make the pronouncement.

After the evening meal, the People gathered and Gruid-na pronounced the two couples joined. The drum made of stretched deer hide that Ermol-na had carried to the cave was brought out and there was music and dancing. Minagle was thrilled because her thoughts were that now she would be free of Reemast's unwanted attention. As sleep time drew near, the two couples took their sleeping mats and oil lamps and found places deeper into the cave where they could be alone for First Night. Minagle felt a sense of freedom that she hadn't realized she had missed. She longed for a bath, but in the cave, she thought such luxuries were unavailable. How she missed home. Life had been simpler when she was younger. She and Domur had swum like fish in the river and gathered greens on the rolling hills. The sun shone from a blue sky and the days were warm. Baambas was beautiful, not life threatening.

Finally, on the fifth day of ashfall, there was a let up. Looking from beyond the cave entrance, there was a whole area of monochrome. The land everywhere was light gray. It was about two feet deep at the cave entrance. Everyone who stood and gazed outside was amazed. Never had they seen such a sight. The plan was to search for meat, and with this view, hunters expected any meat they would find to be dead already. They discussed the ashfall and the women had already begun to make protection for the hunters because the ash was caustic. They made booted pants with straps to go over the shoulder under the tunics. Women were working as fast as possible to accomplish this task. Even Minagle, Domur, Blanagah, and Olintak were enlisted into making the protective gear. The elders showed the younger girls and women how to make holes in the leather so they could run narrow leather strips in and out of the holes to sew the two pieces together. At each end of the sewing line, they tied off the ends with knots. Even the young boys and girls would eventually have these garments so they could gather wood and be protected from the caustic ash and not track ash into the cave when they returned. Every minute counted where meat was concerned.

Minagle and Domur were sent to gather water from its source deep in the cave. They carried an oil lamp and gourds. On their way out on the first trip, Reemast stepped out. "Go ahead, Domur," he said. "I want to have a word with Minagle." Domur thought the request odd, but she demurred and left her friend with her brother. Reemast took the oil lamp and held Minagle's arm tightly. He headed back into the deeper part of the cave. Minagle's heart was pounding and she was terrified. She stumbled but Reemast held her up.

When they reached the place that Reemast had taken his wife their first night, he shoved Minagle to the ground. He raised her tunic and made her lie down. He put his knee between her thighs and separated them. Then he laid himself atop her. Minagle was trembling in panic but kept silent. He put his mouth on her breasts. He began to touch her private parts. Then he placed his hard penis against her and she almost screamed out. "Don't worry, Minagle, I won't penetrate you until you are woman. That has to be soon." But Minagle was horrified that the enlarged hard object she had just seen and now felt against her would someday do just that. She wept. Reemast bit her and then jumped up. He wiped off her face and told her to stop the tears. He pulled her up roughly and helped readjust her tunic. It still galled him that she didn't want him.

They met Domur on her return. Reemast took the filled gourds that Minagle had set down. He would carry them up to the food preparation area. Minagle would go back down with Domur and fill the gourds that waited below. Minagle carried the oil lamp so shakily that Domur asked what had happened. When they reached the water, Minagle's tears could not be stopped. Slowly, with greater emotional than physical pain, she told Domur what had been happening. She was broken. She had hoped that when Reemast joined with Blanagah he'd leave her alone. She guessed wrong. Domur was outraged. She knew her brother and this story did not really shock her. He had teased her unmercifully when she was little. They carried up the gourds and Domur ran to Totamu. She asked her to join them down by the water. Totamu waited a few minutes and then took a few more gourds and went below. Then she heard Minagle's story from end to end. Totamu lifted Minagle's tunic and saw the bite mark on her breast. Totamu was outraged. She took her neck bag and unrolled a tiny bag. She put powder on her tongue and then rolled it around. Then she spat it into her hand. She put the mixture on the bite mark. "Leave this to me," Totamu said. Both girls lowered their heads.

Two hunters had been chosen to go to look for meat. The hunters were Hahami-na and Mootmu-na. Totamu scanned the cave. Reemast was with his wife. Totamu signaled with her hands for Gruid-na and Nanichak-na to follow her to the cave entrance. Both did with no little curiosity. At the entrance after checking carefully, Totamu explained the situation. "This has to stop now and forever," she said.

"Agreed!" both said at the same time with a sharp strike of the right fist into the left palm. Nanichak-na even went so far as to say that it made all men look bad, and that if Blanagah were pregnant, he'd castrate Reemast with no second thought. Gruid-na thought that was a little harsh. Finally, Nanichak-na stated flatly, "I will bring him to our gathering to pronounce our findings. Gruid-na, please, bring the hunters here before they are gone." He left and returned with a puzzled Reemast and all the cave members who sat in total silence in the gathering area. "Sit!" Nanichak-na ordered Reemast. Reemast sat. The hunters outfitted in their booted garments stood at the back of the gathering.

Nanichak-na remained standing and said, "Here is my pronouncement. From this day forth, Reemast, you will never touch Minagle or engage her in conversation or look at her. You will stay as far away from her as possible. If you break this pronouncement, if you say a word to her, if you even look at her, you will be castrated immediately. Then your hands will be severed from your body. You will leave the People to fend for yourself. Your wife can choose to go with you or remain here. You had better hope that no ill ever befalls Minagle, for you will be suspected first. Straighten out your mind web or leave us. That is all I have to say." All people struck their left palms with their right fists except Reemast. Not all the People knew why the pronouncement was made, but they knew that whatever the reason, it was a good one. Reemast was utterly bewildered. Having his way with Minagle was over. He felt that his world was falling apart. For the first time in his life, he experienced fear and the metallic taste it left in his mouth. All he could do was lower his head.

Minagle was shocked. She did not know there was a solution to her problem. This was an amazing pronouncement. She wondered if she could really feel safe again. She'd been mistaken once. All the People had used the force sign except, of course, Reemast. Ermol-na, Nanichak-na, and Wamumur noticed that Reemast had not joined the palm strike. Without another thought, the People got back to work.

Nanichak-na went to where Minagle sat with Domur. He extended his hand and Minagle stood up and took his hand. He carried an oil lamp and walked toward the path that led down to the cave water. They did not speak until they had gone into a round room that was deeper into the cave than Minagle had ever been. There were strange shapes hanging from the ceiling and rising from the floor. Nanichak-na motioned for Minagle to sit. She did.

"I regret what happened to you, Minagle. I wish I had known sooner. I will keep my eyes on Reemast and so will the People. This is not a normal occurrence. In my life, I have only known of two other times this happened. My concern is you right now. It is for the good of the People that you join and have children. I want to know how you feel about that."

Minagle looked at him and smiled wistfully as his great gently sloping brow was nearer to her. He had bowed his head to her. That was unheard of. The eyebrows that so fascinated everyone were near. "I do not know, Great Hunter. Until now, I vowed I would kill myself before I'd ever let any man come near me."

Nanichak-na was startled. No one had ever addressed him as Great Hunter. He felt a glow of pride and then quickly stifled it. He said, "That is what I feared. Minagle, you have let your mind web believe that all men are like Reemast. That is not true. You have to know that the entire People have struck palm with fist for you. Each one of us is bound to protect you. It is now Reemast who is afraid."

For the first time ever, Minagle realized that things had truly changed and her tormentor was now afraid. "I just wanted so much for him to leave me alone."

"Well, now he must." Nanichak-na lifted her face to see her eye to eye and continued, "What I want you to know is that what he did to you was not joining as a man and woman. This was different. When you join, what you and your husband will do is not what occurred to you. Reemast was trying to make you fear him. A husband is tender and caring, not forceful and domineering. I don't know where he got that idea. Can you not see that he treats his wife differently from the way he treated you?"

"Yes."

"I want you to keep that in mind. What happened to you should be kept separate in your mind web from copulating with your future husband. It is two separate things. Look to your parents. Do they not even at this age look tenderly at each other?"

Minagle smiled. Her parents, Grypchon-na and Likichi, were tender with each other. So were Hahami-na and Enut. So were Pechki and Neamu-na. "I see."

"Do you still think you might kill yourself before joining?"

Minagle smiled. "I really want to live, but I don't want to live with fear gripping my throat all day every day. I want to live like I was before this happened."

"My Dear One, what is—is. You cannot undo what has occurred, but you can put it in its right place in your mind web. Sometimes People do really evil things to other People. I don't know why. But the potential is there. Maybe Reemast couldn't handle your rejection. That is his problem, not yours. But he acted on it and that caused the pronouncement to have to be made. You have full protection of the People. In fact, if he tries anything else and is banished, I may follow him and kill him so that he cannot do this evil any longer."

Minagle looked into the dark blue eyes of Nanichak-na. He was deadly earnest. She shuddered when she realized that a great hunter would kill to keep her safe. She didn't wish to be responsible for a death but she didn't want to continue to experience great fear.

"I am trying to tell you that you should consider yourself as safe as anyone who walks through this life. Reemast is in the past. Believe me he will probably know now that he's dead if he tries any more foolishness with you."

Minagle bowed her head. "I will try to put this away where it belongs in my mind web. Thank you for this talk." She lowered her head.

He lifted her face so they looked eye to eye. "Minagle, if you ever want to talk more, tell me. I will talk to you any time you have a need."

Minagle was astounded. High level People didn't normally extend their time to young girls. She bowed her head as low as she could. "Thank you."

"Now, let us go back up and prepare to eat."

The hunters returned just before time for the evening meal. They had in fact found meat. An aurochs and a large straight-tusked elephant both lay nearby to the southwest in the forest. They planned to harvest the following day. It was a good day for the People. Totamu added that the hunters should carefully remove the animal skins. They did not know what would result from the ashfall, and if weather turned cold like in the season-of-cold-days story of Maknu-na and Rimlad, they might need the skins, and whole skins were preferred. There would be a lot of skin preparing, but the season of cold days was approaching and the timing was good.

Likichi left the baby to Ki'ti and took Minagle to her sleeping mat. "I want to talk," her mother said. They were seated. "Long ago, I was down by the creek daydreaming. I had gone alone. It was not a good idea. Suddenly, I was taken from behind and snatched off. The hunter ran with me like the wind. I have never known anyone who could run so fast. I could not see anything but the ground. All I knew is that he was full of black hair on his arms and legs and on his back. I wondered if he was part animal. I probably should have bitten him or tried to gouge out his eyes, but those thoughts never entered my mind. Nobody followed us even though I screamed and screamed. I guess I'd gone too far from home. We reached the edge of a great hill. There were humans there but they were not People. Their heads were shoved up straight above the nose. Their skin was somewhat darker than ours. They were full of hair that was very black. I thought I must be dreaming. They talked in a way I could not understand. Everything I knew was turned upside down. People were talking fast with voices that sounded like dogs barking. They pointed to a place for me to sit and so I sat there. There was one man with white hair who seemed to tell Others what they could and could not do.

That night, the Other who had captured me came to copulate with me several times. He never asked my permission."

Minagle gasped. She couldn't help herself, so she asked, "Were you woman?"

"Yes. Manak was born then. He was baby. It happened and I was miserable, but at least I knew what copulating was and had been with one who loved me. Every night, he would come to me expecting to copulate. There was no preparation; he just did what he chose and that was it. If I refused, he'd beat me and I would have to give in. Finally, I managed to escape. They were faster but I was better at seeing at night and in making care to leave the least in the way of tracks. I made it home. When you were born, the People thought that I had somehow kept the face of the Other who captured me in my mind web. They thought that was why you looked different. But I don't think so. That man had black hair. You were the only child I had who looked like you. I think it was in the copulating. But it doesn't matter. I love you even if you do look different. I think your hair is lovely, like a sky at dusk." Likichi brushed her hand against Minagle's hair. "I just want you to know that sometimes People have to endure hardships that are not in their capacity to control, like this ashfall. Sometimes, joy comes from the suffering, like you, my lovely daughter. My suffering brought me the joy of you."

"That is like what Nanichak-na told me earlier."

"He talked to you about what you experienced?" Likichi was astounded that Nanichak-na had counseled Minagle.

"Yes. He wants me to have a husband and children for the People. He doesn't want my mind web to think wrong things about copulating and what happened to me."

"Did the talk help?"

"Yes, my mother, the talk helped, just like your talk helped. I am less afraid now. For a while, I thought I was alone and there was no help for me. I thought I would have to kill myself if I had to join with a husband, because it was too terrible to think about."

"I'm glad that you understand that joining with a husband and what happened to you are different. We don't have a word for what happened to you. I am just so regretful that it did. If you feel a need to talk in the future, please come to me. I will listen."

"Thank you my mother." Likichi put her arm around Minagle, something she didn't do often, even though she loved her daughter. Minagle nestled against her mother for a brief time and then got up and went to her sleeping mat.

Wamumur walked back from the cave entrance and noticed that Ki'ti had lined up small sticks beside her baby brother who was sleeping. She was talking and talking. He observed briefly and then, using the quiet hunter's walk, he moved where he could hear. To his utter shock, she was telling a season-of-cold-days story to the sticks and the baby. Her memory was incredible for one so young and her inflection was perfect. He retraced his steps and then called to her.

Ki'ti came to him at once, the baby in her arms. She lowered her head.

"How long have you been telling stories, Ki'ti?" he asked.

His question startled her. "I don't know, Wise One," she replied.

"How many stories do you know?"

Ki'ti looked at her hands. She didn't know how to add up the stories. "I don't know," she responded with her head lowered as far as possible.

"Ki'ti, do not worry. I am just surprised at what you are doing." He reached out and raised her head so they were looking at each other eye to eye. "I want to spend time with you and this cave time is good. I want you to tell me every story you know and if there are errors, we can fix them."

"Then I will not be punished for telling the stories to sticks?"

"Ah, you know that rule. Sticks cannot repeat the stories, Ki'ti. Neither can a baby. We don't want the stories told by People to anyone who will retell them. They might retell them wrong. That would confuse our history, and lessons vital to our understanding of the Winds of Change would be worthless."

"I see."

Wamumur leaned his head back and laughed out loud. "I believe you. I will talk to your parents about needing to spend time with you. We will need much time."

Ki'ti lowered her head. She returned to her sleeping mat to play with her brother. She didn't resume the storytelling. She was confused.

Wamumur saw an opportunity to talk to Emaea. He headed toward the cave entrance. "Emaea, may I have a word with you?"

Emaea stopped and turned to see his face light up just as it had in his youth when he looked on her. Wamumur saw that hers glowed in the same way. The Winds of Change had not affected their attraction. "I guess I should extend my . . . ."

"Do not speak of it," Emaea cut him off. "Neither of us can truthfully say we're sorry. Both of us did what we had to do. Every group has to have a storyteller. The Winds of Change have brought us together again. We are old but we are no different from when we were young."

"Speak for yourself. My back is killing me," Wamumur admitted with a grin.

"I meant about the way we feel about each other," Emaea chuckled and pushed at his shoulder.

Then they stood there holding hands.

Across the cave, Gruid-na put his arm around the shoulders of his wife, Veymun, and said, "Finally. I knew this would happen the moment he walked into the cave. It is so bittersweet."

She smiled at him. Ever since Thrullut-na died, they had known that Emaea yearned for Wamumur. They had no idea how to locate him or they might have tried. No one was surprised when Wamumur's sleeping place was empty that night while Emaea's was bulging.

Wisdom moved the sun so the rays of light touched the sky and darkness was slowly dispelled. All but two of the hunters dressed in their booted garments and prepared to harvest. Neamu-na, Hahami-na, Slamika, Manak, Ermi, Kai, and Lamul went to harvest meat. Two of the hunters, Mootmu-na and Reemast, joined Ermol-na to go to the site where he remembered a coal deposit. The home guard was Wamumur and Ekuktu. Reemast had also lost the ability ever to be part of the home guard. The harvesters carried brooms that were used to clean the floors of their homes. They had tried them at the cave entrance and could move ash with them. That is how they had kept an area for the privy. While the men teased each other about their outfits, the sounds of home in the cave were pleasant. The fires from the morning meal had been permitted to die down but not go out. The women had swept the cave floor and tools from the morning meal had been cleaned. Blanagah and Olintak had gone down to refill the gourds of water.

On the way down, Blanagah asked Olintak, "How do you like your husband?"

"He doesn't talk much."

"Now, that's a strange answer." Blanagah looked at Olintak's pinched face and felt genuine pity.

"Well, he is just so silent. I don't know whether he is happy or sad or maybe just has no emotion."

"How was your first night?"

"He went to sleep."

"You have copulated?"

"Only once."

"You cannot be serious!"

"I am. I don't know what to do. Am I unattractive?"

Blanagah stared at her sister. She thought Olintak was more attractive than she was, but she would never have said that. "Of course not! He's the odd one, not you. Are you encouraging him?"

"I do everything I can to arouse him. It seems difficult for him to become erect. It's as if it's too much effort."

"Oh, Olintak, I am so sorry to hear that. Do you want to borrow Reemast?" She breathed a sigh of relief that she had gotten the brother she wanted.

"I think after yesterday that would not be a good idea."

"That's true. We're both in a mess, aren't we?"

"It looks like it. Maybe we were both in too much of a hurry to be wives." Olintak gently hit her left palm with her soft fist.

"Well, we weren't getting any younger and with this ashfall, who knows when we will see People. And if he can't join with you, at least make him hold you."

"I hadn't thought about that. I'll try it."

Wamumur was sitting in view of the cave entrance, eyes focused outside but not really seeing while he listened to Ki'ti tell her first story. He listened with a deep part of his mind web. Any deviation would rattle the web at that depth and he could correct. Ki'ti told the story of the creation of People and their emergence from the womb of the earth. It was not one of the longer stories but she had executed the telling perfectly. He was already persuaded that Ki'ti was the next Wise One, but he forced himself to check out her memories story by story. Skepticism was critical to keep the stories alive and accurate. The outside view began distracting him. He was fine as long as he kept his eyes shut. Occasionally, he'd lapse from his focus and he'd look at her. When he saw how tiny she was, he still wondered at her being able to remember so much so well at such a young age. He had not been that young when he was discovered. In her first story, she was running circles around her father and uncle, and they had studied for many, many years. But she was so tiny. He tried to keep his focus with his eyes shut. He was eager to discuss the story with her afterward to see whether she understood the connection between the emergence from the womb of the earth at birth to the return to that womb of the earth at death. The cycle was embedded in the story but was not specified exactly in the telling. Other cycles would be based on that cycle. He would never have guessed when he carried her as an extra burden on his backpack at the end of the trek that she might be the future Wise One.

Armed with their brooms, Ermol-na had led Mootmu-na and Reemast to the coal bed. They wondered how Ermol-na had been able to find it with all the ash and over all the years he had been away from it. Covered with ash, landscapes lost their unique character. They had begun to sweep away the ash so they could get at the coal. It was tedious work. Ermol-na had a clear picture in his mind web so that the sweeping would not place ash any deeper on any of the area where coal was accessible. It took hours just to begin to see the coal emerging. They had stone hammers and bags made of woven plant fibers that served to carry the pieces of coal. They chipped away piece by piece. Reemast still remembered yesterday. From time to time, his mouth would taste of copper and he would shudder at the pronouncement. Occasionally, he'd chew the edge of his thin mustache. The whole group had basically said that if he approached Minagle, they would kill him slowly. To be castrated, have his hands cut off, and be banished would kill him even if Blanagah joined him. He couldn't understand how the secret could have been revealed. He wondered if someone had been watching, but he didn't think so. He blamed Minagle. Minagle should have been too afraid to talk about it. He wanted to get even with her for ruining his life, but he could think of no way that might not put him at risk of death. All the People, even the little ones, had joined in the palm strike. He swept up ash into the air as if that could create a Wind of Change for his blighted life.

"Hey, Reemast, don't get that stuff in the air. You don't want to breathe it! We don't either." Mootmu-na shouted, riveting Reemast with his piercing blue eyes.

When men reached adulthood, the People didn't tell them what to do. *What was wrong with Mootmu-na?* Reemast wondered. He forced himself to continue the sweeping properly but his inclination was to take his anger out physically on anything he could. He felt a tremendous need for release of the anger and how he wished he could release it on Minagle. He thought of ways and discarded each one for fear of being caught.

Totamu had made a neck bag for Enut and placed a supply of vasaka leaves in it. The leaves were brittle so they broke into smaller pieces. She took it to Enut and explained how often she should use the leaves to help her breathing. She gently tied it around Enut's neck and sat beside her. She suggested she make tea with it because it worked better that way, but chewing was better than nothing. Totamu began to look for lice in Enut's hair. She worked on the hair diligently and found numbers of the little monsters which she smashed between her fingernails. Enut had not cared for herself well for some time. Totamu suspected the cause was her breathing problems, but things would worsen in the confines of the cave if they had to be there long, so getting rid of the lice was critical. She would scan the individuals at meal times for scratching and then check out scalps for infestation. She would try to rid them all of lice. She wished she knew of a way to kill the eggs but was at a loss. She had a very fine comb that her deceased husband had made for her. It was so old now that it was missing several teeth and that did not make it a good tool. She was wistful, momentarily thinking of times past. They normally didn't have a head lice problem when they lived more openly in their tents. They were a clean people. Totamu shook her head as if to bring her mind web to the present and keep it there. She needed to find out if the other People in the cave had a master comb maker. She walked over to Ekuktu. In her hand was the broken comb.

"Ekuktu, I need some information."

"How may I help?" Ekuktu was surprised that a person of this stature would ask him for information. He lowered his head.

"This is a comb made for me to clear out head lice. It was made long ago. We are having problems from head lice in the cave. I need another comb made. Is there anyone in your group with the skill to make one of these with these very tight spaces between the teeth?"

Ekuktu reached for the comb. He examined it.

"May I take it to the cave entrance to examine it better?" he asked.

"Of course. I'll wait here." Totamu sat down.

Totamu did not know that Ekuktu carved as often as he could. People made fun of him because he carved representations of animals. But he had an understanding of wood and could make his carvings look very real. He said he could see the animal in the wood and his carving just released the animal. After examining the comb, he returned to Totamu. He knew there was little likelihood that she knew he carved.

"Whoever made this was expert at carving."

Totamu heard the genuine appreciation in his voice. "He was my husband, and, yes, he was expert at carving," she replied.

"I do carve things that People think are trivial. I love to do it. It relaxes me after a hunt or just from confinement in the season of cold days. But I am told this is a waste of time where I could be more productive. I would like to try to reproduce this comb. It may take awhile, but I would really like to try. I would need to borrow this comb to teach me."

"I would appreciate that very much, Ekuktu. There is nobody in our group that carves well. For them to try would be unproductive indeed."

"I am not this good," he said, holding the comb for her to see. "But I will try my very best."

"Thank you," Totamu said and hit her left palm with her right fist for emphasis. She went to the sleeping mats of her family and began to check that they had been folded properly.

At the skin harvesting, the men had finished the aurochs, and the elephant skinning was under way. Neamu-na asked Manak to carry the skin of the aurochs to the cave and to hurry back to help with the remainder of the work. Manak shouldered the load, which was quite heavy. He struggled with the burden in the deep ash but got the skin to the cave entrance as fast as any might have done. He laid the skin at the entrance and looked for Likichi, who saw him and came to the cave entrance.

"Mother, the first skin is at the entrance. It needs to be swept of ash before bringing it inside."

"Good, Son. I will tend to it. Do you want to take any jerky to the workers?"

"No, Mother. We are too busy."

"Very well. Be safe, my son."

"Yes, Mother." Manak lowered his head.

Manak turned on his heels and left the cave. He wondered as he walked why they always had to be so formal. He had so many questions. Young People were expected to observe and figure things out, not worry the older ones with endless questions that reduced their own problem solving effort. Still, as with the stories, sometimes he really wanted to ask a question when the answer didn't come to him after some thought. He walked quickly through the ash. Hunting, skinning, butchering, and preparing meat were things he understood with great clarity. It was good to get out and be busy doing something profitable after being cooped up in the cave during the ashfall. He thought for a moment of Domur and was glad that he was alone because he blushed at thoughts of her. He wished he could prevent himself from blushing. He didn't do it often, but it was embarrassing when he did. He reached up and felt the beginnings of his facial hair.

At the coal deposit Mootmu-na had filled two bags with coal chunks. He reached for them and Reemast walked over. "I'll take them to the cave," he volunteered.

"No," Mootmu-na stated flatly. "You are not trusted at the cave when few men are there. Don't volunteer for opportunities that would be seen as ways you might create more problems. Consider that you are going to be watched for the remainder of your days. Get used to it. I don't like to have to watch you. Nobody else does either. But that's how it is. *You* chose to require it of us." The last few words were said in anger. Mootmu-na had no patience with the young man. He also had come to an intense dislike of him because of what he'd done to Minagle, and having done that to her, he hurt the entire People.

Reemast was mortified. The People were very serious indeed. He had gone too far, but only if he could, he would go further. This was all her doing. She should have remained silent. How he would like to tear Minagle apart. His fists were clenched. The expressions on Reemast's face were transparent. He had no idea that others could see his vicious thoughts in his face. Mootmu-na understood the evil scowling. Mootmu-na made a mind web reminder to talk to Wamumur. Mootmu-na shouted to Ermol-na, "I am taking the load to the cave." Mootmu-na signaled with his hand in a way that Reemast could not see. The message was for Ermol-na to keep a good watch on Reemast. Ermol-na acknowledged.

Mootmu-na walked with the heavy load. How much nicer it would have been if Reemast had been able to take the load. Why, Mootmu-na wondered not for the first or last time, did the groups of People have to be so fragile. One person could have such a huge impact on the whole group. When the group functioned as was right it could be so strong, but from time to time a person like Reemast would create havoc and weaken the whole group severely. Mootmu-na feared that Reemast might take his anger out on Minagle even though he knew what the punishment would be. He had no confidence that leaving him in the group was wise at all. Time would tell, but he would talk to Wamumur.

When Mootmu-na arrived at the cave, he noticed that Wamumur was listening to a little child. That struck him as very odd, but he did not interrupt. It was obvious that Wamumur was deep in his mind web. What, he wondered, could a child have to contribute? He dropped the bags at the door and looked around for Ekuktu. He didn't want to track ash into the cave living space. He waved to his wife, Amey, and she came quickly.

"My wife," he greeted her quietly, "I am going to dump these chunks out and ask that someone start carrying them to the storage place we talked about last night. More will follow. I have to take the carrying bags, so you will have to use something else."

"I will see that it is done." She hesitated as he seemed to have something else to say.

"Amey, what is Wamumur doing with that child?"

"That little child has been telling the creation story and other stories all morning. As far as anyone can tell, Wamumur has not stopped her once. She sounds like a Wise One when you can hear her. She is just so tiny."

Mootmu-na placed his hand on his chin. "Then she may be a real blessing. None of us has been able to capture the stories right according to Emaea. She has been worried for a long time. Even Wamumur has not found good story-tellers among his People. We may have to band together with a child leading us? Oh, these are truly Winds of Change."

Amey smiled at him. "Stay safe, my husband."

"And you too," he responded.

When Mootmu-na returned to the coal site, there were five people there. Three were strangers. This was possibly not good. To top it off the three strangers were not People. Their heads were shoved forward and they had very black thick hair. They talked in a clipped sharp manner. They wore garments that covered their arms and boots that stopped short of their knees. They carried spears. He hoped his observation skills would be helpful.

Ermol-na saluted him. He returned the greeting. Reemast stood there as if in shock. "I don't know what they want," Ermol-na said and shrugged.

Mootmu-na realized that Ermol-na was unsure what to do, so he dropped the bags on the ground and walked up boldly to the strangers. He gestured as if to ask what they wanted. The humans began to speak slowly and loud. There was no communication. Mootmu-na looked at Ermol-na. "Will you run to the cave and get Shmyukuk, my daughter-in-law. She is young, but she was a slave briefly of these Others. Perhaps she can understand them. Bring her here quickly." Mootmu-na turned to the strangers. He gave them a sign to wait, which they appeared to understand.

Ermol-na returned within a half hour with Shmyukuk. She had been fitted with a booted garment that was too large so the straps had been tied and even with that, the legs drooped and she had to hold them up so she walked on the soles of the boots, not the sides. She did tell Ermol-na that she might be able to understand the Others, and she was afraid of them. As they walked to the coal site, he encouraged her to hide anything that would look like fear. She needed to appear very strong. She spent the time walking to prepare herself to act in a way she didn't feel. It was awkward because guile was not part of the People, but she felt that the People's security was at stake.

When she arrived at the coal site, Mootmu-na asked her to ask the Others what they wanted. Out of her mouth came strange sounds, and the Others appeared to understand.

The dialog went something like this:

Shmyukuk: "What do you want?"

Other 1: "What are you doing here?"

Without translating, Shmyukuk said, "What are *you* doing here?"

Other 1 was shocked: "We are looking for meat."

Shmyukuk translated: "They are looking for meat."

Mootmu-na said: "Tell them the meat is all dead from the ashfall."

Shmyukuk said: "The meat is all dead from the"—and she pointed to the
    ashfall not knowing that word in the language of the Others.

Other 2: "Why are you here?"

Shmyukuk translated.

Mootmu-na said: "This is our place."

Shmyukuk translated.

Other 1: "This is our place as well."

Shmyukuk translated.

Mootmu-na said: "Tell him that his leader needs to come here."

Shmyukuk translated.

Other 1: "Why are you digging rocks?"

Shmyukuk translated.

Mootmu-na said: "Tell him that his leader needs to come here *now*."

Mootmu-na slammed his closed fist into his left hand.

Shmyukuk translated.

Other 2: "We will return." And with that, the Others left.

Mootma-na looked at Ermol-na. "Please go get the hunters here as fast as you possibly can. When they head toward us, then you go to the cave and get every one of the People that can increase appearance of our strength. And hurry."

The People had gathered at the coal site before the Others returned. When they did return, they had an Other with a strange basket woven head covering walk to meet them. The Other stretched out his hand to Nanichak-na and Mootmu-na. His hand was open and empty of weapons. He stretched out the second empty hand. He smiled. Obviously this was not what Nanichak-na and Mootmu-na expected.

"I will try to speak your language," the Other said haltingly. The People could understand. "I am Abiedelai, Chief of the Minguat people. We fled our land for a cave we used once before. We fled because of the . . . ." He lifted a handful of ash. "I suspect you did the same. We did not have time to make much provision before our flight. We occupy Cave Sumbrel. We are—how do you say forty?"

It took a moment before Shmyukuk realized she was needed as translator. She flashed both hands fingers up four times.

Abiedelai continued, "We are"—he flashed his fingers of both hands straight up four times—"counting all living including infants. We are not here to fight. We are here to survive this disaster. We need to agree not to fight each other."

Mootmu-na and Nanichak-na looked at each other. Each had been combing his mind web for anything to guide them in this meeting. They could find nothing. And Wamumur was back at the cave.

"We will meet again tomorrow at high sun to consider this further," Nanichak-na said. "Both of us have been surprised this day. Let us think on this and then talk after we have thought. We will talk here in the open."

Abiedelai raised his right hand. "That is wise counsel. We will meet again tomorrow here at high sun." The Others returned to their cave. The People returned to butchering and coal gathering.

When Wisdom sucked the color from the land, the People returned to the cave having made numbers of trips with coal and meat. The hearth fire gave off a wonderful aroma of roasted meat. The men salivated automatically as they removed their booted garments and shook them outside. A call had to go out throughout the cave for all to assemble for the evening meal. Some of the women were still transporting coal and some were taking meat to the smoking place. Other women had begun to prepare skins. Young children had been called on to help prepare the evening meal. They were bursting with happiness at being called to help. Lamul looked with disdain on his brother who was carving again. *Give him a home guard duty and he'd carve* is what he thought as he scratched his head.

Ki'ti had just completed another story and Wamumur called the storytelling to a close for the day. He complimented her and she blushed profusely and lowered her head as far as possible. For Wamumur and for her, time had stood still as she recited story after story. She even had the stories in the proper order. Neither thought to eat or drink or pass water while the storytelling progressed. Wamumur wanted to go through the entire set of stories before he told the People what he had found. He wanted to know how vast her memory was. What also amazed Wamumur was that Ki'ti had no apparent realization that there was anything unusual about her ability. She seemed totally devoid of pride in her accomplishment. She appeared to take it for granted that she could do this. They had not discussed the meaning of stories but were simply at this point going through the basic memory function of the Wise One. Wamumur was stiff and when Mootmu-na walked by, he noticed and gave Wamumur a hand up.

"After the evening meal, I would like a word with you, Wise One," Mootmu-na said.

"Come to me when you are ready," Wamumur said smiling.

The superior hunters were served and then the hunters. Wamumur was served after the hunters. The women and children followed. There was a quiet that passed over the People while they ate the evening meal. Enut ate little and still wheezed. She was not remembering the leaves. Enut thought it was good to feel tired from doing something rather than nothing. It was good to eat when really hungry rather than just because it was time. She wished it applied to her.

After the evening meal, Mootmu-na and Wamumur walked to the cave entrance and Mootmu-na shared his concern about Reemast.

"It would mean certain death for him if we banished him while things are as they are. What would he eat? Where would he go? If more ash fell, he would die," Wamumur said while his fingers threaded through his beard.

"I understand, but I also have read his evil intent toward Minagle. She should not be required to suffer again for his evil. Reemast hates her. It shows. We already have enough trouble increasing the size of our People because of problems with childbirth; we certainly don't need to have women afraid of men."

"I agree, Mootmu-na. Do you have any suggestions?"

"I have swept my mind web and can find nothing. I was hoping you would have alternatives. I am seriously concerned that if he cannot hurt her, he will hurt someone else. The anger in him is extraordinary. I've never seen anything like it. Is there a way to extinguish anger?"

Wamumur slowly shook his head from side to side. "Why don't we consult with Ermol-na. He saw today what you saw, didn't he?"

"Yes." Mootmu-na caught Ermol-na's eye. He signaled him to come.

The two discussed the situation with Ermol-na. Ermol-na traveled through his mind web systematically. He frowned; he murmured; he wrung his hands. He stood first on one foot with his primary weight and then shifted the balance to the other. He equalized the weight on his feet and looked at the other two men. "What I see is that he has demanded of the entire group that we split our efforts to watch him, something he doesn't want and seems to resent. It takes up too much valuable time. He also has a continued desire to do injury to one of our members. That is clear. We cannot confine him. We are too far from the ocean to trade him as a slave. My only conclusion is that he must meet with an accident for the good of the People."

Wamumur's visage clouded over for a split second. "You have stated the obvious, Ermol-na. I will do the job myself." Wamumur did a strong palm strike.

Mootmu-na held up his hand palm outward. "I offer an alternative."

Wamumur nodded.

Mootmu-na continued, "A Wise One is not the person for this duty. This calls for a -na hunter. Grant permission to me and to Ermol-na to take care of this. Both of us have seen the problem and know how serious it is. Both of us are very strong and have fought in combat successfully. No one need know what happens except the three of us."

Wamumur nodded and the three made very strong palm strikes. Mootmu-na and Ermol-na walked over to the water and drank many full gourds. Then they retired to their sleeping mats early. When the water they drank had coursed through their bodies, Mootmu-na and Ermol-na waked and while Mootmu-na went to signal to Reemast to come, Ermol-na distracted the guard. Ermol-na had hidden a hammer stone under the ash just outside the entrance. While the guard was distracted, Mootmu-na herded Reemast outside and around the curved wall of the cave entrance. While Reemast was still confused from sleep, Mootmu-na hit him very hard on the back of the head with the hammer stone. Reemast fell silently to the ground. One dog whined imperceptibly and the group of dogs shifted and resumed their sleep positions. Ermol-na joined him and they ran to the privy to relieve themselves and returned to pick up the body of Reemast. They put the hammer stone on his belly while they carried him to the coal site. Once there, they dug out a place where there was a deposit of sand. Ermol-na took the hammer stone and with all his force, hit Reemast's head with it just to be sure he was dead. They dug furiously, put his body in the sand, and covered him. This was at the bottom of the place where they had piled up the ash they had cleared from the coal. Nobody would be digging there for a long time. Once they had put the ash back, it was some six feet deep and looked just like it had the previous day. Afterward, they looked grimly at each other and did a strong palm strike. They quietly returned to the cave, very relieved that the guard had nodded off. Ermol-na put the hammer stone with the tools and went to his sleeping mat. A few people coughed, some snored, but none was awake, Mootmu-na noticed. Once Mootmu-na was on his sleeping mat, he took a tiny pebble and aimed for the wall by the guard. He threw the pebble and the guard waked and shook himself and walked around. He would be alert for the rest of the night.

Morning came and the People became animated. There was much back and forth to the privy and when Ermol-na passed Wamumur, there was an instant eye contact and a nod that said all that needed to be said.

As time passed, Blanagah became agitated. She had no idea where Reemast was. He had never been missing from their sleeping mat. She quickly scanned the room and noticed Minagle sitting on her mat stretching. She kept telling herself he'd appear any moment. Maybe he was spending a lot of time at the privy. When the morning meal was finished and there was no sign of him, she went to Wamumur and lowered her head.

"What is it, Blanagah?" he asked.

"I cannot find Reemast," she said. "He was not on our mat when I arose. Has he been sent on some assignment?"

"No," Wamumur said, and then he announced, "Reemast seems to be missing. All hunters, please search every inch of the cave and you two, please check outside." All searchers returned with no news. One searcher came back with the surprising information that there was an additional set of rooms at the far reaches of the cave, maybe more. "Who was guard last night?" Wamumur asked.

Slamika stepped forward. "I was on first shift. Then Kai followed me."

"And did you see him leave?"

"No. I did go to the privy so he might have gone out then." There was very quiet laughter.

"Well, let us see what the day brings," Wamumur said flatly.

When the hunters put on their booted garments, they were very solemn. A hunter was missing. Without understanding from their stories or information from their collective mind webs about times like this one, they had no way to deal with the confusion. Could one simply disappear? And then they were about to confront the Others. They were wary but not anxious. The same was true of the Others.

The hunters left the cave and followed Mootmu-na and Ermol-na to the coal site. There was total silence, except for the quiet squeaking sound of their boots on the ash. Wamumur and Ekuktu remained with the women and children at the cave. There grew an air of expectation and a little anxiety in the cave as not only was there something new in this encounter, but also, Reemast still had not returned.

The Others were not there when the People arrived. Nanichak-na raised his eyes to the sky. "We are early," he said. Despite the heavy cloud cover, the sun was clearly not quite overhead. Ermol-na and Mootmu-na looked at each other, realizing that they had done a very good job of disguising the burial site. Nobody would suspect it was there. It would be unlikely that anyone would walk there, because the land began to slope steeply upwards above the body.

"Ho!" Abiedelai shouted from the top of the hill. The Others descended quietly and orderly.

"What have been your thoughts?" Nanichak-na asked.

Chief Abiedelai took off his hat and raised his own tunic over his head. "We are not here to bargain. We are starving. Our food has run out and we are becoming weak." He nodded to his group and each showed the condition of their bodies.

The People were appalled at the sight. The ribs were prominent and the hip bones of the Others were protruding. Their bellies pressed to their spines. The People had not been able to read their faces, which were hollowed more because they were starving than because they were different.

The People looked at each other, saying nothing but understanding. Nanichak-na said slowly, "Go now. Bring all your people and a bowl apiece to Cave Kwa. We will feed you. Do you know where it is?"

"No. We do not know where it is."

Nanichak-na said, "Manak will stay here. He will lead you."

At that, the People turned and headed toward their cave. The Winds of Change were huge.

Back at the cave, things became very busy. There was no time for anxiety or concern. To feed forty extras required a lot of effort when it was unplanned. The women worked furiously and the men were gathered discussing the possibilities. Girls sped down the cave to fill all available gourds with water.

In the men's circle, Grypchon-na said, "There is another solution. They could stay here. There is much room here. Cave Sumbrel could become the meat preparation area. We could do all the small butchering and smoking there. Meat that has been fully smoked could then be brought here for storage. We could have two hunters guard at night over there or we could devise a way to close the cave off during the night."

The men were silent. Grypchon-na had presented a novel possibility. Each had to run the idea through his mind web. Ermi, Shmyukuk's husband said, "These Others have a different social situation. They have a chief. The speaker must be the chief. He can tell anyone to do whatever he wants and they have to obey him. Here we are all equal."

"You are wise, Ermi." Wamumur said. "We need to set conditions on their coming here and the first is that they lose the chief title and adopt our way of all being equal, at least until they choose to leave."

Slamika, who almost never spoke asked, "To keep our stories true, we need to use only our language. What will we do with them at story time?"

That was met with silence throughout the cave. Finally, Wamumur said, "You have thought well. Yes, we must keep our own language. We don't want to pick up strange words to add to our language. We will deal with what to do with them at story time later. They could go to the lower rooms, but if they join us and intend to stay, then they will have to hear the stories. That is a condition that will form later. Probably by that time, they won't follow the stories that well anyway."

Hahami-na said, "I suggest that we invite them here now. We tell them we will use their cave for the meat preparation, but we tell them that the offer to stay here depends on how we get along. They must accept equality and adopt our ways while here. They will have to use our language. They can decide whether to join us at least temporarily here while they eat. If they choose to join us, they can then go back and get their things. If they need help, we can help. Also the season of cold days will come. We need much food to make it through. Then we need to go north to find land that is free of ash where animals walk the land. That is all I have to say."

All members of the group did a strong palm strike.

The Others appeared over the hill. Manak touched palm to palm the hand of Abiedelai as it was offered to him open and fingers up. Then he turned and began to lead the Others to the cave. As they neared, the dogs began to bark and walk on stiff legs with hackles raised. There was silence in the cave except for Ki'ti and Minagle who tried to calm the dogs.

The Others were shown to a part of the cave between the cooking area and the sleeping area. It was the greater gathering spot. Quickly, food was distributed. The women of the People tried to distribute it by age, first to the elders and then to the younger Others. Chief Abiedelai urged his group not to eat too fast.

The women remained where they had eaten, afraid even of offering to help clean up. The men gathered near the door, with the dogs becoming disquieted again. Minagle quieted them. There were about twenty dogs, so they were something to reckon with.

The men of the Others were wary of the dogs. They had never had dogs, so they did not understand them at all. To the Others, these animals were wolves. Each of the Others tried to situate himself as far from the dogs as possible. The People recognized that and placed themselves carefully between the dogs and Others as a shield.

Chief Abiedelai spoke, "We are grateful for the food. It was well prepared and tasted good. You are good People."

The men of the People lowered their heads. The Others seemed to understand the gesture.

Wamumur spoke, "We have decided to offer to let you stay here temporarily. We would use your cave for meat preparation and then store it here. Your cave has neither the water resources nor the space that this one has. You would be required to help us recover and prepare meat for storage and do the chores that are involved in living. We are unwilling to have two ways of being People. You would have to give up your Chief and live as all equal People while you are here. Our strength is in our working all for the good of all. You will have to learn to use our language, not your own. The season of cold days comes. We must gather much to make it through. When the season of new leaves comes, we will leave this place for land in the north free of ash. That is our plan. We are not willing to change." Chief Abiedelai translated.

The Others looked at their Chief. To the People, Chief Abiedelai said, "Obviously, you have had success, while we have failed. It would be good for us all to join. I have no difficulty trying a different arrangement in the way we interact. We may learn from you that your way is better. We may prefer our own. We have to determine over time if we should remain or leave. Until then, we will totally adopt your ways, but you'll need to let us know clearly what they are. Let us know if we are in error. If we separate after the season of cold days, we will go east." Chief Abiedelai translated for his own listeners.

The people of Chief Abiedelai looked furtively at each other. They had eaten and were grateful, but it sounded like their Chief had been weakened by the food. They had understood him to say they had to learn to use another language. That seemed outrageous. It was particularly outrageous that they had to learn the language of People they considered inferior. But the Chief was the Chief.

"Then your men can go gather your things. Do you need help from our hunters?" Gruid-na asked.

The response was affirmative. Five of the hunters of the People donned their booted garments and prepared to help.

The People and the Others had heard the men. A few of the women of the People began to show the women of the Others where would be a good place for their sleeping mats. The women looked terribly tired and there was great sympathy for the Others who appeared so worn down.

Ki'ti was deeply thoughtful over what was happening. The muscles of her face made a vertical line between her eyebrows. She had already gone through her mind web with the stories and could find nothing that even came close to this experience, except Maknu-na and Rimlad. She was guessing that this would be a new story for their history. She looked up and one of the younger dogs had left the place where it was supposed to stay. It had tried to be unobtrusive and had found her and put its body as close to hers as possible. Its yellow brown eyes scanned hers carefully.

"You can stay here," Ki'ti said as she stroked the dog. "It is the Winds of Change, little one," she said, trying to reassure the dog and herself. The dog licked her and she found that comforting.

Minagle was very curious. Domur had whispered that the Others looked a little like her. Minagle couldn't keep her eyes off them. She noticed that there were just a few of the Others that appeared to be her age. Minagle walked over to where the Others were sitting and knelt in front of Meeka, who was twelve. Meeka was terribly thin. Her black hair was matted and her face was streaked with dirt. Meeka was frightened but tried not to show it. Minagle pointed to herself and said, "Minagle." Meeka had no clue what to do. Minagle tried again, and the girl looked at her confused. Minagle tried again. Suddenly, the attempt was spotted by Chief Abiedelai and he said in the language of the Others, "Meeka, her name is Minagle. Tell her your name and point to yourself." The young girl did it. Minagle smiled and Meeka smiled, too. Minagle offered her hand and stood. Meeka stood. Minagle gently took her hand and led her to Domur. Domur stood. Minagle pointed to Domur and said, "Domur." Meeka said, "Domur." Minagle pointed to Meeka and said, "Meeka." Domur smiled and said, "Meeka." The friendship was making a new threesome. Minagle led both girls to the gourds. Domur picked up an oil light and lit the wick. The three girls picked up as many gourds as possible and headed to the water. Minagle's effort was observed by the other women and it sparked an interaction of name exchanging and learning and preparing the newcomers to help clean up from the meal. The Others were willing to help but seemed to wait for someone to tell them what to do.

Meanwhile, Blanagah was beside herself. She tried not to fret too much but could not understand the absence of Reemast. She rocked back and forth while her arms cradled her bent legs. Any other day, she'd have been admonished for not contributing. She went to Enut and asked if she was well.

"I feel a little better. Thank you." Enut truthfully did not feel better, nor did she wish to lie to Blanagah, but she knew the young woman was distressed over the absence of Reemast. She did not want to add to that distress nor did she wish to discuss her health, so she minimized her own problems. She would have preferred to have been left alone.

"Enut, I am frightened for Reemast. It is not like him to be missing."

Enut looked at her daughter-in-law. Blanagah didn't know the half of it. She responded, "Do not fret. He is a person who has often done things that nobody else would think to do. I don't know why. He may have just gone exploring."

"Mother," Blanagah said almost in tears, "His booted garment is still at the cave entrance."

Enut pondered that information. She began to worry. She had seen the ash off and on when she went to relieve herself at the privy. Surely, Reemast wouldn't have gone out in that without his booted garment. She did not know what to think. Her breathing was laborious, so she didn't spend a lot of time thinking. She listened to her own gentle wheezing. Then she said, "Maybe he is exploring the cave. I heard someone say there were more rooms in the cave."

That calmed Blanagah for the time. She would hope he was exploring the cave and would return with significant information that would help restore his former good standing among the People. Blanagah went to help the women clean up from the evening meal. They had eaten early because the Others were so hungry. Eating early was a real novelty. Enut slumbered.

Meanwhile, the men of the People who remained in the cave were talking with Chief Abiedelai. They wanted to know who the -na hunters were. They arrived at the following new designations: Abiedelai-na, Cue-na, Gurkma-na, Alak-na, Arkan-na, Guy-na, Maan-na, Oho-na, and Gram-na. Abiedelai thought that Lai, Ekwa, Fim, Muttu, and Bolam might feel slighted, but he had selected very carefully and thought his selections were fair. He said as much to the men.

Wamumur said, "Among our People, humility is prized, not pride. No one ever expects to be honored with -na. When the honor is given, it is met with a lowered head and a genuine surprise, not an expectation. These are People that all realize are highly skilled. They are also those who would without thought put their lives on the line, if it were for the good of all. They are wise hunters."

Abiedelai thought. "Then, we should remove Alak from the -na list. All the rest would qualify. I guess I was making age the factor."

Wamumur smiled. "Usually, age is a factor, but it is a lesser factor. Even if someone age twenty years was highly skilled and would give his life for the People, he usually needs more life experience before he has the wisdom to go with the skill and compassion. It is unwise to give up one's life too soon. It takes wisdom to know whether and when."

Chief Abiedelai was impressed that these People put so much thought into their ways of living. He said, "That is such good thinking. Who makes the designation?"

Wamumur realized how large the gap in social understanding was and said, "I think the best I can say is that somehow we all know at the same time. It may follow some achievement, some occurrence, some act . . . but we can see it in each other's faces. It just becomes knowledge that fills each of us as if we were all one."

"Ah," Chief Abiedelai said, leaning against the wall, "I can see that we are very different. My people wait for me to tell them what to do, and they do it because I say so, not because they see that it is for the common good, though I try to make it that way. I can see that all your People think for themselves, while I think for all of mine."

"I would think that would be an awful burden of responsibility and weigh heavily on you. It could also be devastating for your people if you were killed in a hunting accident," Neamu-na said.

"You have much to teach us," Chief Abiedelai said. He was absolutely horrified at the prospect of his people continuing on if he were killed in a hunting accident. The thought had never crossed his mind.

When everyone had returned to the cave and settled in, Wamumur made an announcement. "We have some information that is new to you. Come and listen." Chief Abiedelai translated.

"When we make decisions, we do it through pronouncements. This is a pronouncement: To live together, all are adopting our way. Chief Abiedelai has agreed to this." He looked at Chief Abiedelai, who said, "I agree." Then Chief Abiedelai translated.

Wamumur continued. "Our way is that all adults are equals. We have no Chief. Your Chief has given up his title." He looked at Chief Abiedelai.

"I agree." Chief Abiedelai translated.

"Our way is a way of humility, not a way of pride. We look to the good of all members. We see something that needs to be done and we do it. No one should have to give you orders. You should look for what needs to be done and do it. Do not wait. Do it when you see it needs to be done. We do not tolerate laziness. To seek work is what we expect."

"I agree. We can learn much here," Chief Abiedelai translated.

Wamumur continued, "We have for hunters a designation of -na following the hunter's name. It is for hunters only. It is not for all hunters. It is for the special hunters who are extremely skilled, compassionate, and wise."

Chief Abiedelai translated.

Wamumur continued, "When given this designation, the hunter is expected to receive it with humility, which means a lowered head and without pride—ever. If any hunter were to pride himself in the designation of -na, he would lose it immediately and probably never have it again."

Chief Abiedelai translated.

Wamumur continued, "The only advantage of the designation -na is that the hunter is among those served first at meals. I will name your -na hunters and when I do, I expect the hunter to lower his head in this manner (demonstrated) and remain silent. Your -na hunters are: Abiedelai-na, Cue-na, Gurkma-na, Arkan-na, Guy-na, Maan-na, Oho-na, Gram-na."

Abiedelai-na translated. Wamumur continued, "Do not congratulate these hunters. Simply use their new names. If your name was not called, you are not to feel dispirited but rather know that your time is not yet for the designation."

Abiedelai-na translated.

Wamumur continued, "Those who have just joined us will be fully part of the People. You will have to learn to use only our language. We will stay together during the season of cold days and then leave this place for an ash-free home. Either we all go north together or we go north and you go east. That is all I have to say."

Abiedelai-na translated.

As their names were called, each hunter lowered his head as far as he could. There was a huge amount of emotion associated with the pronouncement, but that emotion was hidden well. Abiedelai-na looked at his men critically. Alak looked irritated at not being named a -na hunter. Oho-na and Maan-na were trying to hide their pride at getting named with the -na designation. The Others had learned to compete among themselves, not look for how they could best work with Others. All of this required great change. They would have to learn a new language. The Others had to deal with massive Winds of Change. But they had already seen that they would be well fed. Some were eager to be tried as equals, while some fumbled, wondering what that meant and how they would know what they needed to do. Some were chagrined to have to lose their elevated ranking among the Minguat. All of the -na hunters had quickly figured out that they had to learn the new language fast. The other hunters wondered what they had to do to become -na hunters.

Abiedelai-na looked at Wamumur and asked why he was not designated -na.

Wamumur smiled, "I am the storyteller. If I went hunting and were killed, all our stories would vanish. All of them are in my keeping. So I cannot hunt. I have to be protected so that our stories continue on."

"What stories?" Abiedelai-na asked.

"The stories are of our history since we crawled up from the womb of the earth," Wamumur responded.

"They also remain in our mind webs so that when something happens, we can go for guidance to what we have learned from the stories."

Abiedelai-na was bewildered. "We have no stories like that. We have only a few and we tend to find them curiosities, but we don't take them literally or seriously."

"I am so sad for you," Wamumur said. He meant it, but from the expression on Abiedelai-na's face, it was clear that it was the last thing he expected to hear. Both realized they were communicating, but that meaning was somewhat elusive.

"One more question if I may ask," Abiedelai-na said. "How did you remember the names I gave you?"

Wamumur said, "The People have good memories. Those of us who tell stories have even better memories and we keep working them so that they stay good. See that child?" He noticed she had a dog on her sleeping mat. "That child recited stories in order yesterday without error, stories that would take many days' walk to tell. Our stories hold ancient memories that help us deal with problems of today based on wisdom from the past. It is a source of answers, so we don't have to go through life unprepared. I think the memory of the Wise One is a gift from Wisdom. We don't earn it. What could a child of" he showed seven fingers "possibly have done to earn that memory?"

Abiedelai-na asked, "And she did so without error?"

"Not only without error, but she also got the inflection right." Again, Wamumur noticed the dog was out of place sitting next to Ki'ti. He wondered what it was doing out of place and why Ki'ti hadn't disciplined it.

"This will be truly a time of learning," Abiedelai-na said and turned away. He saw hunters of the People putting on booted garments. He gently touched Nanichak-na on the shoulder. "What are you doing?" he asked.

Nanichak-na said, "We found an aurochs and an elephant that had died in the ashfall. We are butchering them. We will take them to the cave you occupied."

"Then we will help." He assembled his hunters and told them what was happening. They went swiftly to their tools and gathered their cutting tools. They were ready.

Two of the hunters of the People left ahead of the rest.

Abiedelai-na asked Nanichak-na where they were going. "They are searching for more animals that we can use before they are too rotten."

"Shall I send some of my hunters in a different direction?"

Nanichak-na considered the question. "No, Abiedelai-na, you should tell your hunters what is happening and watch to see what your hunters do."

Abiedelai-na understood and did what Nanichak-na said. Abiedelai-na's hunters looked at him. Suddenly, Arkan-na and Cue-na looked at each other. "We will go to search for carcasses also. We will go to the east since they go to the southwest." Abiedelai-na translated.

Abiedelai-na and Nanichak-na both smiled broadly. The remaining Others followed the butchering hunters. It was good. Totamu looked through slitted eyes from her little alcove in the cave where she sat cross legged and wondered whether the good would last. She pulled her cover tightly around her shoulders as she shivered. Though the stories obligated them to care for those in need and wanderers, including Others, it did not remove in the least her inherent distrust of Others. She leaned over and spat upon the ground.

Chapter 2

*The Winds of Change were blowing, but life was goo*d, Shmyukuk thought. Wamumal, Mitrak, and Shmyukuk had padded the wall behind their sleeping mats and they were relaxing while their infants nursed. Shmyukuk was fascinated by Wamumal's twins, Ekoy and Smig, whenever she had the chance to observe them closely. She hadn't known that twins were a possibility in childbirth. Wamumal and Shmyukuk's infants were the same age, a year; Mitrak's infant, Ketra, was two years old. Trokug, Shmyukuk's infant, still enjoyed playing with his mother's black hair when he nursed. She shifted forward and began to delouse his hair. She noticed some attached eggs and tried to pull them off with her fingernails. She wiped the smear on her tunic.

Ey, a fifteen-year-old girl married to Arkan-na who was more than twice her age at thirty-three, was anxious. She was young but she had been joined with Arkan-na after his first wife died in childbirth. Ey had been horrified to have to join someone of his age with children some of whom were older than she, but soon got over it because of the gentleness and kindness of her husband. She had not known him until her group and his gathered to exchange mates. She had to leave her family and mother children older than she could have birthed. Her first child, Tita, was emaciated as badly as her mother, and Tita was about the size of a year-old child, not the two-year-old that she was. Ey, out of desperation, walked over to the nursing mothers and signed that she would like to sit with them.

Wamumal smiled broadly and signed for Ey to join them. Shmyukuk grabbed a skin and set it up for her to lean against between herself and Mitrak. They were appalled at the terrible thinness of Ey and Tita. Trokug,

Shmyukuk's one-year-old, had nursed to the point that he had fallen asleep. She laid him beside her and murmured. How, she wondered, do you communicate when you don't speak the same language? She did, of course, speak the language of Ey, but she had been strictly forbidden to use it because it would slow down their learning the language they had to adopt. She pointed to her baby. They had already learned the names of each other but the names of the children remained to be learned. She said, "Trokug," while she pointed to her infant. Ey said, "Trokug." Ey then said, "Tita," and pointed to her own infant.

To Wamumal's amazement, Shmyukuk said, "Tita," and pointed to herself saying her own name. Ey looked at her carefully and then handed Tita to Shmyukuk. Shmyukuk offered her breast to the tiny Tita. At first, Tita languished. Shmyukuk remained calm, knowing that the infant would either suckle or not and there was nothing she could do but offer to drip a bit of milk on the infant's lips. Shmyukuk reached out and patted Ey's hand. She was so pathetically thin. Shmyukuk had lived as a captive of the Minguat for a while. She knew these Others were a thin people, but the size of Ey made the normal Minguat look fat. Ey could do little but smile back. Finally, Ey placed her hand on her chest and patted Shmyukuk's shoulder. She knew the word for grateful, but she had difficulty saying it. The infant began to suck. Slowly, tears fell from Ey's eyes. Mitrak noticed and touched Ey's shoulder, signifying compassion.

After a while, Shmyukuk placed her hand on Ey's hand. She said, "I nurse Trokug." She reinforced what she said with every hand signal she could think to use or create. "You bring Shmyukuk Tita. I nurse Trokug; you bring Shmyukuk Tita." Finally, Ey understood that Shmyukuk was offering a wet-nurse service. Ey lost more tears. She had all but given up on her daughter. Perhaps now she would live. Wamumal lost a few tears also. Her friend never ceased to amaze her. She would have been glad to help, but she had twins and that took all she had. While Ey rested, she thought of some in her group who had lost their children on the trek. She had been the only one to have kept her baby. At least ten or twelve babies had died. It had been a trek of many tears and there had been no time to mourn. She had all but given up on living until they had run into these People. Why had they been so kind? She could not understand. But she was grateful to the deepest center of herself. All of the babies drifted off to sleep. Barriers were breaking down. Mitrak told Shmyukuk that she would help feed Tita also. Little did Shmyukuk, Mitrak, or Wamumal understand what the other women had experienced. How it would have torn their bellies had they known.

Meanwhile, Totamu had asked the women who had agreed to make the booted garments. With the ash and the need to keep it out of the cave because it was already making people cough and it irritated skin, booted garments were critical to the health of all. She had shown the new women how to cut and construct the garments, but she was a person who checked to be sure that the garments were being made correctly. Where she saw error, she talked to the women and gently showed them how to fix the error. In their own language, two of the women spoke open resentment of Totamu's apparent authority when all People were supposed to be equal. They also resented any authority from inferiors, which is how they viewed the People. Abiedelai-na overheard them and called them. He was acutely aware that Shmyukuk knew the language of the Minguat. He feared that she might hear slurs from his Minguat. He didn't know whether any other People knew his language.

Aneal and Rayla got up and went to Abiedelai-na. "You have spoken our language!" he said accusingly.

"Yes," Aneal said, "but it was between us."

"That must stop now," Abiedelai-na said in his language, using his right fist to strike his left palm after he mentally sorted out the right/left pattern. "This is the last time you will use our language while we are all together here." Abiedelai-na was acutely aware how close his people were to death by starvation. He was not going to tolerate insurrection—not while they had an agreement that had been made that would save his people. "Further," he said, "you were talking in an unkind manner about Totamu."

Rayla frowned and pouted. "She's got us making booted garments for children. Our children died on the trek. Why am I making something for their children? It's not fair. Besides, since when do we take direction from inferiors?"

Abiedelai-na grabbed Rayla by the arm tight enough that it would later bruise. "You ungrateful girl! And you," he said to Aneal, "these People did not take the life of your children. We would all be dead if we had remained in our homeland. We almost didn't make it to safety. These People have brought us in and fed us and offered to take care of us through the season of cold days. We would have starved without them. To help keep this shelter free of ash, the garments are necessary. Have you not heard people coughing, as it is? Imagine ash in here. Your husbands are wearing booted garments now. Their legs will not be burning from the ash because they are protected. The cave is protected from ash because the garments are left at the cave entrance. And, you fools, some People understand our language. They can hear you. You want us thrown out of here? You will work to the good of the group or I will personally throw you over my shoulder and carry you naked two days walk from here and leave you to fend for yourselves. Is that clear?"

The girls were shaken. Abiedelai-na was usually such a kind, gentle person for a Minguat. This seemed out of character to them. What he said stung. Neither had considered the need to keep ash out of the cave or that their husbands were benefiting from the work of the women who already lived in the cave. They had been self centered, selfish. Worse, they might be overheard and understood where their view of the People as inferiors was concerned. They would not wish to be responsible for the Minguat's having to leave the cave in the cold.

"Finally," Abiedelai-na said, "I do not want to hear our language from your mouths unless or until we separate at the end of the cold time. Remember that there are People who can understand our language. You just cannot use it. So if you want to talk to each other, you'd better get to learning their language." He let go of Rayla's arm and walked off. He no longer was Chief, but he knew that his authority was still there, just like their language—just in case. All knew that if they parted company with the People, Abiedelai-na would be Chief again, so his word was still law. He also knew and so did the girls that he would be good to his word if they continued with their language or their ungrateful attitude. He was always looking to the good of the group. Fortunately for the Minguat, most of the women heard what was said and by the time night fell, everyone in the cave would know even without a pronouncement. A new level of caution would overlay whatever they said or did.

Oho-na and Grypchon-na had gone out early to look for carcasses. Oho-na was becoming tired and thirsty. He had forgotten his water skin. He was slowing. Grypchon-na stopped and examined Oho-na. "You are thirsty?" he asked.

Oho-na nodded.

Grypchon-na pulled a water skin from his pouch. He held it out to Oho-na. Oho-na looked surprised. He wasn't sure that if he'd have been among his own, the Minguat, whether anyone would have shared. They might have just made fun of him and let him go thirsty. He reached for the offered water pouch, lowering his head as far as possible. He drank the least he could to slake his thirst. Grypchon-na put the water away and pulled out two pieces of dried meat. He gave the thicker one to Oho-na. That wasn't lost on Oho-na either. Oho-na had never met such selfless people. He was amazed and deeply grateful. Never again would he leave the cave without water and food. He wondered how he could have forgotten. He had much time to think and he was spending a lot of that time looking at the manner in which both groups had been operating. Oho-na looked up. He squinted, "There," he stuttered as he pointed a little to the northeast in the monotonous monochrome landscape.

Both walked to the place. Sure enough, behind a little rise in the earth there was the carcass of another elephant. This time, it was the elephant with the large mastodon-like head roll and tiny ears. Grypchon-na grinned at Oho-na and then he kneeled and continued eating his dried meat. They had carried four long sticks and after they finished their dried meat, they put three of the sticks arranged in a tripod tied with a skin strip at the site so that it could be found more easily later. On the way back to the cave, they took the fourth stick to drag it through the ash to mark a path to the elephant. Their day had begun successfully.

Most of the men were on the meat butchering and preservation detail. Cave Sumbrel was busy and all the found carcasses had been butchered and moved to the cave. A few men had gathered sticks and were smoking meat already. There was little chatter and much work. Each knew that for the season-of-the-cold-days survival, they needed to gather as much meat as possible in the least amount of time. They were fortunate that insects were not present. It appeared that maggots would not be a problem.

Manak had been sent to the cave for additional cutting tools, and he returned with information that another elephant had been located. Manak, Slamika, Lamul, Gummo, and Ekwa were eager to go to the next carcass. Manak had reported that food was being prepared at the cave and would soon be ready, so the younger men had to return to the cave to eat and then they could go for the next carcass. Chamul-na had to smile. He knew that Manak was no slacker but he was genuinely pleased to see him take this critical food gathering so seriously. He was a grandson to approve.

Before they had reached the cave on their trek, Emaea's People had gathered a huge supply of wood for cave use. It was stacked near the cave entrance and covered with skins as they had anticipated the ashfall. Since some of the new small booted garments had been completed, Minagle, Domur, Aryna, Meeka, and Liho had gone stick and wood gathering. They could easily see where Cave Sumbrel was by following the trail etched into the ash on the ground. They carried wood there as quickly and as much as possible. The girls tried very hard to shake off as much ash as possible from the wood before depositing it at the entrance to Cave Sumbrel for smoking. The girls were talking among themselves as well as they possibly could and the Minguat acquisition of the language of the People was being acquired expeditiously by the young. There was a lot of laughter. Minagle felt a return to earlier, happier times.

At the cave, Blanagah was still struggling. She could not imagine what to think of the disappearance of Reemast. She had even taken a light and gone to the depths of the cave seeking her absent husband. Finally, Mootmu-na, her father, told her that it was time for her to begin to realize that it would be unlikely that Reemast would return. He said that he suspected the young man was dead somewhere. Of course, he *knew,* but said it was clear that the situation was abnormal enough for his daughter to begin to give up hope. He also assured her that Reemast's People did not seem overly concerned, which underscored the thought that the young man was probably dead. In some fundamental ways, Mootmu-na breathed a sigh of relief. The subject was closed. He no longer needed to pretend where Reemast was concerned. Blanagah had collapsed into his arms, but both knew that though she missed Reemast, she really didn't know him well, and it would soon be time to get on with her life and find a new husband.

Wamumur called Ki'ti to him as soon as he had a break in his administrative duties. He noticed the young dog stuck to her like it had been tied. "Little Girl," he began, "What is this dog doing out of its assigned place?" He tried to sound stern, but he was inwardly eager to know what her response would be.

Ki'ti lowered her head. Then she looked straight into Wamumur's eyes and said, "Wise One, this little dog has asked to be my friend. I need a friend. I want the dog for a friend. If the dog makes trouble, I can get rid of him, but I ask from the innermost part of my belly to be allowed to keep the dog as my friend."

Wamumur noticed that the dog sat right beside her. He looked at her, nothing else. He had seen no reason to deny her request except that never had such an idea of friendship with a dog been discussed, nor was it in the stories, but he wasn't dealing with an ordinary child or ordinary circumstances and he knew it. The Winds of Change were blowing. "For right now, Little Girl, keep the dog. I will tell you tonight. I must think. Now we must work. Are you ready?"

"I will go to the privy and then I will be ready," she said, doing her utmost to please the Wise One. Why, she wondered, did he call her Little Girl? Her name meant Falling Star. Ki'ti, Falling Star. Seenaha, Mootmu-na and Amey's three-year-old, was a little girl, not she. She ran to the privy and the dog bolted for the place designated for dogs for the same purpose. She returned to Wamumur and they seated themselves in the same places as before but not before Emaea arrived with food and insisted they eat before starting another storytelling session. They did and Wamumur noticed that Ki'ti gave the dog a bit of her food. He frowned so she did not repeat the dog feeding. The dog snuggled against her side.

Ekuktu, still on cave assignment because Nanichak-na knew that he was trying to carve a louse comb, was working on the comb and finally took it to Totamu for her approval. Totamu smiled broadly at Ekuktu and took the comb into her hand. She looked at it from every angle. Then she asked Ekuktu to kneel before her. She combed his hair with the comb. "It works!" she exclaimed when the teeth pulled out a louse and some eggs. "Will you make many of these?" she asked.

"How many?" he asked.

She raised one finger "for each woman in the size she needs for her and her husband and children and" she showed two fingers "extra of each size for each. Those with thicker hair will need a tiny bit more space. I think that the thicker hair might clog these teeth."

"That's a lot of combs!" he said, startled.

"It will keep you busy for a long time during the season of cold days, will it not?" Totamu said.

Ekuktu smiled at her. She knew he loved to carve. Totamu used the comb to get the rest of the lice and eggs from Ekuktu's head.

"Now," she said. "Tell your brother, Lamul, I want to see him after evening meal. Do not say why, but I will tell you. He is not pleased that you sit here and carve while he is out working. He thinks you play. He also has a head full of lice. I shall relieve his itching tonight so he may thank you." A smile curved her lips.

Ekuktu lowered his head. "You are too kind," he said.

Totamu kept the new comb knowing he had the old one and probably by now had the complete design in his mind web. "Nonsense," she replied. *Someday*, she thought, *he'd also realize how important keeping the peace was to survival.* Tonight, Lamul would learn.

While the young girls headed back to the cave from their wood collecting, Domur asked Liho why she looked so different and where she got her yellow hair. Her use of language was halting but she managed to convey that she had been brought into the group one season of cold days ago. She lived among People who had yellow hair before that. Vanya, who was now sixteen, had asked his grandfather, then Chief Abiedelai, at a gathering of the groups to get him a blond headed wife. He thought the color was wonderful and it attracted him very much. His grandfather got a young girl, one not ready for joining, because Vanya wasn't ready either. The girl was adopted by Arkan and Ey and would someday become Vanya's wife. Liho was that girl.

Minagle and Domur were fascinated. They had never heard of people reserving a wife or husband for that matter. Neither had they heard of adoption. They found Liho interesting with her gold hair and gray eyes. Her eyes were so pale that sometimes they wondered whether she was really alive. She was very thin, like all the Minguats. Even if she ate a lot, she wouldn't gain the stockiness of the People, they surmised. They were really happy to have her and the Others for friends. There was much to learn for both sides. Domur really wanted to take a comb to Liho's hair. For all its interesting color, it was ratted terribly. The People did comb their hair and if the young People didn't keep their hair rat free, their mothers would do it and not too pain free. The boys who were not yet joined had hair trimmed to shoulder length, parted down the middle, and they wore strips of leather tied around the head to keep hair from the face, and that was a lot easier to take care of. Joined men let their hair grow long. Domur knew that Ekuktu had been carving a comb. She wondered about that. They all had combs but not like he was carving. Domur wondered why the Others didn't take better care of their hair.

People began arriving at the cave. Manak brought a message from some of the superior hunters that they begged those in the cave to go ahead and eat without them. They would be a little late with the meat preparation and would eat when they got to the cave later. It became clear fast that there would be a time before all would eat together again while the meat preparation was in progress. There would be a huge number to feed while the season of cold days rested on the land, so they had much to do, hopefully not too much. Women began to serve the -na hunters who were present and then moved on to the hunters. Wamumur was served and then the women and children. There was excitement in the cave because not only had Oho-na and Grypchon-na found a small straight-tusked elephant, similar to but a different species from the larger straight-tusked elephant, but also Ermi and Guy-na had found two aurochs to the south of the first find and Oho-na and Grypchon-na had found an elk and a bison on their second excursion. At present, food might not be the freshest but it certainly was plentiful. There was even some variety.

While she ate, Blanagah began to search around for the available men. The People had no more choices unless she wanted an old man like Chamul-na who was supposed to be almost forty-eight or Nanichak-na who was a lot older. In those cases, it would be their choice, not hers. It seemed that the available men were Vanya and and Ghanya. She just could not find men who were emaciated appealing, just as the old men did not really appeal to her either. She had also heard some talk about Vanya and Liho, but Liho was just a child. So she realized there were one or two choices and that was it, unless they met other groups of People and in the ashfall, that was unlikely. Then, she shocked herself that she was considering Reemast dead. A horrible cold and empty feeling washed through her belly. Was he really dead? He had seemed so vital.

Lamul finished eating and Ekuktu told him that Totamu had wanted to see him. He went begrudgingly to her. He wanted to flee to gather meat.

"You asked to see me?" Lamul asked with his head lowered.

"Yes. It will take only a short time. Come sit before me." Totamu kneeled behind Lamul. She pulled out her comb and began to comb his hair. Lamul felt foolish, but he dared not move. Totamu combed, pulling hair from time to time. She would take the comb and push out lice and eggs into the fire and he could hear them pop occasionally. Totamu kept on. When she finished a little later, she said, "Now that should feel better. You certainly look a lot better. It may take a little while for you to feel the difference.

"You are telling me something?"

"Yes," she answered tersely. In her belly she was smiling.

"You are telling me I have treated my brother badly?"

"Yes," she replied.

He lowered his head. "Thank you. You are a good woman. I will make things straight with my brother."

"That is good." Totamu walked over to where Shmyukuk was nursing Tita.

Tita was still being slow to nurse, but had just latched on and Shmyukuk wondered if Tita needed to be fed more often until she got better. She asked Totamu and Totamu thought she should try. Totamu began to make her rounds of all the People seeking to know whether there were any unmet needs. Totamu had thought that there would be no difficulty for the People since the Others had to learn their language. What she discovered is that teaching was as difficult, if not more difficult, than learning.

When she passed Nanichak-na, she asked, "Don't you think that once the Others have learned our language, we should learn theirs? It might be to our advantage later."

He smiled. "Wamumur and I talked of this same thing early today. We have to keep our language clean for the stories but we would know which words were strange ones. I think we should learn their language so that we understand them and those like them. Knowing two languages would give us advantages that they will have and we won't, if they stay or leave. We will talk about this more when they have about mastered our language. Right now, they have to merge with us, not the other way around."

"I see," Totamu said and smiled inwardly. And she did. If the tables had been turned, they would have been ruled by a chief. These Others were like them and different. They did not work in a unified manner for the good of the group. They were having to learn the concept. Had the tables been turned, they might have been taken in as slaves instead of equals. They might have been the last to eat instead of cared for to regain their strength. It was good that things went as they had. Suddenly, she felt old and tired.

Wamumur approached Ki'ti quietly. He stood there looking into her pleading eyes. "You may keep your dog as your friend. We will see how that goes. The dog must stay out of the way of People. That is all I have to say." He knew her work for the past few days had been perfect. How could he deny her? She was giving the People exactly what they needed.

Ki'ti lowered her head while her hand touched her new friend. "Wise One, do you want to know his name?"

Of course he was curious but he didn't want it to show, "What is it, Little Girl?"

There was the term again but she smiled and said, "This is Ahriku, the Great Wolf," almost as introduction. Her face shone with a light that he had seen nowhere since before Baambas started coughing out plumes. It was the light of joy. He asked himself what he was doing allowing her to have a dog in the cave but then shrugged and walked away.

Ki'ti didn't ask Wamumur why he called her Little Girl although her curiosity burned to know. The People were supposed to observe in silence and think to find answers. She knew it had something to do with survival and the need for each individual to be able to think for the good of the group, but somehow it was hard for her to put all the pieces together. How much easier to remember the stories.

Totamu was performing her morning walk through the home cave. Finally, she settled down and called to Ki'ti. The girl went quickly to her, accompanied by Ahriku. Totamu motioned for her to sit in front of her. She did and the dog sat beside her. "Is Wamumur permitting you to keep the dog with you?"

"Yes, Izumo."

Her great grandmother lifted an eyebrow almost imperceptibly.

Ki'ti noticed that Totamu had a stone in her hand. Made of chert, it held a sharp edge when hit by a hammer stone. "Turn and face the fire," Totamu told her. Ki'ti obeyed immediately. She felt the comb in her hair and Totamu began to delouse her hair. Ki'ti bore with it in silence. She had some tangles. Totamu put the combed out material on top of an old piece of leather. Later, she would toss the material into the fire. She combed and combed. At one point, Ki'ti thought the lice might be better than the pulling.

"Now," Totamu said when she reached the end of the combing, "I am going to cut your hair."

"No, please, Izumo, I will look like a boy." Ki'ti was holding her hair down against her skull.

"Nonsense. I am going to cut it shorter than boy's hair anyway. We are not living in our normal homes and the lice are bad. We will have short hair while we are here." And she began to cut away over Ki'ti's protestations. She left no hair longer than her thumb. Totamu carefully placed the clippings on the piece of leather. Some in the cave were fascinated with what Totamu was doing. The men who were eager to get back to their work saw this as a great time to evacuate the cave.

Minagle, who had been gathering water with Domur, Aryna, Meeka, and Liho, noticed what was happening when they brought the gourds up. She held her arms over her head and said to the girls, "I will be next. I have always tried to keep my hair neat. I like it long like this."

"You can be sure that it will grow again," Aryna offered.

"Yes," Minagle said, resigned but not pleased.

She saw Totamu rise and shake the leather into the fire. She also noticed that Totamu had picked up the largest gourd and was following them to the lower level with Ki'ti and the dog. Ki'ti's hair looked like the hair of a year-old child. At least it didn't look like boy's hair. Totamu went further into the cave than the girls who were filling the gourds. The water was about two feet deep where the girls gathered water for drinking. It was deeper and swifter where Totamu went. She told Ki'ti to remove her tunic and she did. She pointed to a place nearer the wall and had Ki'ti stand there while she poured water over her head. The water was cold. Ki'ti ran her fingers through what was left of her hair. She reveled in the water. Totamu continued to pour gourds of water over the girl until the child had used her hands to wipe the dirt and ash off her skin from head to foot. Then she shook out Ki'ti's tunic and slipped it over her head. She combed the girl's hair and smiled. "You look almost like People," Totamu smiled.

"I feel wonderful!" Ki'ti had to admit. She and the dog scampered back up to the living level of the cave.

Totamu walked up the ramp-like path. She searched for Minagle and found her. She did the same thing with Minagle that she had done with Ki'ti. Then she cut the hair of Likichi and Enut and Pechki. Enut asked her to cut Domur's hair, so even Domur was not spared. The girls looked at each other and didn't know whether to laugh or cry. They felt wonderful after having bathed, but the way they looked with short hair was something to get used to. Minagle's hair was thick. She had felt her hair instead of lying down on her head as it did on the People—hers stood straight up. She kept trying to press it down but she had to give up. Way down deep inside she realized again how different she was. It hurt.

Totamu looked up. It was Emaea. "Yes, Emaea?" she said expectantly.

"You have done well, Totamu. I ask you to cut my hair and the hair of the girls and women in my group."

Totamu was overwhelmed. Praise from Emaea was treasured and never expected. "Please," Totamu gestured for her to sit down. She cut Emaea's hair and then poured water over her at what she now considered the bath. Emaea pulled her own tunic over her head and once clothed, she hugged Totamu.

"Tell the women and girls I will cut their hair tomorrow. Tell them after we eat in the morning to come to me. That is all I have to say."

Emaea smiled. She would inform them, but they'd probably know as soon as they saw her with her short hair. How good it felt to be clean and have all that hair gone for the present.

Totamu went to Pechki and held out the comb and sharp cutting tool. Without a word, Pechki began to comb Totamu's hair and delouse it. She worked diligently, not wanting to leave a single louse in her mother's hair. She used the same piece of hard thick leather that Totamu had used to put the hair and lice on. She was gentler than Totamu, but she was just as thorough. When Pechki finished, she dumped the contents of the leather into the fire and went with Totamu to the bathing area and poured water over her head until Totamu was satisfied. The two short-haired women looked at each other and laughed heartily. After all the trekking and working to set up life in a cave, they felt clean and that life was good. It was good to be clean.

The cave inhabitants were beginning to settle down for the night. Some of the hunters were still at Cave Sumbrel working on meat preparation. The light was beginning to fade, so they had begun to pack up to return to the home cave.

Nanichak-na touched Chamul-na's shoulder. "We will have to have our hair and beards cut off when we return home," he jested. The women could not have overridden Totamu, but the men could.

"That and our manly hair probably," Grypchon-na entered the conversation and there was coarse laughter in the cave. His point was that he saw Totamu as having a willingness to control people, sometimes to a fault.

Nanichak-na said, "I have no lice there. Have you?"

Grypchon-na and the others men agreed that the lice were only on their heads. They wondered why the lice seemed confined to that one location when there was hair in other places.

The men filed out from Cave Sumbrel ready for food. They were tired and had already discussed the unlikely need of posting guards. All washed their hands and arms in the water in the cave before they left Cave Sumbrel. They all left the cave as it was without gating it. The day had been a long one. When they arrived back at the home cave, they were surprised at the number of women who had shortened hair. Oddly, some felt it was appealing and, certainly, the clean bodies were appealing. As tired as they were, the men ate and then went to their sleeping mats. Wisdom would restore color to the land early, and they wanted to use as much time as possible while it was light to gather the meat and prepare it for stocking the cave.

While the men ate, Wamumur found Totamu. "Would you?" he asked her. "I want all the hair cut off my head and face. Right down to the skin." He handed her his prize cutting tool that was the sharpest he had ever made. It was of black flint that he'd had since he was a child.

Totamu nodded and Wamumur sat. He was not a person that she would have told to wait until the morning. She did not even begin to delouse him. To remove all his hair gave lice no place to be. They would fall off with the hair she cut. She realized that he had gone one step further than she. But cutting hair so close to the skin also gave her a challenge. How to do that without cutting him? She worked slowly, getting a feel for how she would do this. The tool at first felt odd to her. It was large. Little by little, however, she began to get a feel for the tool. It had one very sharp edge and soon she learned to shave instead of cut the hair. She was successful in shaving the hair and not the skin. When she finished, she and Wamumur went to the area she had set aside for bathing. He pulled off his tunic and slipped to a kneeling position, since he was too tall for her to reach above his head otherwise. The cold water pouring over him was like a balm to his fatigue. He reveled in the feeling of getting clean, though he felt a bit strange to be hairless on head and face.

Totamu helped by scrubbing part of his back that he couldn't reach. After he stood, she poured water over his legs and feet. Then he shook out his tunic and replaced it. They walked up the ramp together. The Winds of Change were touching so many parts of their lives.

When the two re-entered the living part of the cave, some of the women gasped. The men controlled themselves barely. Wamumur's new look would take some getting used to. What Wamumur suspected is that his days of scratching head lice were over. Thanks to Totamu, he would sleep well.

Ki'ti curled up with Ahriku and was asleep long before many in the cave. The buzz of the last minute clean ups and unrolling sleep mats was short-lived and the cave settled for the night.

As Wisdom returned color to the land, the hunters were up early. They ate quickly and got outside to begin the day. They had used up all the posts and narrow runners and cross poles that they had taken to construct drying racks and meat holders and skin stretchers. They had used all poles available from the two groups of the People and the Others. Mootmu-na announced that he would be going out to look for new supplies to construct more meat racks. Without a word from any of the men, Hahami-na, Kai, Ermol-na, Gummo, and Guy-na went to him and began to put on their booted garments. Wamumur smiled. The mixed group was working as one, at least for the present.

Cave Sumbrel was a large cave with a wide entrance that curved like Cave Kwa, only with a more significant curve. The cave had a ceiling opening midway into the cave in the shape of a circle with a diameter bigger than the men were tall. Through the hole, one could see the sky. To avoid a breeze, it would be necessary to go to the very back of the cave. The men had built a fire under the ceiling hole and that created a draft that circulated the air even more effectively. It was a great shelter for drying meat. Abiedelai-na had brought their huge chunk of salt. Pieces of it were stirred in a large bowl of water for a dip for the meat strips. The men kept meat from the ashfall for themselves where after-death blood had not pooled, saving the meat where it had pooled for the dogs. The two types of meat were stored separately.

The operation was as efficient, if not fragrant, as the men could make it. Having the new drying racks would help with the enormous amount of meat they were putting up. The men were surprised to see Flayk, Amey, Olintak, Aneal, Mulop, Seacah, Dolk, Tap, and Rayla arriving at the cave so early. They were there to begin to work the skins. They had brought their tools and gathered toward the back of the cave to work. They completely separated flesh from skin. To remove the hair, they soaked the skins in urine. To soften the skins, they soaked the skins with brains and salt. To keep the odor down, they burned the flesh in the fires. Little scraps of hides were kept in water-filled skin bags to deteriorate into a form of glue once the water was boiled off. Beyond that were drying frames where skins were tied to finalize the process and dry. They were talking among themselves with much stuttering and looking for words, but making a huge effort at language learning. Gummo noticed that Tap, his wife, still had long hair. He smiled, considering that the long hair wouldn't last long.

Domur, Minagle, Aryna, Meeka, and Liho were out gathering wood when Domur noticed some low growing vegetation sticking through the ash. She brushed off the ash with a stick and found a blueberry bush that had fruit attached. She asked Liho if she knew how to get back to the home cave. She nodded that she did. Domur asked Liho to get something to hold the blueberries. Domur said blueberry several times so that Liho would remember the word. Liho grinned with understanding and took off at a run. Domur began to shake the bush. The other girls found similar bushes. They were delighted. Tonight they could have a real treat. Liho returned with a plain bowl made of carved wood. Quickly and with great care, the girls began to fill the bowl. Liho started to eat a blueberry and was reproved by Minagle. The area had a number of blueberry bushes and the girls soon filled the bowl and Meeka carried it carefully back to the home cave where it was emptied and she returned with it for more. It took until high sun for the girls to pick clean the blueberry bushes in that area. Minagle carried the last blueberries to the cave. The other girls returned to their stick gathering, feeling well satisfied. Minagle joined them after delivering the blueberries.

Totamu noticed Blanagah sitting hugging her knees on her sleeping mat. She went over to the girl and touched her shoulder. "What are you doing?" Totamu asked.

Blanagah did not respond.

Totamu shoved her. "Get up and put on a booted garment. Go to Cave Sumbrel and work on those skins. There are not enough people working the skins and there's a need for someone to stretch skins and you're strong," she said loud enough for the entire cave to hear. Blanagah was frightened. Rarely were orders issued among the People. When they were, it was due usually to laziness or obstinacy. Blanagah got up and desultorily headed for the cave opening. It was bleak inside the cave without Reemast; it was bleak outside the cave with all the gray monotone; it was bleak to do skins. However, she would prefer to do skins than have Totamu escalate her attack. She did what she must automatically. Suddenly, every woman in the cave who was not inextricably involved in an activity that was critical to the group's welfare gathered tools and left for Cave Sumbrel. Even Enut prepared to join them.

Totamu stopped Enut. "Your cough is bad. Stay here." Totamu doubted that Enut would have enough breath to make it to the cave. Her cough had gotten a lot worse even with help of the leaves. She wondered whether Enut might die soon. Enut retreated to her sleeping skins. Her awareness was at a low level. She responded simply to directions from others.

Shmyukuk had been nursing Ey's infant much more frequently and the baby girl was showing signs of life. It gave Shmyukuk a strange sense of fulfillment that she'd never experienced. Ey had gone to work the skins along with Likichi. Shmyukuk, Wamumal, and Mitrak were caring for all the infants of whom there were seven: Frakja was Likichi's two-year-old boy; Mitrak's two-year-old daughter was Ketra; Wamumal's year-old twin boys were Ekoy and Smig; Trokug was Shmyukuk's year-old son; Tita was Ey's two-year-old daughter; and Seenaha was Amey's three-year-old daughter.

Wamumur was back listening to stories with Ki'ti and she had just finished the last story. She had not erred. Now, Wamumur was ready to move to the second stage of the examination. He wanted her to discuss the meanings or significances of the stories. As they began to discuss the significances, Ki'ti began to fail. It was one thing to know all the words and inflections but the significances, those were something else. He then realized that he would have to begin again. She would tell the first story and then they would discuss it in detail. He knew that with her memory, there would be little problem getting her to remember the significances. Even greater understanding would come in time as she repeated to herself or to another the significances. He would have to be sure that she understood the finer points. But he knew he had his replacement. On that, he could rest assured.

Wamumur was intrigued with the dog. It seemed to have one desire in life—to be near Ki'ti. It did not bother anyone in the cave. The two seemed to have a special bond and that was captivating to the old man.

Totamu went to Eki and motioned for her to follow. Eki was one of the newcomers and was working with Munjun to cook the meat for the evening meal. Totamu deloused her hair and then cut it. That was followed by a trip for bathing and then Totamu sought out Pu. Pu had left for the skins. She looked for the other women who were new and could not find one. Then she realized that Blanagah had left with long hair. Totamu smiled to herself.

Her comments to Blanagah had been very effective. Then she remembered Munjun. Munjun had been turning the large roasts that were speared and cooking slowly over the fire. Munjun had just returned from the privy and Totamu went to her. Munjun kneeled at the roasting pit and Totamu began with the delousing. Munjun had white hair but it was not the white hair of Totamu's People which was fine and very white. Munjun's hair, Totamu noticed, still had some black in it and the white color was more gray than white. It was thick hair.

Down in the bathing area, Munjun was replacing her shaken out tunic when she beamed at Totamu and said haltingly, "I you thank." Totamu smiled and put her hand on Munjun's shoulder. "It's 'thank you'," she said.

Munjun looked at her, "Thank you."

Totamu smiled and lowered her head. *It's good,* she thought. *It is good.* She patted Munjun's shoulder.

When the women gathered to begin to return to the home cave to help with food preparation, they divided up who would stay and continue working and who would go for food preparation. This division was handled well for the women who returned to the home cave did so willingly and those who stayed to work the skins did so willingly. No one seemed to notice that nobody who had long hair willingly returned to the home cave.

Totamu had taken some of the grains they had and mixed them with blueberries that had been washed ash free earlier. When the women arrived, she had two of them take the grains and the blueberries and mix them together with a little honey from the gut bag and then roll them into little round balls and place them on a long sheet of leather to dry out. They would have a very special sweet treat.

Totamu sent Wamumal to Cave Sumbrel to bring a long-haired woman back with her. Wamumal quickly put on a booted garment and went to do Totamu's bidding. When she reached the cave, she said, "Totamu has sent for the first of you for haircutting."

Feeling that she needed to show an example even though she didn't want to, Pu arose and followed Wamumal. As they walked back to the home cave, Pu touched Wamumal's head and asked the best she could how it felt to have short hair. Wamumal, smiled and said, "Wonderful! No louse bites all day." Pu understood. Pu's arrival surprised Totamu. She expected People, not Others. She was secretly pleased.

By the time the evening meal was ready, all but two women had been shorn. As soon as Totamu finished at the bath with one, that one would return to Cave Sumbrel and send back another. Totamu had been surprised that she had had to summon the women. They were supposed to have presented themselves after the morning meal. At least, the People were supposed to. Totamu had pushed the Others and made no apologies. Totamu, however, did not dwell on the shortcomings of her People's running away that morning rather than being shorn. She might have done the same thing had she been young. Totamu was an administrator of sorts. If People neglected what they were supposed to do, she took it upon herself to poke and prod or do whatever was necessary to make the group function as optimally as possible.

The evening meal was a great success. The roasts were wonderful and the blueberry-grain-honey rolled delicacies were really special. There were enough treats for one more night. All People enjoyed the unexpected luxury, except Frakja, who stuck a piece of the treat up his nostril and had to endure the discomfort of having it extracted.

After the evening meal, Totamu caught one by one of the Others and cut their hair. She was surprised that the Others did not object, since she had no permission to cut their hair but then she thought, they are accustomed to being told what to do. Pu had indeed set an example. She smiled and kept on with her work to eliminate head lice.

Ki'ti sat beside Wamumur after they ate. She looked up at his shaved head and beardless face again as if getting used to it was taking a while. At least he had his eyebrows. He felt her eyes on him and looked at her.

She could contain it no longer. "Wise One, why do you call me Little Girl?"

He put his arm around her and asked why she hadn't been able to know why. She frowned and said it might be easier to understand if he was calling someone else Little Girl.

"Very well," he said, "I'll tell you. You are our next Wise One."

"No, that's impossible!" she protested, shocked.

"Why so?" he asked.

"I am not that important, Wise One," she said with her head lowered.

"Little Girl, look at me."

Ki'ti looked into his eyes as he continued, "Wise Ones don't select themselves. Wisdom searches the People and selects the Wise One. Wisdom does not search for someone who deserves the mission but rather the person Wisdom chooses is the one Wisdom chooses. Wisdom didn't choose you because you have a better or worse mind web than someone else. You are able to remember the stories because Wisdom *gave* them to you. Wisdom is wiser than either you or I will ever hope to be. You cannot argue with Wisdom.

You have a mission and you have to fulfill it now that Wisdom gave you the stories. Also, there will be a time when I die. Your mission is to follow me. The People must have a Wise One or we lose all our knowledge. You have the knowledge but not the understanding right now. It is my job to give you the understanding. But there is great danger in knowing that you will become Wise One and in being one. The danger is that you can come to see yourself as more than you should. People think better of themselves than they should all the time. For a Wise One to do it threatens the life of the entire People. It is very tempting to get puffed up with pride, and then you are not only worthless but the People can also perish because of it, because you think of self first. You have to guard against it for the rest of your life. I call you Little Girl to remind you now and in the future that you are to kill your pride every time it raises its head. You will remember my calling you that. You will remember my warning about pride. A prideful Wise One is a fool. You are critical to the survival of the People but that makes you servant to all, not chief. Sometimes you will want to do other things and you will have to deny yourself. Do you understand my words?"

"Yes. Wise One, did you ever have to deny yourself?"

Wamumur chuckled to himself. "See that woman there?"

"You mean Emaea?"

"Yes, I do. When we were young and of the age to join, our groups met. It was a very long time ago. We wanted to join. We burned for each other. I know you don't understand that yet. But we had to part."

"Why, Wise One?" Ki'ti looked sad.

"Because she is the Wise One of her group and I am the Wise One of ours. It cut our bellies to the core to have to split—I felt as if my belly bled for years, but that is the way of Wisdom. Our bellies were cut for the rest of our lives—until I walked into this cave and we were together again. Other times, you want to do other things. There were times when I wanted to hunt or explore. Those are things that are denied a Wise One. We end up protected. Even when we don't want to be protected." He looked off into the distance farther than the walls.

"So that is why you haven't joined now that you're together again? In case you have to part?"

"You are very perceptive when the subject is not yourself," he acknowledged with a small laugh.

"So you are starting to get me used to having to deny myself by calling me Little Girl?"

"Very good, Little Girl."

"But it makes me sound younger than I am," she continued to protest.

"Yes, it does. Imagine how you'll feel when I call you that and you are" and he flashed thirty. He seriously doubted he'd be alive when she reached that age.

"You wouldn't do that?" she said questioningly, horrified.

"I will do anything I can to keep you from pride," he vowed. "The very feeling of resentment you are having right now is pride, Little Girl."

"I like Falling Star a lot better than Little Girl," she said. "Please tell me that the People won't start to use that term."

He smiled. "They won't unless I tell them to do it. Right now, your words are pride, Little Girl." He was becoming testy.

Ki'ti lowered her head. "Forgive me?"

"Yes. Start thinking about your pride and begin killing it off. Right now, you are concerned with what you want and what you like. Get rid of those feelings. That is not what being a Wise One is all about. Put first in your mind that the People are more important than any want you'll ever have. You are servant."

After a while she asked, "Do the People know I will become Wise One someday?

"Some have thought it out and know, but I've told no one yet. I will have to do it soon because you have to be protected. In fact, there is no better time than right now."

Wamumur rose and asked whether anyone was missing from the cave. Blanagah wanted to scream that Reemast was missing, but she held her peace. No one was missing. Then he began the pronouncement. It was directed to the People, not the Others as much, but he made it to the whole group. Wisdom had selected Ki'ti as the next Wise One. From that moment forth she was to be protected. The People knew what that meant and each took it seriously that instant. The hunters who were learning the stories would not be relieved of their duties to continue to practice the stories, but the next Wise One would be Ki'ti.

Ki'ti did not realize that never again would she be able to go anywhere without hunter escort lest some wild beast or person snatch her. Her life was making an enormous change. She would never again know privacy, though to the little group of People, privacy wasn't really a major issue, but she was not permitted even to go to the privy alone since it was outside the cave. For her, it might be easier at this age than when she became woman, but it would not be easy—ever.

She left Wamumur and went to her sleeping mat. She was very tired and now she had full realization that the last few days had been a test of her, Wamumur hadn't wanted to listen to season-of-cold-days stories at the end of the season of warm nights. But she should have known that Wamumur did not waste his time days on end with a child for no reason. She just hadn't questioned. She ran her fingers through the fur on her sleeping mat. She stretched out and hugged Ahriku to her belly. What would her life be? Her mind raced into sleep.

Blanagah returned from the privy and sat on her sleeping mat. She noticed that Olintak and Slamika were moving under their skins and she knew what that motion meant. Good for Olintak, she thought, and then returned to the ache in her own belly. She pulled the skin over her and tried to block all thought and sound.

It was not long before the entire cave was asleep except for the lone guard at the entrance.

When Wisdom returned color to the land, the hunters were up quickly, eager to get on with the meat preparation. The women served the morning meal as swiftly as possible. There was a feeling that this would be a good day. The women hurried to get to the skin preparation. There were some lovely aurochs skins.

Manak virtually inhaled his food and then came and kneeled before Totamu. "Izumo," he said, "Would you cut off my hair like you did for the Wise One?"

"If you wish," she said. "You will have to get the tools from Wamumur."

Manak rocked his feet back to standing and went to Wamumur who was at the cave entrance. He asked if he could take the tools to Izumo who would cut off all his hair as she had his. He agreed and told Manak where the tools were. Manak was bald and his little facial hair was gone quickly. He then raced to the Cave Sumbrel to get his assignment for the day without taking time for a bath. He noticed that he felt wonderful to be shaved, but the air on his naked head felt a little strange, but at least nothing was moving or biting.

When Totamu finished with Manak, Ekuktu asked for the same head and face shave. Totamu agreed to do it. She had gone earlier to return the tools to Wamumur and he suggested she keep them for a while since it was likely she'd need them again. He was right.

The young girls gathered and began to put on their booted garments for their stick gathering. Ki'ti joined them and when Wamumur saw her with the girls putting on a booted garment, he strode over and picked her up by the straps on the booted garment, holding her out from him as if she were a bug.

"What are you doing, Little Girl?" he asked roughly. "Did last night mean nothing to you?"

She wished he'd put her down. She felt utterly foolish dangling there and the dog didn't know whether to bark forcefully or tuck tail and run, so he watched and shivered.

"You are to become Wise One. You do not go off with a few girls. You are to start learning. Now, take off the garment." He put her down and turned and moved to his favorite area of the cave.

Ki'ti lowered her head and shed tears. Minagle put her arm around her sister. She whispered, "Your responsibility is more important than ours, my Sister. Go and do well."

Ki'ti removed the garment and went to kneel before Wamumur.

"I will try to do better, Wise One," she said.

"Let's get something straight. Until I die, you will be by my side all day every day unless I tell you differently. You will learn what it is to be Wise One. That is your mission. You have no choice in this and your pride will prick at you for some time to come. The sooner you get control over it, better yet kill it, the sooner you will be happy."

"Wise One, I really don't want to be a Wise One. I am not fit."

Wamumur grabbed her by the back of her tunic and tossed her across his legs and swatted her very hard on the bottom as if she were an infant. "You have no choice. I do not want to hear those thoughts again ever. Things are what they are. How dare you call yourself unfit when Wisdom gave you the stories? You blaspheme Wisdom! You cannot change this. If I must treat you like you're an infant, I will. Wisdom chose you. I didn't. Do you think I would fight Wisdom? Never!" He paused. He had lied. He recently fought Wisdom on the trek. *Fortunately,* he thought, *no one knew.* "Now, start getting used to how things will be. You cannot change this. To fight it, you have to fight me and the People. Worse, you'd have to fight Wisdom. You will lose. Make this easier on yourself. Obey." He picked her up and put her to his side. Ki'ti's head was as low as she could get it. She knew then and there that she had better quickly control her mouth and learn to curb or kill her own pride. But how, remained to be clear.

Wamumur remembered his blasphemy when they trekked to avoid the eruption. He felt bad to discipline the child for what he'd so recently done himself. He knew better when he did it. He felt he had to be sure she knew not to blaspheme. He still felt wretched. It ripped his belly.

The girls had seen with horror from the entrance what was happening. Each was so relieved that they were not in Ki'ti's position. They knew their roles and it was easy to do what was expected of them for the good of the People. They didn't have the stories in their mind webs and were grateful not to have to change lives as would be required of Ki'ti. They scurried on their way to get out of the cave.

Once out looking for sticks, Liho and Meeka asked about the Wise One and what they had just witnessed meant. The other girls tried to explain it. They answered questions for a very long time because the ways of the People and the ways of Meeka and Liho were so very different. The girls were also afraid that they might anger Wamumur and end up swatted. The other girls reassured them that there was no chance of that. The role of Wise One carried tremendous responsibility and the person designated had to give up a lot of their own wants. Ki'ti was just new at it. She'd be fine but she wouldn't have a girl's life from now on. She was young to become a Wise One so it would probably be harder for her, they thought, and it probably wouldn't help that Ki'ti was really strong willed. They understood that right now, the Wise One would be very strict with her. They also agreed that they were glad they hadn't been selected by Wisdom.

Manak and Ermi were scouting for meat. Suddenly, Manak thought he heard something. He signed for a quiet stop. Both listened intently and sure enough they both heard the same strange noise. Then Ermi pointed off to the north east. Each one could see the elk. As they watched, they realized that the animal was not covered by the dust but apparently it was blind. They had the location poles but without sharpened ends. Manak motioned for Ermi to remain watching the elk and he would return.

As fast as he could, Manak ran to the home cave to get his spear and his father's. He didn't know where Ermi kept his spear. In his haste, he'd forgotten to ask. His father's spear would suffice. He raced back to where he had left Ermi. The two made quick work of the blind elk. Then they marked it with the poles and raced back to the meat preparation cave. They told the hunters of their find—live meat

All of the hunters gathered and talked. Finally, Manak and Ermi were given new assignments. They were to take gathering poles and make a trail through the ash. They were to try to follow the elk's path. What they were to do is to follow for a day to see whether they got out of the ashfall. At the end of the day, they were to return home. They were cautioned to watch the sky in case there was more ash to fall. They needed to get food and water from the home cave. Nanichak-na told them to pack the foodstuffs on a dog or two. It was an adventure and both young men looked forward to it. Other men were sent immediately to the elk.

When they got to the home cave, Manak and Ermi were still excited. Women packed foodstuffs for them and included a supply of the blueberry treats. Water bags were filled to the brim and the men left with the dogs and lots of water. Each had a small sleeping cover rolled and tied which they carried on their backs. How exciting it would be to find that a day's walk would get them out of the ashfall!

Totamu was kneeling beside Enut. She was worried about her granddaughter. Enut's coughing was more and more rattly, and she appeared weaker and weaker. She had hardly eaten anything that morning.

"Are you using the leaves?" Totamu asked. She tried not to show the alarm she felt.

"Yes. They don't seem to be helping. I am just so tired." Enut was lying down.

Totamu put her head gently against Enut's chest. She listened carefully and scowled. Totamu took some skins and lifted Enut enough to get her lungs elevated. The raspiness of her breathing really concerned Totamu. Enut was warmer than normal but not burning hot. Totamu was beside herself. She concluded that the old age sickness was getting Enut way before her time. Lots of old people died when their lungs filled with water. Granted, Enut did have totally white hair, but she was thirty-three. Her sister, Likichi, had brown hair without a hint of white at thirty. Thirty-three was young to die. She kept racing through her mind web tying to find a remedy for Enut but she could find nothing more than the leaves she was already using. Enut coughed gently.

"Izumo," she said softly, "don't worry over me. I'm going to die soon. I know it. I have had a good life. When I die, will you ask Likichi to mother Domur?"

Totamu knew not to pretend differently when someone said they knew they were dying. She took Enut's hand in hers, "Of course. You do know that Domur and Manak want to marry?'

"Oh, yes. Then will you mother Domur?" If Likichi had mothered Domur, then Manak and she could not have married because they would have had the same mother. That was considered incest even when one of the brother/sister pair was adopted. It would be prohibited.

"Of course," Totamu said.

"Thank you, Izumo. I want you to know that I love you very much. I have talked to Hahami-na and he knows all that I've said to you. Live long, my Izumo." Enut shut her eyes and went to sleep. Totamu watched her for a while. She seemed to be doing no worse, no better, so she went to attend to cave affairs. Totamu hoped the condition would improve but she could not shake the feeling that Enut would die soon.

The sleeping mats had been rolled up and were at the edges of the cave, so Totamu began to sweep the floor of the cave to get out any ash or dirt that might be on the floor. She was careful to sweep away from Enut, but otherwise she was vigorous in her method. Wamumur watched her and wondered. He was listening to Ki'ti's retelling the first story so they could discuss it. He would have to be tough on her until she lost the strong will she seemed bent on showing. He was realizing what Totamu had been fussing about. Teaching was hard.

From time to time, Ki'ti wanted to shed tears from the morning's time with Wamumur, but she kept her mind on the storytelling and tried to forget her feelings. Her right hand occasionally reached down to touch Ahriku and that reassured her that a tiny part of her world was comforting. Ahriku would lick her hand in return.

Totamu came closer and stopped near them. "Little Girl," she said, "I was ashamed of you this morning."

"Izumo, I ask forgiveness. I wronged the People." She hung her head.

"Very well, Little Girl, but I don't ever want to see that again. The People depend on you."

"I will obey, Izumo." Ki'ti lowered her head. She wanted to weep but dared not. Then she lifted her head and asked permission to go to the privy. Wamumur got up and agreed to accompany her. He winked at Totamu as they left the cave. Totamu swept the place where they had been sitting.

Manak and Ermi had not returned when the evening meal was served or when Wisdom sucked the color from the land. That meant that the ashfall covered some real distance from where they were. Even when Wisdom returned color to the land, the young men had not returned. By high sun, they were back at the home cave returning the dogs and preparing to go to work.

"Did you sleep?" Emaea asked.

"No, we kept going. Hoping," Ermi said.

"Then you will lie down and sleep," Emaea said as Totamu joined her.

"But I feel fine," Manak protested and was joined by Ermi.

"Listen to what I tell you," Emaea said firmly. "You will lie down and sleep until the evening meal. Do not argue. Do as you are told." Manak and Ermi could have refused but neither had the temerity to counter Totamu whose silent support of Emaea was unquestioned. They were men, but Manak was still close to childhood and Ermi was trained to accept orders. And the men were tired.

Both young men walked down to the bathing area and washed off and then found their sleeping mats, got a cover, and went to sleep.

Lamk and Sum, eight-year-old boys, had been assigned home cave coal duty. They were provided baskets to fill with coal and take to the home cave. Pechki showed them where to store the chunks down in the lower part of the cave. The boys worked tirelessly. They talked haltingly of the ashfall and wondered whether it would continue. They talked of the game that had been found. This was a true adventure to them. Sum was learning the language quickly from Lamk. They had been in the cave at Ki'ti's tough time and each time they walked by she was mortified. They would look at her with sympathy, which made it worse. Then she would remind herself that even feeling bad about herself when people looked at her with sympathy was pride and she would try to calm her feelings. Why, she wondered, did she just not accept the sympathy? It wasn't easy! Pride was complicated. Everywhere she looked there was her pride staring back at her. She wondered whether she would ever become Wise One with her deficits. At that moment, Ahriku's lovely golden eyes looked into hers with adoration. For the first time that day, Ki'ti smiled.

"Thank you!" she said with enthusiasm.

"For what?" Wamumur asked, puzzled.

"Wise One, I was thanking Wisdom for giving me a dog to help me go through this learning."

"Then, Little Girl, today you have learned at least one thing. Gratitude to Wisdom is good." Wamumur put his hand on her shoulder.

"Wise One, do you love me?" she asked boldly.

"Yes, Little Girl, I do. This responsibility would be a lot easier if I didn't," he admitted. "Do you love me?"

"Yes. It rips my belly when I feel that I have disappointed you." She looked deep into his eyes and he knew her words were truthful.

"Then, obey me."

"Wise One, I am really trying." Again he saw truth in her words.

Wamumur said nothing else. He was miles away wondering in his secret mind web what their offspring would have been like if he and Emaea had been able to have children. If he could have had children with her, he would have liked them to be just like Ki'ti. He shook himself from the daydream and got up to go outside. He signed to Ki'ti and she joined him.

When they returned, he told her that she could go to be with the younger people. She felt awkward after the morning but realized that she had to interact with those in the cave so she might as well do it. Let her pride die.

She went to sit near Minagle. Minagle put her arm around Ki'ti's shoulder and told her she loved her.

"I love you too, Minagle, and I am sorry to shame our family so."

"It was no shame to me, Sister. I am happy that you will be the Wise One but I know that the learning will be hard for you. It would be hard for anyone. You are very young. Mother says that Wise Ones aren't usually found until they are almost" and she flashed two tens. "So your childhood just got cut short. But then all of us have a childhood cut short in this ashfall. Is your bottom sore?"

"Yes," she replied softly, "very sore."

"You'll get over that soon. I am sorry for you but you do have a strong will and a mouth quick to speak." Minagle smiled at her sister. She covered her sister's hand with her larger one.

"I wish Wisdom had chosen you," Ki'ti whispered.

At those words, Minagle shuddered inwardly, knowing she would have shared her sister's feelings if she'd been selected. She said, "I wouldn't say that aloud, if I were you. Actually, you should never say that out loud or think it. Wisdom chooses whoever Wisdom will. We are not to question Wisdom. Saying that makes you look like an infant. That's probably why you were treated as one."

"That's what Wise One said, but see, you already know that. I didn't."

"Sister, you do know it now and you just said what you said. That is your danger. You have to control your mouth. I don't have all those stories in my mind web. You have them for a reason, to show that Wisdom chose you. Now you have to learn all the other information that Wise Ones have to know."

Ki'ti realized that she should be silent.

"I'll always be your sister and love you," Minagle tried to reassure her.

"Thank you, Minagle." Ki'ti lowered her head.

"What's the dog as your friend all about?" Minagle asked.

Ki'ti's visage brightened. "I think Wisdom gave me the dog to comfort me through this time. Ahriku is my dog's name. Ahriku is my friend."

"I see," Minagle said, but she didn't really.

Liho came over to where Minagle and Ki'ti were sitting. She was fascinated with the dog. "Can I touch the dog?" she asked, searching Ki'ti's eyes.

"Try it," Ki'ti replied.

Ahriku looked questioningly at Ki'ti as Liho extended her hand toward him. She told him that it was okay. Ahriku permitted himself to be stroked.

Liho then stood back and watched the dog. She was fascinated but would not have wanted to try to have a dog herself.

Sum and Lamk were returning to the cave. Lamk turned off to the privy. Before going in the cave, Sum met Keptu. He said to Keptu very quietly in the language of the Minguat, "We used to think the People were really dumb. They aren't dumb at all, do you think?"

Keptu looked startled that Sum had used their language and had asked the question he had. "I don't really think about it much," she replied in her own language in a whisper. "Do you think all our Minguat could be so wrong? But I really like Lamk. He's smart."

Sum and Keptu shrugged as if the question were too difficult to understand. They went into the cave hoping to find some food. Sometimes food was available between meals.

Totamu went to Hahami-na and said quietly, "Enut has spoken to me."

"Did you agree?" he asked.

"Well, first I reminded her that Domur and Manak want to join. I approve of joining them. Enut asked me to mother Domur so that the two young People can be together as husband and wife."

"I should have thought of that," Hahami-na said with his head lowered.

"My friend," Totamu said, "there is too much in the Winds of Change for all of us right now. The only one who seems to have a solid, coherent memory right now is Ki'ti."

"Poor Little One. To be chosen so young. She is trying so hard and keeps blundering." He ran his hand over his bald pate.

"Wamumur is being harder on her than he might be if it had been someone that he didn't love so much. I think he is also being hard on her because she will be woman. She is a strong willed little girl right now. She keeps saying things that should not be spoken against Wisdom."

"I bet his calling her Little Girl rankles her." Hahami-na smiled.

"Oh, yes. Until she controls that part of her pride and learns to keep her mouth shut, she may find it hard to sit." The two shared a laugh at Ki'ti's expense. They felt for her but each had run up against Ki'ti's strong will more than once.

Before the people in the cave settled for sleep, Totamu had completed all of the women's hair and had shaved the heads and beards of more than half of the men. She was relentless and seemingly tireless in her delousing effort.

Soon, all the members of the cave were settled for the night. Little shadows from the fire played against the ceiling and walls. Tiny sparks rose and vanished. Ahriku snuggled next to Ki'ti but seemed restless. He'd get up to make a circle and then settle back down. The single guard, Neamu-na, at the entryway looked out at the night sky and hoped that the ash had finished falling. He remembered that Manak had said that the ashfall as far as he went was only lower by a few fingers than at the cave. He worked at making a hammer stone. He was not as good a toolmaker as Ermol-na but he worked at it knowing that he had a responsibility to his tools whether he was very skilled or not. North seemed a good way to go when they left, he reasoned. It was opposite the direction of Baambas, but he wondered whether there were other mountains to the north that might explode. He heard a person make a strange sound late in the night. He looked around but saw nothing unusual.

Chapter 3

Totamu was awakened by a horribly loud, high pitched sound that seemed only vaguely familiar. She shook herself trying to slough off slumber. What was that noise? Others in the cave who had not already awakened were raised from sleep at the sound that pierced the space. Totamu realized the sound was coming from Domur and that clued her in immediately to the cause. She crawled across the mats to Enut and, yes, Enut was entering the next world and was with them no longer. Hahami-na was trying to comfort his daughter, who seemed inconsolable, while his own belly was torn with grief.

Totamu noticed that Hahami-na had failed to shut Enut's eyes, so Totamu gently closed the eyes, never again to see those beautiful blue eyes that had sparkled with life. She had been expecting Enut's death, but even when expected, she always found death was never easy to accept. Tears flowed silently from her eyes. She put her arms around Hahami-na and Domur. Then she saw Slamika. He, too, was weeping but in silence. Domur was making enough noise for them all, she supposed, as she kneeled, sitting on her feet before Enut's body.

Nanichak-na and Mootmu-na ratted around in the tools and found some strong bone digging tools. Each had taken a short broom, which was stiffer than a long broom, and a digging stick that was pointed and a tool of bone that scooped and they had gone to the cave entrance to put on their booted garments even before they ate. Nanichak-na had noticed what once had been a small glade before the ashfall turned the world into a monochrome landscape. He knew that Enut would not last long with the cough she had, and he had thought that the glade would be a good place for her burial. He had already discussed it with

Hahami-na, who was pleased with the site. Consequently, he and Mootmu-na were ready when the time came to do the work needed to make the place in the ground for Enut's journey to the next world. In the overcrowded cave, the burial would have to be done immediately. They left and headed toward the glade.

While the activity surrounding Enut's death was busily going on, the Others quietly slipped away from the cave to go to work on meat and skin preparation. The Others feared death and did not handle such times well.

It did not take long for everyone in the cave to know what had occurred. Minagle had replaced Hahami-na in comforting Domur and she was joined by Aryna, Meeka, and Liho. Hahami-na was busy locating Enut's small bag of personal tools. They would be given to Domur.

Totamu took a soft piece of leather and went to the large gourd of water. She immersed the leather and made it wet. She twisted it tightly to remove most of the water and returned to Enut, washing her face off with care and tenderness. Her granddaughter! Death had a strange way of choosing people. Who'd have thought she'd outlive her granddaughter. But then she had out-lived Reemast, Enut's son. Totamu thought about Reemast. They had killed him, she was certain, and with reason. But she had no idea who had done it. Normally, she would have known. He had crossed a line that was uncrossable. It was really sad. Had they not killed him, he might have murdered Minagle or someone else. There was a difference between killing and murdering, she knew, but death was death.

Totamu looked at her hands as she touched the hands of Enut. Her own hands looked so old. *When,* she wondered, *had they lost their flesh? When had her veins become so large? When had she gained all those wrinkles in her skin? When had her skin defined the bones in her hands instead of the other way around?* Her knuckles were huge. Her nails were broken and dirty. Normally, she had been careful to keep her hands clean. To prepare food and to stay healthy they had learned long ago, keeping hands relatively clean was important. Enut's hands did not look old at all. In a wisp of thought, Totamu realized that while she'd fled the volcano, been busy around the cave cutting hair of those in the cave, and tended to administrative duties, she'd neglected herself.

A few of the women in the cave came by to offer sympathy and assis-tance. Totamu didn't want any of either but tried to remain civil. She ached but had a responsibility and would fulfill it to the best of her ability. Focus on the work was also for her a balm for her pain. She wanted to make it so that when the men came to take Enut to the place for her burial, all would be ready. They had no flowers. There was nothing to add to the grave to send with her. When they left their home place, they had left anything that wasn't critically needed, even the red ochre for keeping skin in death. Totamu's eyes watered again. Then she remembered that Enut had eyed the shells on her dress. Totamu used the sharp cutting tool and removed one of the shells from her dress. That would do very well to send with Enut as a token of their love. She took a piece of leather from her bag, folded the strip, threaded the strip through the hole in the shell, and pulled the ends through the loop. Then she tied the ends of the leather together and slipped the necklace over Enut's head. *That would do very well*, she thought.

Pechki came over and looked at what Totamu had done. The two women hugged.

"You have done well, Mother. How can it be that I have lost a daughter and a grandson in just a few days?" Pechki's eyes were reddening from crying.

"Our People dwindle, Daughter. I do not know why this has to be. We do try so hard to take care of each other. Maybe it is time to join permanently with the other People to increase both our numbers? I have heard some talk, but in this case you and I, we have been hit hard with sadness. No one else seems to have become so sick. Look at that face. She seems to be sleeping, does she not? Just sleeping."

"Except, Mother, she is too still. Even in sleep we move. I remember when Nanichak-na's wife died. That hit me hard, but not like this. This is terrible."

"Dear One, we NEVER expect to outlive our children and grandchildren. What am I doing here at my age when my granddaughter's son is dead? No, we never expect the younger ones to leave first. It feels unnatural. But when I chase questions I cannot answer, I turn it over to Wisdom. There are things we never understand."

"Mother, your gift to Enut has not been unnoticed by me," Pechki said as she fingered the necklace Totamu had made. "I thank you so much. There are no flowers that we can put in the place of departure for her, but this more than makes up for it."

They hugged again in silence.

"Did Hahami-na tell you that I will mother Domur?"

"Yes, he did. That is wonderful because I know she wants to be free to join with Manak and he wants her. That's the only way to do it."

"So you're not opposed?"

"Mother, how could you ever think such a thing?"

"Pechki, I long ago learned that people have wide varieties of opinions and you can never be absolutely certain where another's desire is unless you ask, and even then you don't always know for certain. Do you want to finish cleaning her up? The rag is here."

"Of course, Mother, thank you."

A few of the Others had been getting the morning meal going. It gave them something to do when they were at a loss to grieve as the People were grieving for someone they didn't know.

Domur continued to wail and it was unnerving some of the cave inhabitants. Finally, Hahami-na walked over to Domur, and he made her stand. He took her to Totamu. "You have lost a mother," he said as if making a pronouncement, "But you have also gained a mother," he said while taking her right hand and putting it in the hand of Totamu.

She looked into Totamu's eyes and her wailing became silent with only tears falling as understanding pierced through her pain. She had wept for loss of a mother, certainly. She had found Enut with her eyes oddly splayed and wide open and her mouth open and her jaw hanging oddly. Domur realized her mother was dead. By tradition, daughters who were not yet women were passed to the mother's sister when the mother died. Manak was Likichi's son. Having Likichi for mother would have made Manak and Domur ineligible for joining. Domur's wailing was two-fold. She had lost a mother and expected to lose her choice of future husband. The Winds of Change had all but taken her will to live. When she realized she'd been passed to a new mother two generations removed from Likichi, Domur realized that she and Manak had been spared separation. Her relief was enormous. With her relief came her silence.

Totamu smiled wryly at Hahami-na. "We should have done this sooner."

"Yes," he agreed with a shrug, and left to go outside to help Mootmu-na and Nanichak-na. He needed to expend some energy after what he'd experienced.

When Hahami-na reached the grave site he found that the two had made a lot of progress. All the ash had been removed and they had dug an area with the digging sticks. The larger bones, scapulas from various large animals, were being used to scoop the chopped up earth to the side.

"Any quieter in there?" Nanichak-na asked while looking carefully at Hahami-na to see whether it appeared that he had need of comforting.

He nodded. Realizing that there was not much need for him there, he asked, "Have you seen any stones that would be useful in protecting the grave?"

Mootmu-na stood up straight. He put his hand to his head in thought. "There are some stones in the back of Cave Sumbrel. Back there where the women put the skin stretchers. There aren't many rocks, but I estimate there are enough for good protection."

Hahami-na lowered his head and turned to Cave Sumbrel. "Be right back," Mootmu-na said to Nanichak-na. "I want to send Slamika to help his father. It will give him a chance to participate."

Nanichak-na nodded and smiled wistfully. *What a sad day*, he thought.

When Mootmu-na arrived at the home cave, he found Slamika kneeling on his sleeping mat, sitting on his feet, bent over with tears still falling from his eyes. He stooped down and put his hand on Slamika's shoulder. Slamika looked up with red rimmed eyes. There was an emptiness about him. Olintak was beside him but had not been able to comfort him at all. She was distraught because she could not reach him. Mootmu-na looked into her eyes trying to tell her this would pass.

"Your father needs you, Slamika," Mootmu-na said quietly. "He is gathering protection stones from Cave Sumbrel and is bringing them to the grave site which is downhill. You can find it from Nanichak-na's scraping and digging sounds. Here, let me give you a hand up," he added.

Slamika didn't want to do anything but grieve, but he also would not have dreamed of failing to respond to a need of the People generally, certainly not his father's need specifically. So he gave his hand to Mootmu-na and got up and went to put on his booted garment. He walked outside to the privy and then headed to Cave Sumbrel. It was a grim day. *Even when Wisdom returned color to the land these days, all was gray*, he thought.

Mootmu-na prepared to return to the glade, but turned and asked Amey to bring him some meat for Nanichak-na and himself, maybe Hahami-na and Slamika as well. She quickly placed plenty of meat in a woven basket with a lid and handed it to her husband. "Be safe," she whispered.

"And you," he whispered back.

Ki'ti had been hiding on her sleeping mat. She did not remember ever experiencing death. Oh, People had mentioned that Reemast was probably dead, but she hadn't seen him. Others had died when she was too young to remember. She'd seen Totamu tie a leather strip under Enut's chin to the top of her head. It kept Enut's mouth from hanging so grotesquely. But Enut still didn't look right and it frightened her. She sat on her mat with her covering cape-like over her head holding Ahriku in her arms tight to her chest. She noticed Wamumur approaching and was alarmed.

"You have your first assignment, Little Girl," he said. "When we go to the grave site today, you will tell the first story."

Ki'ti was startled. "Now?"

"You know the story, don't you?"

"Yes, Wise One," she replied. "I must go outside."

"I'll accompany you. Come on," and with that, he held out his hand. She took it and headed for the privy. Ahriku bounded to the cave entrance and the opportunity to relieve his bladder.

"Will the Others be there?" she asked, curious.

"Yes, but they don't know our language well enough to follow the story. Don't worry. This is something we have to do. And I assign you to do it."

"Yes, Wise One."

"Now, go take some food and review the story in your mind web."

"Yes, Wise One."

"Little Girl, are you well?" he asked. Her answers were not typical.

"Yes. This morning had me frightened. That is all."

"There is no need for fright," he stated flatly.

She wanted to reply flippantly, but bit her tongue. "My understanding hasn't caught up with my responsibility," she said, having thought out what she considered would be an appropriate reply.

"Well thought out," he complimented her. "But that's not what you were going to say."

"You see into my mind web?" she asked quite daunted.

"Only sometimes," he said. "You did well."

Ki'ti felt a sense of relief. For days she had felt under attack. A compliment was a welcome respite. She realized, too, that she hadn't fooled him. But she had held her tongue. For perhaps the first time in days she was proud of herself, realized it, and wondered how anyone could ever kill pride. She ruminated. Is that what it would be like to be an adult? Would she forever be forcing herself to speak appropriately instead of from her first thoughts? She didn't want to grow up if that's what it meant, and then she realized that would be something never to say aloud. Wamumur would strike her if she did. She finally knew that. That thought was contrary to the natural way things were; it was contrary to the health and well being of the People; and it was probably not true, if she really examined it. She realized that for a moment, she had permitted herself to believe a lie of her own making. For the first time in her life, she felt alone, really alone. Chilled. In the midst of all these people, she felt terribly alone. But she also felt enlightened. Her punishments were to keep her from believing lies she'd created for herself. She went to the sitting place where she had gone through the stories. She shut her eyes and began to tell the story in her mind.

Wamumur was sitting on the rock staring at the floor. Ki'ti put her hand on Wamumur's arm and asked, "Wise One, do you ever feel alone when there are many people around you?"

He touched her head and smiled, "Both Emaea and I know that feeling well. It comes with being Wise One."

Mootmu-na, Nanichak-na, Hahami-na, and Slamika all stood at the grave site and ate the meat that Mootmu-na had brought back. There wasn't a scrap left. None of the men had realized they were hungry, but the food helped. Hahami-na and his son returned to the cave to bring more protection stones to the grave site. It did appear that there were just enough of the stones to keep Enut's body safe from any animals that might come later to try to dig her up.

Mootmu-na looked up as the two men went to gather rocks. Hahami-na put his arm around Slamika, something that was certainly permitted but rarely done among the men after a male child entered puberty. Mootmu-na smiled broadly, gesturing to Nanichak-na to look, when he saw Slamika tentatively and then strongly place his arm around his father. It was good.

Back in the cave, Wamumur took his right foot and nudged Ki'ti's foot. She looked up, pride over her assignment for the day vanishing.

"What have you forgotten?" he asked.

She felt the fear from earlier creep up her spine. What had she forgotten? She mentally walked through her mind web from the time she encountered him that morning to the present. Then she realized he'd told her to eat.

"I'm not hungry," she blurted out, and then realized she shouldn't have said that. "Forgive me, Wise One." She lowered her head.

"Eat," he insisted and left her to go to talk to Emaea.

She got up and went to find something to eat. Ey saw her and fixed her a bowl of food. She handed it to Ki'ti who took it and thanked her. Ki'ti was not hungry but she dutifully ate what was in the bowl. Noticing that Wamumur's back was to her and that Emaea could not see her, she did share some with the dog, unaware that Totamu and some in the cave noticed.

Hunters and women who hadn't already departed left for Cave Sumbrel to continue working. They couldn't spare time since getting provisions for the season of cold days was critical in light of the meat's coming from the ashfall. Along with the strips, the men also were curing meat in the form of smoked legs. Legs were hanging in the cave with fires underneath the smoke hole. The drying strips were off to the sides. They would be there for a long time. Some of the drying strips were ready to take back to the home cave for storage in the nice, cool, dry room in the lower level away from the flowing water. Women had carefully swept the future storage room clean, which included the ceiling, walls, and floor. The room was huge. The young girls who had been gathering sticks were given the task of taking the dried meat to the cave and placing it carefully where they had been told to put it on mats. None of the hunters had gone looking for meat because they felt they should attend the departure of Enut.

The men had dug down to a level of about four feet. The sides were caving so they tried to scoop carefully. Then Mootmu-na helped Nanichak-na climb out of the hole, and Nanichak-na gave Mootmu-na a hand to help him out. The work had been beneficial to both of them. They headed for the cave with their tools and the bowl. They would bring the tools back later when it was time to cover Enut's body.

The women who tended the children noticed the tools when the men returned to the cave. Mitrak jumped up since Shmyukuk was nursing Ey's infant. Mitrak would alert the hunters and the women at the other cave that the grave was ready and it was time to gather there. She put on a booted garment and headed to Cave Sumbrel.

Wamumur walked over to Ki'ti. "Little Girl, I do not want you feeding the dog from your food. You know that. I should punish you. I should also punish you for trying to get by with something I don't want you to do when my back is turned. Both are not good."

Ki'ti hung her head. *Would this never end?* She wondered.

He continued, "What I will do and this is certain. If you feed the dog again away from the other dogs, you will have to make him stay with the others. If he refuses to stay, I will break his neck. Your friend will be gone. Is this understood?"

"Yes, Wise One." She lowered her head horrified. She knew he was serious.

"You will never have an unobserved moment again in your life. Get used to it. If I don't see you, many other eyes will. When you disobey me, you put the People at risk. It is as if you lied. To lie is to try to fool People and yourself. It is also to steal, to steal an identity, a thing, an opportunity that is not yours. A Wise One holds to truth only. The People know that. They depend on it. Your life must be an example of Wisdom, not corruption. Nothing else but Wisdom. I will hear of your doing things that I have told you not to do, if you try to do things secretly. Don't try. You will become Wise One." He hit his left palm with his right fist hard. "I do not want to strike you for doing things that are not good. But I will." He did another hard palm strike. "If necessary, your former experience will be nothing compared to what is possible. Is this understood?"

"Yes, Wise One." Her voice was very low, but he heard her. Once she had seen several men in turn beating Reemast within an inch of his life when they saw him squeeze to death baby birds he'd found in a nest. They didn't kill him but for a long time he'd been badly hurt. She suspected that is what the Wise One meant. It frightened her.

"Your childhood has been cut short by Wisdom. You do not argue with Wisdom. You accept. You are to learn. Learn!" he said definitively.

He started to walk away and turned, "Soon, we will go to the grave site. You will stand in front of me. When I tell you, you will begin the first story and go through it to the end. Do you understand?"

"Yes, Wise One," she said while her belly was ripping into thousands of pieces. She must, she knew, protect Ahriku at whatever cost to her. No longer would she sneak her food to the dog. Ahriku's life was too precious to her to risk it.

Mootmu-na and Nanichak-na took two straightened poles and put the carrying leather on them. It made a stretcher for taking Enut's body to the grave site. Those two and Hahami-na and Slamika would carry the stretcher.

The People and the Others gathered outside the cave. Those who were inside the cave went to the entrance to put on booted garments. There would be no one left in either cave. All would attend.

Solemnly, they walked to the grave site. Some were crying but the noise of it was negligible. It was as if the ash swallowed sound. The People were expected to balance their grief with understanding that Wisdom decided when one of the People would die. It was a tough balance when you were close to the person who died. Wamumal could not easily carry both her children, so Ekuktu carried Ekoy while she carried Smig. The stretcher had been lowered to the edge of the long side of the grave when they arrived. Enut laid there, appearing serene. The necklace was lovely.

Wamumur began to speak of the loss of Enut and what she meant to the People. She had been a good mother, a solid supporter of the People always ready to help, of good nature, who prepared unique and very tasty aurochs, and so on. Then, he started the circle. Whoever chose could either speak or nod to the next person to speak.

Totamu picked it up. "Enut was my granddaughter. She was an obedient child," she said, staring straight at Ki'ti, "and she was also friend to everyone. She raised" she flashed three fingers "children to adulthood, while she had to live through losing" she signed ten "children to illness, war, accident, or in birth. She saved me from a serpent's bite on more than one occasion. I approve the way she lived her life."

Pechki went next, "Enut was my firstborn. She was one of only two of my children to make it to adulthood. She was respectful and had a wonderful sense of humor. She could find the best in situations that were not good. I turn her over to Wisdom. I will miss her sorely. That is all I have to say." Then she sobbed.

As each of the People spoke, Abiedelai-na began to grow in discomfort. He had already become uncomfortable with thoughts of how close the Minguat had come to annihilation when they met these People and were taken in. Here, one person had died in relation to the ash. His Minguat had lost ten infants and two children. Until now, Abiedelai-na had been supremely confident in the ability of the Minguat to overcome anything the world had to bring their way. He had confidence in his own leadership. But that confidence was falling apart and he knew it, as he looked at the lifeless body of a woman named Enut that he didn't know at all. These unpretentious People who had food when the Minguat were starving, these compassionate People who welcomed them and fed them as if they were family, these humble People who asked almost nothing in return—they had taught him so much. Knowledge and feeling were two different things, however, but what he felt from all this was vulnerability. He realized that the natural world was fine when things were fine but when things were tough, the world stood on its head. All the prior thinking and order were irrelevant. This must be what the People meant when they talked of the Winds of Change. He'd been asked, "What would your people do if you were killed in a hunting accident?" And he'd had no real answer. There wasn't one. He didn't know. He could guess that the hunters would fight to assume leadership. The best leader might not win. Yet, here in the midst of all this calamity, these People were conducting life as normal though all nature strove to undo them. They didn't have a leader, yet they thrived. He'd always felt so superior but now so inferior. It was his fault that they were late in leaving their home near the mountain that spit out all the ash. He had not guessed what would happen until he almost imperiled all of them on the trek. He found himself wanting to be like them, the People, as they called themselves. He wanted the strength that came from many good minds working on problems. He wanted the bonds they shared. Instead, he cursed himself. He knew that if the tables had been turned, they'd have made slaves of the People and wouldn't have cared what their feelings were. He was vulnerable, ashamed, and convicted of his own evil. Evil? Yes, he thought, he hadn't enslaved these People but had those People come to them, he knew he would have enslaved them, and his men would have enjoyed their women and possibly killed the men. Abiedelai-na shuddered. He had always thought the Minguat were superior to the People. He wasn't at all sure he still didn't consider them inferior.

Ki'ti ended the circle with, "My aunt carries away part of my heart."

The circle had been completed. Wamumur said, "Now, Ki'ti tell the first story."

She stood there. He put his hands on her shoulders, since she liked to shut her eyes when she told the stories. She began in the most adult voice she could muster, loud and strong:

"In the beginning, Wisdom made the world. He made it by speaking. His words created. He spoke the water and the land into existence, the night and day, the plants that grow on the dirt, and the animals that live on the dirt, and those that live in the water and in the air. Then he went to the navel of the earth. There he found good red soil and started to form it into a shape with his hands. He made it to look a little like himself. Then he inhaled the good air and breathed it into the mouth of the man he created. The man came to life. Then he took some of the clay left from the man and he made woman. He inhaled and breathed life into her. Wisdom created a feast. He killed an aurochs, skinned it, made clothing for the man and woman from the aurochs, and then roasted the aurochs for the feast. The man and the woman watched carefully and quietly to see how he killed the aurochs, how he skinned it, how he made clothing from its skin, and how he roasted it. They paid good attention and they were able to survive by doing what they had seen done.

"The People were special and Wisdom pronounced that the man was to treat the land and the water and the animals and the woman the way he wanted to be treated—good. And the same was true of the woman. And it went well for a long time. But Wisdom hadn't made the People of stone. He had made them of dirt, knowing that they shouldn't have lives that would go on too long for they might get prideful and forget Wisdom. That is good because People should not be without Wisdom. They would die.

"That is why the People return to Wisdom when they die. They are placed in the earth and Wisdom knows. When Wisdom hears of a death of the People, Wisdom waits until the grave is filled back. He waits until it is dark. Then he causes the earth to pull on the spirit of the dead to draw that person's spirit back through the dirt of the earth to the navel from which all People came, the navel of the earth where the red clay for making the first man was. The dead spirits depart for the navel of Wisdom. That is where they reside for all time. All People's bodies return to the dirt, but their spirit, that essence of the person made by the One Who Made Us, is pulled back to Wisdom in the place where first man was made, and Wisdom keeps all those he chooses with him there, safe and loved. There is a cycle Wisdom made: a cycle from the navel to the navel. He keeps the spirits of those whom he chooses and he destroys those whom he hates. Wisdom hates those who hate him, those who ignore him, those who would be hurtful to him or to the land or water or to those living things Wisdom made including People."

Wamumur squeezed Ki'ti's shoulders. He was well pleased.

The People and the Others had watched and listened as this tiny child spoke strongly and forcefully and downright believably a story that related to the death of Enut and what would happen. She kept her eyes shut during the telling but her face shone as if it had an internal light. It did not escape the onlookers that right beside Ki'ti sat a dog whose eyes never left her face as she told the story. Wamumur had been hard to read because he'd kept his eyes on the top of the girl's head. He was listening, the People knew, to assure that she told the story correctly. At the end of the story, they were amazed that a child that size could remember what she had, and word had it that she knew each and every story and could tell them as well as this one. Of all the People, Minagle stood probably the most in awe of her little sister. *Who could have known?* she thought. She also felt a pang of concern for her sister. Recognizing how good she was at this, Wamumur would see her as a treasure belonging to the People and he would really be tough on her, probably tougher than he had been.

Abiedelai-na was the only one of the Others who understood the story. Finally, he understood a lot. The People were what they were because of Wisdom. Wisdom would be displeased if they were unkind to others. His people had no Wisdom. When they were unkind to others, they could actually consider themselves wise for having bested another. They had a word that meant wisdom but it was not a God. It meant smarter than fundamental knowledge. Clever. If you were superior in knowledge, you were considered wise. Somehow, these People concluded that Wisdom was totally separate from knowledge. Wisdom was like a person, he concluded. In fact, for the knowledgeable, it might be harder for them to become wise. He would want to learn more about this Wisdom. He questioned whether the Minguat were missing something.

The People each took a handful of dirt and tossed it into the grave, being careful not to cover Enut with it. They milled around briefly, telling the family that they were sorry that they had lost Enut. Then each one returned to their duties. The Others observed and told Hahami-na, "I'm sorry for your loss," as they'd seen the People do.

Back in the cave, Mootmu-na stowed the stretcher and he and Nanichak-na took the needed tools and headed back to the grave site. They were surprised that Hahami-na and Slamika both joined them. There they began the process of refilling the hole and putting the protecting stones atop the grave. Nanichak-na took a moment to add another hole to his garment, signifying the loss of the wife of his son.

Wamumur seated himself and Ki'ti joined him.

"May I speak?" she asked.

Wamumur looked surprised at the request, but nodded.

"I know that I have been fighting becoming a Wise One. I found the idea not good. I wanted to run away when there was nowhere to run. But out there, when the words began to come from my mouth, Wise One, it was like Wisdom speaking through me. I felt huge. I feel like I'm about" she flashed ten "arms tall, not with pride right now, but with joy that somehow Wisdom used me to tell the story. Does that make sense to you?"

Wamumur picked her up, placed her on his lap, and hugged her so tight she struggled for a second to breathe. "That is what it is, Little Girl! That is why you don't feel alone. You were at-one with Wisdom. That is the joy that is returned to you when you give yourself to Wisdom. There is nothing else in the world that compares with it. I have to think it's what Enut is experiencing now that she is on the way to Wisdom's navel. There was no way to prepare you for that, but that also means that Wisdom has definitely chosen you. Some People who tell the stories never feel what you speak of. And now, you are not to speak of that feeling to anyone but me or Emaea. There is no one else here who has any way to imagine what it is to have Wisdom speak through them or what it is to be at-one with Wisdom. There are many ways of being at-one with Wisdom. Having Wisdom speak through you is only one. You will learn. Keep silent about being at-one with Wisdom. That is only for you to discuss with Emaea and me." He helped her get off his lap, and then he did a powerful palm strike.

She did one in return, sealing the order.

Gruid-na approached Wamumur. "May I speak with you, Wise One?" he asked.

"Of course! Do you wish to go outside?"

"That would be good."

"One moment. Little Girl, do you need to go outside?"

"Yes, please," she admitted.

"Go then and I will follow. Then, you are to come inside and sleep awhile."

"But I'm not . . ." she stopped the words, "Yes, Wise One," she said.

Gruid-na walked with Wamumur behind the child. "She is interesting, isn't she?" he asked.

"You don't know the half of it," Wamumur said.

"I am here to put forth an idea from my People. It's something all of us have discussed and we want you to think about it before we present it to all of you."

Wamumur wondered what was coming and he was utterly unprepared for what followed.

"Your group of the People is getting very small. Ours is small. If you put our two groups together we are a little stronger. I do not favor large groups, but both of us have groups of People too small for protection if it were needed. I suggest that our groups join as one People. We also approve of you and Emaea joining if you choose to do that, and there would be no need to separate again ever until death. We think your group will approve. What do you say?"

"I think, Gruid-na, that you already know my answer. I'd have to be without Wisdom to say no."

"Good, then I intend before the day is out to have discussed this. Perhaps Nanichak-na will have a pronouncement tonight?"

"No, he will not. "

Ki'ti passed between the two men on her way to her sleeping mat.

"What did I tell you to do?" Wamumur asked.

"I did not forget. I must sleep," she replied.

"Good. Do not get up until I call you."

"Yes, Wise One." She and Ahriku raced off to her sleeping mat.

"Looks like you have her well in hand," Gruid-na said with a grin.

"Look again, my friend. She is like Baambas. Under that tiny exterior lies a giant of a will to do what she wants when and how she wants to do it. It will take years to get that softened."

"Then I shall have fun watching."

"Oh, Gruid-na, I want you, not Nanichak-na, to make the pronouncement."

"That would be an honor, Wise One."

"Thank you, Gruid-na. I cannot tell you how touched I am." Wamumur actually wanted to lose more tears but could not permit himself to do that. He and Emaea had waited for about forty-five years to hear that they could join. Why it came so late in life was a good question; but that it came at all was a total mystery—or Wisdom. He looked up to see if he could locate Emaea. He saw her eyes and knew that she knew and had, no doubt, been watching him. They shared a smile.

When Gruid-na approached Grypchon-na later that day, he was surprised that the man said he had something to add to the pronouncement if it could be agreed. He said he and Likichi had thought of it and discussed it already.

"You see," Grypchon-na said, "Teaching Ki'ti will be a full time effort. For the girl to have to be split between two sets of parents gets to be confusing. The girl obviously is the next Wise One. She should be mothered by Emaea and taught by Wamumur. They should not have to ask permission from Likichi and me for her time. It's not like we wouldn't see each other. But her life now is really under their control, or rather the control of Wisdom through them."

"Will you talk to them?" Gruid-na asked.

"I am tied up with this meat preparation," he replied wiping sweat from his brow on his arm. "Will you do it so it can be part of the pronouncement tonight?" Grypchon-na asked.

"Of course."

Gruid-na finished his searching for the rest of the men and then spoke to the women. There was not one objection, only joy at the idea. Then Gruid-na went to find Wamumur. He had trouble locating them until he went to the lower part of the cave.

"May I interrupt you two?" he asked with a laugh.

"Of course," Wamumur said. "We were just being young."

All three laughed.

"Well, this may make you younger yet!" He had their attention. Gruid-na went on to lay out Grypchon-na's proposal. Both of them were awestruck.

"That would simplify things a lot," Wamumur said, not showing the deep joy he was feeling. His dreams were manifesting themselves, although he knew Ki'ti was a handful. At such an advanced age for him to join with Emaea and to have a child, he was so overjoyed he feared it would spill out.

"That would not only simplify things, but also it would make two old People fill up with joy," Emaea said. "No," she added, "I think overflow with joy is better said," she paused. "They really want to do this?" she asked.

"Actually, it was their idea. They saw what we all saw this morning. Did you see how her face radiated Wisdom as she spoke—even with her eyes shut?" he asked Emaea.

"I did and I knew that I was witnessing an amazing thing. I think even the Others knew that something fantastic was occurring. The Winds of Change are blowing hard here."

"They are. It is strange that you had me agree to do the pronouncement. When I got to Nanichak-na he agreed with you that I should do it."

"Wisdom," Wamumur grinned.

Gruid-na wanted to say that he'd had about as much Wisdom as he could handle for one day, but he knew that would be out of order. He held his peace.

"I know what you were thinking, Gruid-na," Emaea said.

"Go back to being young again," Gruid-na said as he turned and went back upstairs.

"Wait a minute, Gruid-na," Wamumur called to him. "You get Likichi and Grypchon-na to tell the little girl. Tell them to make her know that she is not being rejected."

"I will tell them. Can they awaken her now?"

"Of course, we'll be up soon." And Wamumur's arms encircled Emaea and they were transported to a different world and time briefly.

When Grypchon-na and Likichi got the news that they needed to be the ones to deliver the message to Ki'ti, they braced themselves and awakened the child. They let her become fully awake before they told her that she would be mothered by Emaea. They were not rejecting her but they knew the Winds of Change and it was time for that move. Wisdom had made it clear.

Ki'ti covered her face and cried quietly. "Is it because I shamed you?" she asked.

Likichi threw her arms around her daughter and assured her that they fully approved her. Likichi said, "When you told the story with your eyes shut today, did you not feel something wonderfully strange and new?"

Ki'ti had promised not to tell people about what happened to her, but she did answer, "Yes."

"That is why we are doing this. Emaea and Wamumur both live in the world you were in today. They can help you grow into it. We cannot. We don't know that world." Likichi put her fingers to Ki'ti's mouth. "Be careful not to say something which you should not say, Dear One."

Ki'ti's eyes clouded with tears as she looked at her parents. "You will still be here? Minagle will still be my sister? My brothers will be my brothers? If I want to talk to you, it is permitted?"

"Of course, we will be right here. But the mothering will be done by someone who can truly mother a Wise One. Someone, for example, who knows after storytelling you must sleep. I had no idea."

Ki'ti's eyes pierced her mother to the bottom of her belly. "You are sure they can mother and father me better than you?"

"Yes, because you are going to be a Wise One. Now, didn't you need to sleep?"

"Yes," she admitted, "but I didn't know it. I felt like I could go on sleepless forever. Yet I am tired even now."

"These are things they are better equipped to handle. It would be inefficient if they had to come to us to tell us when you need to sleep. Do you understand?"

"Yes. It is hard to learn to be a Wise One."

Her mother laid her fingers to Ki'ti's lips again. "Don't, my Dear One. Don't think like that. Wisdom chose you and that ends it. Nobody can help you but you yourself. The only way you can help yourself is to give up your own wants and give Wisdom what is Wisdom's due. We all understand that, but usually it takes us until we're grown to understand. For you it is very early. And that's why we have done this thing. We do it because we love you and we respect Wisdom. Ki'ti, you must do your best. Do not shame us now that this has happened. Do not shame your new parents. Instead, make us all approve you. Will you do this?"

"Oh, Mother, I will try with all I have in my belly to do as you wish."

"Very well, now and for the future, you address your father as Grypchon-na and me as Likichi. Do not call us Mother and Father again."

Tears welled up in Ki'ti's eyes. Her back was as stiff as a board. "Very well, Likichi and Grypchon-na, does that also mean I have to move my sleeping mat?"

"Yes, but not until after the pronouncement."

"What will my sister think?"

"Your sister will understand," Grypchon-na said with assurance.

Ki'ti picked up her dog and hugged him tight. "Grypchon-na, will you please accompany me outside?"

"Of course." He and the dog followed her outside.

"My husband, what is troubling you," Pu asked in another part of the cave. Abiedelai-na sighed.

"You look like a lake troubled by rough wind. What is it?"

Abiedelai-na looked around. No one was near enough to hear that he spoke very quietly in his language to his wife. "I feel vulnerable for the first time in my life. I don't know how to get over it or whether I can."

"What is giving this feeling to you? You've never seemed anything but invincible to me."

"What is giving me this feeling? My wife, because of my blindness, I almost lost the Minguat. As it was, many children died. We almost starved to death. If these People hadn't taken us in, we would have died. I have been blind to so much."

"My dear, it cannot be so bad. We are fine. You brought us to these People and we didn't have to fight them because you took off your shirt."

"But Pu, you don't get it. One of the men here asked me what would happen if I lost my life in a hunting accident?"

"You're too good a hunter for that."

"I used to think that myself," he said as he shook his head from side to side looking at the floor. "But in truth, I could have an accident as easily as another. Then the hunters would fight to see who would be the next Chief. We could have a disaster."

"My Dear, we aren't hunting right now."

"Wife, we will have to make a decision after the cold time whether to leave or stay with these People. I think we should leave, but some of the way they choose to live makes them far stronger than we are. I want to learn about this. I don't want to feel vulnerable like this again. I have seen what our way can do to us. I don't like it. All they think about is the good of all. I have thought of the good of the Minguat, but I have thought alone. They think as a group. They have all of the minds working on the same issues. It is a better way. They share responsibility so that no one carries it alone."

"Don't you think that if you decided to use their way, our hunters would fight you? Don't you think they prefer our way? They are not used to having to think things through the way these People are. These People are nice when they disagree. Can you imagine our people disagreeing nicely? And then from the beginning of time we've said we're superior to the People. You can't change that by issuing an order. It's part of us. We're living for the future right now because we are still too thin and weak."

"That is why I feel vulnerable, I think. Some of our heritage is needlessly time consuming or destructive. Until I met these People I never understood that. It could bite us when we least expect. Like this volcano event."

"Well, you cannot let it eat your belly. You have a long time until the cold time ends. It's not even here yet."

"True. I'm thinking that if there is a way to return a favor to these People for saving us, it is to go east when the season of new leaves comes. Down in our innermost selves, I know we do not mix well."

"My Dear, the evening meal is served. Let us go to eat and ease yourself. Give yourself time to think things through. You'll see that our way is superior after all, I'm sure of it. I agree with you that we should separate, but for very different reasons."

After the evening meal and the clean up from it, Gruid-na stood and called to the group. After they gathered, he said in a loud voice, "Today, the two groups of the People have joined. Wamumur and Emaea now join as husband and wife. Totamu now is the mother of Domur. And, Emaea is now the mother of Ki'ti. That is all I have to say."

Ermol-na began to play the drum and there was dancing of the People and the Others.

Totamu smiled and nodded to no one in particular. It was good. She approached Nanichak-na and reminded him that his tunic was about to come apart. "Give it to me and I will fix it tonight," she told him.

He smiled. He returned moments later wrapped in his covering for sleep. Totamu took the garment and managed to get it repaired before all had turned in for sleep. When she handed it back, he lowered his head, "Thank you," he said. Nanichak-na loved the garment. He slowly ran his fingers over the holes he'd made in it lingering in the last one. His tunic was a summary of his life. Totamu did not understand the depth of his feeling about it or even what it meant to him, but she knew not to repair any of the holes he'd obviously made in it. In a place where privacy was more an idea than reality, the People did not probe the personal thoughts of another. People would share what they chose to share and safeguard what they didn't. But when Totamu saw him moving his fingers on the holes and lingering on the last, she suddenly understood why the holes were there.

Totamu tapped Domur on the shoulder and motioned for her to follow. She and Domur would share an evening of closeness, sitting shoulder to shoulder, sharing bits of Domur's life with Enut that were important to Domur. Totamu had not forgotten how to mother.

The evening was good. Wisdom sucked the color from the land, while the firelight danced lively on the cave walls and the group was one in dance and happiness. The Minguat had been strangely affected by the day's events. Most could not put their experience into words but there was a slight shift in their view of the People. It was time for all to start thinking about sleep. It had been a huge day.

Ki'ti carried her sleeping mat and her cover to Emaea. "Where do you want me to sleep, Mother?" she asked, feeling awkward.

Emaea savored the words without emotional display. "Here, against the wall will be good," she told Ki'ti. "Come here, Little Girl," she said.

Ki'ti dutifully went to her. "Before you go to your sleeping mat at night, I want you to come to me. Give me a hug and kiss my cheek and I will kiss your cheek. If there is anything you want to talk about and haven't, let it out then. Do not go to sleep in anger or frustration. Little Girl, do you have questions? Are you angry or frustrated?"

Dutifully, Ki'ti hugged Emaea and kissed her cheek. She received Emaea's kiss. She looked into blue eyes and asked, "How long will it take before my belly stops hurting?"

Emaea was seated and she pulled Ki'ti to sit on her lap. She wrapped her arms around the little child. "Time controls part of it, Little Girl. You control the other part."

"I?" Ki'ti asked.

"Yes." Emaea stroked Ki'ti's hair, "You see, the sooner you let go of what is past and begin to learn to accept that you are going to be a Wise One, the sooner your belly will stop knotting up and hurting. It could be a day or two or it could be a very long time with you sickening."

Ki'ti rested in Emaea's lap while Emaea stroked her gently. Very, very quietly, Emaea hummed to her. The sound floated her off into sleep. Wamumur fixed her sleeping mat and he gently put her on it. He covered her along with the little dog which had snuggled up to her belly.

"She will be fine," Emaea said. "There has been so much for her to get used to so fast. Imagine being called to be a Wise One at age," she flashed seven. "You and I had childhood, not an ashfall. I cannot conceive of how she feels."

"Well, I can," Wamumur said, "and it isn't easy for me to live with it. At the same time, I love her dearly and deeply. I also know how important she is to us. And I know I have a responsibility to help her overcome pride."

"And I appreciate that as much as you." Emaea sat next to Wamumur holding his hand. "*We* have a responsibility, my husband." She looked into his eyes. They both had eyes that were shining as brightly as they ever had. Tonight, a dream had been realized, not a Wisdom dream, but a human dream as old as time itself.

The cave noise slowly lowered. Totamu thought just as she closed her eyes for sleep that she only had a few more men to finish up removing facial and scalp hair. Then she'd see how well that worked for a solution to the head lice problem. She smiled and was asleep. Grypchon-na and Likichi held hands as they lay on their backs side by side. It had been a rough day with Likichi's loss of her sister and their having Emaea mother Ki'ti. At least there had been a way for Manak and Domur to have a joining in the future with Totamu mothering her instead of Likichi. Likichi thought about mothering. Among the People, the mothering links were fairly fluid, because all was done for the good of the group. Ki'ti was too young to have seen the shift in mothering, but it was not uncommon in the least. Poor Dear, she thought, the Winds of Change were tougher on some than others. How wonderful, however, to know that the next generation would have a storyteller, and who better to prepare that person than Wamumur and Emaea? Wisdom had smiled on them.

Blanagah had set her sights on Ghanya. He was one of the Others, but if that's the best she could do, that would have to do. He had picked up a little weight but still looked terribly thin. He appeared to be a good worker and everyone seemed to like him. He was one of Arkan-na and Ey's children. She'd found he was age sixteen, and his black hair, now all gone, was like Minagle's. In fact, now that she thought about it, Ghanya looked a little like Minagle. She would have to work her way into his consciousness as they both worked in Cave Sumbrel. If they joined and the Others split off from them, it would mean that he'd have to go with her People. That might be tough, but time would make that clear. She twisted and turned and finally drifted off into sleep.

The fire crackled as it died down. The flickers of the fire were dancing exaggeratedly on the cave walls and ceiling. They had been fortunate to find the cave when they did, Chamul-na thought, as he shifted to a softer place for his hip. He was watching the flickering and thinking of mortality as he drifted off to sleep. Beside Ki'ti, Ahriku twitched as if he were running but he didn't disturb Ki'ti's sleep.

The guard, Ermol-na, had gotten some stones to reshape while he guarded. He was hitting them with a deer antler tip and little pieces were littering the floor. In the morning, a woman would sweep. He needed to resharpen some of his tools, and it was a good way to stay awake.

In the morning, Manak and Ermi met on the way back from the privy. They had enjoyed their journey to see where the ash ended and thought it would be good to go again but maybe for ten days out and ten days back. Before the morning meal, the men gathered and discussed it. They favored a five-day trip and wanted a trail left in the ash so they could follow the trail in the future if they found a way out of the ash. They also wanted day cache markers so that they could eventually place food along the trail. What the men saw as unwise was for Ermi to go. His wife had an infant. He should not go for so long. Cue-na said that he thought one of his Minguat should go. Fim volunteered and was accepted to accompany Manak. The two would eat, pack their minimum necessary items, and leave as soon as they could get ready.

With the stirring in the cave, Wamumur, Emaea, and Ki'ti sat on their sleeping mats and stretched. The three went out to the privy and then returned to the cave. They straightened their sleeping mats and put them against the wall. Each went to get some food and they ate as a group quietly. Ki'ti knew that this day would start an examination of the significances of the stories. She would have to learn them well. She was determined that this would be a day when she would do her very best.

Wamumur took a skin with the hair on it and placed it on the rock near the entrance. He sat on it. Ki'ti went over and kneeled to his side, sitting on her heels.

"Begin with the first story," Wamumur said, "and include the significances."

Ki'ti was off into the world of the stories. When there, she was prideless, her focus on getting the story and the significances right for the People. Self was irrelevant as she perfected her information. There was pleasure in the learning, so much so that it removed her from her surroundings. Only when Ahriku licked her did she surface, and then only to touch the dog, and then to submerge back into the concentration needed to do the integrative memory work she had to do to gain understanding.

The hunters had eaten and gone to the other cave. The women were getting prepared to leave to work the skins. Wamumal, Shmyukuk, and Mitrak were to care for the seven youngest group members. Tita was making marked improvement and Ey was delighted. Even Ey was looking a little better. The routine of the cave had become established. It was good.

Minagle, Domur, Aryna, Meeka, and Liho had been given a couple of bowls and sent with sticks to see whether any more blueberries were available. They were cautioned not to stray too far into the woods. It took awhile but they did find another group of blueberries and they picked those bushes in no time, taking the bowls back to be emptied repeatedly. These blueberries were better than the first group. They wondered why that was. Their laughter brought vibrancy to the desolate scene. Since the ashfall, there had not been a single bird song or noise from any living thing except the cave dwellers.

Manak and Fim had five dogs and they were ready. Their own packs were bulging with water bags and extra sleeping skins and food. They were excited as young men can be to have a chance to prove themselves in their survival to an ash-free world. They headed out following the track that Manak and Ermi had made earlier. That would take them a long day. Fim was twenty-three and felt much older than Manak, but in this case, Manak had been on the first part of this trek and he hadn't. There was little need for leadership in any case except to be sure that they did not deviate from north as the direction in which they headed. They wanted to be away from the volcano. Fim knew that in the Minguat ways of doing things, one would have been designated leader. Here, no one was. It felt strange. Maybe that was why he still felt no integration with the People.

They quickly passed the place where they had found an elephant and continued on. "It all looks the same," Fim remarked.

"Yes. Later you'll see that the land rises and falls. But that's all I've seen. I haven't even seen a river." Manak readjusted his pack. It was heavier than any he'd ever carried.

They walked onward, dragging the stick so that they had a trail to follow on their return. The land rose slightly. They could tell not visually but rather the way their legs felt. They would have wanted to run if they hadn't been laden down with packages and had their feet encumbered with the boots. Neither liked the boots but would not have taken them off. They didn't carry enough water for washing their legs and feet. The men did not stop until it became dark. They had promised to sleep, so they did, drinking water to get them up so that they did not sleep overlong. Neither lingered into sleep.

In the cave, all were getting settled down. Blanagah had made advances to Ghanya, only to discover that he definitely wasn't interested. That came as a shock to her. Little did she know that he found her differences unattractive. He had looked around and thought Minagle was appealing but she was not woman and he really wanted a woman of the Minguat or a similar group, not from the People. He felt superior to the People but hid it well. He had been cleared for joining by Abiedelai-na, but his cousin, Vanya had not. They were the same age. He often wondered how the Chief made his decisions. Vanya was his friend. Vanya was a little more daring than he, and they had great hunts together. At the present, he felt he could wait a while longer until they were out of the ash and were able to meet with the Minguat for exchange of women and men. That's how it had always been. He was in no hurry. One thing was certain. When people joined, they ended up with babies and he didn't feel ready for that responsibility in this time of ashfall. It was permitted for him and Blanagah to copulate even when they were not joined, but he didn't want her to think he was interested, so he refused all her proposals. At one of the men's meetings at a gathering of the Minguat the previous year, he'd heard one man say he had to join with his wife because they had been copulating before joining and she stuck to him like she'd been tied. The group wouldn't have approved if he'd refused. So Ghanya did not look to females but instead stayed with the men to work and talk. He dozed off to sleep easily.

Likichi did not find sleep easy to come. Her daughter slept across the cave and that would take some getting used to. But her largest concern was that Manak was off on an adventure, which pleased him tremendously, but she thought it could be dangerous. There was just a nagging in the back part of her belly. She would have to trust that Wisdom called them to do what they were doing and that Wisdom would keep them safe.

Manak was awake before Fim. He made water and got a piece of dried meat. *It was really good*, he thought. He stood scanning the landscape as far as he could see but the ash seemed to go on forever. Fim opened his eyes and stretched. They were only on the second day of the trek. He hoped they'd find good news soon. He took some meat and remarked, "This is good. It is from the ashfall, is it not?"

"Yes," Manak said. "This is better than some of the other dried meat we've had. I like it a lot."

Manak began to harness up the dogs. "How about helping?"

"Manak, I do not know these dogs. I feel awkward around them." In no way did he want Manak to know he feared the animals.

Little did he know that Manak saw straight through the subterfuge. "Oh, sorry, Fim. I forgot. I'll tend to them." And he did.

The men trekked for days until finally, on the fifth day, they reached the top of a very tall hill. "What is that?" Manak asked.

Fim stared and stared. "I wish we were just a little closer. It looks like normal land." He looked at Manak with his eyes very large.

"See that hill over there, the tall one?" Manak asked. "Do you think we could make it over there without too much time spent? I think we could see better from there."

Fim said, "If you'd like to go, I'll go. We have no elders to stop us. I think it might give us the answer we seek."

The two headed off still dragging the stick, which they traded off from time to time. By nightfall, they had made it to the top of that hill, but Wisdom sucked color from the land and it was too dark to see. So the men bedded down and would wait to see what Wisdom's return of color to the land would reveal.

In the morning, the two arose at the same time. Their excitement was obvious from the quickness with which they reached their feet. Each wanted to see what they could see from this vantage point. In the far distance to the northwest, they could see great mountains. What was the most exciting was that to the north they could see where the ashfall ended on the hills. There was green! Color! It was good. Manak squatted down. He took a digging stick and moved the ash where he stood to the ground. As they had walked, the ashfall was much lower. Only two fingers of ash remained on the ground where they stood. The news was good and bad. The bad news was that the land north of them was hilly. The hills seemed to go on forever. But there were no huge mountains mixed with them. *They could traverse this land, but they definitely needed to wait for the season of new leaves*, Manak thought.

They packed up their things and began the trip back to the cave.

"If they had said we could be gone for ten days we could have discovered so much more," Fim said flatly.

"It may be that they will let us return to start caches for the exit from here. There is a lot we can do when we face cold season confinement."

"What is cold season confinement?"

"That is spending the entire season of cold days in one place."

"Why would your People not leave here right now? Get out of this hideous place to where game runs free?"

"Part of it is in our stories. We have a volcano story. The People know from the stories that after a large volcano explodes, there is a time of great cold. Baambas was much bigger than the volcanoes in our stories, so the cold could be worse. We will have our cold season confinement to build up a great store of food to keep us and the dogs during the cold and get us to our new place in the season of new leaves with reserves until we hunt well there. We don't know what our new place will hold in store for us. So we prepare for the worst. You've noticed how dark the sky has been? That will cause the cold. If we left now, think of all the meat we'd miss. Right now, we have time on our side. The ash-covered meat is not spoiling, but it's drying instead. Also, your people need to fatten up. We can have a lot of food built up so that when we do leave, we don't suffer. We have time to find the game at the next place without being frantic to find it. It is our Wisdom."

"I keep hearing a lot about wisdom. To us wisdom is being really smart."

"To us it means the One Who Made Us."

"Wisdom is the One Who Made You? Why don't you just say so?"

"Because Wisdom has a name that is special, just for only certain times, we don't use it lightly. The One Who Made Us is a very special name. We say Wisdom to avoid using the very special name, so we won't use the name wrong by forgetting. We also avoid using the name because it might make us prideful that Wisdom did, in fact, make us. He made us with hands, not words. He made everything else with words. He called the animals into being, but with his hands he made us. To Wisdom, we are very special."

"Wisdom made *magic* use of his words? Is that what you're saying." Fim used the word magic from the Minguat language because he didn't know the word in the language of the People.

"I don't understand the word 'magic.' Wisdom usually creates by speaking things into existence. For People, his hands made us instead of his words. Wisdom is not like us. Wisdom is the creator of all that is. We are the created. That is all."

After those words, they walked in silence for hours. They dragged the stick behind them on the way back to leave a double trail.

"There's the first day back marker," Fim said.

"We must be walking back faster than we walked when we came," Manak observed.

"Do you want to continue?" Fim asked.

"That is good," Manak said and the two continued walking until Wisdom sucked out almost all color from the land and it became too dark to see well. The next day of the trip was much like the first. It definitely was quicker. They continued on and arrived back at the home cave by the last part of the fourth day. Everyone gathered around them to find out what they had learned. They told of the five days walk and how they finally reached the land of the hills. Midway through the hills, they saw the ashfall no longer stole the color from the land. Fim suggested they leave at once. The men gathered and discussed the information for a very long time. Fim was startled to hear that Abiedelai-na was not interested in leaving for the land immediately. Cue-na, Gurkma-na, and Arkan-na of the Others all argued for leaving. Their Chief was listening to the People who spoke slowly and kept referring to Wisdom. Finally, they all agreed to spend the cold season confinement together. They knew what they had at the home cave, and they had no idea what would be in store for them if they moved. The stories of additional ashfall after a big ashfall bothered some of the People. The idea of great cold was considered carefully. They would all remain together during the season of the cold days. All did the palm strike. It was good.

In the cave, time passed imperceptibly, until the nights began to become very cold. Their clothing was not designed for cold temperatures. It would be necessary to make clothing that would withstand the cold. Even days became much colder.

One day, the People were finding the weather colder than they could remember. In the evening, Manak shouted to the people in the cave just as they were beginning to prepare for sleep. "Ash is falling again!"

The men roused from their sleeping mats and went swiftly to the cave entrance. They looked out on something falling from the sky, but it was not ash. Outside, they could see their breath. Fascinated, a few went into the precipitation and came back to the cave watching the white precipitate turn liquid. Vanya tasted it and said it was water. Others tried and agreed. All were moved with curiosity. What was this solid white rain that fell from the sky and turned to water? Inside, they didn't see their breaths. They returned to their sleeping mats, wondering what tomorrow would bring. What they found was about an inch of white rain atop the ash. The children were taken with the white rain, but it was so cold that they did not really enjoy being outside of the cave for long. The men and women going back and forth to Cave Sumbrel found the white rain could be slippery. It was not welcome.

Overall, the cave inhabitants got along amazingly well. When it was time for storytelling, they had to shorten the time during the day when the People listened, because the Others did not have the same attention spans that the People had. They became cross when sitting in one place too long. But that was not a problem. Surprisingly, the ashfall meat was exceptionally good, so there was no difficulty for everyone to get enough to eat during the cold season confinement. There were some small quarrelings over space and occasionally an outbreak of irritation would develop, but there was plenty of work to do designing and creating warm clothing, so contention was minimized. All adults contributed ideas as the occasion had demanded the best thought possible. One thing was certain, they needed head covering. The People had not seen a head covering until they saw Chief Abiedelai the first day, the day when he took his shirt off. The variety of head coverings created was diverse and some had merit and others did not. Trial and error was beginning to show what was practical and what was not. They also discovered that there was sometimes a need to cover hands as well as arms and shoulders and heads. When the men gathered wood and were out for any length of time, their fingers would begin to tingle from the cold. That was seen as not good, so they would return to a cave to warm up. Having to keep warming up was needlessly time consuming, so they asked for hand coverings.

Totamu had found that the head lice issue was definitely better with the shaved heads. It was better on the short haired females, but not altogether gone. Combing and washing hair seemed to help a lot. She wondered about shaving the heads of the women but feared insurrection. Men had their heads and faces shaved regularly when hair began to appear. They had no head lice at all. Totamu was attaining mastery at shaving.

Sometimes, particularly just before the evening meals, small groups of the Others would chuckle among themselves in a way that slightly unnerved the People, but they dismissed it as Minguat custom. After all, Abiedelai-na could be seen doing it.

All began to anticipate the season of new leaves and the departure for the green hills.

Meanwhile, the Others had taken a trip to the east and found that fewer days were required to reach a land free of ash. They could do it in four days.

During the season of cold days, the People began a routine of carrying meat and caching it along the route to the hills. Cue-na, Gurkma-na, and Alak and their offspring began trips to the east to prepare caches for their leaving. Arkan-na and Ey had decided to remain with the People with Abiedelai-na's permission. Abiedelai-na would revert to Chief Abiedelai, and when they split, he and his wife would go with the Others. Arkan-na's decision to remain with the People angered Vanya because he wanted to join with Liho, but Liho was adopted by Arkan and Ey and they would not give up being her parents. Neither would Alak and Munjun relinquish parenting Vanya. So Vanya's dream of the blond haired girl would be gone in the Winds of Change.

The People had begun to learn the language of the Others, but they knew they had much more time since Arkan-na and Ey had opted to remain with them.

Chapter 4

Wisdom returned color to the land. Departure was imminent and the People were very excited. Poles were used to make stretchers for transporting meat, skins, and other necessities. In a manner of bravado, the Others had refused to carry as much meat per person as the People. They were very confident that soon they would have all the fresh meat and seafood they could use, and they were tired of the dried meat they'd eaten while they endured the cold season confinement in the cave. So they carried two stretchers of meat and that was all. After all, they had caches along the way just as the People had and could see the sea from the last cache.

On the other hand, the People would carry the remains of the meat, which was huge, and the skins which also were significant in size. It would take the hunters more than one trek to their new homeland, but they did not want to be without or to waste what they'd gathered. They had a story about the ant. Ants were prepared and put lots of food aside underground so that they did not go hungry. Ants did not waste what they gathered. Wisdom taught the People to learn from the ants and other living things. It was another way to hone their observation skills and learn from Wisdom. The animals were there for food, certainly, but also to teach.

Wamumur felt sad for the Others who were leaving. Abiedelai-na had tried so hard to understand Wisdom, but each time they tried to discuss Wisdom, Abiedelai-na either got sleepy or kept disagreeing or became irritated. Perhaps Wisdom did not choose to reach out to Abiedelai-na. Whatever the case, Wamumur was saying farewell to Chief Abiedelai. The People watched as the Others left. Aryna would look behind her waving to the girls, but none of the Others looked back. They were going to the sea.

Arkan-na and Ey stood and watched their own people leave. Guy-na and his wife, Alu, stood beside Arkan-na and Ey. Lai and his wife, Inst, joined them to watch. "They never looked back," she said, emotion tinging her voice.

"That is true, Inst," Arkan-na replied, "but you can see why they did not. They have great pride. They live for pride. We have found a better way, but one they cannot understand. Wisdom will lead us. It is good." Having been one of the Others, he could understand.

Ghanya grieved the loss of his friend. He would not know that two days after arriving at the sea, Vanya would be caught in a rip tide and be carried out to sea to drown. His body would never be found. He had not heeded the season-of-cold-days story that urged People to be careful in new surroundings. To let new surroundings teach slowly. Of course, he probably barely understood the language of the People, let alone the story.

The People packed moderately and began the trek. Ahriku was back among the dogs led by Ki'ti and Minagle. He had his packs securely fastened to his back. The People followed the path set by those who prepared the way months earlier. Within five days, they could see the end of the ashfall.

"I can smell green grass!" Lamul shouted exuberantly. And so the People could. The scent of chlorophyll wafted to them on the breeze. A lifegiving scent. The People threw up their hands and walked in little circular motions in joy at the scent. They inhaled it, almost hyperventilating with pleasure. It was hard to sleep that night, the excitement was so great. They spent the night there and would go to the new land the following morning.

When they awakened, the People were bursting with excitement. The land free of ashfall beckoned. They were ready. The day was spent first going downhill and then climbing uphill. The way was steep so they had to walk carefully. When they reached the grassland, the People rested. They sat on the grass that was free of ash and some stretched out to gaze at the sky and others lay on the ground as if preparing to sleep on their bellies. Little children had not seen or remembered grassland and they were searching out this amazing green vegetation, first one piece and then another. They felt it, smelled it, and tasted it. It was good.

The People ate and then resumed their trekking. The People had removed their booted garments once they cleared the ash and were able to make much better time. They shook the garments and folded them across their backpacks. They had no need for those clothes during the trekking but the Others, who had gone with them and were still quite thin, kept their capes about them during the trek for they felt a chill that the trekking failed to dispel.

They all wanted to get the ashfall well behind them so that if another eruption occurred, they would be protected by the mountains that had spared this location. They trekked for the remainder of the day and stopped by a small pond for the night. Hunters scouted the area around the pond for vipers that might be lurking, but they found none. When Wisdom returned color to the land, they continued trekking, always heading north for five more days. Then they found a place where there were numbers of caves beside a stream. They followed the stream for several more days and finally found a place that they chose as their new home.

The caves were just off the stream. They were large and there were many of them. There was a hill paralleling the caves on the other side of the stream which formed the other side of a tiny valley. The space of the valley was about 12,000 forearms in length and about 1,600 forearms wide.

The People put the things they had carried in the largest cave and some of the hunters left to scout out the possibilities for hunting while others went off in different directions to be sure that the cave was in a safe location. It took a while for them to find some flat land that looked ideal for grazing. They saw no animals but that did not cause them alarm, because there were fresh feces from grazers as a few of the hunters could attest by lifting their feet. It appeared that there were no other groups in the area. It was high sun and it was warm for the weather they'd been having.

There were rhododendrons near the caves and children had to be warned not to chew or eat them. There were some willow and some berry bushes, blackberry, from the looks of it, and blueberry. There seemed to be one cashew nut tree and plants that might be rhubarb. The women were suspicious that some of the plants had been purposely placed where they grew. Placed there by People. They wondered why anyone would do such a thing. After consideration, they agreed it was a wise thing to do. It made gathering easy.

Some of the women, hungry for greens, had gone to hunt for what the place might have available. They found a good variety including plantains and dandelion greens, and they put them in baskets to carry back to the cave for the night's meal.

Little children were cautioned to remain near the cave and the adults there and the older ones were charged with gathering wood and kindling for the fire from the treed valley that paralleled the caves. Ghanya and Manak had been asked to stay at the cave as guards. They quickly scoured the area to be sure no snakes were visible. Then they kept an eye on Frakja and Ketra, who were both three, and Seenaha, age four. The two-year-old children and

117

Tita were with their mothers at the cave. Ghanya noticed something very dark in the ground across the stream from where they were walking. He stepped across the stream and discovered that they had some coal placed right across from the cave. *That would be very convenient*, he thought. In the caves, they had good fires using a mixture of wood, some coal, and some bones. Sometimes, they'd have more than one fire in the caves, depending on the smoke hole. The mixture lasted longer than wood alone.

Wamumur and Emaea walked along the rock sheltered walk. Caves led back inside the rock walls, some to a great depth. They were exploring the caves and letting the walls speak to them. Ki'ti followed along wondering what the adults were doing, and knowing she was to stay with them. Behind her trotted Ahriku.

"There was much fire there," Emaea said quietly. "The People must have been here for a few years," she said, having pointed to a place near the entrance.

Ki'ti was not sure what Emaea meant so she walked to the cave wall and touched the rock and there on her fingers was the trace of soot. She looked quizzically at Emaea. "How did you know there was smoke there? I could not tell since the rock wall is dark already."

"Come stand here, Little Girl. See how the light on the rock is shiny and then gets dull?"

"Yes."

"That's how I knew. The wall does disguise the smoke well, but if you have seen smoke on walls for a long time, you start to know the signs that tell it's there and for how long."

"So that's a thing of knowledge, not a thing of Wisdom."

Wamumur reached out and put his hand on her shoulder. "Good, Little Girl. You are using your mind web well."

"Little Girl," Wamumur said, "I give you permission to go to Manak to ask him to watch over you until I call you. Do not go beyond where he can see you at all times. Ki'ti, keep your mind alert for vipers. We have not been here long and must be very careful."

"Yes, Wise One," she said with a grin on her face. She fairly flew to Manak with Ahriku hot on her heels. Manak caught her in his arms and hugged her. She told him what permission she'd been given and Manak now watched little children and the future Wise One. He showed her a little place in the stream where she could play in the water. She went to the place and found she could stand in it to her knees. She pulled off her tunic, shook it out, and laid it on the bushes by the stream. She stepped into the stream and sat in the deeper water. She could bathe. She cupped handfuls of water and threw it at her face. She bent over and immersed her head in the water and grabbed some sand and rubbed it through her hair. Ahriku ran through the water, swimming when it got too deep. The dog seemed to enjoy the experience as much as Ki'ti. She rinsed the sand from her hair and then sat back down in the water, luxuriating in it and staring into the sky. It was still a darker than normal sky even though they were in grassland away from the ash. She wondered if the ash blew around in the sky for a long time and glided in the sky over places where no ash lay on the ground. Ahriku sat on the bank and watched her.

Seenaha noticed her splashing in the water and she came to her. Ki'ti removed Seenaha's tunic and washed her in the stream. Ketra could not be left out so she arrived and suddenly the little stream was alive with children. Frakja would not be left out. Manak decided to join the children. The water was barely deep enough for him to bathe, but he did his best. Clean skin felt wonderful. After the long trekking, it was delightful to laugh and relax in the stream. The laughter did not go unnoticed by the adults or other older children.

Wamumur and Emaea looked at each other. "When was the last time we really heard laughter like that?" Emaea asked.

"It must have been before we started running from Baambas. It is good, Emaea," Wamumur said. "It is good." He bounced a playful double palm strike with a grin. Emaea laughed and mimicked the gesture.

Soon, mothers brought the little ones to the stream where they enjoyed the water as much as those who were already there. Minagle and Domur left their chores to join the water laughter. Lamk and Sum and Keptu ran to the fun along with Meeka and Liho. Manak and Ghanya laughed that one of the first tasks would be to widen the bathing area. It might be enjoyable to be able to come down on a hot night and get into the water, if there would ever be a hot night again. Manak had never known a season of new leaves this cool. He wondered whether it was the move north or the cloudy sky they'd had since Baambas blew. It was warm enough to bathe, but not to stay overlong in the water.

Wamumur and Emaea walked over to see what was causing the laughter. They looked down on the young ones splashing and bathing in the water, and they smiled contentedly as Wamumur put his arms around Emaea. "It is good," he said. "It is good!" she responded. They shared a prolonged smile. There was a joy that immersed the both of them. Later, they would bathe there themselves, their smiling eyes communicated.

Ghanya had been sitting on the bank watching the People bathe and play in the water. He was troubled to see Meeka, Liho, and Ey naked.

"Come on in!" Manak called to his friend.

"I cannot. You are naked!"

"What?" Manak shouted back. "Do you bathe in your clothes?"

"No. But we have, or at least had, separate places for males and females to bathe. I am not accustomed to seeing females naked."

"Look, my friend," Manak called again, teasing. "Did Wisdom make you different?"

"Manak!" Ey interjected slightly acerbic, "Among the Others, it is not custom to look upon nakedness. He is doing what he has been taught to do."

Manak lowered his head to Ey first and then to Ghanya. Then he said, "Ghanya, I am sorry for teasing you. I shouldn't have done that. But you are one of us now. We bathe and enjoy the water together. We think nothing of how we are made, because Wisdom made us. We didn't. He made you, too. So please, reconsider and join us. This water is wonderful and it is great to be clean!"

Ghanya struggled with the very ideas of being naked and bathing with unclothed females. It seemed all wrong. But he had no argument for why it was wrong. All his life he had been very serious and careful to do what he'd been told. For the first time in his life, he pulled off his tunic and stepped into the water with females. Within minutes, he found himself laughing at the antics of the little ones forgetting briefly that he wore no clothing. From time to time, he would become self conscious, but then, he kept telling himself, he was part of this group now. And a small voice inside would say he should question that. For now, he would be part of it, even if that meant bathing with females.

People were coming back from their trips out to collect plants or look for grazing spots where hunting might be good, and for presence of other humans. The women at the water gathered the little ones and all of them headed toward the cave. The evening meal needed to be prepared.

That night, they would feast on dried meat and grains boiled with plants. Some plants would be put in their bowls washed but uncooked. Those who hadn't bathed were looking enviously at those who had. They wanted to know where the bathing place was.

Finally, when things calmed down and everyone had bathed, the entire group gathered near the fire to hear of the day's findings. The dogs seemed restless by the entry. Ki'ti sat in Emaea's ample lap and relaxed. Liho leaned against the side of her father, Arkan-na. Manak and Domur were sitting together touching shoulders. To the surprise of everyone, Ghanya and Minagle were seated side by side. When she noticed, Likichi elbowed Grypchon-na. They smiled at each other, content. Both of them thought Ghanya was a very nice young man. Most of the young ones were either asleep on their sleeping mats or they were sitting with their parents dozing in the semi-darkness.

Suddenly, Ahriku began to growl louder than was permitted. His neck arched and he stared down at Manak's sleeping mat. The hair on his neck stood on end and every hunter in the cave became alert. Ahriku began to bark, which was definitely not permitted, but in this case was allowed. Rather than discipline the dog, Manak, Slamika, and Minagle went to see what was bothering the dog. Nanichak-na went to the tools and picked up a sharp-edged rock. Hahami-na went to the place where spears were stored. He pulled out a snake stick, one with a forked tip, just in case. Manak carefully moved the mats until he uncovered a large brownish viper. It had beautiful markings—square shapes laid tip to tip along its back. On its sides were triangles with two eye-like dots within the triangles. Ahriku was behind the snake's head when Hahami-na placed the forked spear just behind the snake's head in one thrust. Nanichak-na then cut the snake's neck, killing it. He left a bit of skin that kept the head attached to the snake body. He carried it outside and hung it in a tree where it continued writhing. When Wisdom returned color to the land, he would see to the burying of the head a good distance from where they lived and the snake body would be displayed over bushes as a lesson to other snakes.

Ahriku ran to Ki'ti and shivered. She hugged him and put him on her lap. Slowly, the people in the cave regathered to hear the day's news.

Nanichak-na started by telling about the two grazing lands they had found to the north and northeast. The meadows were huge and there were numbers of animals out there ready for taking. Gruid-na mentioned that they had the same experience going due east and south east. There were mountains to the west and southwest. They wondered about the need to go back to get additional provisions from Cave Kwa and Sumbrel, but the group discussed it and decided that one or two trips back there would suffice, if they were in what appeared to be good safety.

Arkan-na spoke to the security. Those who checked the security had gone north, east, west, and south. They had searched somewhat in between those directions. They had found no trace of living humans anywhere. Occasionally, they'd find a firepit, but they seemed to have been used long ago since the wind had blown dirt over it, almost covering the rocks. Ghanya mentioned finding coal just outside the cave. Grypchon-na said that some day he would have to take Wamumur and Emaea and Ki'ti for a little over a day's journey to see something which he would not describe, but said he had found a place of the spirits or giants and they should see it. The women did not mention the plants they had found, assuming that too mundane a topic for the group.

It was decided that Guy-na, Lai, Ghanya, Kai, Ermi, and Manak would return to transport what meat or other supplies they could. They would leave the poles and skin stretchers since they had ample material to make them where they were going. The People wanted them to wait until they had rested, but the young men chose to leave in the morning. They would carry little food and water, because the caches had been left over half full.

All agreed that the choice of place to live was good. In small numbers, people broke up the gathering and went to their sleeping mats, unafraid that vipers would be a problem with Ahriku in the cave. Ki'ti was sound asleep so Wamumur bent down to pick her up with assistance from Emaea. He placed her on her sleeping mat where she was immediately joined by Ahriku. Emaea put the covering over both of them. Then they stretched out on their sleeping mats. "It feels so wonderful to be clean," Emaea said. Wamumur smiled and touched her clean skin. All over. They joined and then slept well.

Olintak jerked and sat up. Slamika rose on an elbow and asked if she was well.

"I don't know. I must have been sleeping. It felt like someone kicked my ribs."

"Are you carrying a child?" Slamika asked, partly excited about the idea and partly afraid.

"I don't know. Ow! There it goes again. Put your hand here."

Slamika put his hand on her belly. She really didn't look as if she were carrying a baby yet.

"Ow! Did you feel that?"

"Yes, my wife. I think you have a baby in your belly. Ask the older women tomorrow."

"Do you really think that's what this is?" she asked naïvely.

"I really think that it is. Ask tomorrow." Slamika was in awe that they might have a baby. He was delighted and at the same time he was concerned that Olintak would do well in childbirth. He didn't want to lose her. He treasured her.

"I will." Olintak lay back down and tried to get accustomed to the kicking.

When Wisdom caused the sun to fade the darkness, the hunters were preparing to take the stretchers on their trek back to their former caves to bring back all the meat and skins they could carry. The men were in their prime and were eager to make this contribution. They knew the route now and expected to be able to travel a lot faster than they did on the trip to the new place without older and younger People to slow them down. They chose the largest of the stretchers to make the trip worthwhile. They ate and said their farewells and left. Their wives were not nearly as excited about their leaving as they were.

Lamul asked Hahami-na if he might have the honor of burying the snake head. He would be accompanied by Gruid-na. He was given an affirmative nod. They chose a location in the forest to the southeast. They were experiencing showers off and on, but hunters never were slowed by rain. Lamul severed the head from the remaining skin and put the venomous head in a leather wrap for protection while carrying it. He and Gruid-na left the area for the forest.

Olintak sought out Totamu. When Totamu recognized her, Olintak said, "Please can you help me? I have a lot of discomfort in my belly. I feel that it is kicking my ribs."

"Are you pregnant?" Totamu asked.

"That's what Slamika thinks. I do not know. He said to ask."

"You don't look pregnant. When was your last flow?"

"I don't remember," Olintak said, surprised that she hadn't thought about that.

"Is it kicking now?" Totamu asked.

"No."

"Well, I think Slamika is probably right." Totamu hugged her.

Olintak was beaming as she returned to roll up the sleeping mats. A baby. She smiled at Slamika across the cave. They shared a silent understanding.

Totamu also smiled. For some reason, it had not been easy for the People to become pregnant, to hold the baby to term, and to raise children to adulthood. When around the Others, it never ceased to amaze her how large their families were. Not so with the People. It wasn't just her group of the People, she mused. The People just seemed to have small success in reaching adulthood. Mootmu-na and Amey had the most success of any of the People she'd known with seven offspring. That was almost unheard of among the People at that time. And Ekuktu the father of twins. Now, Olintak pregnant. Yes, Mootmu-na and Amey had raised a lot of children and were grandparents of three with another on the way. *It was good*, she thought. It was good. She did a palm strike.

Wamumur and Emaea told Ki'ti that they planned to explore the area to learn of any messages that Wisdom had for them in this place. She was to pay close attention and watch what they did because some day she would have to do the same thing. People never stayed too long in one place.

123

Olintak found Blanagah and went to her side. "My sister, I have good news."

"What is it, Olintak?" Blanagah wondered.

"I am pregnant."

Blanagah looked at her wide eyed. "Are you really? That is wonderful news. Are you excited?"

"I can't believe it. Yes, I'm so excited I could burst!" Olintak hugged herself.

"Don't burst! I want to see my niece or nephew," Blanagah teased them to laughter.

"Last night, I thought I must have eaten something awful. It was kicking me in the ribs."

"Well, you don't look like you have anything in your belly." Her sister eyed her critically.

"If you'd been my ribs, you'd have no doubt." Olintak smiled.

"I am happy for you. What good news. Does Slamika know?"

"He's the one who told me to check it out today. Yes, he knows. He too is very happy."

"Would you like to come with Inst and me today to gather dandelion greens? She's missing Lai already, and he just left to bring food and skins from the cave."

"I would like to accompany you two. That would be good." The women each took a piece of leather for a covering if it rained. Each carried a basket.

Nearby, Pechki put her arm around Minagle. "I noticed you and Ghanya sitting close at the gathering last night. Is there something between you?"

"I think so, Izumo," she answered her grandmother, looking into Pechki's dark blue eyes with her brown ones. "I like his seriousness and his responsibility. He is like Manak, mature. He is so thoughtful. Sometimes when I've struggled with something, I find him there with a helpful hand. Also, when he puts his hand on my shoulder, well, I get all mushy inside."

"It sounds like the two of you are attracted. I don't suppose you've talked of joining?"

"Oh, but we have! One of the things I like about him is that he doesn't want to copulate until he joins. He said problems can come from that. He thinks about things. I like that."

"What kind of problems?" Pechki asked intrigued.

"Apparently Blanagah was interested in him maybe for joining or maybe for copulating. He didn't say. He did say that he wouldn't choose her and refused to copulate with her because he didn't want her to think that he would join with her. He thinks that females can get tied to a male just because of copulating, tied somehow when they're not even joined."

"That may have some real truth," Pechki said. "He sounds smart, Minagle."

"Last night, he told me I was beautiful. He told me he would like to join with me when I am woman. Is that good?" Minagle asked very seriously.

Pechki cupped Minagle's chin. "My Dear, that may be very good. I think you will need someone who thinks carefully as you describe. How do you feel about him?"

"I want to be close to him whenever I can. I still feel a little frightened from the time with Reemast. Is that wrong?" Minagle asked with imploring eyes.

"Oh, my Special One, I still ache for you that you had a bad experience, but you need to put that behind you. It happened, but Ghanya is not Reemast, nor is he anything like him. What Reemast did was grotesque. Not at all what copulating is about. Those things you know, but you need to take it from knowledge of bad experience to moving forward in life doing what those in life do. Otherwise, you're like a tied dog. You cannot go anywhere through life."

"So you think that Ghanya and I could join and be happy?"

"That is for you to decide. I would expect so."

"I really think he is wonderful," she admitted with a smile that warmed the heart of her grandmother.

Her grandmother smiled slowly, savoring the time spent with Minagle. She was pleased that Minagle and Ghanya had found each other, especially if Minagle felt comfortable about it.

The hunters had gathered. They planned to hunt in the lower grazing land. They had seen some antelope and thought that might be good.

Wamumur and Emaea began their walk. They had inhabited the first large cave they'd found. It was situated to the south, the direction from which they arrived at the place. One of the things Wamumur and Emaea really liked about Cave Kwa is that it had water inside. They wondered whether any of the caves had water. Caves seemed to line this rock walk ledge and go quite a distance. They would first check all the caves that they hadn't checked the day before.

When they reached the twentieth cave down, Emaea noticed a different feeling. There was a very gentle movement of air. She motioned the others to be quiet. She listened carefully. The dog's ears were tensely erect and he looked deep into the cave. Emaea turned into the cave. She noticed that the cave seemed to have a break in the back toward the left. She walked in and went to the break. There was a bit of a ramp down and the cave opened into an enormous room. Wamumur and Ki'ti and the dog followed her into the

125

huge room. There was a ceiling hole which let light in. Going off to the left was another room and then another. In the very last room, there was the water that Emaea sought. That is what caused her to stop at the cave. She had sensed the water. *Perhaps this is where they should live,* she thought. She put her hand in the water and tasted the water. It was good. Wamumur was also thinking they should move to this cave. The safety of this cave was special because there was a vestibule of sorts and then a narrow entrance to the big cave. That could provide safety that they had never had. The cave was larger than any cave they had ever seen. Not only did the hole in the ceiling let in light but also it would be a great smoke hole. The cave was ideal.

As they continued to look around, Ki'ti asked, "What's this?"

She had found a tiny shiny yellow selenite stone that appeared to have been worked somehow.

Emaea took it and examined it. Then Wamumur. The two adults looked at each other.

"It's an owl far from home," Wamumur mumbled with great feeling. "Very far from home." His voice trembled as memories showered him.

"What do you mean?" Ki'ti asked. "It looks like an egg at first, not a tool. I had to learn to see it. At first it just looked like a pretty rock."

They walked out into the sunlight. The stone seemed to glow from the inside out. It resembled an owl. Whoever carved it had made it smooth, amazingly smooth.

The three sat on the rock walk ledge looking out over the stream bed below. Wamumur seemed lost in thought.

Wamumur shook himself loose from his mind web travel and said, "When I was very young, I lived near rocks like this. It was very long ago when I was your age," he looked at Ki'ti. "I was stolen from my home. I was brought to the People and raised as a special son. I ached for my People. But I never saw them again. We traveled and traveled. We went south and then east. So I think this rock came from the west somehow. Far, far away. Since we have moved so far north, I'm estimating that this may have come from that way, west. I had a happy life after grieving for my own family. By the time I met Emaea, I had all but forgotten the old life I had." He squeezed the rock in his hand. "I hadn't thought of that old life until now. This rock. It probably came from mountains near where I was born. We were called the Band of the Owl. I remember that. It's like finding part of my childhood and that childhood is so far away that I cannot remember it except in little brief images. We don't name our groups, but the group I was born into named itself the Band of the Owl. We each had one of these. I cannot remember the name of the man who carved it. I don't know what happened to my owl." He seemed submerged in thought again. Then he said, "These rocks are so fragile. I wonder how this one survived."

Emaea was dumbfounded. She'd known Wamumur for so long and never knew he'd been stolen. What things she still had to learn about this man! Emaea held out her hand for the stone. Wamumur gave it to her. She looked at the way the stone captured light and found it fascinating. It did in fact resemble an owl now that Wamumur had mentioned it. She could see the large eyes and the circles that feathers made around owl's eyes. She could also see the beak. The wings were marked and there were feet. It fit neatly into her palm. Without knowing it was an owl, she, like Ki'ti, might have thought the pretty yellow rock contained only random marks. She realized Ki'ti had a point. You have to learn to see. She handed it to Ki'ti. The girl took it and looked at it marveling. In the light, it was so much more alive than in the half-light of the cave.

Ki'ti gave the owl to Wamumur. "This should be yours, Wise One," she said.

He took it and thanked her. The offer and the owl meant much to him.

"We should continue," Emaea said.

They got up and continued down the rock walk ledge examining caves. When they reached the twenty-fifth cave, Emaea stopped, almost running into Ki'ti who was in front of her. Ki'ti had come to an abrupt stop.

"This is not good!" Ki'ti stated flatly, accompanied by a resounding palm strike and moan.

"What do you mean?" Wamumur asked.

Ki'ti was shivering. "Not good," was all she would say. Ahriku sat staring at her face with a little shiver that showed his uncertainty and an almost perceptible whine.

Wamumur walked past her into the cave. He could feel the creepy feeling himself, though it was not as strong as it appeared to Ki'ti. He rubbed his upper arms unconsciously. Emaea felt something that was not good as well. The adults sought the cause of the feeling, but Ki'ti simply stood just outside shivering. Emaea noticed a hint of a foul odor in the cave but could not imagine the source of Ki'ti's reaction. Wamumur lit a firebrand he carried with him and moved to the back of the cave. In the far back of the cave, Wamumur found a body of a human. *Had the hunters not checked the area for humans?* he wondered. Who was this? It was a man and he was mummified. He was different: neither People nor Other. He wore pants and boots and a tunic top with fur left on the leather. In some places, the fur was black and in others it was white. He had a head covering and a spear. He was very tall. Wamumur turned the body to the side and found that he had been speared in the back, not once but three times. The spears had been removed. Emaea removed the jacket. Dried blood was all over his tunic.

Emaea marveled at the jacket. It was lovely. It was made of rectangles sewed together. The rectangles were sewed from the top down the garment on the front and back, long enough for an arm, and then the bottom had been stitched together under the arm. Clearly, the black and white fur came from a single animal since there was no seam to bind the two colors together. It was the first truly sleeved garment she had ever seen. The work was beautiful. It was stitched with some very fine material in a strand. It was brittle, but she assumed that when the man wore it, there would have been no brittleness. The tunic was made of soft skin with a collar at the neck that seemed to tie above the head just like the jacket. Beside the man was a green bag with a shoulder strap.

"How long?" she asked.

"Oh, he's been dead for years and years and years," Wamumur estimated. He looked for Ki'ti. "What's the matter with her?" he asked.

"I'll see what I can find out," Emaea offered. She knew when Wamumur said years three times that the man died a good bit before Wamumur had been born. How, she wondered, could something so old affect someone so young?

She went outside and took Ki'ti back down the rock walk ledge and sat with her in the light. "What is the matter, Little Girl?" she asked.

It took awhile for Ki'ti to respond. "I felt like I could see it."

"See what?"

"There were" she held up five fingers "men." They were chasing another very tall man. They were Others. The man they chased was different but not People, not Others. The Others were dripping evil." Ki'ti shivered.

"What do you mean dripping evil?" Emaea asked, fascinated but not understanding.

"Black clouds drifted behind them as they moved to kill him. It looked like the black clouds dripped. They had found the man walking along the hill over there and they chased him here and killed him. He had done nothing to cause them to kill him. He tried to talk to them, but they wouldn't listen."

Emaea was amazed. Ki'ti knew there was a man in the cave who had been killed, when she hadn't set a foot in the cave? She knew he was tall? Not People; not Other. How, Emaea wondered, could she have "seen" something that existed a long time ago? How could she have known he was murdered when she and Wamumur hadn't known he'd been killed until he turned the body on its side?

"Mother," she said shivering, "He was a good man. He was taking curing plants to his family. His family was sick up there (she pointed to the mountains). He got the curing plants from someone to the east. He just wanted to save his family. Why did they have to kill him?"

"Hush, Little Girl," Emaea had pulled her on her lap and held her in her arms. "Shhhhhhhhh." She rubbed her arms trying to warm her. The girl's skin was very cold.

Wamumur came outside. "This looks like a bag for transporting herbs, a little like Totamu's. I wonder how they made it green." He had the bag in his hand. "That man was an arm taller than I, maybe more."

"Little Girl," Wamumur said with authority, "why are you so upset?"

"Wise One, I do not want to see those Others come here and do evil to the People. I fear them."

"Little Girl, what you talk about took place long before I was born. It is old. You are outside our time. Wake up from your dream. Those people, the Others who did this, they are gone. Long, long before I was born. A long time ago. If you are going to see things like this, you have to make it clear to yourself what time you are in. Otherwise, your mind web can become disorganized."

Emaea looked at Wamumur. *Does he see this way, too?* she wondered, but she chose not to ask. Later would be a good time to pursue it, not now.

"Wise One, can we take the bag to his family?"

Wamumur looked at her wondering whether she'd heard a word he said. "No! I told you, you are in the wrong time."

She got slowly off Emaea's lap. She stood before Wamumur making herself as tall as she possibly could. "He can sleep again, if his family gets the bag. I know where they are. He is troubled."

"Little Girl, his family is dead."

"I know and you know, but he doesn't."

"What makes you think you know where his family is?"

"I only know that I know. I can show you. We need to get the curing plants to his family." She stood first on one foot and then another, twisting her hands together. Her eyes were partly dilated.

Emaea looked at Ki'ti and knew something was very wrong but could not understand exactly what the problem was. She was troubled by the way the child moved and acted and her eyes were too dark. This was, she thought, beyond her expertise.

"You can do nothing of the sort," Wamumur asserted positively. "We will bury him and that will be that. Do you understand me? He and his family are dead." As far as he was concerned, that was the end of it, and he failed to wait for an answer. Wamumur was getting irritated with Ki'ti's assurance and forcefulness. He didn't pick up on her body language or anxiety as he thought he was dealing with an obedience issue and having never parented, he didn't realize he had to deal with multiple issues at one time, especially with the young and willful and spiritually driven.

Wamumur and Emaea headed back to the home cave. The green bag was swinging on its shoulder strap from Wamumur's arm. They would suggest a move to the new cave that afternoon. Wamumur wanted to get a burial party for the mummified body.

Emaea had taken the man's jacket to share with Totamu and Pechki and anyone else who wanted to look at the sleeved design and two toned pelt before it was buried with the man.

Back at the cave, things moved swiftly. Women took brooms to the new cave and were busy getting it prepared. Some of the men started hunting for a good place for burials. Ki'ti could not take her eyes off the green bag that Wamumur had laid atop his sleeping mat. She reached out and touched it. Touching it seemed to make it come alive again for her. She could see other things: The man's wife and children. Their cave. She wanted to weep. The man was the saddest person she'd ever seen. He urged her. She filled up with a certainty, a certainty that she must at all costs get the bag to the man's family in the mountains. She put her head through the shoulder strap to carry the bag. That's how the man had carried it. On her, it almost dragged the ground. She didn't even look around. She never considered hazards or consequences. She went to the end of the rock walk and began to scale the hill. Getting up there was not easy and she shoved a lot of dirt and small rocks to the ground below in her climb. It took her a long time to scale the hill and then she began her trip downhill to the next hill. She was unaware that her tunic and arms and legs and face were full of dirt. She went on as one possessed. She did not reflect on the wisdom of her choice, only that it must be done. She was driven. Soon, she was topping the next hill. She pushed on with a strength she didn't know she had.

Suddenly, Emaea realized she didn't know where Ki'ti was. Her dog was with the dogs, but she was missing. She asked and someone had seen her heading toward the south end of the rock walk awhile ago. She was carrying a green bag. Emaea called to Wamumur. He came fast, noticing the alarm in her voice.

"Ki'ti is missing. Someone saw her heading toward the end of the rock walk with a green bag. The south end of the walk. I cannot find the green bag."

"Wait until I get my hands on that child!" Wamumur said exasperated. "Men!" he called out.

He told them what had happened and what he suspected. Nanichak-na and Mootmu-na and Ermol-na volunteered immediately to go to find her and bring her back. Wamumur wanted to join them but knew he'd hold them back with his slowness.

The hunters grabbed water pouches and left quickly. It didn't take long for them to find the trail at the end of the rock wall. They were excellent trackers but they'd need good skill as Wisdom had begun to suck the color from the land. When the men saw the loose dirt, they were shocked that she'd chosen to go straight up a steep incline. Only a little further there was a turnoff that was a gentler incline, which the men chose to use. She was headed, perhaps, the way a bird might fly to the place.

The men followed her over the first hill and down and up the next. She had walked through shrubs and grasses. She never thought to cover her trail but in the reduced light it was not easy to follow. The mountains were nearby and they were into them before much time passed. They noticed that she was going through a pass that they would never have seen without knowing this country well. She kept going straight up. It was getting to their leg muscles. They called out to her but either she didn't hear them or she just didn't respond. They all knew she was their next Wise One. She had to be found. *What,* they wondered, *was the matter with this willful child?* They kept on and on. They reached a large meadow and realized she'd gone straight through it, something wise hunters would never have done. They ran across it as fast as they could. The Others would have been quicker, since they seemed to have been made to run. Wisdom continued to suck color from the land. That was not good. In the mountains, dark came quicker than in the hills or flat lands. The men were pressed to find her. Alone in the mountains at dark, she could be prey to any number of animals.

They had reached white rain. It was lying on the ground in patchy places, not falling from the sky. The men urged themselves on. They noticed Wisdom was about finished sucking color from the land.

Suddenly, Ermol-na said, "Look up there." He pointed to a place far above them.

There was a single cave with a fire going.

"Is that her, or Others?" Nanichak-na asked nobody.

"Shall we go there?" Mootmu-na asked.

"I think it is Ki'ti because the fire is so small. Let's go." Ermol-na said as he moved quickly to find the path up.

With difficulty, the men found the path that led to the cave. It was well concealed. They wondered how Ki'ti had located the place, and the hunters shared a glance that without words showed how in awe they were of the child's ability to know things. They were slightly shaken. It would have been far more comfortable to have found her wandering and not finding the place. The path appeared not to have been used for a long time. In some places, trees grew on the path. When they finally reached the top, they saw Ki'ti talking to three bodies in the cave. They were partly skeletons and partly mummified. Animals had not disturbed the bones. She had built a little fire and was seemingly unaware of the presence of the men. The men found the whole thing unnerving.

Nanichak-na, the oldest of the three men, wasted no time. He grabbed the back of her tunic and jerked her up. Ki'ti was startled, as if awakened from a dream. Nanichak-na carried her to the side of the cave, put his foot on a small rock, and laid her across his leg. He swatted her bottom over and over forcefully but taking care because she was small and girl. She wept, screamed for mercy, and wept some more. He did not hear her. As a seasoned hunter, he knew anatomy, human as well as animal. He was careful to strike with force to make a memory but where he would do no internal permanent physical damage. He offered her to Mootmu-na, who took her and repeated the same punishment. Finally, Mootmu-na handed her to Ermol-na. Ermol-na also administered punishment. Ki'ti was very sore and utterly heartbroken. She was definitely returned to the present time period.

"Now, we will go home," Nanichak-na stated flatly. Mootmu-na and Ermol-na carefully put out the fire. Nanichak-na held her hand tightly. They began the long trip back to the home cave. The men had not remembered that Ki'ti had carried a green bag to the cave, so the bag remained with the dead man's family. She was at peace, having delivered the bag. Now, the man could rest. The pain didn't matter. *She had done what she had to do, even if the hunters didn't understand*, she thought.

It was very late when they reached the home cave. Good to their word, People from the home cave had moved to the much larger cave that had been found earlier. The men presented Ki'ti to Wamumur. Nanichak-na was holding her left hand and Ermol-na had her right hand. Both held her hands too tightly.

Nanichak-na said, "We found her in a cave up in the mountains. She was talking to three dead bodies. Fortunately, she'd built a small fire. Each of us has punished her severely."

"Thank you. You are good men," Wamumur said, grateful that his daughter had been returned, but very angry that she had run off and used the precious time of three hunters, and that she had disregarded what he'd told her.

He took her by the hand to the cave where she'd gotten so upset. She was shocked. The terrible feelings of earlier were there no longer. She said, "The man really does know."

"Sometimes we know things we aren't supposed to know, Little Girl. It is one thing to run into mind webs of humans that get hung up in life or death, it is quite another to act on them. You deliberately disobeyed me. I know that you would tell me that you *had* to do it. That is a lie you let yourself believe. Get that straight. For you to go running off alone in the mountains when Wisdom is sucking the color from the land put you at great risk. An animal could have eaten you for its evening meal easily. You didn't think about that, did you?"

Ki'ti hung her head and said nothing.

"You took valuable hunter time to find you. What gave you the right to take up time of your uncles? You are our next Wise One. You are not permitted to run off alone in the wilderness. We could lose the stories that keep our People safe. Our hunters could have met with injury or death."

Ki'ti stood still, her head was as low as it would go. Now that she no longer felt the presence of the man, she could understand. Before, she only knew one thing. She had to get the bag to the people in the cave. Did she have two mind webs? She tried to understand.

Wamumur took a green branch from a tree beside the rock walk and pulled the leaves from it. He bunched her tunic up, holding it at her neck, and he began to use the branch as a switch against her skin. Her back and bottom and legs were covered with lines. Again, she had cried out and begged for mercy, but there was none.

Wamumur threw the stick off the rock walk toward the stream. Ki'ti breathed a sigh of relief thinking her punishment was finally over.

"Now, Little Girl, get this clearly. If you ever go where Emaea and I cannot find you, I personally will take your foot and put it on a rock. I will then hit your foot with another rock. You will never walk normally again, and you won't be climbing mountains. You had better learn from this. You will do what I tell you, and you won't do what I tell you not to do. I know that you want to tell me that the man is calm now. I *know* he is. Does that make what you did right? No. You have a responsibility to us, not to a man dead for years and years and years—no matter how much he tries to influence you. Do you understand?"

Ki'ti kept her head down and did not speak for fear of weeping.

"I asked you, do you understand?"

"Yes," came a tiny voice.

"I can't hear you," Wamumur said.

"Yes!" she responded louder.

"I can't hear you!" he shouted.

"Yes, I understand!" she said as loud as she dared.

"Very well. And you like to walk on good feet?"

"Yes, I like to walk on good feet!" she replied with increased volume but avoiding haughtiness.

"We will talk tomorrow about these ways we have of understanding things in other times. Now, you will present yourself to your mother. I don't know what she will do."

"Yes, Wise One," she replied, thinking she could take no more punishment. She began to see that getting that bag to the dead people might not be worth the pain she was feeling.

The two walked back to the new home cave in silence. Ki'ti walked over to Emaea who was sitting next to Totamu. Emaea turned Ki'ti around in silence. She pulled her tunic off over her head. Then Totamu began to apply salve to the injured skin on her back, bottom, and legs. Ki'ti tried to stand there stoically, but tears of shame began to course down her face. It was clear that everyone in the cave knew how thoughtless she'd been. It hurt as much as the punishment and now the salve did. She could feel the eyes in the darkened cave boring into her. Why had she listened to the dead man? She had no answer and that frightened her. If she listened once, what could prevent her from doing that again? Maybe the punishment? She wondered. It really, really hurt. And the eyes in the dark, that hurt just as much. She had let her own People down. She wondered, would this kill any of her pride? She was ashamed, but she knew pride still lurked in every pore of her being.

Minagle came over and asked for the tunic. Emaea handed it to her. She took it down to the cave where the water ran and washed it out. There was blood on the tunic. Not woman blood, just blood from her punishment. Minagle's heart ached for her sister. Why she would have done something like that was more than Minagle could understand, but she could reach out to her sister by washing her tunic. When it was cleaned, she carried it back up to Emaea who put it on a pole to dry.

Ki'ti remembered to hug and kiss her new mother before she went to bed. She didn't want to talk and Emaea understood that well.

Emaea had unrolled Ki'ti's sleeping mat and the girl stretched out on it on her belly. Ahriku was at her side immediately. Emaea covered her with her sleeping cover. Ki'ti cried herself silently to sleep. Ahriku licked salt tears from her face. He also licked salve from some of her wounds.

Emaea went outside and sat on the rock walk edge. Wamumur came and sat beside her.

"What happened today, my husband?"

"Have you never slipped in time and known what happened to someone someplace in another time?"

"No," she replied.

"Well, I have. It is so real that it is hard to separate from the present. Ki'ti is so young for this to be happening. It would be more difficult for her to separate the times. What she saw was real. I have no doubt of it at all. Had she not tripped into the other time first, I might have. But I know when and how to stop."

"She saw the man on a mission to take healing herbs to his wife and children. He was doing no harm when some of the Others saw him. I guess they didn't want a stranger in the area where they were living. So they killed him instead of warning him to stay out. His dying thoughts were probably of getting the bag to his family. I got that much myself."

"She said they were dripping evil."

"Ah, now that is something else. She was seeing inner feelings expressed externally. You and I would see that immediately in body language. There are other ways to see it, to know how a person feels or what their motivation is. She seems to have been given a lot of abilities at a very early age. I don't blame her for doing what she did. The ancient wishes of those who are dying float around and can be very convincing. She didn't seem to get much of a measure of personal safety from Wisdom yet. She was punished severely because she must first do what she is told, no matter what. Obedience is critical. That is her safety at least for now. I have warned her that if she runs off again, I will hit her foot on a rock with a rock so that her walking will be impaired from then on."

"Oh, in the name of Wisdom, would you really do something like that?" Emaea, horrified, recoiled.

"Yes, definitely and in the name of Wisdom. She cannot go running off like that for her own safety, so hunter's time is not abused, and for the well being of the People. She will become Wise One after us, but she has to live to do it." He did a strong palm strike.

Wamumur took Emaea's hand and caressed it. "I hated doing what had to be done. Wisdom knows I hated it. I don't want to hurt her. But we live where a life can be ended just for failing to think briefly. I was so worried waiting for the hunters to return with her. I was terrified that they'd return with her dead body. There are cobras out there and other vipers and all manner of large animals, including rhinos. She could so easily have been killed, or one of the hunters. She must do what she is told. Can you think of any other way to reach her?"

"I have to admit I'm at a loss. The hunters told Totamu and me that when they reached the cave, she was talking to the bodies of the dead people and didn't even hear the hunters when they spoke to her."

"She was deep into the mind web she got caught in."

"Well, what will keep her from getting caught again?" Emaea asked confused. "I remember seeing her with her eyes dilated and anxiety showing in her wringing her hands. Those must have been signs that she had entered that other time. Either that or maybe that was a sign that she was not able to be obedient because of the stressful tug of the man from long ago."

"When you first get caught in the mind web of another in another time, you know you have one foot in the real and one in some other time. She needs to stay in this time and not allow herself to go wandering in another time. She must refuse. She can do that. Curiosity is what permits wandering in another time web. I will discuss this with her tomorrow. Curiosity can be deadly. The other thing that will help is the punishment. She will hurt for days, but she will remember forever."

"I am glad that I don't have that ability," Emaea said and then wondered whether she meant it.

They looked at the stars for a while and then went inside where most of the people were already asleep.

In another place, when Wisdom returned color to the land, the hunters heading south on the ash had made two days in one compared to the trek to the new place. They were eager to get the meat and return so they traveled as rapidly as possible. The Others could move a lot faster than the People, but they kept to the speed that the slowest member could travel comfortably. The trek was monotonous in the monochrome landscape where silence reigned. They were eager to reach the cave and get it over with. They were going at a much faster rate than with the whole group. Soon, they realized they'd have to put on the booted garments, because they were nearing the ash. They were delighted to find when they reached the ash that the lines and the footsteps of the many People had left a clear trail. The men hoped to get to the cave and back before wind or rain obliterated the trail. They continued to move as quickly as possible.

In eight days, they had reached the caves. The men were tired and that evening they packed the meat and a few skin drying frames and tools on the stretchers they'd made. They packed to the limit of the stretchers and slept through the entire night before making their turnaround. On the return trip, however, the People pushed themselves to be quicker, since they knew the Others could move a lot faster than they could. They would make the return trip in seven days. They could see storm clouds forming in the south when they reached the green grassland, and they all breathed a sigh of relief. They had enough food to keep them well within a safety net.

The People had made the home cave and environment a convenient place to live. The rock walk led from cave to cave. It was one with the rock wall that overhung the walk, creating a covered promenade that stretched the entire length of the cave system. In a rain, they could walk from cave to cave and never get wet, and it rained more than they were used to. A bath area had been scooped out in the stream and the plants around it that had any height were removed. The area was open to light and gave no refuge to animals or water snakes.

Wamumur and Emaea had continued to explore the area with a much more subdued Ki'ti, followed by Ahriku. Ki'ti was getting past the physical pain but she still was embarrassed by her own behavior. Fortunately, she had no more encounters with other mind webs. Wamumur and Emaea were very careful to watch her for any behavior changes that might indicate spiritual entrapment.

While the men were gone, Domur became woman. She began her flow the day the men left. She was so eager to see the return of the men. She wondered how long after the return she and Manak could join. Her dream was so close. Minagle was fascinated with it all. She knew the joining of Domur and Manak would be very special. Her best friend and her brother. How wonderful!

Blanagah, meanwhile, was not happy. She wanted to have a husband but none of the eligible males was interested. Ghanya had obviously decided on Minagle and it appeared that there was something between Meeka and Lamul. Frequently, she pondered her situation. She did not want to end up without a husband. But the idea of one of the older men did not appeal to her. Sometimes, she would dream of Vanya, not having any idea that the young man was dead at sea. She wondered why People saw her as undesirable and guessed it was because she had been joined already, if briefly. Maybe she was just too desperate. Maybe she was just too unlikeable?

She was out in a meadow picking plants for the evening meal when Hahami-na saw her. He waved and walked over to her.

"Are you well, Blanagah?" he asked.

"Quite well, Hahami-na, and you?" she responded wondering what he wanted.

"Also, quite well. Are you finding what you seek?" Hahami-na asked.

"All but the dandelions. Normally they are everywhere. I can't find any."

"Would you like some help?" he asked. "I have seen some."

"That would be very kind," she said.

"Here, let me carry your basket," he offered.

"I don't want to trouble you," she replied.

"It is no trouble," he said, taking the basket from her. He noticed how the wind played in her short wavy brown hair. She was attractive and her life, like his, had been touched with sadness. His red hair streaked with gray was just coming back in now that shaved heads were not required anymore. She could see that he was balding.

As they walked to the place he knew dandelions grew, she found herself becoming more and more at ease with him. When the hills were steep, he offered his hand to steady her. When he saw something he thought might interest her, he pointed it out. He even found some other greens that would be good for the evening meal and helped her harvest them. When they reached the place where Hahami-na had remembered the dandelions, again he helped her harvest them. He carried the basket on the return trip.

"Blanagah, you and I share a recent loss, you of your husband, me of my wife. I know how you must have felt. You probably know how I have felt."

"Yes?" Blanagah replied.

"There are few options for joining in a group as small as ours. I want to ask while we are away from the cave whether you would consider joining with me." There, it was out. He had tried to do the best presentation he could. Now, he had to wait for an answer. He stared at the ground.

Blanagah was not too surprised after the afternoon they had spent. He was so kind and considerate. She thought a bit and then said, "Hahami-na, I would be honored to be joined with you."

Hahami-na was filled with joy and Blanagah's joy was rising. She would be joined and have children and Hahami-na was a good man. It was good.

When they returned to the cave, Hahami-na met Wamumur and Nanichak-na and he told them his news. They could be joined that night or any other they chose. Hahami-na would have to discuss it with Blanagah. They talked and both decided that night would be good. Both were lonely and wanted to be close to each other. The meat offering was waived. For the immediate present, the People decided that the offering of meat would be unnecessary for any joining.

Blanagah couldn't wait to share the news with Olintak. She found her at the bathing area. Olintak was delighted for Blanagah. She knew Hahami-na would be wonderful to her. He was a good man. She smiled wondering whether Blanagah would have children with red hair. She had already wondered whether her children would have red hair.

Mootmu-na and Amey got the news from Hahami-na. They were delighted. The move to the cave was good. Suddenly, there was a shout. Ekuktu was signaling that the men were returning from the caves with the meat. Everyone looked at everyone else. How could they be back already? All rushed to the trail. Sure enough, the men were on the way and all were there. The People were exuberant. Quickly, the women added to the food being prepared for the evening meal. This was a time to celebrate.

The men arrived and laid down the stretchers. The meat was immediately transported little by little to the second cave in the series where the place had been cleaned and mats had been placed on the floor. The cave had been prepared several days ago. Food from the trek had been placed there already.

The men were weary. They embraced their wives and some went directly to the bathing area. Domur approached Manak at a run. He caught her in his arms and swung her in a circle.

"What is different about you, Domur?" he asked.

"Does it show?" she asked

"What?" he asked.

"I am woman," she said gleefully.

"Tonight?" he asked with a smile for her alone.

"You'll have to check. Blanagah is joining with Hahami-na tonight. There is no reason for us not to join tonight. Let me know and I will sweep a cave for our First Night."

"What about the meat offering?" he asked.

"That has been waived for the present, but were you not moments ago loaded with meat?" she teased.

He went off to check with Wamumur about joining, and Domur found Blanagah and asked whether she would be sweeping a cave, and if so, which one. Blanagah said she hadn't chosen yet but would take a quick look and they could both check the caves and decide. Each got a broom and found caves that were nearby but not close to each other. Both women swept carefully. Before the evening meal, their caves were ready. The men had brought the sleeping mats and covers to their caves after preparing the hearth and stacking wood, and all was set. They all hoped that the pronouncement would be made just after the evening meal so they could have a long night.

"How is Little Girl?" Manak asked Domur. "I haven't seen her. Normally when I arrive from a trip somewhere, she flies to meet me on the return."

"Come, walk with me," Domur said. She led him in a north direction on the pathway along the rock wall. As they walked she told the story to him of Ki'ti's running to carry a bag to a cave, directed by a dead man she thought wanted to get a bag of herbs to his family. Only the man had died long before Wamumur had even been born. Somehow, she'd gotten mixed up in an ancient mind web. Hunters had been dispatched to find her and bring her back. Sure enough, she'd found a cave and there were dead people there, an adult and two children. It was in the mountains where there was white rain on the ground. She told of the punishment meted out to the girl, and of Wamumur's threat if she ever did that again.

"Ah, that little one. What on earth possessed her to do that?"

"Wamumur said that sometimes it's possible to get caught in the mind web of another outside our own time. He said that most people would be so afraid that they would leave it alone and run the other way. Not so with Ki'ti, who believed it and lived it."

"How awful," he said. "I am glad Wisdom made us as we are."

She smiled at him and they embraced. "I cherish you, my dear," Manak said to her. "Will you please not bless me with a Ki'ti?"

"I'll do my best." She smiled at him with a huge smile that drank his soul.

When they returned to the home cave, Manak went to find Ki'ti. "There you are," he said.

Ki'ti hung her head. "I have shamed you and my family," she admitted.

He put his hand under her chin and pulled her head up so he could look in her eyes, "Little Girl, what you did was not good, but I love you. I will always love you." He stood her up and turned her around. He lifted her tunic and examined her back. "Ah! You really got punished, didn't you?" He dropped the tunic horrified at the bruises and switch marks. He'd never known anyone to have had that much punishment. Of course, he didn't know about Reemast's death and he'd forgotten Reemast was punished severely for killing baby birds.

"It still hurts," Ki'ti replied.

"Will that make you remember to obey Wamumur and Emaea?"

She looked into his eyes, "I will do my best."

He stood there leaning in her direction with his hands on his hips. "That isn't good enough!" His words were caustic. From a distance, Emaea was listening.

"What do you mean?" Ki'ti asked, drawing away from him.

"It means obey Wamumur and Emaea. There isn't any doing your best. You simply obey. I know you understand me." Manak was fierce looking.

"I understand." She spoke quietly. She was hurt that even Manak was irritated.

"No, that isn't good enough." He was sterner than she had ever seen him.

"What do you want from me?" she asked twisting her hands and furrowing her brow.

"I want a promise. I want a promise that you will obey Wamumur and Emaea. No equivocation. Simply promise me."

Some of the mothers began to pick up the little ones to take a stroll outside. Some adults went outside just to provide privacy if that might help.

"But if I promise you and fail, then you have a right to punish me. I don't want to do it."

"Little Girl, promise me. Now!" he insisted. In the cave where normally People spoke quietly, Manak's voice was rising and drawing attention. A few more People went outside.

She started looking about.

"There is no place to run, Little Girl. Promise me. You have to promise me so that you have no little crack to crawl into to avoid obedience to your parents. That part of your pride you can kill. I know you well, Little Girl. Or should I call you Baby? You must promise me or you put the People at risk. I have not lived with you for so many years not to know how your mind web works. I want the cracks sealed up. No more rebellion. Now, promise me."

Ki'ti looked down at the floor. Nobody knew her as well as Manak. At first, he'd found her willfulness amusing and a diversion, but now he was making it clear that he wanted from her the one thing she didn't want to give. Worse, she thought, he was telling everyone in the cave how her mind web worked. The part of her mind that was not good.

"Now," his voice thundered, and she jumped, startled by the sound. Grypchon-na and Likichi were fascinated. They knew there was a strong bond between Manak and his little sister, but neither had any knowledge that it was so strong. Only Manak would have known about some kind of crack she might use to avoid obedience.

Ki'ti was shivering. She did not want to promise. Finally she said, "Okay."

"That's not good enough," he thundered.

"What do you want?" she asked, trembling.

"You say out loud so everyone can hear you: I promise Manak that I will obey my parents unequivocally. That's all."

"I promise," she whispered.

"That's not good enough. The whole thing and loud."

Tears were streaming down the girl's face. After what seemed a terribly long time, she said loud enough for all in the cave to hear, "I promise Manak that I will obey my parents unequivocally."

Then he went to her and picked her up in his arms and hugged her. Wamumur felt that of all the People there, he had just learned the most. Who would have thought that Ki'ti kept little cracks that she could dive into to avoid obedience. How did her mind web work? What was the source of the rebellion? Sometime he would have to talk to Manak. And thank him.

What Manak didn't really grasp is that he changed the life of Ki'ti that evening. He gave the People an obedient storyteller. Ki'ti had bundled up all the changes wrought by the Winds of Change and though she loved the People, her life had changed so much and so fast that she kept reserving a part of herself for only herself. When she became overwhelmed, she'd run to that place and build her will stronger and stronger. She would rebel for no viable reason. She had begun to become a menace to herself and therefore to the People. Somehow, Manak had seen right to the core of the problem. She loved him so much that she eventually capitulated and with her capitulation, a new and different Ki'ti emerged, the special one that would one day be their Wise One in fact.

Manak in his youth could not know that he had profoundly changed his sister. He could hope, and that's all he did. He had startled Domur, but as time went by, she could see the difference his time spent that night meant to her and to the People. No longer would the People wonder about the willful child. Ki'ti's change was that significant.

Tension reduced in the cave and the evening meal was served. The meat was tasty and the plants the People ate filled a strong need. They could virtually feel the nourishment from the green plants they'd done without for so long. It was great to have plants growing again. As soon as the four who were joining had eaten, Chamul-na rose to make the pronouncement that Blanagah and Hahami-na were joined and that Manak and Domur were joined. Ermol-na brought out his drum and the People sang and danced in the gathering area of the cave. The newly joined couples danced toward the shadows and quietly left for their chosen caves to the north, and others would not go down there until the next day.

Emaea took Ki'ti by the hand and they went to walk the field just southeast of the rock walk.

"Oh, Mother," Ki'ti began, "I am so sorry."

"Shhhhh," Emaea put her fingers on Ki'ti's lips. "We are just going to walk right now. You have much to sort out. Ease your mind. You have promised. Look forward, My Dear, not backwards. Do you not know how many People love you?"

As they walked, Emaea wondered whether others had been so affected by the Winds of Change that they were like little volcanoes about to explode. She mused on the problem with Reemast. His pride, unlike Ki'ti's, had been obvious. Ki'ti's was more hidden. Had he been suffering from the Winds of Change or was he just demanding to get his own way? She felt a little old and tired. Somehow, she demanded of herself that she know the answers. If she didn't have them, who would? And then it occurred to her that in the case of Ki'ti, the person who had the answers was her brother. He had watched out for his little sisters and knew them well. It did amaze her that Ki'ti could be as complex as she was at her age. It was possible that she didn't need to have all the answers, if she could learn who did have them when it was necessary. Or perhaps, there was no way for anyone to know all the answers. What bothered Emaea was that Ki'ti had learned about walking in another mind web outside of present time. She wanted to go with Ki'ti to the cave where the bodies were. She would really like to take the body of the man they had found to be with his family forever. She wondered whether that idea was as absurd as Ki'ti's taking the green bag. She wondered whether People ever really became adults or whether there remained a child in each adult and only the skin and bones got larger and older. The walk was good, but she began to lead them back to the home cave. Soon, it would be time for sleep. From the field, she gazed at the row of caves. Three lights. Her heart filled with joy. It was good!

When they returned, they found that many in the cave were laying out their sleeping mats and getting ready for bed, since Wisdom had sucked all the color from the land. Emaea loved the new cave. Before she was willing to sleep, however, she took a piece of very soft leather and cut it in a small circle. She then poked holes around the edge of the leather with a medium sized stitching awl for sewing. She threaded a leather strip through the holes. Before she drew the edges of the circle tight, she picked up the little yellow owl and put it into the soft leather pouch. She tied the ends of the leather strap into a secure knot. Wamumur came over and sat on his sleeping mat. Emaea slipped the pouch on the leather strip over his head. It was similar to what Totamu had made for Enut, only this one was not an ornament.

"What is in this?" Wamumur asked.

"It is your owl, My Love," she answered with a smile.

He reached out and hugged her.

Ki'ti came over and dutifully kissed Emaea and hugged her.

"May I have one of those?" Wamumur asked.

Ki'ti went to him and leaned down and kissed his cheek and hugged him. He pulled her off her feet and drew her into his lap and hugged her tight. "I do love you, Little Girl," he said with feeling.

For the first time in a long time, Ki'ti felt safe and secure. Somehow, she knew everything would be fine. She did not pull away but rather rested her head on Wamumur's chest. Her head hit the hard little owl and she looked at him quizzically. "It's my little yellow owl," he explained. "Now, Little Girl, you need to go to sleep and your mother and I need to take a walk. You will do what I say?"

"Yes, Wise One. I promise to go to my sleeping mat and sleep." And she did.

Wamumur and Emaea walked out under the stars. The night was lovely. Just cool enough to cause him to place his arm around Emaea. "You have been thinking about something. What is it?" he asked.

"My Dear," she responded, "I am probably as crazy as our daughter, but I think we should take the body of the man and put it with his family in the mountains."

Wamumur didn't know whether to laugh or cry. "Whatever made you think that?" he asked.

"I think it was that you and I were separated for so long and now we're together. They have been separated longer than you and I were. And we can do something about it."

"Are you off in some mind web time thing?" he asked.

"No, but I wish I could do it once so I'd know what you and Ki'ti are talking about."

"You don't want to know."

"Oh, yes, I do," she said firmly.

"I fear that if I take you there and we return the body, you will experience it. Worse, I fear that Ki'ti will experience it again. Those people are dead. Can we not leave them dead?"

"How would you feel if you were that man and Ki'ti and I were in that cave?"

"Ah, you think like woman!" Wamumur said, sounding exasperated.

"In case you haven't noticed, I am woman. Would you prefer I were man?"

"Ah, but you drive me wild sometimes," he said, embracing her and silencing her with a kiss.

They returned to the cave. Wamumur was ruminating about returning the body to the cave. *What would these females think next?* He wondered.

The people had settled down for the night. Wamumur could hear Emaea breathing. She still had some residuals from the ash. He was unsure what to do about her unusual request. After much time thinking, he decided to get some hunters to accompany him to move the body there. It would get rid of any connection with the event where they lived; it would satisfy Emaea's curiosity; and it would give him the opportunity to teach Ki'ti how to resist temptation to fall into other mind web traps. He was not sure whom to ask to go. And after his decision was made, he drifted off into slumber.

Chapter 5

After Wisdom returned color to the land, Wamumur went outside. He stood on the rock walk surveying the stream bed and the tiny valley that lay between the hill and the place they now called home. The morning was lovely and there were fewer dark clouds. Still, it was cooler than most seasons of warm nights had been. It was great to see color in the landscape return. He did not think he could have tolerated for long the lifeless monochrome vistas they'd left. Sometimes, he longed for home as they knew it by the river before Baambas. It was such a simpler time.

"Good morning," Mootmu-na said on his way out to the privy.

"Morning," Wamumur said, abbreviating the wish.

Mootmu-na returned shortly. He stopped to see what Wamumur was looking at. Nothing seemed different to him, so he asked.

"Nothing much, just taking in the morning. I do have a strange request of you. Would you be willing to accompany Emaea, Ki'ti, and me to take the body of the strange man to the cave where you found Ki'ti?"

"Sure. I don't really think that's strange. To have his body here when we know where his home is—we do know that was his cave, right? Well, it seems fitting."

"Mootmu-na, I am convinced that Ki'ti has the story right. How on earth would she have found the cave otherwise? I also had the same senses about the man. Yes, it's his cave. This would give me a chance to teach Ki'ti to resist falling into other mind webs. She will feel it again and I can keep her out of it."

"You can do that?"

"Yes. Well, I can tell her how to do it. She actually has to do it."

"Then, by all means, let's do it. I'll get Nanichak-na and Ermol-na to come as hunters. I'll ask Ghanya and Lamul to carry the stretcher. You want to do this today?"

"If it is convenient." The names that Wamumur had chosen had changed through Mootmu-na's intervention, but it didn't matter to Wamumur. Mootmu-na's selection was good.

"We have enough meat so that few hunters need go out today. Today is fine."

"Good. Then, when you are ready . . . ."

"We have to dig up the body, and we'll have to fix it to the stretcher. Some of the hills are very steep."

"I cannot believe I'm doing this," Wamumur said. He put his fingers against his forehead.

"It's your world. You understand these things. If we hunters can help you teach Ki'ti what she needs to learn, that is good, very good."

Wamumur went into the cave and wakened Ki'ti. "Get up, Little Girl," he told her and gave her a hand. She got up and slipped on her tunic. Ahriku yawned and stood. She went out, while Mootmu-na guarded her, and then came to sit with Wamumur on the rock walk edge.

"We are going to take the body of the strange man to his cave today," Wamumur said, trying to sound as if this were a perfectly normal thing to do. "I want you to go and to feel again the tug of temptation to fall into the mind web trap. I want you to learn that when you feel your feet in two different worlds, you reject the strange one immediately. You NEVER *need* to know what these strange mind webs are saying. NEVER. You do need to learn to resist the temptation to pursue them out of curiosity. Do you understand?"

"Yes, Wise One. I really risked my life and interfered with the lives of others when I fell into the mind web of the man with the green bag. I am still sore to prove that I did wrong. I would like to learn to recognize when that extra mind web is there and how to resist. I do not ever want to go through this again. You said you NEVER need to know what another mind web is telling you. Is that really true for all situations?"

"Yes. There is NEVER any reason for you to pursue these things. You live here and now, not somewhere else before in another time. Once we get that body removed from here, this place won't have as strong a connection to what happened. But when you think of it in the light of the present day, what reason could you have to need to know that a man was killed here?"

"None. Wise One, the pull was so strong. I think when I went to the cave, I'd have done it no matter what happened."

"That is what I want you to resist. I am not sure what the knowledge is that you gain—it may come from the dead or from evil spirits that attach themselves to the dead or to a thing. All I can tell you is that the temptation they set in front of you is NEVER for *your good*. Sometimes, it causes People to do things that get them killed."

"Do you know what it is to fall into these mind webs?"

"Yes, Little Girl, I do. I walked in the one you experienced to verify what you were saying. What you said was accurate. But look what it had you doing. Going to a cave in the mountains unprotected while Wisdom sucked the color from the land. Not safe. Stupid! You cannot ever again permit anything outside yourself to take over your mind web like that. You could have run into a rhino or a cobra. You're no hunter! Understand?"

Ki'ti shuddered wondering what she'd have done if she'd seen a cobra in the cave where she took the green bag.

"Yes, I understand I cannot do that, but, Wise One, how do you resist?" she asked.

"You resist by telling the other mind web to leave you alone. You call on Wisdom to protect you. If there are People around you, call on them for help, but they may not understand what your problem is."

"Wise One. We are fortunate. You now have Emaea and I have both of you. Was it hard to be Wise One when there were no others but you?" Ki'ti was sitting right at the edge of the rock walk swinging her feet from side to side. Her hands were by her legs with her fingers cupping the edge of the rock walk. She stared down to the ground below, but she wasn't focusing on the ground.

"Ah, the questions you ask! Yes. You mentioned feeling alone. For years and years, now that was alone! I had to learn about mind web traps by myself. Once, I almost lost my life. There was no one to teach me. I was older than you when I was recognized, but the Wise One before me didn't live long after I began to learn. It took a long time for me to learn that calling on Wisdom could provide protection."

"How do you call Wisdom?" Ki'ti asked. Ahriku was cuddled up to her side and as she moved her legs, the dog would become unsettled. Ahriku got up, walked in a circle, and settled down again.

"You can call out loud to Wisdom as you would to someone outside whose attention you wanted to get. You can also call out in your mind so others do not hear. You see, I think Wisdom is a spirit who is like a person. I think Wisdom knows what we do and what we think. I don't really understand, but I get glimpses of Wisdom. And I know that when I call on Wisdom, a peace comes on me and suddenly, if I cannot figure out what to do, what I should do becomes clear. Is this making sense?"

Ki'ti nodded.

"Wisdom is always there with you. You only need to reach out. Once, I called on Wisdom when a lion stalked me. For some strange reason, the lion lost interest and left me alone."

"So if I got tempted into another mind web, I can call Wisdom?"

"Yes. Now, promise me that if you find yourself in that situation, you'll call on Wisdom."

"Wise One, I promise you, if I find myself tempted by another mind web, I will call on Wisdom."

"Good Girl," he said. "You may have need to do that frequently today when we go to take the body of the man to be with his family."

"Should I be afraid?"

"No. You have me and Emaea and the hunters and Wisdom. You also have some understanding you didn't have earlier."

"Wise One, was it fair for you and the others to punish me when I didn't even know about mind web traps?"

Wamumur was unprepared for the question. He looked down at her and her eyes were looking right into his. "Little Girl," he said looking down to her, "You weren't punished for giving in to the temptation of the mind web trap. You were punished because you disobeyed. I had told you we would not take the bag to the cave. You disobeyed. You went to the cave despite what I had said. To be punished for disobedience is appropriate. It is fair. But I will tell you, life is not fair. Get used to it."

Ki'ti sat on the ledge even after Wamumur got up and went to find Emaea. He learned that the People Mootmu-na had chosen for the trip were in fact willing to participate. All were going about the normal business of life while Emaea prepared food for the eight People who would be heading to the cave.

They began the hike as soon as the body was secured to the stretcher. The men knew a way to reach the hills without taking the virtually perpendicular steep route that had been Ki'ti's starting point at the end of the walk. They went just a bit further to the south and used a gentler slope. They reached the hills and the ups and downs and then the mountains began.

"This really is beautiful country," Emaea remarked. "I love the rise and fall of the land but I'll admit that these mountains are getting to the backs of my legs."

"Mine, too," Wamumur said quietly.

Ki'ti was enjoying the walk, seeing it from eyes different from when she went there to take the green bag. She could see butterflies and birds and little mammals that scurried when they saw people. Mootmu-na pointed out a cobra absorbing warmth from a large rock. As the walk progressed through the open field, they heard a bark. Ahriku's head turned toward the woods. They all expected wolf pups. Everyone stopped and was very quiet and still. There at the edge of the forest was a very small deer. It barked again as if to draw attention to itself. It had antlers that went straight back and curved inward and it also had little fangs. The deer was about as tall as the distance from a man's elbow to his hand. They continued walking and the deer continued browsing.

"Wise One, do deer normally bark?" Ki'ti asked.

"No," he laughed. "That's something new for me. Have you ever heard deer bark, Emaea?" he asked.

"That was the first," she replied with a smile. She was thoroughly enjoying the walk. Her thoughts, however, were not on the present. She could not believe that Wamumur had agreed to her request. Even she thought her request was strange.

They walked through the pass and shortly arrived at the flat land below the cave. Lamul and Ghanya put the stretcher down.

Ghanya walked around looking up. "How are we going to get the stretcher up there?" he asked no one in particular.

Ki'ti grabbed tight to Wamumur's hand. "It's starting," she whispered.

"Good," he said, "now ignore it."

"It's so hard!" she complained.

"What did I tell you to do?" he asked.

"You said to ignore it."

"I mean what did I tell you earlier."

"You said to tell it NO."

"Do it!" he said.

Emaea stared up to the cave and suddenly she began to sense something strange. Was that a woman up there staring out? No, her mind was playing tricks on her. She thought that she was just picking up on Ki'ti's concerns. Then she felt as if she slipped in time. She was feeling and seeing what the woman above was feeling and seeing. She was curious. She looked toward Wamumur.

He noticed her expression and was prepared. "Tell it to quit, Emaea. If that doesn't work, call on Wisdom."

Ki'ti smiled. "Wise One, it works. When you call on Wisdom, it works!"

"Good, don't let it come back," he said to her, "Emaea, don't let your curiosity carry you away. Break the connection!"

Emaea, with her years of self discipline, found it difficult to stop her own curiosity. This was definitely a new thing but from the way Wamumur was acting and what had happened to Ki'ti, she realized that this was dangerous territory and she broke the connection.

The hunters were looking at the Wise Ones as if they'd lost their way in their mind webs. They were not experiencing any of this. It made the hair on the backs of their necks stand on end.

Mootmu-na and Ermol-na were trying to help Ghanya answer his question. "Do you think you could strap the body on your back and make it up there?" Mootmu-na asked.

"I don't know. Maybe I should climb up there first and then answer that question," Ghanya said.

"He is happy," Ki'ti whispered to Wamumur.

"I *know* he is, and I told you to break the connection," he said sternly.

"Well, that's how the connection arrived. I broke it. It hasn't returned."

"Are you telling me you couldn't block it before it began?"

"Yes."

"Then call on Wisdom now and ask that any connection like that gets blocked."

"I will obey, Wise One."

The men kept wondering about the climb and, finally, Lamul said, "We might have enough rope to tie to the skins to haul him up hand over hand from there. His body doesn't weigh much, it's just awkward."

The men untied the rope from the stretcher and from their cover that they'd put on top of the body. Fortunately they had used rope liberally to tie the cover over the body and around and around the stretcher. They untied every piece of rope they had. They tied all the rope pieces together. Ghanya took the rope looped over his arm and climbed to the cave. He slowly lowered the rope and it just came to the ground.

At that point, Emaea went to the body and took the covering and put it on the ground. Two of the men laid the body of the man on the covering. Emaea then took the corners of the cover and tied two ends together and then the next two ends together. She slipped the rope through the openings made by the tied ends. She took the rope and made a knot that would not slip apart while the men pulled the body up.

Ghanya had begun to pull the body up alone. Lamul climbed up quickly to help. The man's body was laid beside the body of his wife. Lamul tossed the piece of leather that had been used as a covering down from the cave.

"Wise One, may I go up there?"

"No, Little Girl, this is as close as you will be permitted. That is true for now and forever. Never again will you go up there. Promise," he insisted.

"I promise," she said sincerely.

Emaea did not ask. She simply climbed up the tortuous path to the cave. She looked about her for a few minutes. She realized the cave was much deeper than it appeared. She went inside. The bodies were in the vestibule, not the main cave. The main cave was furnished, but it had no water. To live there would have required transporting water. She wondered at what she saw but was disconcerted at the pulling of the different time. She called Wisdom to break the connection. Then she descended. She could feel the very strong pull of the dead or spirits or whatever it was, even when she was on the lower ground.

She really had to fight it, but she could understand Wamumur's words of caution. It would not do to become caught in the mind web of other people at another time. They had their own world to be concerned about. She had hers. And she'd experienced enough to know she didn't want to pursue it. At least, she had satisfied her curiosity as to what Wamumur and Ki'ti meant about slipping in time. She had looked out from the cave and had seen a huge expanse and realized how much danger Ki'ti had put herself in by taking the green bag to the cave. It astounded her that Ki'ti had gone straight to the cave. There must be more she didn't understand about different ways of knowing things, but her curiosity had been quelled by her experience. As an adult, she was acutely aware of the danger posed by this time capture and she understood why Wamumur was so adamant about Ki'ti and her leaving it alone.

"Wamumur," Emaea asked when she returned to the ground level, "Do you think that Totamu would be interested in the green bag?"

"My Dear, I don't want anything in our lives from that place or the man. They belong here in their time. We belong at home in our time." He did a strong palm strike.

"I understand," she replied, and she did.

Going back, Lamul would carry the poles for a while and Ghanya ties and leathers, and then they'd switch off. The hunters took a good look at the environment in the mountains and concluded that there was not really a good supply of meat to harvest from this area of mountains. Even the deer were tiny and they didn't gather in herds. As Wamumur and Emaea watched Lamul and Ghanya, it took them back to their earlier days and they enjoyed that. Each felt that the day had been good. They and Ki'ti had all learned a good deal.

Blanagah had returned to the busy home cave. She and Hahami-na had decided to remain a few more days in the separate cave at night, which had always been an option to newly joined couples. She was glowing. When she found Olintak that morning, she was smiling from ear to ear. She could not stop talking about how wonderful she found Hahami-na. Unlike Reemast who had pursued his own needs, Hahami-na had been considerate of hers. That was indeed a new concept to Blanagah. The men teased Hahami-na that he had a certain spring to his step. Domur also was radiant. Her love for Manak seemed to double from the time she saw him arrive back with the meat from Cave Kwa to the present. And his for her. They participated in the chores and then would wander off to be alone.

Those who had been to the cave of the man with the green bag returned and quietly fit right back into daily life. No one questioned Wamumur or the others about their trip, though it wasn't a secret at all what they had done. Most thought they had gotten rid of the body to keep the new Wise One safe and let it go at that. A few were just happy to get rid of the strange looking person who must have been very tall.

Lamk and Liho walked along the stream until Lamk stopped and picked up a tool that obviously hadn't been one of theirs. The tip was broken but it was a blade in the shape of a long leaf the length of his hand. He thought it was beautiful. He took it to his father, Mootmu-na.

"I found this," he said beaming.

Mootmu-na looked at the tool. *It had been crafted by a master*, he thought. The stone was a yellowish brown with dark flecks in it. It had a shine. Too bad it was broken.

"Where did you find it, my son?" he asked.

"By the stream. Liho and I were walking down there." Liho accompanied Lamk to see what Mootmu-na thought of the tool.

"Ermol-na," Mootmu-na called, "come take a look at this."

Ermol-na's curiosity was aroused. "What have you found?"

"Lamk found it, or was it you, Liho?" Mootmu-na asked.

"It was Lamk," she said. "He has good eyes for finding things," she said matter of factly, not intending flattery.

Lamk smiled at Ermol-na.

"Good work, Lamk," Ermol-na complimented him.

"We can learn a lot from this tool. In fact, I could fix it so we could use it." As he viewed it from all angles, Ermol-na was already mentally reworking the broken tool. He was impressed with the style of knapping which differed from his own. It almost seemed to his eye that more than one person had worked the tool. Maybe one was right handed and one left handed, he thought, or maybe there was no preference for either hand but each hand knapped a little differently? He was curious.

"Take it, Ermol-na. Let us see what you do with it. Now, my son, and you too, Liho, would you like to show me where you found it?" Mootmu-na asked, trying to pry a piece of meat from between two teeth. *Those two teeth were always trapping something*, he thought, as he followed the children from the cave.

"We were right around here," Lamk said, drawing an arc over the land about waist high with his open hand.

"Here's the place where you took it from the ground, Lamk," Liho said squatting down by the damp earth. Sure enough, the stone tool had left its shape in the damp earth.

Lamk's brown hair had begun to come back and was about fingernail length all over his head. Liho's very light blond hair was about finger length and was wavy. The light made it shine like a halo in the daylight. As she looked at the stream bed wondering whether there were more tools, Mootmu-na looked down at the two of them considering their youth. What things they would see, he mused. He was glad that there were two of them, male and female that age. It wasn't always the easiest thing to find someone near one's age with whom to join. As he was aware, when two of widely spaced ages joined, often one remained alone in old age. But then he smiled at his own thoughts realizing that his daughters, Blanagah and Olintak had lost to hunter's death their first choice of husbands, and Blanagah had lost her second. He wondered whether he should revise his initial opinion of age-mates. Looking at Lamul and Liho, he wondered whether these two would eventually join as friends like Manak and Domur.

Nanichak-na walked by with Arkan-na on the rock walk above. Mootmu-na could hear Nanichak-na ask, "Have you ever seen short deer with antlers and tusks? Deer that bark?"

Arkan-na got a big laugh out of that. As they passed, Nanichak-na was explaining what they saw on the mountain. Mootmu-na smiled.

"Look here! Is this another?" Liho called to them.

Lamk and Mootmu-na went to the place where Liho stood across the creek from cave side. There was another stone tool, broken, like the last. The tools were different from what they made, but Mootmu-na could see uses for the tools and thought that Ermol-na might find things he could use in the tools he made from what they might find.

Ki'ti heard the call from Liho and walked over to the place where they were examining the newest tool. Immediately, she knew that the tool had been made by the man in the cave. She knew those blades had been attached to long sticks. She ran to Wamumur.

"Wise One, you must help me!" she said breathlessly, failing to wait to be recognized before speaking.

His face registered the shock of her intrusion into his conversation with Chamul-na.

"Wait. You are being rude," he admonished pushing her aside. He finished the conversation with Chamul-na, and then turned to Ki'ti.

"What is the matter with you?" he asked gruffly.

"I heard Liho call about another tool, so I went to see what the noise was all about. I was not even close when I saw the tool in Mootmu-na's hand—and I knew it had belonged to the mountain cave man. I didn't seek the knowledge, Wise One. I promise. It was just there. Help me."

"You can start by curbing your curiosity. Did the unwanted knowledge stop when you left?"

"Yes, Wise One. It did."

"Good. Then you turned away fast?"

"Yes."

"Let me show you something about sensitivity. If I brush against your arm here, does it make a great impression on you?"

"No, brushing my arm does not make an impression."

"Now, let me rub your arm briskly. Now, when I brush against your arm, do you feel it more noticeably?"

"Yes," she responded, fascinated.

"Remember when you fell last year and scraped your leg?" Wamumur asked.

"Of course, I remember."

"How about when things touched the skin on your leg when it was hurt?"

"It was awful. It would bring tears to my eyes sometimes."

"You could say that your arm and your leg get sensitive to touch when rubbed hard or injured?"

"Yes."

"Before you became involved with the mind web of others, your mind web was like your arm before I rubbed it or your leg before your accident. You have been involved very much with the mind web of others. Your sensitivity to picking up those signals is very high right now, like your arm becomes more sensitive when rubbed hard. You need to avoid all occasions that would keep that sensitivity going. There are at least two tools that have been found. There may be others. We cannot run up to the cave to keep getting rid of these things that might remind you of the mind web trap. What you have to do is to turn off your mind web to curiosity right now. You need to let time pass so that the sensitivity to the mind web of others gets like your arm after it stops feeling the tingling of having been roughed up or your leg when it was injured. Do you understand?"

"I do understand, Wise One. I really do. That makes a lot of sense to me. I think my time would be better spent if I go to work on the stories again."

"Little Girl, I am very proud of you. You have come to a great conclusion! Focus on them strongly and on the significances for days to come. Stick with it. Then you will not be tempted and your sensitivity will subside."

"Wise One, I saw the tool used in a different way from the way we use tools. Do you want me to tell you?"

"Ah," he said with exasperation, "I thought we just finished this conversation. And do you remember that I once told you that nothing from another mind web is for your good."

"Yes. But what if this could help our hunters?"

"Little Girl, are you questioning me when I told you that you NEVER need to know what another mind web has to tell you?"

"I remember. I will go to do my story work. How, Wise One, do people forget?"

"You don't. You focus long and deep on things that matter. Like the stories. And with different mind webs, you don't permit yourself to think that they have anything to offer. They do not. If we are to know about different weapons, Wisdom will lead us, not a strange mind web."

Ki'ti threw her arms open wide and hugged him. Her exuberance always surprised him. Wamumur felt hope that the special little one was making good progress. *This was a sign of premature maturity*, he thought. For her to choose to return to the stories was definitely wisdom if not Wisdom. Same was true of her willingness not to continue to try to bring up information from other mind webs.

Emaea had been busy nearby in the cave and had overheard the conversation. She had learned much about the need to avoid the mind webs of others and how to do it simply by listening. Curbing curiosity was important in this instance. She found it interesting that curiosity about some things brought great Winds of Change, like the clothing that was being made for the season of cold days. In other cases, it could lead to one's undoing. There was, she thought, such a huge need for Wisdom. It bothered her for some odd reason that she didn't know what the green bag contained. Somehow, she was convinced there was information that would make a good contribution to the People. She was hesitant to follow up due to Wamumur's negativity.

Wamumur knew there would likely be more tools in the area. He walked down there to see the last tool that had been found. Like the first it was beautiful as well as being useful. He suggested that they continue to look for tools in the same area. The one thing that had not been found in the cave with the dead man was any tool at all for self-defense or for securing meat. People did not roam the country anywhere without proper tools. He had a feeling but not a mind web connection that what had been found were the tools the man had made.

Meeka, Minagle, and Ghanya joined the search for more tools. When they finished, some fifteen stones were found and taken to Ermol-na, the closest person the group had to a master knapper. The men of all ages gathered to examine the tools. They were a bit confused on the use of a few, but mostly they knew what their uses were. The Winds of Change were blowing again. The new tools would make a difference in the way some tools were made from then on. There was much to learn here. Veymun and Pechki exchanged glances. They enjoyed seeing the men examining the tools.

Pechki made the call for the evening meal. Everyone came to the cave and prepared to eat. The cave gave off a wonderful aroma and People realized that it had been a long time since they had had the means to season food. With the lack of ashfall, they had begun to eat as they had in the past and it was good. Now they could find plants for seasoning. There was a lightheartedness in the cave as the People ate. There was a feeling that for a time at least, life would exist without great stress and in peace. The prospect of peace generated light laughter and playfulness that, like the spices, had been gone for a long time. This was not lost on Totamu.

Totamu had been terribly stressed over the incident with Ki'ti. Certainly, she understood that the child's behavior could not be tolerated, but she felt the men had been excessive. She kept telling herself that she had not traveled to the cave and seen where Ki'ti had gone alone, but she had misgivings that she did not voice to anyone. She wanted to reach out to comfort Ki'ti but when she saw her settle down and begin to work on the stories again, she felt that things were returning to normal. She had heard bits and snatches about mind web traps and had no clue what that meant. Maybe, she thought, she was just being overprotective. She had never questioned Wamumur's judgment until this incident. She would be silent and bide her time. She knew from life that was wise.

Totamu also thought of the Winds of Change where the Others were concerned. Bathing was something the Others had done infrequently where her People had bathed almost daily before Baambas. The Others had separate bathing areas for males and females, which her People had not. She thought that having separate areas for bathing would make it easier for thieves to steal women. It seemed almost antisocial. But now the Others were bathing regularly and not making any significance of males and females. It was good.

Totamu listened to Ermol-na, Lai, Chamul-na, Neamu-na, Guy-na, Grypchon-na, and Gruid-na discussing the new tools. Even Ekuktu, as young as he was, had some input and the older men listened. Totamu was surprised. Ekuktu was an outstanding wood carver, but tool maker? She wondered whether this might be another factor in the Winds of Change. Maybe his seeing wood helped him see stone, she thought.

She heard Ekuktu say that the way the bottoms of some of the points were made would make it easier to attach them to the tips of spears. Hunters were fascinated and Ermol-na agreed to try it.

Totamu saw Blanagah and Hahami-na leave the cave when Wisdom had about sucked all the color from the land. Shortly afterward, she noticed that Manak and Domur left. She was surprised that both couples were taking the extra time away from the general cave. She noticed that Ki'ti had stretched out beside Emaea with her head in her lap. Emaea was stroking the girl's brown wispy hair. That dog was right next to the girl's belly. Totamu could not understand the connection between the girl and the dog.

Pechki walked over to Totamu. She kneeled behind her mother and began to massage her shoulders. She knew that often Totamu's shoulders ached. Her mother would say little about it, but she would appreciate the massage.

Veymun was talking quietly to Amey about Olintak's pregnancy. Amey could feel the one she carried in her own belly move about as they talked. So far it just fluttered. They were both very excited about Olintak who had been such a quiet one always waiting for her sister to do things first. This was one time that Olintak was first. It didn't bother Blanagah at all now that she had found happiness with Hahami-na. *Who would have thought it possible*, they wondered. Hahami-na was thirty-eight and Blanagah was fifteen. But then Arkan-na was thirty-four while Ey was sixteen. Both of them were very happy and Ey was the only one of the Others whose infant survived the trek. They had always tried to pair People by age, but the two women began to question its importance. Then, they agreed that it might be more a function of the two people involved than age. There was so much to wonder about when the Winds of Change were blowing.

The People began to settle for the night. There was still some coughing in the cave but nothing like what it had been in Cave Kwa. Totamu was the worst off, still having some chest tightness, so she continued to use the leaves that helped her loosen up. Gruid-na and Nanichak-na had occasional coughs, but it didn't seem to affect their ability to breathe easily.

The People did well in the new location. They fell into the rhythm of the land and learned quickly when to hunt and what to hunt. They saw deer, some large enough to bring to the People for food, and monkeys, many of which really made them laugh, and serpents, which struck them with fear. The giant elk was a major food source, and with the size of the group, it behooved them to go for large animals when they could. The animals were magnificent. Other animals in their area were bears, and the occasional sloth bear, hyenas, rhinos, horses, elephants of several varieties, hippos in the lowlands, water buffalo, aurochs, antelope, gazelles. Food was plentiful and the People used the whole animal so the hunt was always about more than food. It was for tools and skins and glue and other things like bladders for carrying liquids and brains for working skins. The location had dangers, certainly, but it was a great solace after the ashfall entrapment. Because of the way the land was laid out, a large variety of animals migrated on a route that went by the northeast part of their territory. They were confident that this was the place Wisdom would have them be. The women had planned to use the skins they'd been given and the ones that they were getting after each hunt to make season-of-cold-days clothing like the ones the strange man had worn.

Just looking at the man dressed as he was, they could infer the pattern of the garments: tunic, jacket, pants, and boots. They hadn't seen any hand coverings that the People would make. During their speculation, they assumed the man had been killed while the weather was too warm for hand coverings. It was apparent that the man had a headcovering as part of his jacket. With white rain standing in piles on the mountains nearby, they reasoned that the season of cold days would be hard and cold. They must be prepared. Emaea had seen the woman in the cave. She told them the woman either had on a tunic that must have come to her ankles or she was wrapped in a fur blanket. She wore boots. She said the fur was left on and worn so the fur was inside. The women found that really strange and, before they made women's clothing, it would require a lot of thought.

They liked the way the man's jacket closed. The fronts overlapped, which would add warmth and keep wind out, and there were two loops that were sewed on one of the overlapping pieces near the edge. On the other side of the jacket, there was a loop with an animal horn drilled and threaded into the loop. The animal horn, when threaded through the loop, would keep the jacket closed. It was a unique idea for a closure. The seams were sewed together in a way that they didn't understand. The fabrication seemed to Emaea to have a lot to teach. She continued to long to discover the contents of the green bag. Was there sewing material in there? But the man carried it. Did the woman have a sewing bag up there? So much of the fabrication of the clothing of the man with the green bag was a real surprise to the People and another of the delights of the Winds of Change. Was there more that they were missing?

Emaea watched the hearth outside the cave where Mootmu-na was crafting a new spear. Lamk was beside him, watching carefully to follow what he saw his father do. The fire had been banked down. He would put the spear over the smoldering fuel and turn it much slower than he would turn meat if roasting over a hearth. Emaea could hear him tell Lamk, "You're not cooking it like meat. You want to get the moisture out, not seal it in. That makes the point harder. Hold this." Mootmu-na handed his spear to Lamk. He went to the spear holder and pulled out a smaller version of his spear. The tip had been pointed but not hardened. "This is for you." He held out the shorter spear. They traded. Lamk began to harden his own spear. He thanked his father, lowering his head as far as possible.

It was a warm season-of-colorful-leaves day so Emaea decided to get Pechki to join her for a walk to the cave of the man with the green bag. She had shared with Pechki that there might be some way to learn about the seams in the garment of the man with the green bag, if they could find the sewing bag of the woman or if the green bag held sewing supplies. Totamu overheard the plan and asked to join. Pechki quietly asked Neamu-na to join them for protection and the four slipped away quietly. They went up by the gentle slope and reached the path to the cave easily. Pechki and Totamu obviously weren't thrilled about the climb so they waited below while Neamu-na and Emaea climbed up. Totamu was a little short of breath during the hike so she had been using her leaves to chew. She pulled out another. In the cave, Neamu-na and Emaea looked into the green bag and found nothing that a hunter wouldn't have with him except for a gum-like substance that neither was familiar with.

Emaea explored the little cave and discovered that the woman was resting against what was likely her sewing bag. It was decorated with zig-zag designs from a continuous thread of something. They carried it down to share with Pechki and Totamu. The four of them examined the contents and Emaea wanted to know what the filament was. It was looped. Neamu-na laughed out loud. "You know what that is," he assured them.

"I do not," Pechki said emphatically.

"Look again, and think of butchering while you look at it."

Totamu tried to figure it out, but she was stumped. So was Emaea.

Then Pechki laughed. "Now I know what it is! It's sinew that has been separated into threads. That's what they used to sew the seams together! They must have kept it wet to get the filaments apart. What a clever idea! I wonder how they kept it from becoming brittle while it was worn."

Emaea was filled with a new feeling. It was a joy that filled her belly. Wisdom had made it clear to her that there was something in the cave, something that would have as much use to the women as the points the children had found had meaning to the men and their tools. Now, they could make the seams that the man with the green bag had in his clothing and Pechki would know how to do it.

There seemed nothing else in the bag that was helpful except the strange pointed bone that was very thin, encased in a piece of leather. It was Neamu-na who figured out the use.

"If you lined up the leather pieces and used a thin awl to poke holes in the leather so they matched, you could use the bone tool to draw the sinew in a loop through the matching holes," he said.

Instantly Pechki got the visualization. "Think of the time that would save!" she exclaimed. Her mind was busy sewing. "You'd probably have to put rendered fat on the sinew to keep it from getting brittle like the one holding the man's jacket together."

Totamu mused, "It's interesting how cunningly they made beautiful garments." She was fingering the zig-zag pattern on the sewing bag.

Carefully, they put the things back together and Neamu-na climbed back up the hill to put the sewing bag back. Then they returned to the home cave with their new knowledge.

That evening when all was quiet, Emaea explained to Wamumur that they had been to the cave of the man with the green bag and and learned helpful information that they could use in sewing. She compared the find to the stones the children had found. Wamumur looked long into Emaea's eyes.

"I have been terribly self centered, my loved one. I have had to be the only Wise One for so long that I have discounted your insight. I hate myself for it. Will you forgive me? I will slow down in the future and not make the same error."

"Of course. I have to admit it felt really special to find that my insight was right."

"And I'd have deprived you of that feeling, one I enjoy myself. I am so sorry." He obviously was. Emaea leaned her head and shoulder against his chest and reached for his hand.

Ki'ti had listened to the conversation. The double standard for what she and Emaea were permitted to do did not escape her. She realized that it hadn't taken hunters to go after Emaea, but still underneath it all she smarted from her treatment when she went to return the green bag. She also chaffed that he'd told her that there was never good to come from minds of long ago. Did that apply only to her? Did it also not apply to Emaea and the hunters? She remembered Wamumur telling her that life wasn't fair. She agreed, and she permitted a tiny spark of anger to smolder way down inside. She lifted her pup to her lap and stroked him.

Totamu thought of the trip she'd just taken. How Ki'ti had found the cave was beyond her understanding. She had gained understanding of how very dangerous it had been. She began to soften her views of how the hunters had treated her and Wamumur's punishment for disobedience.

Manak, Lamul, and Ghanya had been scouting the area near the cave. They had discovered a cave at a good distance from their home which seemed to attract many of the snakes like the one that had entered their cave. When they found a hole above the cave like their smoke hole, they lay on their bellies and peered down into the cave. They could look down and see uncountable numbers of the snakes writhing in the cave below. Hardly a piece of cave floor showed.

The People continued thriving into the season of cold days. Olintak had her baby boy, Keemu, after much lengthy hard labor over a two-day span. She and Slamika were silly about the baby. Both had anticipated its arrival and were so happy that some members of the group wondered about their mind webs. The baby had red hair and deep blue eyes. He was a very happy little one and slept well at night. There was an anomaly in his birth. Keemu had six toes on each foot. His hands were normal, but he did have six toes. The sixth toe apparently was the littlest toe. It would not cause problems for the People, so the odd feet were overlooked. After all, Ghanya had two toes on each foot that were joined together with skin between them almost to the tip of the toes. He had never had any problem with them.

Domur was pregnant and she and Manak seemed to be almost as silly about their baby that would come as Olintak and Slamika were about theirs. Totamu wondered at times if there wasn't too much leisure time, but the laughter and happiness in the group is something she would not trade for more seriousness. Totamu's cough was a little worse but not even close to the cough that had taken Enut's life. Enut had a wet raspy cough that gurgled. Totamu's cough was rough and dry. She was convinced that it came from the ash. She had learned that when the cough came, she was very short of breath.

If she spent much time resting, the cough would eventually go away and she could breathe better again. Having to rest in the daytime irritated her. The leaves helped her breathe better, but the effectiveness seemed to decrease as time passed. She wished she could find a cure, but had no prior knowledge of this affliction. It was not the sickness where people would eventually cough up blood or drown out of water. This was a tightness that came and went. Sometimes her breathing whistled. She wondered about it but did not consider it a serious matter, only one to be endured.

The day had progressed well. Men had gone out to check their snares along the stream. They returned with animals whose meat could be added to the cooking bag and animals that would provide special decorative additions to the garments the women made. The women had been wise. They had learned well from the strange man. The garments kept the men warm. They had fashioned hoods for the jackets that were better designs than the one the man had. The pants they wore were much better designed than the booted garments. The footwear made of strong elk skin was lined with rabbit fur and grasses to keep the men's feet warm. The men also wrapped their feet inside the boots with skins with the hair still on. There was much teasing about how wide boots would need to be for Keemu with his extra toe. Garments were designed to last long and serve the wearer. The greatest design work was on the front and that might mean a trim of white around the opening of the hood or a special horn closure. They had already discovered that when they had a very cold spell and white rain, they could put the booted garments on over the other garments and that kept them very warm indeed.

Gruid-na had taken all the youngest children, boys and girls, to another cave where he had set up a stretcher with leather on it against the back wall. First, he had the children throw stones aiming for center of the circle he had made from blueberry juice on the stretched leather. He had also made small slingshots and had the children practice hitting the circle on the leather with stones passed from the slingshots. He would demonstrate the technique while the children watched carefully. Then he would ask hunters who had a spare moment to demonstrate. Then the children would try. Any error on form was caught and dealt with immediately so that the child didn't learn the wrong form from the beginning. They knew that with muscle memory it was critical to get it right from the outset. Correction was for making the child's efforts good for future hunting, not for making them feel badly. It was accepted appropriately so that no feelings got hurt. The children wanted to do well in hunting and this was the first step. When a child's pebble finally hit the spot, it was worth a celebratory moment, but this was not overdone. They were discouraged from keeping score. Children were encouraged only to make their best effort each time to hit the mark. When they consistently hit the mark, they went to the next phase of training in another cave where a target was pulled by a line of leather in one place or swung by a rope filament in another. They had to hit moving targets. When the weather was good, boys and girls would practice outside with a four-string throw. It was made of four strings knotted at the top and had rocks tied onto the ends of the strings. This tool enabled them to snare birds in flight. To practice this, someone would throw a leather pouch into the air and attempts were made to snare it.

Sometimes before Wisdom sucked color from the land, the men would go to the hunter school caves and practice to keep their skills polished. Children eagerly went with them and lined the cave edges to watch. The activity was one that took place during the seasons of colorful leaves, cold days, and new leaves whenever hunters were free. Children would practice when no hunters were using the caves.

Ki'ti had spent all day practicing in her mind web the story for the night. It was one which they could finally get a fuller appreciation for the significance, now that they had experienced the cold. It was the story of Maknu-na and Rimlad. She wanted the story to be error free and was finally confident that she had it. She was very tired. She wondered whether telling the stories made Wamumur tired. Inst noticed her and she took a tender piece of dried meat to the girl. Ki'ti was touched. The kindness had been so unexpected. That might give her some energy. She took the meat gratefully with her head lowered and thanked her. She took a bite while Inst watched her. Her smile gave the answer she sought. It was very good.

Olintak had just fed Keemu. The little red-haired, blue-eyed baby with the six toes had stolen everyone's love. He was adorable and so happy. It was almost as if he embodied the joy and hope of the People for better times. He had a laugh that seemed to start at his toes and bubble all the way up. People would stop what they were doing to listen to his laugh. If they didn't laugh aloud, they almost always smiled.

The women announced that the evening meal was ready. The cooking activity in the cave had increased. The cold weather made everyone hungrier. Ki'ti found that she could eat easily all the food she'd been given despite the fact that she'd had the piece of dried meat already. When the clean up was finished and the infants had calmed down, it was time for the story.

They assembled in the large gathering place and quiet settled on them like the loss of color in the tops of trees in the setting of the sun, imperceptibly but not slowly.

There was no news to pronounce, so the story could begin. Ki'ti had been given a soft covering to sit on. She sat cross legged in front of the People with the fire off to one side. Her tunic bowled in front and Ahriku curled up there. Her shadow was huge on the cave wall. She began:

"Notempa was one of the greatest of the great ones that Wisdom called on the land. He had long white hair and a fierce face. Clouds would gather at his head and get slowed up there making ovals in the sky. People loved to look at Notempa. The People had been visited by two Others who called themselves traders. They brought exquisitely beautiful purple, shiny shells from the salt water. The shells were large and made wonderful dippers or food holders. They had an edge with holes so that the dippers could be tied for travel. Some of the People desperately wanted dippers, but the traders told them they had to trade something for the dippers. Some of the People thought they should just be given the dippers for their hospitality. They didn't have anything to trade but they wanted those dippers. The People knew that hospitality was required by Wisdom. Strangers were to be taken in and cared for well, so not to anger Wisdom. Strangers didn't have to recompense for hospitality. While the disputes over the trading occurred, Notempa fumed. Smoke arose from his head and the smoke smelled like bad bird eggs. Many times Notempa fumed, letting the People know that they were supposed to remember Wisdom's hospitality.

"While the People argued with the Others, Maknu-na and Rimlad went hunting. They didn't like the excessive squabbling over the dippers. They ranged far to the north, farther than they normally went. They could see Notempa in the great distance. One day they saw that the smoke had become a great column. It rose high into the clouds. Notempa shook the land and made a great noise that they could hear even where they were. They could see the cloud still rising but parts of the cloud column had started to look like a tree falling back to the earth from the sky, while other clouds were racing down the face of Notempa and coming right at them. The falling smoke cloud came toward Maknu-na and Rimlad at great speed. They were terrified. They could feel the warmth of the cloud coming at them. They could hear it. They grabbed hollow reeds and jumped into a pond to try to save themselves from the wrath of Notempa. Maknu-na and Rimlad put the reeds in their mouths. They submerged themselves in the pond and only the reeds kept them breathing, which was not very easy. Both expected to die.

"After a long time, the air seemed to clear and they raised themselves from the pond. The whole landscape was the same color. An ugly gray. It was hot and smelled awful. They looked at Notempa. Notempa had been so angry that he had blown his own head off. No more white hair, just an empty place cut off at the neck.

"Rimlad and Maknu-na looked at each other. They knew that their group of People was gone. They could not have survived the horrible downrushing hot cloud they'd seen. While still in great fear, they realized Wisdom had spared *them* specifically. And they wondered why. They walked as far north as they could to get away from the terrible fury of Notempa. The air hurt their breathing passages. The caustic gray gritty material burned their feet and legs and arms. They desperately pushed on. When one would tire, the other would urge him on. They feared Notempa and they didn't want to die. They found animals covered in the gray material, dead, and they ate raw meat from those animals.

"On the third day, they found a group of People living beyond the dead land. They were taken in and cared for well. These People at first had thought the travelers were ghosts of the dead because they were very pale colored from head to toe, until they washed up and were given clean clothing and food and what they wanted most, water. They had bad coughs which finally went away. The People gave them good bedding and let them sleep. Maknu-na and Rimlad were treated differently from the way their People had treated the traders of the Others. They were ashamed when they thought of their People and the travelers with the dippers.

"They were asked to live with these People who took them in and accepted the generous invitation. The air didn't clear from the explosion for a long time. There were many years of very cold weather. The People who lived had to make clothing for cold weather. Sometimes people would have a toe or finger turn black and fall off when it was very cold. If the frozen member got too bad, they would slowly sicken and die. One man cut off his black finger and took a white hot stick from the fire and touched the sore place with it. His hand healed very well.

"For years, along with the cold weather, they also had beautiful sunsets. The colors of brilliant orange and red and purple and yellow were like none they'd ever seen. However, the cold didn't last forever and the sunsets were only there briefly. They learned of Wisdom's wrath when People failed to offer hospitality freely to travelers. First, Wisdom made Notempa get very hot and explosive and then he would cause the world to turn icy cold. Never again would the People fail to offer hospitality freely to those who were traveling by. After a long time passed, People said that Notempa's head was growing back. Wisdom would not forget the People. And Maknu-na and Rimlad realized they'd been spared so their story would become a story for the People, a story to remind them of Wisdom's rule of hospitality. That was all a very long time ago."

When Ki'ti finished, you could have heard a mouse squeak. The People had just gone through a similar event, but they had been spared and they had offered hospitality. For the first time Arkan-na and Ey, Guy-na and Alu, Lai and Inst, Ghanya and Meeka understood why the Minguat had been given such wonderful treatment from the People. This story made it very clear. They did not want to anger Wisdom who had unleashed a volcano to make it clear to the People that hospitality to strangers during their travel was not only expected but also required. They experienced a feeling of gratitude to the traders of long ago, even to the group that didn't want to extend hospitality without recompense, to the individuals who took them in, and ultimately to Wisdom. They had lived through the last year, thanks to Wisdom's story.

Likichi was so proud of Ki'ti. She had matured so much in the last months and no longer seemed angry and rebellious. She seemed to have accepted her role and was obedient to it. Likichi knew that it was inappropriate to tell her former daughter how proud she was of her, but she was. Totamu was also experiencing the same feelings. Ki'ti had told the story well. It was good. Totamu had to admit that her concerns over Wamumur and the hunters and Manak were unfounded.

When the People began to bed down for the night, Ki'ti went to Emaea, who held her arms open wide. No words were spoken right away, but they hugged for a long time. So much had happened in the training of Ki'ti, some of it very hard, but she was going to be, Emaea was convinced, a Wise One that even Wise Ones would respect. Emaea had watched the faces of the Others who had joined them. She had noticed that the last time they had heard the story in Cave Kwa, the Others had not seemed to understand. Most of the Others had been restless and wiggly during the telling. Not so with the ones who stayed. This year, there was no doubt that they were moved to their bellies.

On a beautiful, clear, very cold day, Manak, Ghanya, Lamul, Grypchon-na, and Kai dressed warmly and hiked to the cave of the snakes. They each carried water, a spear, knives, and also they brought two small torches and a portable cinder. They climbed to the top so they could look down into the cave. The five men lay on the snow looking for snakes.

Grypchon-na scanned the scene and asked, "Where are they?" They'd heard about the snake cave from the young men and were interested to see the same sight.

"There were so many that you couldn't see the floor in some places!" Ghanya insisted, slightly defensive.

"I'm going down there to look around," Lamul stated with a tone of consternation. He was clearly confused.

"I'll go with you," Manak offered. The two retreated down the hill to the cave opening.

At the cave opening, they used the cinder to light the small torches. Lamul led the two inside. The other men watched from above. No snakes were found in the first cave but the musky smell of snake was very strong. Lamul made his way to the opening toward the back and found another room and then another. The two young men looked knowingly at each other as the odor of snake all but overwhelmed them. Inside the next room, they found the snakes all intertwined and seemingly asleep. Quickly, they retraced their steps to the cave entrance.

Looking up at the smoke hole, Manak shouted, "You must come down here to see this."

Grypchon-na, Kai, and Ghanya made it to the cave entrance as quickly as they could. Lamul led them quietly to the room of the snakes. Kai was gagging at the odor as he peered into the room.

"What in the name of Wisdom is this?" Grypchon-na inquired of no one.

"Wouldn't you like to set fire to the lot of them?" Ghanya asked.

"No!" Manak rejoined a little too fast. "We'd have Wisdom attacking *us*! I'd rather deal with snakes than Wisdom!"

"I don't understand," Ghanya said. "You killed the single snake that invaded the cave where we live."

"For our self defense, it is permitted. For food, it is permitted. But Wisdom does not permit us to annihilate groups of defenseless animals simply because we fear them. Wisdom made us superior to them, Ghanya, but Wisdom also made the snakes. It is our assignment to care for living things, not exterminate them," Grypchon-na tried to explain.

"More of your stories?" Ghanya asked.

"Yes," Grypchon-na added without further elaboration. "I'm ready to get out of here. What we have learned is that in very cold weather, snakes sleep like bears. Where we lived before running from Baambas, these same snakes did not sleep because they didn't need to protect themselves from the cold."

"And," Kai said smiling outside the cave, "they definitely stink when you put a lot of them together!"

All the men laughed a little too loud and a little too long, for the smell was terrible. Manak and Lamul carefully extinguished the torches. They were reusable so they carried them home.

On the way back, Grypchon-na said, "We must avoid this place in the season of new leaves and warn others to do the same." They named the hill Serpent Hill and they would warn all to avoid it in the seasons of new leaves and colorful leaves.

The season of cold days passed uneventfully. Thanks to the clothing inspired by the man with the green bag, the People had not suffered from the cold. Actually, they had thrived. The season of new leaves had turned into an early season of warm nights. When Wisdom returned color to the land, Ki'ti got up, rolled up her sleeping mat and cover, and went outside where she sat in the daylight on the rock walk. The sun on her skin felt wonderful. She was watching Ahriku frolicking with the other dogs across the stream. After romping and playing near a deadfall tree, Ahriku rose up and dived down with his forelegs. His snout was busy under the limbed part of the tree until he arose with his prize, a vole. The others came to the deadfall to see what they might find. Either there were no more or the voles had been alerted to danger. Ahriku ate a part of the vole and then left the other part for whichever dog would get it. He returned to Ki'ti's side after stopping at the stream to drink. The two sat side by side motionless looking out in the same direction. Ahriku took his cues from Ki'ti.

The men were rousing and getting some food before they departed for a hunting trip. There were two groups of hunters and they chose to go off in different directions. They all agreed to return before sunset. There was a lot of noise coming from the main cave even though the People spoke softly when they were in the cave. *The business of numbers of people rising and putting away sleeping mats and eating was a happy noise,* Ki'ti thought. She got up and went inside to get something to eat.

Ermol-na, Guy-na, Ghanya, Kai, and Grypchon-na headed to the open field to the south. There was a dropoff there and they hoped to run a rhino over it. They had discussed the plan for days and it seemed sound. If the animal went over the dropoff, they thought, they would reduce their risk of personal injury in the kill. As they walked the trail they'd begun to form when going back and forth to the site, Guy-na pointed out a large antelope well hidden in the trees. This was the largest antelope, a beautiful animal, and it looked a little like a large horse. The humid landscape was just getting into full sun in the mountains. In some places, it appeared that clouds were rising from slumber on the land. Sounds of waterfowl from the small lake further south reached their ears. Birds welcomed the day with song. It was a beautiful day.

As they approached the field, the men did see the rhino they'd seen on earlier trips. It was a small rhino, but that didn't make it a small mammal compared to humans. It was dangerous to hunt these animals. They had extremely good hearing and sense of smell, but they couldn't see well. They had one horn and thick folded tough skin.

The hunting party began putting their plan into action. The rhino was oriented with its head toward the dropoff. Guy-na crept to one side of the beast, and Ermol-na, the other. They carried leafy branches along with their spears. Arrayed behind the beast were Grypchon-na and Ghanya carrying rocks and spears. Kai maneuvered around in front of the rhino to the ledge at the dropoff. He kept below the level of the land so that the rhino would not smell him. A slight breeze blew from the ledge toward the rhino.

Kai's objective was to taunt the animal and then at the last moment squat in safety of the ledge just under the dropoff. There was a slight indentation by the ledge and Kai planned to slide into the indentation. Guy-na and Ermol-na's goal was to keep the beast headed to the dropoff. If needed, Grypchon-na and Ghanya were to spur the beast from the back end.

At the signal from Ermol-na, the hunters began their plan. Kai stood up and called to the rhino. The beast was alert immediately. The others remained totally still. The beast pawed the ground. It looked from side to side. Kai threw small pebbles at it and called to it while jumping about on the ledge. It edged forward toward Kai. He yelled and yelled at the rhino while Ghanya and Grypchon-na used slings to hit the back legs of the rhino with stones. The rhino finally spotted Kai. It had had enough. It began to charge Kai, who waved and yelled at the animal. In seconds, the animal covered the distance to Kai. He squatted and headed into the depression behind the ledge. He just about made it, but the rhino began to stampede and went headlong over the ledge, its hind leg catching Kai's leg. The bone in Kai's leg broke but the skin remained intact. The rhino crashed onto the land below, breaking its own neck. Ghanya was sent back to the cave at a fast run for a stretcher and some women to help with the meat, and other helpful carriers, first for Kai and then for butchering and transporting the meat and skin.

Ghanya arrived at the home cave breathless. He explained what was needed. Hahami-na and Ekuktu grabbed the poles and a skin for the stretcher and headed out immediately. Totamu gathered her tools for healing a broken leg. She had given initial splints to Hahami-na along with some leather ties. She also gave him a leaf for Kai to chew immediately. She started a tea that would reduce pain so it would be ready when Kai arrived.

Women gathered and picked up tools for skinning and the ones the men would need for butchering. They began to follow the path to the field.

There was a lot of excitement in the cave. They hadn't had rhino for so long that some People in the cave actually began to salivate thinking of it. Mitrak was busy laying out soft skins on the ground for Kai close to the cave wall where he wouldn't be in the way. Shmyukuk offered to watch Ketra when Kai arrived, so that Mitrak could keep her mind on Kai only, when he first arrived back. Veymun went outside to find a tree branch that would serve as a crutch for the man. Amey raced out to help her, bringing a tool for cutting branches.

At the field, the men made a temporary splint for Kai's leg so they could get him back up to ground level. He was in a tremendous amount of pain. He was also irked that he had not been speedy enough to avoid the falling beast. He felt that somehow he had let the others down. When Hahami-na and Ekuktu arrived with the stretcher, the men placed Kai on it. They gave him the leaf from Totamu to chew, and added the splints to his leg because the temporary one was not very well done. Then they headed to the home cave with Kai.

The men went down to the rhino kill and began to watch for hyenas, though it was early for those brown mottled, bad tempered beasts. They waited for the other men and women to bring all the tools needed to begin the butchering. They would have some great rhino evening meals and then a lot of meat to put up for the season of cold days. With the exception of Kai's accident, it was good.

After Kai had been returned to the home cave, Ghanya began a run to the other hunters. He could follow their tracks to the north field. He traveled quickly through the forest, sometimes leaping high over windfall and laughing out loud when he encountered monkeys in the trees at one point. Their curious faces and shouts at him struck him as humorous. A few monkeys threw their feces at him, but he was too far from them to have been hit. Light slanted slightly through the trees and made a lovely sight which was not lost on Ghanya. Finally, he arrived at the field and looked carefully for the other hunters. He could see them at the far end of the field. He continued his run. He arrived to find that they had felled a deer. He told them about the rhino. They quickly suspended the deer from poles and began to head to the cave with it. They would hand it over to the women and go to help butcher the rhino. They wanted to be sure that all useable parts of the rhino got back to the caves before any scavengers decided to get their share.

Kai was lying on the skins sipping the tea that Totamu had prepared. It did help. She took the splints off carefully to clean the wound and apply healing herbs to the skin before setting and re-splinting it. Moving the leg caused Kai considerable pain. Fortunately, the skin was not broken through except in one small area that Totamu found. She washed it, put honey on it, added some herbs, and was confident it would heal well. Totamu told Chamul-na that she needed help with the leg. Chamul-na had done this before, so he was definitely her choice. He lumbered over to Kai.

"This will hurt, Kai," he said with feeling. "You need to be absolutely still."

Kai gritted his teeth. He didn't doubt it would hurt. He wanted to be strong to show his manliness, so he drank the rest of the tea and hoped he wouldn't cry or shout out. Chamul-na handed him a stick to bite. Chamul-na placed his foot in Kai's crotch and took the young man's leg in his hands. He could see that the leg was out of alignment. Totamu knelt beside Kai, ready with a length of tree bark and wide leather strips. When Chamul-na pulled the leg bones apart and slid them back into the correct position, Totamu's callused hands worked efficiently and effectively. She placed soft leather first and then the bark around the leg to hold the bones in place and wrapped the leg with deer skins to hold the bark in place. Then she placed the straight sticks for holding the leg steady on either side of the leg and began to tie them in place to support the wrappings. She kept checking to be certain that she didn't make any of the wrappings too tight. She didn't want to add to Kai's problems by cutting off his circulation. Once the splints were on, she wrapped the leg round and round with more wide skin strips. She also wrapped his foot to prevent him from wiggling his foot.

Kai managed not to cry or scream while the leg had been straightened and splinted. He relaxed finally in a pool of sweat, exhausted, and took the stick from his mouth. Except for his injury, the hunt went as they had planned it. He kept trying to think how he might have avoided the injury. He was surprised at how fast the animal had moved. Finally, from the tea and the leaf he'd chewed and the earlier release of adrenaline, he drifted off to sleep on the extra soft skins, while remembering the excitement of the hunt.

Totamu got up and touched Mitrak's shoulder. "He was brave. Because of his bravery, we have rhinoceros. He was also brave when his leg was being straightened. That is very painful. I hope he will be able to walk again. He will have to keep weight off his leg. You will make that clear to him?"

"Of course. Thank you so much," Mitrak said. She was worried about her husband, but she was proud of his taking the pain so well. She was frightened about his bravery with the rhino, but she would never have said it aloud.

"When he wakens, he will need more tea for pain relief for a while. Here are the leaves to use. One leaf for each drink. You can use the leaves twice. I will leave you five of them. When he needs to relieve himself, get two men to help him. It will be a long time before he is ready for a crutch. He also is not to put any weight on the leg. It could make it so he cannot walk in the future if he puts weight on it now. The others will have to bear his weight for him. Do you understand all this?"

"Yes. I do. Thank you again."

"My Dear, don't keep thanking me. I thank him that I'll be able to eat some rhino. He did that for all of us and we are all grateful. Please, give him our thanks."

Mitrak lowered her head. She put the leaves aside and went to get Ketra. She was surprised when Shmyukuk offered to keep the little one beside her and her family that night. Ketra would enjoy it, Mitrak thought, and it would help, so she agreed.

The men from the north field arrived at the home cave, bringing the deer. They took some dried meat and a number of water skins and headed back for the rhino butchering. On their way they passed some of the men bringing meat to the preparation cave where there were women ready to start the preservation. Drying racks had already been set up. A couple of large pieces of rhino were set aside for the night's meal. They were taken to the home cave and Veymun and Pechki got the pieces ready for roasting. They had to cut them down some so there were about 8 large roasts when they managed to fix them to the spits for roasting.

When butchering such large animals the men were bloody messes when they finally arrived back at the home cave. Although they'd tried to clean themselves, the busy area of the cave was the bathing area. They had to bathe themselves and wash off their clothing. It was noisy and joyful as they spoke of the day's events and the bravery of Kai. For the first time in her life, Emaea had participated in a small way and was part of this after-hunt bathing ritual that until she'd participated, she did not understand. She enjoyed the noise and good-natured fellowship.

After the work in the meat preparation cave was completed, the dogs were ignored or invited—depending on whom might be asked—to enter the area to clean up the floor. New meat was as big a treat for the dogs as for the people. When the dogs finished, the floor was astonishingly clean.

That night there was a great feast. It was late by the time all the meat was placed in the meat preparation cave. Much had been accomplished by the hunters that day. After the evening meal, Ghanya found Minagle sitting on the rock walk edge. He joined her. The trees were losing their color at the top as Wisdom sucked the color from the land. Minagle shivered from the cool wind that blew across her shoulders.

"I wouldn't have shivered if I still had all my hair," she said, touching her short shining hair.

"It'll grow back," Ghanya assured her while he put his arm around her to warm her. He found her attractive in an exotic way. Her hair was always clean and shining. The Minguat had never thought as much about cleanliness and grooming as the People. It did make a difference, he admitted to himself. Minagle even smelled good.

"I know it'll grow back. I just wish it would hurry," she assured him, resting her head on his chest.

With his free hand, he reached for her hand. He had never felt like this. She was so special to him. She made him feel wanted, needed, strong, gentle, intelligent—in a word—special. But then, she was People even if she didn't look like it. He shoved the idea aside.

"You ran fast and far today, I hear," she said.

"I like to run," he responded. "Do you run?"

"It is not something women do, or at least I've never seen any woman run."

"You are made more like me than like your People. It is possible that you could run easily. Sometime we will take a long walk and we'll find a place and you can run to learn whether you enjoy it."

"I'd like that, Ghanya."

She noticed he still had some blood from the butchering in his ear. She spit on her fingertips and reached up to remove the dried blood. Ghanya was touched. He smiled at her.

"Now, we'd better get you inside. You have bird skin from the cold. See the little bumps on your arm?"

The two laughed gently as they returned to the cave.

Ki'ti was leaning against the side of the cave on her sleeping mat with Ahriku at her side. She had been pondering how important it was for Wise Ones to have exemplary behavior. She wondered whether People would honor Wisdom less if the Wise One had less than exemplary behavior. She thought that it did make a difference. It had a profound impact on her to realize that her own behavior might affect how the People honored Wisdom. It frightened her to think of the huge amount of responsibility placed on her, but it also gave her a deeper seriousness and more conviction that she needed to stay strictly obedient regardless of what her exuberant spirit would have her do unchecked. She began to see the edges of what it meant to have a leadership role among the People. It was a heavy burden.

A moan permeated the cave. Mitrak quickly poured hot water over the leaf in the bowl and carried it to Kai. She let the tea steep and then helped him sip the brew. He looked at her with grateful eyes. He made it clear that he needed to get to the privy so Mitrak explained what would be involved. He looked ashamed to have to lean on others, but realized that if he put weight on his leg before Totamu told him it was okay, he was asking for a limp at best in the future, at worst not being able to walk at all. His pride for the moment had to suffer for his strength for the People in the future. Mitrak asked Lamul and Manak to help Kai to the privy. Both were more than willing to help out. Manak and Lamul made a seat with their arms and carried Kai. Both agreed that was easier than being human crutches. They returned him to the cave and gently placed him back on the skins. Kai finished the remains of the brew and Mitrak covered him. He asked where Ketra was and Mitrak explained.

Far in the back of the cave Amey had gone into labor. This would be her eighth child if it lived, but despite her fertility, she sometimes lost a baby before it was born. She had six stillborns that did not count as children. This one looked abnormally large in her belly.

The men had been meeting. They had convinced themselves to build a barricade at the field that would limit the options of animals in the direction they could take, making them go where they wanted them to go. What they had difficulty with was knowing why Kai had a broken leg. That would have to wait until Kai could explain. They were convinced that running an animal off the cliff was a good idea. They just needed to think it through a little better. Nobody wanted to chance another broken leg.

Flayk said to Pechki, "The stranger with the green bag had a garment made of black and white fur. What animals do you think his garments were made from?"

Pechki looked up, "I have no idea. It had to be a big animal of each color, because the material was not pieced together. It wasn't rabbit."

"No, it seemed to be a lot thicker and longer than rabbit fur and the skin was a lot thicker."

"I think we have a lot to learn yet about this land."

"I agree. Sometimes I miss our old home, not the cave in the ash, but the home we used to have," Flayk said

"I know what you mean. We could fish there so easily and the fish were good in addition to the other things we had. And it didn't get so cold."

"Veymun said it was cold because of Baambas. Somehow, the ash in the sky keeps the sun from being as warm as it might be. It happened in the story."

"True. I wonder how long it will last. In the story it was many years"

"Well, I hope it's not too long," Flayk said. "Look back there. It looks like Amey is in labor."

"Let's go help," Pechki replied.

Suddenly, the earth shook. People tried to steady what might fall over. It didn't last long. Everyone waited to see whether another shake would follow, but the single event seemed to be all. Not even the water skin that was kept hot had fallen. All was fine.

"Do you want some meat?" Mitrak asked Kai.

"Yes, that might be good. Now, tell me it's rhino," he half smiled, "for revenge."

"It is," she smiled back. Quickly, Mitrak got some meat and put it in his bowl. She brought it to him and helped him rise up to a sitting position.

Kai took the bowl and began to eat. It was still warm and tasted good. He hadn't realized he was hungry.

Wamumur walked from the men's meeting area to sit with Emaea. He had noticed for days now that Ki'ti's behavior had made a huge turnaround. Wamumur asked Emaea what she thought about the permanence of the change, and neither had a clue because they had never parented and did not know what to anticipate. They also were not sure that having parented would tell them what they wanted to know about Ki'ti. They had, however, learned to take life as it came, so they were comfortable with not knowing. Both hoped it would last.

Totamu walked past Chamul-na and said, "You did a very good job today on setting that leg. It seemed to be a pretty clean break."

"It did go back together very well. Surprised me. That is a strong and tough young man."

"What would you expect of Mootmu-na's son?" she laughed.

"Mootmu-na is a pretty tough old bird," Chamul-na said with a glance at Mootmu-na. "Guess it makes sense. Kai was brave to be the person to call the rhino."

"I think so." Totamu walked to the back of the cave to check on Amey's progress. Pechki and Flayk had brought some skins and a leather strip to hold in her mouth for pain. They had gone for more leathers and a large gourd for water to wipe the infant and Amey.

In yet another part of the cave, Blanagah was settling down with Hahami-na. She glanced at his red and white hair and wondered again whether she'd have a baby with red hair or brown like her own. She was still miffed at having had her hair cut, but it was growing in fast, faster than a lot of the other women. She knew that Hahami-na was tired. He had been going back and forth with the meat from the rhino to get it to the cave before nightfall. She massaged his shoulders and back. Then they stretched out together and he was asleep before her head was even down on the mat.

Neamu-na took guard duty and the cave began to settle down for the night. The fire died down so that the shadows did not dance as high on the cave walls as they did earlier. There was great contentment in the cave overall.

In the far back of the cave, Totamu and Amey struggled to bring forth the baby. As often as Amey had delivered, she'd never had this problem. The baby was obviously stuck. This occurrence was happening with more frequency among the People. Totamu tried to grasp the head without success. Amey was exhausted. They struggled through the night. Finally, Totamu took the desperate step that she knew she must. She hit the baby's head with an elongated rock hammered by a stone, breaking the skull and the baby was born dead. She felt utterly sickened, but she was not willing to lose Amey. The remains of the baby were wrapped and ready for quiet burial, and Amey was cleaned before either woman slept.

When Wisdom faded the night's darkness, Minagle went straight to Likichi. "Mother," she whispered, "I think I am woman." Likichi could see the evidence and she quickly gathered the skins and the ties she had put aside for this day. She told Minagle to go to wash far downstream and to return quickly. Minagle flew to the stream. She washed quickly, pausing to chat with no one, and returned. Her mother showed her how to put the absorbent plant material inside the skins and then how to attach them to herself so they wouldn't fall off. The girl was fascinated. She'd seen others wear these things, but to consider it herself, she never had. Likichi flashed five. "That's how many days it usually lasts. Keep yourself very clean, she urged Minagle. Instead of using the bathing area, go further downstream. You do not want to get your flow in the water People bathe in."

"I understand," Minagle assured her.

"Keep checking to find out how your flow goes. When the absorbent material is used well, throw it in the back fire where cooking is not done and repack with more. We keep a large supply in the bag over there," Likichi pointed to the bag that held the absorbent material from plants. "From time to time, gather some of the absorbent and contribute to the bag. It is something we all do."

"I will do that, Mother."

"Do not tell anyone you're woman until the flow ceases."

"Won't some of them see this undergarment and know?" she asked

"Of course, but that is how it's done."

"Very well, Mother. I will obey."

Minagle had very mixed emotions about being woman. It meant, no doubt, that she and Ghanya would join. She dearly loved the young man. But she also had concerns about how well she'd do in copulating. It still frightened her when she remembered Reemast. She knew she had to get past that, but doing it and knowing it seemed to be as far apart as a mountain top and the bottom of the sea.

She walked down the rock walk toward the north. It went for a long distance, far beyond the area most People used for living. She walked to the end where it broke off into a ledge about twenty feet above the ground. The ground below was covered with spiked rocks that were very sharp. It was not a place where people walked. She sat down to try to sort out her life now that this complication had occurred. She heard footsteps behind her.

"My Minagle," Ghanya said quietly.

She turned to look at his face, "My Ghanya," she said using the greeting they had established.

"I noticed." He said the two words quietly and with love. He knew all too well what she must be experiencing.

"Mother said it must not be discussed, but everyone knows when a girl becomes woman."

"Yes. In our former group it was announced."

"Ghanya, I love you with all my heart, but you know what happened to me when Reemast was alive. I am terrified that it could cause me to be not the best woman for you."

"Minagle, I know what happened. There was no way to keep that quiet. You have to know that I would never force you to do anything you didn't want to do."

"But I don't want to be a child all my life. I want to be fully woman. Please, don't treat me differently because of what happened, just help me."

"What bothers you, My Minagle?"

"It's just that when he took me down in the cave and came so close to penetrating, I looked and saw what was about to happen. It scared me out of my mind web."

"Let me see if I understand. What you *saw* frightened you?"

"Yes. His little penis was huge!" She gulped.

Ghanya put his arms around her. "My Minagle. Do you not know that a man's male member swells greatly for copulation? That's just how it is. It may hurt somewhat the first time, but it gets better. It is a source of pleasure for both men and women. Now, I think that when we copulate, you should shut your eyes at first. That might help keep the memories away."

"Shut my eyes?" The thought had not crossed her mind.

"You said what you *saw* frightened you."

"That's true."

"Then, I suggest you don't look."

She laughed. She wondered whether it might make a difference. They hugged.

"We will do whatever is necessary to become two people who love each other as much as the parents we have and the other adults here. I have never seen such a group of people who love each other. It was not so where I grew up."

"Oh, Ghanya, that is sad." Her brown eyes looked with sympathy into his.

"That is why we are here. Your People have a better way," he knew what he was supposed to say, he just wondered if he could believe it. "Now if I can just help you find a better way, I will have contributed something back." He ran his fingers through her hair. It had grown to about a hand in length. He pulled her head toward his and kissed her. She melted. They walked back a little way to the stairs that had been built into the rock wall at the far end. They followed the path down the hill and took the curve around the rock wall. From there, they could climb up and sit atop the place where they lived. From there, they could see past the hill and out to the larger valley below. The valley was where the stream turned into other streams and they all headed to the river beyond. It was also home to a very large lake. Only a few men had been to the river or the lake. They sat there holding hands and not speaking. Finally, Ghanya rose and held out his hand to Minagle. "I must help with the meat. You should get back also."

She gave him her hand and he pulled her up for a last hug before they headed to the steps and the rock walk. Minagle felt that everyone knew she was woman. There was no way to conceal it. Why, she wondered, did her mother make it something to hold in secret for so long? In the cave, she went to a place where she would not be seen and checked the absorbent material. There was little dampness there, so she assumed rightly that it was not time to change it. In some ways, she felt that she and Ghanya were the only two people on the earth. She could not have found a better person to share her life with, she was convinced.

Seven days passed since her flow began. It ended on the fourth day, and it was whispered about that Minagle was woman even though by then everyone knew. Meeka was utterly frustrated. She was the same age as Minagle and she was not woman. It did not seem fair.

Grypchon-na would make the pronouncement that night that Ghanya and Minagle would be joined. It was an exciting time. Minagle went to the cave to sweep it clean. She had chosen a cave at some distance from the main cave. She swept the walls and the cave floor twice hoping to remove any spider that might have been in the cave, and she took the wood that Ghanya had laid outside and began to place it for a quick starting fire. He had already made a circle of stones for the hearth. She returned the broom to the main cave and gathered their sleeping mats and covers. Her chosen cave was one of the smallest. They could easily have their sleeping area out of sight from anyone who might pass by, though passing a cave with newly joined couples was forbidden. The fire right in front of the cave would keep them warm and not smoky. Later, she took a water bag and a bowl of meat to the cave. When she walked in with the meat and water, she smelled something. It was a sweet scent. She looked around and discovered that there were wild rose flowers surrounding the sleeping area. She guessed right that Ghanya had surprised her with this special gift. He didn't think like anyone she knew. She realized how thoughtfully he was trying to help her not to be frightened on their first night together.

The group feasted on venison and the pronouncement was made. Grypchon-na began drumming and Ghanya and Minagle participated because dancing was obligatory. Shortly afterward, the two slipped off to their cave hand in hand. When they reached the cave, Ghanya picked her up and carried her through the entrance. She giggled at the gesture. He laid her on the sleeping mats. He had started the fire just before Grypchon-na made the pronouncement.

"My Minagle," he said.

"My Ghanya," she said.

They fell into each other's arms. Soon, they were out of their tunics and were touching. Ghanya had learned what the men teach of how to arouse a woman, and he began slowly. Minagle responded well. There was joy in their foreplay. It was slow and she found she craved more—until they reached the point of penetration. Ghanya was gentle and did everything he could not to frighten her. But despite her receptivity, she re-experienced the past. She panicked. She rolled over and drew her knees up to her chest. She wept.

Ghanya wondered what to think.

"You looked, didn't you?" he asked.

"Yes. I'm sorry! I forgot. And then . . . ."

He lifted her to his lap and cuddled her while Minagle fought the demons of the past. It hit her suddenly. The picture she had carried all the years was of a male member surrounded by red hair close to her pre-pubescent female parts. She'd had no hair! This night, she remembered, had been of two adults with black pubic hair. The pictures didn't match. Finally, she implored him to start all over again.

"I've had a good hard talk with myself. Please, let's resume."

Ghanya hoped that this time would be different. "Promise me you'll shut your eyes," he asked.

"I promise," she said.

They began again and when it came time for the ultimate penetration, Minagle, true to her word, kept her eyes shut. She was not immune to the heat of wanting him, it wasn't that. It was Reemast intruding that bothered her. She had fought her demon and made it clear to herself that this was the man she loved, not the boy she feared. She had conquered something basic, something that had frightened her for years, but she had won. This time, she felt initial pain, but then she felt a filling internally from this person she adored. This was joining! Finally, she understood. This was truly different. She contained him. His love poured into every part of her being. It was powerful but not frightening anymore. It was gentle and kind, not threatening. She held onto him as if never to release him. The demons were gone. She was woman.

As they lay there drained, Ghanya breathed a sigh of relief that he thought only he could know. Little did he guess that a cave full of adults were hoping to know what he knew at that moment. He and Minagle were truly joined. It was good. In fact, it was so good that Minagle was asking for more of the same. Ghanya could not believe it, but he joyously complied. The two spent a full seven days in their cave. In some ways they did not want to return at all, but that was not the way of the People.

Chapter 6

Wamumur and Grypchon-na walked along the stream on a brilliant season-of-warm-nights morning. Birds were singing and the dogs frolicked in the area where they were permitted. Children were splashing at the stream. Men and women went about the busy work of cave life.

"I think we should take that trip," Grypchon-na said.

"What trip is that?" Wamumur asked curious.

"I told you when we first moved here that I'd seen a place I wanted to show you and Emaea and Ki'ti."

"I do remember. It was a long time ago."

"True, but I still want to show you. I'd like to know what you make of it."

"Why not plan a trip to gather medicinals and spices and other botanicals that we might need or have use for? That would give a purpose to the trip." Wamumur couldn't get his mind web around a trip that had no objective other than to look at something.

"That could be arranged. I know that Totamu wants some more of the leaves she uses for her cough."

The men talked about the possibility of the trip for a while and finally decided to do it. There was nothing holding them. The hunting trips had been very good and they could spare the time. They would leave the next day. By the end of the day, the traveling party was set: Likichi and Grypchon-na would go; Nanichak-na would join the party; Mootmu-na and Amey wanted to participate; Lamul volunteered; Ghanya and Minagle decided to join; and Wamumur and Ki'ti would go; but Emaea refused to leave the home group just in case there was a need for her. All agreed that was wise, but Wamumur would have enjoyed sharing the trip with her. He did know that Emaea was concerned about Totamu.

The next morning, all was ready. The dogs were laden and the group's food was carried on a stretcher. Three of the older dogs remained at the cave site. They would be good watchdogs, but their days of long travel were over. The men also had backpacks in addition to the stretchers. Women carried lighter backpacks. Totamu had supplied numbers of baskets for the plants. She asked them to dig up the plants root and all. Basically, Likichi knew what Totamu wanted. She also would recognize plants they'd never seen and would bring those in another, different set of baskets.

There was great excitement among the travelers for their trip. None of them had ever had to scout out a new land until Baambas. They had lived in the same area with seasonal moves for generations and generations. They had found a new place to live, but scouting the area was new. In their old homeland, they knew the area within a twenty day trek radius of their home. In this place, they had barely scratched the surface.

The People said farewells and the little traveling group left. Ahriku was lightly burdened and he walked right beside Ki'ti's left foot. Grypchon-na led the way. First, they followed a path to one of the northern fields where the men hunted. They walked across the field, startling some birds and causing monkeys to chatter in the flowering tulip trees. Then they stopped at an overlook and surveyed the lowland valley below. It seemed to stretch forever. Grypchon-na had an amazing memory of the route he took when he was scouting the area for wildlife. He took the little group the same way. They descended through a growth of birch trees and alders to the lower valley and followed a stream and then branched off crossing another stream. They followed animal trails for much of the way. All watched to be sure that the little dogs made it across the stream. They walked and walked, getting very warm in the afternoon. Finally, as evening fell, they found a rock shelter to use for cover for the night.

Amey and Likichi began preparing the night's meal as soon as the men made a fire at the hearth. Minagle brought the women whatever they wanted for the meal and Ki'ti tried to be helpful, but it was clear that making the evening meal was not her skill. She wanted to be helpful so Wamumur suggested she tend to the dogs with Minagle and then take Ahriku to hunt for wood. He cautioned her to look for snakes and to watch Ahriku for signs of snakes. She was delighted to have some way to participate and, fortunately, there appeared to be no snakes. She feared snakes.

They bedded down for the night and then rose early the next morning to continue their journey. As they walked, Likichi would occasionally stop them to dig up plants. She was very serious about looking for them and she had Ki'ti looking also. Ki'ti knew many of the plants that Totamu used. Minagle had a lesser knowledge, but she too looked. At one point, Minagle called a halt. She had found a number of the plants Totamu used to help her breathing. She also found some that were similar but different and they gathered many of both. Ki'ti found some other ones, much smaller, but they were known to ease pain and thwart infection, so she gathered a supply. The men waited patiently, sitting at the edge of the forest.

For days, they traveled, always northeast. Then, one night, Grypchon-na said, "Tomorrow you will see the place where the giants played."

Likichi looked at him as if he'd become lost in his mind web.

Wamumur asked him to repeat himself, because he was sure he didn't understand.

"Oh, you understood just fine. This is a place that is so different from anything I ever saw that I thought you should see it. Maybe it has a story that can add to the ones we already have."

Ki'ti was getting very excited. New things always intrigued her. Wamumur was concerned enough after seeing her face light up that he said, "Little Girl, remember the problems that curiosity can create for you?"

She shrank back and thought about his words. She did remember. She quelled the exuberance and brought it under her reason.

They ate their evening meal and settled down to sleep as soon as supplies were repacked and ready for morning. Wisdom had removed all the color from the land. Ki'ti lay on the ground looking at the heavens. The stars were so huge and plentiful that it could almost take her breath away and she was familiar with them. Ghanya was having the same reaction to the beauty of the night sky. Each knew that some people had a capacity for joy at seeing things of beauty while others were not affected. They could not understand indifference to the view that was above them.

When Wisdom restored color to the land, the group rose and ate. They packed up and began their walk. Off to the west, two huge live oak trees provided unused shade. A good bit before high sun, they could see strange gray shapes looming ahead. The gray shapes were stone and they had been shaped in amazing ways. Some looked like trees without branches. Others looked like bridges. Some were huge stones piled atop other stones, sometimes huge stones above much smaller ones. Some appeared to have been cut evenly across the bottom and placed atop other columns. The closer they got, the more amazing the scene became. They got close enough to walk among the pillars. The group stayed together, and they spent hours walking among the pillars. Atop a pillar once in a while they could see a tiny piece of vegetation growing as if it mistook the top of a column for the ground below. For once in her life, Ki'ti was speechless. The place did not call her to a mind web not of her own, but it took her imagination and expanded it beyond anything she could conceive. This was totally beyond her.

"Do you see why I thought of giants and playing?" Grypchon-na asked.

Wamumur looked at him. "I cannot wrap my mind web around this place. Never have I dreamed of such a sight. It is astounding. I wish Emaea had come."

The group spent the day at the place where the giants played. They could not seem to take it in. Ki'ti was trying to make mental pictures of the things she saw. She wanted to describe them for Emaea. She would stand and stare at a single view for a long time, trying to remember every detail.

Ghanya walked up to her and said, "You're trying to capture the image like you capture the stories?"

She was always fascinated when he'd make a statement and then raise the tone at the end to turn it into a question. "Yes," she replied. "I want to be able to share this with Emaea."

"It is lovely in a strange way?"

"It is. There is a special beauty here."

"I'm glad you can see that, Ki'ti."

She smiled a genuine large smile at him. How, she wondered, had he known she loved the beauty in things? Did it show somehow?

Ghanya left her for Minagle. "Your little sister is really special," he said.

"She is. She's had a hard time, but she seems to be doing a lot better recently."

"You love her a lot?"

"Differently from the way I love you, but yes, I love her a lot. I watched out for her for most of her very young childhood. I still think of her as a very young child."

"In some ways she is. In other ways, she's like a little old lady!"

"Oh, poof," Minagle said as she shoved her elbow into Ghanya's ribs.

The men had built a hearth at the edge of the stone pillars. They had gathered firewood for a small fire and the women were getting things ready to cook the evening meal. Wisdom was beginning to suck the color from the land. They had a novel experience that day. They would never forget the images they put in their mind webs.

Ki'ti was sitting with Wamumur watching the color leave the treetops at a distance.

"Wise One," she asked Wamumur, "why does Wisdom suck the color from the land?"

"So the things he made will sleep and be rested for the next day," he replied.

"Why did Wisdom make us need to sleep?"

Wamumur looked into her eyes. He yawned and said, "So we don't get filled with pride and see ourselves as being Wisdom for ourselves. We depend on Wisdom and we need to know it."

"Does Wisdom sleep?" she asked.

"No, Little Girl, Wisdom keeps everything he made working all the time. Wisdom doesn't need sleep, but you do, so get ready for a good sleep tonight."

"What do you make of this, Amey?" Likichi asked, slowly sweeping her hand with her finger pointing to the strange shaped rocks.

"I honestly don't know. I can see why Grypchon-na wanted the story-tellers to see it, but it's over my head."

"It's over everyone's head, I think," Likichi said, and continued, "I have been intending to tell you that I think Lamk is turning into a fine young man, but of course, you know that."

Amey said, "That's nice to hear. He reminds me of Manak."

Likichi thought of her son. "Now that you mention it, I can see that."

"Manak is a fine young man. I hope Lamk turns out like him. I wonder whether Manak will be a father when we return home," Amey said smiling.

"That's the only shadow on this trip. I want to be there when the baby is born, and I might miss it." Likichi raised her arm and wiped sweat from her brow on her forearm.

"I can see why you wanted us to see this, Grypchon-na," Wamumur said. "But I don't know what to do with the knowledge."

"Why do you have to do something with it? Why isn't it enough to have seen this place and let it go at that?" Grypchon-na asked.

"I don't know," he replied. "It's so perplexedly different that you'd think that you'd have to do something with it."

"Well," Grypchon-na laughed heartily, "it looks for once like I figured something out that stumped you. I knew what I had to do. I had to show it to you!"

Ki'ti didn't know whether to laugh out loud, so she did what she'd seen Minagle do a year or so ago. She covered her mouth with her hand and grinned. Across the fire, Minagle winked at her.

They settled down to sleep. For Ki'ti, sleep did not come quickly. She was fascinated with the silhouettes of the stones against the night sky. *What were these things?* she wondered. And finally, finding no solution, she fell asleep.

The next morning, they ate and got underway. Grypchon-na led them northwest. There was a part of the country he wanted to explore. He'd seen a section of it and wanted to get a bigger view. They walked steadily, rising a little over time. They entered a forest of hardwood trees where they discovered a path, albeit overgrown, a path that seemed to have been there since ancient times. The path was oriented north to south. They headed south. Somehow, Grypchon-na hadn't seen the path when he was in the area the first time. The path made progress much easier. Elevation change was significant through the hilly country. At one time, they'd pass through lowlands where citrus shrubs grew and they'd pull some lemons to carry home. Then they'd pass through elms and hickory hardwoods to birch and alders to pine and spruce and firs. The change was gradual with the different vegetation mixed until certain trees predominated. There seemed an endless variety.

They entered into a forest of bamboo. They were fascinated with the plant and the girls pulled up some of the smaller trees so the plants would fit in collection baskets. As they continued through the bamboo, all of a sudden, they saw a creature moving ponderously. They froze in place to watch, alert to possible danger. The animal appeared to be a bear. Its coat was black and white. The ears, arms and across the shoulders, and legs were black. The body from the arms down was white. The face was white. There were black circles around the animal's eyes and it had a black nose. Likichi knew for the first time the source of the material for the garment of the man with the green bag. The animal showed no fear. It watched them as it was watched. Clearly, it was eating bamboo. From the signs that Totamu had given her, Likichi didn't think that the People should eat the leaves that the animal was eating.

They continued along the pathway winding through the forest, until they came to a stream that was bordered by a rock wall and caves. Large rhododendrons edged the rock wall, along with pines and a few hardwoods. Grypchon-na signaled them all to stop and to be still and silent, including the dogs. Grypchon-na and Nanichak-na used hunters' stealth and surveyed the rock wall and caves. When they determined that no one currently was there, the others were allowed to examine the caves. It was so like their home it surprised them. It was clear that others had occupied the place long ago. Wamumur put his hand on Ki'ti's shoulder to warn her to use caution. She understood and called Wisdom to protect her.

They could see hearths where the people had made fires. Ki'ti's inhalation was heard by all. "Look at that!" she said louder than she intended, pointing.

All looked at the aurochs carved in the cave wall. It wasn't fancy but the shape of the wall was like the shape of the side of an aurochs. The carver had simply supplied the straight and curved lines that drew attention to the animal's shape that the wall didn't show. Never had any of them thought to do such a thing. But there it was, a seed of things to be. The visualization in tangible form of a memory. It was a thing to behold. Ki'ti worked feverishly to store as much information about the image as she could. Words could give form to the memory of a story. Lines could give form to the memory of an image once beheld. It was academic training hurled at her in an immense amount in a tiny fragment of time. The same thing was happening to Ghanya. Something in him responded to the image in ways that set off a harmonic to which his whole being vibrated. This was something he wanted to do. It was inborn. In a flash of inspiration, he had learned to see and to supplement.

"Oh, there!" Ki'ti exclaimed. She pointed this time to a panda on the wall. This representation had the panda's leg and arm shaped by the cave wall and a part of its head and ear. And there was a sprig of bamboo. It was more fantastic than the aurochs.

"Wise One, can we please look at the rest of the caves to see if there are others?" she asked.

He nodded and took her hand. They went to the next cave. Ghanya was still stuck on the panda. The second cave was image free. They moved to the third cave and found a barking deer. It seemed to come alive, caught in the light from outside. The next cave was huge and had numbers of rooms. Wamumur sniffed to see whether he could detect any living thing. Nanichak-na hurried to stay with the two of them. It was dark so Wamumur looked for something to form a light. Nanichak-na called to Grypchon-na and asked for a light. Grypchon-na came with an oil lamp and a coal that was carried along to light fires. He got the lamp going. They went further into the cave and sure enough, in one room, there were more images. These were not the fantastic painted images that would come later in time from the Others but they were not lesser by any means. A few lines here and there and the animals leapt out of the rock. Ghanya finally reached the room of the animals. Here was a rhino, there a gazelle; here a serpent, there a monkey. A hyena crouched in a corner. A straight-tusked elephant raised its trunk.

Ki'ti gasped. On the far wall there was an animal that she had never seen. It looked like a winged serpent with four legs. It seemed to be exhaling fire. The fire was red dripped color from the cave staining the wall. Never in her life had she seen or imagined anything of the sort. You actually couldn't see the image unless you stood in a certain place in the room. If you walked around, it would disappear. Everyone in the group walked around looking and seeing and not seeing. How, she wondered, could someone make a thing on the wall and have it appear and disappear? The little group of travelers couldn't seem to make themselves leave the room of the animals. Ghanya couldn't believe how just a few, very few, lines could make something that was an idea leap to life. It amazed him. He would like to have met the artist. Sadly, the man lived hundreds of years before Ghanya.

They went to the remainder of the caves but there were no more images. In one cave, Minagle found a little bag. She took it to Ghanya who carried it to the group. He opened the bag and dropped a tiny little yellow owl into his hand.

"Look at this," Ghanya said.

Wamumur said, "Look at this," and took the little owl from the bag at his neck. The two were identical. Wamumur put his away.

"What should we do with it?" Ghanya asked.

No one spoke. Some thought that since Wamumur had one, it should go to either Emaea or to Ki'ti. Amey put out her hand. Ghanya placed the little yellow owl in Amey's hand. She tucked it into her bag. Nothing further was said.

The little group continued following the ancient path. The path threaded its way through a pass in the mountains. They arrived at a flat place near the summit of one mountain as evening fell. They stopped near a tiny rock overhang, barely enough to shelter them from the falling dew. The men made a hearth and a fire and the women began to gather the food for preparation of the evening meal. Lamul noticed a small four-horned antelope. He fluidly loaded his slingshot with a small round rock, releasing it and hitting the deer's head in a sensitive area, and the deer collapsed. It was not dead but could not get up quickly, so he raced over to finish the kill. The women began to prepare the area to camp. Lamul returned with the antelope and the men got it skinned and readied for roasting as fast as they ever had. They would eat well that night. It might be a little late, but when they ate it was good. They looked into the starry sky and wondered at the things they had seen. Ghanya and Minagle wandered off a bit from the group and spent time being man and wife in the grasses with more abandon than they normally practiced in the community cave.

Amey had talked to every member of the group asking about her thought as to what to do with the owl. She thought it would be a right thing to do to make a pouch like Wamumur had and thread a piece of leather through it and make it for Ki'ti to wear around her neck. Everyone approved wholeheartedly. That night, she presented it to Ki'ti. The girl wept and threw her arms around Amey. Amey reminded her that the whole group was in accord with the idea. Ki'ti went from person to person and hugged them and thanked them. She had never had a personal item, except for the dog and her tunic. This was an unbelievable honor in her eyes. It was also a tie to Wamumur as storyteller.

When Wisdom returned color to the land, they began again, following the path downhill for a long time. The day was lovely and there were many plants to gather. Most were familiar but there were some strange ones. The baskets were almost stuffed full. The women thought that Totamu would be pleased.

Grypchon-na said at dinner that evening that they should arrive home the next day or the day after that at the latest. They were well pleased. The trip had been incredible but they were all tired and longed to be home. They slept that night under an overhang and it rained a little. Fortunately, none of them got wet, including the dogs. The next morning, they arose and ate some more meat and began their walk. Suddenly as they walked, Nanichak-na said, "This area looks very familiar. I know where we are!"

Grypchon-na asked, "Where then?"

"Look up," Nanichak-na said. There above them was the cave of the man with the green bag and his family. The group knew they were almost home. Soon, they arrived at the home cave and the People raced out to welcome them back.

Minagle ran to Domur. In her arms was a very tiny baby. "Totamu said she thought the baby was early," Domur explained. "But she is fine." Likichi went to her to see the infant that she'd just heard was a girl. She looked at the tiny face. She looked a perfect combination of Manak and Domur. But she was so tiny. She couldn't tell whether the infant had blue eyes or green ones like Domur.

Wamumur found Emaea. He raced to her and surrounded her with his arms. For a brief moment, the two were the only ones in the world.

"My Husband, I have missed you," Emaea said when she could speak.

"I have missed you also, My Wife," Wamumur said with great feeling.

"How is our child?" Emaea asked.

"She is well. I approved of her on this trip."

"That is good."

"It is good," he reaffirmed with a palm strike and a bit of a sigh of relief.

Likichi and Amey took the plants to Totamu. The three women sat on mats on the floor and began to examine the plants. Meeka and Liho joined them and offered to help hang any plants that needed to dry. Totamu asked them to get the drying rack and put it up along with the pole. She had the girls hang the new plants on the long pole that fit from one projection to another on the cave wall, not the normal drying rack. The young girls were delighted to be able to help.

First, Totamu went through the plants that were unfamiliar. She was the most surprised at the bamboo. It brought up a memory that she couldn't quite grasp. Perhaps, it would come to her later. She told the girls to take the leaves to the fire and drop them in. Then she told them to dry the plant.

From another plant, she chose to keep the leaves and burn the root system. There were clues with each plant and as she went through, she explained to Likichi why she did what she did. She stopped at the plant that looked like a close match to the leaves she used for breathing. "Take this leaf, Meeka, and steep me some tea," she said. Meeka hurried to do as requested. Liho took the plant to hang on the pole.

Then, Totamu moved to the next set of baskets. She was delighted. The women and girls had obtained a wonderful supply of plants she desperately needed and hadn't felt well enough to gather. Meeka brought her the tea and Totamu drank. In a few moments, she was far more open to breathe than she had been in a long time. Perhaps the plant, seeming similar but somehow different, had something that would help over the long run since the potency of the leaves she'd been using seemed to have decreased. Maybe it was just different enough to give her more time.

Ki'ti and Minagle had unpacked the dogs and they raced to join the ones who had remained at home. Even Ahriku, as much as he doted on Ki'ti, went to join the others for a while.

Nanichak-na and Chamul-na had been planning to take a different trip. Chamul-na had to wait while Nanichak-na accompanied the others on what would be referred to as the trip to the place where the giants played. Chamul-na and Nanichak-na planned to travel due north. Now that they had found the ancient path, Nanichak-na suggested they simply follow it. They knew now that there were signs of human habitation along that trail and they wanted to know if other humans lived in the north. It wasn't so much that they wanted to meet other humans as much as they wanted to know where other humans were. It was a trip more for security than social purposes. After all, they'd found an established path, a rather wide one at that. Likewise,

Ermol-na and Arkan-na had talked of following the river to the east for the same reason. If People were around, they reasoned, they might be located near rivers. It had struck all of them as strange that they had so far seen no sign of people anywhere, only traces of those from the long ago.

Nanichak-na assured Chamul-na that he had no need to rest up before they started, so they packed up only what hunters needed for travel and left the home cave quietly. From a distance, Chamul-na saw the cave of the man with the green bag for the first time. He was shocked that a child had been able to find it while Wisdom was sucking the color from the land. It was well hidden along the hill. In daylight, he couldn't even see the path leading to the cave until Nanichak-na pointed it out. Chamul-na was interested in the ancient path leading north. It seemed once to have been used routinely because the surface was so hard.

"How old do you think this path is?" Nanichak-na asked.

"More than I can count from the first looks of it," Chamul-na said. "It will be interesting to see whether trees have grown on it. Do you remember?"

"I don't remember seeing any trees of great height. There are some small ones, but they don't really block the path. I expect that since the ancient times animals have also used it."

"That would make sense."

The two walked silently as they got further into the woods, first, mostly birch and alder and then becoming more pine. The path followed a stream that flowed north. The path was midway up the hill, however, not at the water's edge, and it continued uphill. Birds called out and occasionally a small group of monkeys would shout out their presence to the world. Nanichak-na told of the great bear with the black and white fur. Chamul-na hoped he would see one. Nanichak-na also told him about the cave with the animals and it surprised him when Chamul-na asked to stop by so he could see the animal that appeared and disappeared. In all his life as a hunter, he'd never seen an animal that was snake-like and had four legs and huge wings and breathed fire. He also hoped not to see a live one.

The two men were walking swiftly. The fragrance of the evergreens permeated the air, giving it a strong poignancy. Nanichak-na much preferred hunter travel to travel with those who were older or younger and unseasoned. With just the two of them, they could probably eat well not by backpacking food but rather by finding something along the way of small size daily. They often would start out when they awakened, packing up and eating their morning meal of dried meat while they walked. At night, their evening meal was something small that they managed to find on the trail during the day. They had plenty of dried meat if nothing living was available, but that rarely happened. They did not hunt animals they could not consume when on hunter travel.

Nanichak-na said, "It is interesting that the Others who joined us can outrun us with ease, but for the long treks, they don't have the endurance we have. I noticed that with Ghanya. He can run like the wind for a small part of a day, but day after day on the treks, his legs tire, especially if the going is uphill."

"I wonder why that is. I have noticed that we seem to have stronger leg muscles for trekking."

"I don't understand it really. We are so alike but there are slight differences. With Minagle who seems to be part of the People and part of the Others, she tires not quite as fast as Ghanya but she lacks the endurance we have, unless it's because she is woman."

"She does look like there is some of the Others in her. Do you suppose it was from when Likichi was stolen?"

"I think so. I haven't really ever discussed it, but with the Others joining us, it makes Minagle stand out more."

"Yes. She's like Shmyukuk. They look like sisters."

"They do, don't they?"

"I think when we hunt, it is good to have some of the People and some of the Others together. Some of us cannot move as fast as the Others. We work well together."

"I think it is good."

"It is good."

Nanichak-na asked Chamul-na whether he really wanted to see the cave with the animals.

"Of course," he replied.

"Then we have to turn off here," Nanichak-na said. There was no obvious path, but the caves could be seen from the main path for those walking south. The caves were blocked from view for those northbound on the path. The view was obscured by a projection of rock.

The two went to the caves and Nanichak-na said, "I have no light. Did you bring one?"

"No. I have an ember, as you know."

"We will have to make a torch if you want to see the animals."

"Here, let me put one together. Are these the caves?" Chamul-na grabbed a Y-ed pine branch.

"Yes. The entrance to the rock walk is down there."

Chamul-na was busily twisting last year's ferns and mosses around the branch and securing it with a long vine. As they reached the big cave, Chamul-na stooped down and set the torch afire. "This won't last long, but it should do the job," he said.

"It's in here," Nanichak-na said leading him to the second room. "There, look at that wall. That's where the monster is."

Chamul-na raised the torch and then jumped at the sight of the monster. He slapped his leg since he was not free to do a palm strike with a torch in his hand.

"Now, walk over here and it will disappear."

Chamul-na did. It disappeared. Even the red that looked like fire was gone in shadow.

"That's the most unusual thing I've ever seen," Chamul-na said in awe.

"I agree."

"Did it affect the Wise Ones like the man with the green bag?" Chamul-na asked.

"Not at all. They were just as fascinated as we are. They had no explanation for how the images got here."

"Look at that elephant, Nanichak-na! You could swear it was real." He slapped his leg again.

"It's unbelievable to see these things on cave walls, yet here they are. I wonder what it's all about."

"We'll probably live our lives without ever knowing."

"Sadly, you're probably right. I'd like to know," Nanichak-na said wistfully.

Chamul-na laid the torch in the hearth in the front room. The hunters traced their way back to the path down the slight incline. They were on the way again. Both were still fascinated with the path.

"Now, here's an elm tree on the path, but this tree couldn't be any more than" he flashed fifty "years old."

"I agree. What strikes me is that the path seems so tramped down. It looks as if it were used for a long time and then fell into disuse. The part of the path I've seen is not terribly overgrown. It's just a mystery to me. Wait!" Nanichak-na said. He took a couple of pebbles and tossed them to the ground. He reached over and pulled a few seeds from a tree nearby. He dropped them to the ground. "When the seed hits the path, it bounces. The path is so hard it doesn't give the seed a place to grab. Any wind that blows here would sweep them away. Is that the answer?"

"I don't know," Chamul-na responded, "but it sounds as good as any answer."

The path descended to the edges of a lowland but did not leave the trees and shrubs. It continued on beside a stream that flowed north. They followed the stream on the path that rose to a higher elevation again, putting them high above the stream. Having the path available made travel much easier. After a few days, they began to see more bamboo and the black and white bears.

"Are these the bears you saw?" Chamul-na asked.

"Yes. They are the source of the garments of the man with the green bag. Those garments look like season-of-cold-days garments."

"I agree."

In some places, the bamboo was falling into the area of the path but it was not growing on it. Finally, as the evening drew on, the men began to look for food and a place for the night. Suddenly, Chamul-na shot out his arm for halting and silence. Slowly, he took his spear and positioned it. He gauged the area for success. He gave a bloodcurdling shout as he threw the spear. The spear caught a very young boar in the neck.

"We have meat!" Chamul-na exulted as if he were a young child, not an old man of forty-nine.

Chamul-na gathered up the young boar and said, "You should not have strayed so far from your mother," as if the boar could hear him and learn.

Then he took his spear and the boar and joined Nanichak-na on the path.

"Good work, my friend," Nanichak-na said, followed by a palm strike.

"Thank you," came the reply and the hunter lowered his head with a grin.

They found an open place for the night. The sky was clear so they did not concern themselves that they had no protection over their heads. Nanichak-na gathered stones for the fire pit and Chamul-na started piling wood for the fire. He found a good couple of Y-shaped sticks for a spit and a stout green cross bar to thread through the boar for cooking over their fire. The men worked as they had countless times on hunter travel. No one need say anything. They simply did what had to be done. It was part of them.

After Wisdom had sucked the color from the land, as usual, they walked to the crest of the hill above camp to view in a 360° circle. Smoke arose from nowhere. It had been the same every night. There was no sign of human habitation.

"Could it be that we are alone in all this wilderness?" Nanichak-na asked. "Surely, the path builders had descendants. Surely, if they could build this solid path, they could make fire, and we could see the smoke rising when we observe from high points."

"I find this most odd," Chamul-na said quietly. He did a quiet palm strike.

They stretched out for the night. It was quiet for a forest. The stars were blazing overhead. There was a slight fragrance on the breeze and just before he fell asleep, Nanichak-na wondered what flowers were blooming.

In the morning, they continued on. It rained. It had rained a lot since they'd moved to this new site. They had grown accustomed to it. They thought this must be unusual because the mosses they associated with rain forested areas were not growing in this place. They saw several huge elk moving in the hardwoods and in a grassy field there was an aurochs. They came across elephants eating trees in the forest.

"This place at least has life, if not people," Chamul-na said.

"I keep thinking because of the path that we will find some people. This is so strange."

Onward, they continued until on the seventh day, the path turned up from a valley to the left and they arrived at a dead end at a large river.

"Wow! What a river!" Nanichak-na said with enthusiasm looking down. His palm strike was loud.

"What is that?" Chamul-na asked.

The men went to the rock platform to their left and noticed that a huge rope had been hung across the river. It was the largest rope they'd ever seen. They could not span the circumference with a single hand of theirs; it took two. They saw that there had been two ropes but one had broken. The rope that remained had ropes dangling from it, ropes that might have supported some kind of flooring they thought. It looked like the path might have continued across the river on a bridge made of ropes. Both men got queasy at the very idea. They certainly made ropes and had constructed bridges, but never bridges of rope like this. The knowledge and understanding of these people who had left the area amazed the men. Those people could make cave walls alive with animals and build paths that grew no plants and bridges out of rope that dwarfed what they had ever built. Of course, neither would have said it, but they would have been terrified to cross that large river high in the air on a bridge made of rope.

They sat down to drink in what they were seeing. Chamul-na wondered whether there was a way to the river to fill water bags, and he found one. He took two water bags and descended to the river. When he came back up, he noticed that Nanichak-na was dozing so he took two more water bags to the river to fill them. He sat in the sun by his friend and let the sun warm him. The shadowy forest had been cool and they hadn't felt it much because they were on the move. When they settled down, it would have been chilly if not for the sunshine.

Chamul-na wondered what weapons the bridge builders might have. If they could build a bridge like that, could they have superior weapons? He scanned the area where they were resting. There was nothing that left any trace of humans or for that matter any other type of living thing.

Chamul-na returned to the river and walked about by the water's edge. He looked for footprints or any other evidence of life. Nothing but plants moved. No prints had been left from any living animals. Yet the hunter felt watched. He knew that feeling and knew that animals he'd watched had felt it as well. What could be watching him? He wondered.

He climbed back up to the platform. Nanichak-na was snoring. Chamul-na smiled. Obviously, Nanichak-na didn't feel watched. Chamul-na tried to shake off the feeling but he was unable to do so. Chamul-na looked again at the other side of the river and there in the woods stood the tallest ape he'd ever seen. He put his hand on Nanichak-na's shoulder and hushed him. His friend looked where directed and stared.

"What in the name of Wisdom is that?" he whispered incredulously. "It must be twice our height. It looks like an ape but stands like a man."

"In the name of Wisdom, I have no idea! I've been feeling watched. Let's get out of here, *now.*"

"I think that's a great idea," Nanichak-na said while gathering the few things he had to carry.

They walked away as rapidly as they could without running.

"I hope there aren't any on this side," Chamul-na said quietly.

"Well, if it's an ape, it could swing itself across that rope."

"I didn't think of that. Thanks a lot."

"I think we've seen enough for this trip. What do you think?"

"I think," Chamul-na said, "I think, we've seen no people. I hope that isn't the reason. But it's far away from where we live.

"That's true. This is a strange new land, isn't it?" Nanichak-na asked.

"True. And I've had my fill of strange new things for a while."

"I agree," Nanichak-na did a strong palm strike.

Chamul-na sealed the palm strike.

They walked long into the evening to put distance between the creature and themselves. There was something about an ape that looked like a man that frightened them both. It seemed all out of joint with nature. They were not embarrassed to admit to each other that they were afraid—

they were. What they saw had frightened them greatly even though it only observed them instead of threatened. Had there been young men with them, they might not have been so outspoken about their own fears, but when it was the two of them, they were open and honest to a fault. They had been friends too long. The moon was full and the stars were out. No clouds drifted overhead. They walked steadily through the night. Occasionally, they stopped for water and to get some dried meat from their traveling packs. They ate while they walked, both engrossed in thoughts of what they'd seen.

"You know, Chamul-na, I find an ape far more troubling than a lion or a bear. Why do you think that is?"

"I don't know but I feel the same. Maybe it's that there appears to be some kind of kinship in there? I don't know. Which would you fear the most—the fire breathing flying snake with legs or the ape?"

Nanichak-na thought and then said, "The ape. I know that's real. Surely, apes didn't make this path? Did they make the animals on the cave wall? Did they build the bridge?"

Chamul-na looked at him with consternation.

For a long time, they continued in silence. There were night noises as they walked along, but they were night noises that they knew. Not ones that were strange or frightful. Finally, when Wisdom restored color to the land, Chamul-na felt a need for sleep. They found a very small cave and the two went inside. They decided to build a fire for warmth, smiling at each other like boys, neither fooling the other. They built a large fire at the mouth of the cave and both fell asleep quickly.

By the time the sun was directly overhead, the men awakened and continued their walk home. They had found no answers about other people or how the path came to be and managed to remain in place for what appeared to have been a very long time.

When the men reached the part of the path in the field of the man with the green bag, some fifteen days had passed. As they walked into their home cave they were greeted by an outpouring of people. They went inside and were fed and they told their story of finding no people. They told of the path that went on and on for days and days. They told of how the path ended in what appeared to have been a bridge made of rope, something the People had a very hard time trying to visualize. What they didn't share was the ape. They could not have known that at that time, the only apes like that left were north of the river where the broken bridge was. And there were fewer than twenty.

The other hunters had arrived back already. They had followed the river to the east of them. It first went south and then north and then east. There was no path to follow but they could go along the river bank and did. They traveled for a long time and having seen no people for days and days, they returned. The little group of people felt very much alone. What would they do if those who were young needed to find other people with whom to join? It presented a dilemma. Hopefully by that time more People would be in the area.

The hunters who had been at home during the trips had talked to Kai and had built the barricades they felt would be helpful in the field to force animals to go off the cliff. Kai had explained the need to dig out the cave under the ledge so that it was deeper. He also said that he was not prepared for the speed of the rhino when it started after him. He should have disappeared quicker. And finally, people needed to get their legs inside the cave. He felt that people should practice enticing an animal and then disappearing so that they could do it without sticking their legs out. The cave had been dug back into the hill further and several people willing to volunteer to entice the animals had practiced to gain a skill of getting quickly to safety. The next day, hunters would go to try the field again. Aurochs had been seen in the field, and the People wanted to increase their stores for the season of cold days.

Ki'ti sat beside Domur. She was delighted with the baby. She found it so hard to imagine ever having been that small. She just wanted to watch the baby's face.

"Do you want to hold her, Ki'ti?" Domur asked.

"Could I really hold her?" she fairly whispered.

"Of course."

Domur laid the baby carefully in Ki'ti's arms. "Relax your arms. That's better. She just lies there right now. It will take time before she is able to turn over, so she isn't going anywhere."

"How'd you decide on a name like Tuma for her?"

"Oh, we just toyed with names and that one sounded right to Manak and me."

"What does it mean?"

"It is a flower that used to grow back home. As often as I've looked, I have never seen one here."

"So now you have one."

"Yes, Ki'ti, now we have one."

"What color flower was it?"

"Pink."

They both laughed as they looked at the tiny pink face.

Ahriku walked up to Ki'ti after being with the other dogs. He quietly took in the scene and lay down beside her, right next to her leg.

"Is Manak hunting tomorrow?" Ki'ti asked.

"He is and he is going to call the aurochs."

"Are you frightened?"

"Yes. Are you, Ki'ti?"

"I am now, but when I was a little child, I wouldn't have been."

"Ki'ti, you are a little child."

"No, Domur, I just look like one. I was one until the night of the green bag. Then I grew up."

"Do you really think so?"

"I *know* it. Everything changed in me then. Manak also contributed when he made me promise to obey unequivocally. I threw away my childish ways. I do have a responsibility and it is like a heavy weight on me. It will always be like that. So, no, I'm not a child anymore." Ki'ti did a palm strike with her arms around Tuma.

"Well said, Ki'ti. I'll remember that." She sealed the palm strike. Ki'ti was not a child any longer despite her years.

Totamu was sitting with Pechki, Alu, and Veymun. They were enjoying the time after the evening meal and the time before going to sleep. In the season of warm nights, it was a delightful time. There was still plenty of daylight and there were few demands on women at that time of day. Rain made the air smell wonderful.

"I've been wondering and wondering what my mind web was hinting about bamboo. I finally remembered," Totamu said.

"What's that?" Veymun asked.

"It was so very long ago. Veymun, you might remember. We were children. We had bamboo rafts for the lake. We only had them a short time. I don't know why they stopped using them."

"I do remember that. The men would use them for fishing." Veymun put her hands on her head as if that would help her remember.

"Well, we have that big lake down in the lowland. I'm thinking if we made some bamboo rafts we could fish there and supplement the meat we have with some fish both fresh and dried."

"What a wonderful idea."

"We will have to wait. The bamboo has to dry for a long time before it can be used. Remember? Before it dries, it's too heavy and it sinks. If we got the wood now we could make rafts next season of new leaves or warm nights," Totamu said.

"Even so, what a great idea. The men could bring a supply and put them in a cave and next year, well, we could become fisherwomen."

Gruid-na, Veymun's husband, stopped by the women. "I just heard mention of something for us to do. What do you have in mind?" he asked.

Veymun smiled. "Totamu mentioned something about the bamboo from our childhood. Do you remember the bamboo rafts?"

"Yes, I do. That is far back in my mind web."

"Well, she was thinking if we got some bamboo and put it in a cave it would be ready for raft building for the season of new leaves or warm nights. We could put them on the big lake down there to fish. We could supplement our meat with fresh and dried fish."

"What a wonderful idea. I'll share that with some of the men who aren't hunting tomorrow. We could gather some. It isn't far."

Totamu said, "Do you remember it has to be cut while it's green? The pieces have to be cut the same length except the crosspieces have to be shorter. You can't cut it well when it's dry. Our fathers used to burn it, not cut it. When burning it you must," she paused, remembering, "you must make a hole in the part to be burned to prevent explosion."

"I didn't remember, but now that you're saying that, I do have it in my mind web. This is a great idea."

Gruid-na went to meet with a few of the men who were not hunting the next day. Ermol-na and Ekuktu would join him in gathering bamboo. The hunters who would try the ledge dropoff again were Manak and Lai, the callers, and Grypchon-na, Mootmu-na, Slamika, and Hahami-na to goad the animal from its sides and back.

The People in the cave began to settle. Ki'ti had been sitting next to Emaea trying to explain what the place where the giants played looked like. She had taken a stick and drawn lines in the sand on the floor trying to convey the idea. Emaea tried to envision it, but it didn't work. When she drew the images of the animals from the cave, Emaea could visualize that, and she was fascinated. The animal that she had trouble visualizing is the monster that breathed fire. Emaea said that was probably because she could imagine no such thing and thought it wasn't real.

The next day began with shouts and cries as a few of the women tried to sweep a snake from the cave. Wamumur, realizing the snake was not poisonous, went over and picked up the snake and carried it to the end of the rock walk and let it go. He sympathized with the animal who repulsed People simply by its form.

The hunters were up and eating. Their expectations of a great hunt were evident but not spoken. There was a feeling that if they spoke about it, the hunt would go poorly. It was as if words spoken had some malevolent power of their own. Each hunter took care that their favorite weapons were in good shape the days prior to the hunt, but they checked again that morning. Finally without a word, but as if a signal went out to all, they congregated at the cave entrance ready to leave for the field.

The men filed out silently and headed toward the path they had made that would take them to the field. The day was bright and a slight breeze was blowing from the east. That would keep their odor from the animals. As they approached the field, they saw the two aurochs grazing. Manak went to the north and skirted around to the ledge where the cave he would use for escaping was located. He could raise his head just enough to see the other hunters getting positioned behind the two beasts. They had spears and slingshots ready. At a signal from Mootmu-na, Manak showed himself above the ledge and began taunting the aurochs. He tossed stones and yelled and danced. The display did not impress the beasts sufficiently for them to discontinue grazing. The hunters were mystified, but Manak continued.

Finally, Manak took his slingshot and put a few pebbles in the cup and let them fly. He hit one aurochs right near the eye, causing it to bleed. He let fly a few more pebbles and hit the snout of the other beast. By then, he had their attention. He continued taunting and using his sling until finally one of the aurochs had had enough. He let fly another set of small pebbles and the beast began to charge him. He kept his head and raced for the ledge and went over in the way they had practiced again and again. The beast actually tried to stop but the forward momentum of the huge body was too great and the animal went over the ledge, bellowing at its mistake. Manak watched as if it were in slow motion, relieved to be inside the cave that had been hollowed out deeper as Kai had suggested. It worked!

He raised up and looked at the second aurochs. It was nervous and looking from side to side. The hunters had crouched in place and were immobile. Manak climbed back up to the level of the field. He began to taunt the remaining aurochs. The cow made noises of frustration. He hit the cow's head with pebbles. It too finally became angered sufficiently that it began to charge. Again, the beast went over the ledge.

To the hunters, this innovation was almost too good to be true. They were safer than they had ever been when hunting these animals. Certainly, it wasn't risk free. There was risk, as Kai gave testimony. But they had learned a different way of gathering meat that didn't result in hunter death, at least not yet. That, too, was something they didn't discuss out loud.

Slamika was sent back to the cave for butchering reinforcements and tools. He stopped first at the place where Kai was sitting. He recounted the hunt. Kai was disappointed that he hadn't been there, but he felt some pride in knowing that he had given them ideas for safekeeping of the hunter who called to the beasts. How he wished that he could help with the meat preparation, but he knew that to be a hunter in the future he had to follow Totamu's requirement that he refrain from putting weight on his leg, until she told him he could. He knew it wasn't any time soon. He would ask Ermol-na for one of the tools the children had found and some stones and a hammer stone, and while unable to hunt, he would try to learn to make tools like the ones they'd found.

Guy-na, Arkan-na, Chamul-na, Neamu-na, Ghanya, Lamul, and Ermi gathered at the cave entrance. Wamumur knew he would have to remain at the cave. He wondered who would stay behind with him. The men drew straws. Ghanya and Ermi drew the short straws. They would set up the preparation cave and guard the home cave. The others gathered tools for skinning and butchering. They headed quickly to the field. They were joined by Pechki, Likichi, Meeka, Liho, Lamk, and Emaea also decided to go. Emaea had always wanted to participate but as the only Wise One, she had been protected. Now that they had three Wise Ones, she made the decision that her time of protection was over. She would go. She would accompany the women who helped at the butchering stage. She would participate completely! She felt a new sense of freedom that had been denied her for years. Again, the Winds of Change could be felt. For the first time in her life, Emaea would return to the cave bloodied and specked with gore, needing a thorough wash before joining cave life. It was a tremendous adventure for her. In the past she'd been a partial participant. This time she was part of the entire process.

The People worked feverishly for the next couple of months. Much food had been gathered, dried, and stored for the season of cold days. Wood had been gathered as well as coal. The cave was ready for the cold. And cold came gently at first and then in a fury they had never seen, but then they were not new to cold. Ki'ti soon would begin the stories of the season of cold days. Alu and Inst both discovered they were pregnant. Alu had lost a baby on the trek to Cave Sumbrel. Inst had never been pregnant. Both were very excited. Over the seasons of colorful leaves and cold days, Totamu found that the new plants were much more successful at easing her breathing. She wasn't back to normal by any means, but she was better. She had moved her sleeping place. She was grateful to be as far away from the smoke of the hearth as possible, but in a place so as not to become too chilled.

In the season of colorful leaves, Liho and Lamk had built shelter lean-tos for the dogs by cutting slender trees in the understory and covering them with dirt and vegetation. They had done a good job of building and the winds didn't take off the roofing. The dogs definitely used the lean-tos. They still curled up, but it appeared they were more comfortable. The older dogs gravitated to the center of the lean-tos. Ahriku continued to stay by Ki'ti's side.

The men had gathered fifty bamboo canes each approximately six-man strides long. They had gathered thirty crosspieces that were about three man strides long. They had all been placed in an empty cave where the floor was relatively level. They were ready for the women when it came time to make rafts. The wood would have to be carried to the lake, but that would not be a problem. Even some of the younger women could carry them when they dried out. The men assumed the job was theirs, but they never knew for certain. What they did know is that the women would wait until the season of new leaves to gather the vines they'd use to attach the bamboo canes together. Everyone who had enjoyed fish before the ashfall looked forward to the fish they could have by the upcoming season of warm nights.

Chapter 7

The season of cold days was fierce. Hardwoods had lost most of their leaves. Wamumur had pulled on his pants and boots and jacket in addition to his tunic. The pants, boots, and jacket were made in the style of the garments of the man with the green bag. They were designed for warmth. He walked the rock walk, something he did most mornings. It gave him some exercise and freed him from the busy noise of the cave. Chamul-na walked with him this morning. He, too, was dressed in the new style for the cold weather.

"Wise One, there is something I think you should know, but I don't think the People should have to know."

"What?" Wamumur asked, troubled with where the conversation was heading. He picked a small end branch from a tree next to the rock walk, pulled back the bark, leaned against the rock wall, and picked his teeth.

"When Nanichak-na and I went north on the ancient path, we came to a dead end at a rope bridge."

"You told of that," Wamumur replied shifting his back to avoid a sharp rock.

"Yes. What we didn't mention is that while there, Nanichak-na went to sleep. I kept feeling watched. You know what I mean?"

"I do know what it is to feel watched. Go on." Wamumur was leaning against the rock wall more comfortably.

"I looked across the river and saw what was watching me. It was an ape or hairy man. Twice my height."

"Surely you exaggerate!" Wamumur laughed genuinely, believing that Chamul-na was teasing.

"I assure you I do not exaggerate. The hair stood up on my neck. I waked Nanichak-na and he had the same response." He did a strong palm strike.

Wamumur got serious quickly. "Why did you wait so long to speak?" The old man stood straight, no longer leaning on the rock wall.

"We didn't speak because we didn't want to frighten anyone. The beast is on the other side of the river days and days and days from here. It didn't threaten us, only looked at us. It didn't follow us."

"So why are you telling me now?"

"I've been thinking a lot. I think there is a story there somewhere with a significance that says that you don't build bridges unless you welcome what is on the other side to come to your side. Is this making sense?"

"You think somehow that the man that is twice your height is responsible for the people's having left this place?"

"You've gone further with this story than I did. I just feel really burdened to know and not to share."

"Chamul-na, I don't know what to make of this. Are you suggesting I create a story based on what we don't really know?"

"I don't know what I'm suggesting, but I feel a lot better now that someone else knows."

"I will think on this, Chamul-na. It is good not to withhold information."

Wamumur went back to the cave and sat with Emaea. He told her the conversation that had just transpired. From her sleeping mat, Ki'ti had heard every word. She held her little bagged owl tightly in her fist. Ahriku got up and looked at her and whined so quietly that it was all but inaudible. He knew that she was terribly stressed. He licked his whiskers. His large teeth were startlingly white.

Ki'ti got up and walked to Wamumur and Emaea. "Would you walk with me?" she asked. She began putting on warm clothes.

Her new parents noticed she was disturbed. As soon as Emaea put on warm clothes, they got up and went with her, wondering what was disturbing her.

When they got far down the rock walk, Ki'ti stopped and asked whether they could sit. The three sat on the edge of the rock walk with Ki'ti in the center.

"You will have to punish me again," she groaned.

"What are you talking about?" Emaea asked concerned.

"I overheard your talking. I know the answer to Chamul-na's thoughts about the story."

"Have you been in someone else's mind web, Ki'ti?" Wamumur asked bruskly.

"No. I have listened to my owl."

"What?" Wamumur asked. He had no idea what she meant.

Ki'ti took the owl from the pouch and handed it to Wamumur. "Feel it. Can you hear it sing?"

Wamumur looked at her. "Little Girl," he said, "I feel nothing. Are you letting your imagination run wild?"

"No. Would you please let Emaea try it?"

Emaea took the little owl and held it in her hand. She could literally feel a vibration from the owl. Was that what Ki'ti meant by singing, she wondered.

Emaea asked, "How do you hear the singing?"

"When I lie down at night and the bag slides to the earth, I can hear the singing. It sings quietly but it sings the same song repeatedly."

Emaea leaned down so that her head was on the rock walk. She put the little owl near her ear. To her amazement, she could hear a buzzing sound. She sat up and handed the owl to Wamumur. "You try it," she said noncommittally.

Wamumur laid himself down on his side and placed the owl on the ground near his ear. He could hear some buzzing but could not make out any words.

"I hear buzzing," he said.

"I heard what sounded like a word or two in our language," Emaea said.

Wamumur said, "Let's shorten this. Little Girl, tell us what the owl told you."

"Are you going to punish me for listening?" she asked.

"Little Girl, what did I just say to you?"

"Forgive me, Wise One," she said and began.

"The owl was made" she laboriously flashed 200, "years ago. It was made by a man named Torkiz who was a stone worker. He made animals come to life from stone. He came from where Wamumur came from, a place called Onesto."

At the sound of Onesto, Wamumur was startled. He blanched. Emaea noticed but remained silent. Ki'ti accurately brought up something his mind web had forgotten. She was right. That was the name of the place where he first lived. He could see the place beside a small river where the land gently rose in soft hills behind. On the hills hardwood forests grew with plenty of bamboo and shrubs. It was warmer there.

Ki'ti continued, "The owl has not sung since the stone worker died. It recognized the owl that Wamumur has, and it began to sing. The owl I have belonged to Torkiz, and the owl Wamumur has belonged to the woman Torkiz loved, Ilea.

"The people where Torkiz lived feared him for creating animals from stone because the animals were so real. They drove him away. After he was gone, they found he had carved," she flashed 100, "owls from yellow stone that seemed to have a light inside. The people didn't like Torkiz but they came to love the yellow owls. Eventually, the people who drove Torkiz away became the Band of the Owl and they carried the little owls in pouches around their necks like the stone worker did. Only he carried three of the owls. The third owl is broken.

"The stone worker traveled to a far country. Here he lived beside the People called Kotukna. They were People like us. They lived in our caves. The old stone worker lived alone in the cave of the animals. Later, a few of the Kotukna including Ilea lived with him there. It was the happiest time of his life. There were more of the Kotukna living in the area. They used the ancient path for visiting. It was the main path. There are other paths, too. They go west. The main path was there when they came to this area. The owl doesn't know who built the path.

"Other humans came. They looked like a mix of the People and the Others. They lived on both sides of the big river. They were the Mol. They lived all over this area in small groups, and they wanted to visit without traveling to the source of the big river, so they made the bridge. Some of the Mol died making the bridge. They were very tall people. The man with the green bag was Mol. They built the bridge and used it for a long time. When lesser ropes gave out, they repaired them.

"Then two things happened. Big giant hairy human-like apes moved into the area on the other side of the big river. And a group of the Others moved up from the south. The Others were determined to kill the People. The People never knew why.

"Once, it got so bad that even during the season of cold days in the white rain, the People moved north on the ancient path. They left things behind just to get out before the Others killed them. One of them, a woman, left the owl that is around your neck, Wise One. The leather band holding the pouch broke and she didn't know it."

"At the same time, the man-like apes were frightening the Mol near the bridge. The Mol and the Kotukna fled west into the tall mountains. The stone worker hid from the Others in a well-concealed cave. He was too old to flee.

"It is said that a hawk fed him until he died. It was not just a single hawk but generations of hawks. While concealed and alone, the old man would come down from time to time to the cave of the animals where he worked the fire breathing flying snake with legs.

"It is said that one day the Others found that cave and they lit a firebrand and explored it. They saw the fire breathing flying snake with legs. It matched one of their legends and frightened them so badly that they left the area following the lesser river to the south all the way to the sea.

"It is said that it is not wise to build bridges for they will be used for good and for evil. Things are divided for a reason according to Wisdom. The river divides the two lands."

Wamumur and Emaea were dumbfounded. Ki'ti was a conduit for information that none of the others really accessed. Her ways of knowing were vastly more expansive than theirs. They could not build enough barriers to keep her from the information. Wamumur tried to determine whether this information was dangerous. He also wondered whether the information came from Wisdom to be helpful to the People. He could not compare it to the mind web trap, but he had no experience with this buzzing owl. He felt caution was imperative.

"Little Girl, why did you fail to report this until now?"

"Wise One, I feared more punishment and I reasoned that it had not urged me to do anything at all, so I listened. It sings only one song, the song I just told you."

"Little Girl, concealing things is like lying. Do you understand that?"

"No."

"Well, I am telling you it is. You are forbidden from this day to conceal anything else. You are also forbidden to participate even as a listener to these other sources that others don't hear or understand. Do you understand me?"

"Yes, Wise One, I do understand."

"Didn't you have unsettling feelings about listening to the song?"

"Yes."

"What am I going to do with you, Little Girl?"

"Please spare me, Wise One. I promise to report anything that is not normal that communicates from this moment for forever."

"Can you make the owl stop buzzing?"

"I don't know."

"Take my owl. Does it buzz?"

Ki'ti put the owl to her ear. "Your owl is silent."

"Then," Wamumur said, "trade owls with me."

Ki'ti surrendered her owl and kept his. She put it in her pouch and put the pouch around her neck.

"Little Girl, you are not to speak of any of this. I cannot verify what you've said. Right now, I don't want Emaea to get into this stuff. So you will remain totally silent on this. Is that clear?"

Emaea felt invisible somehow.

"Yes, Wise One. I shall speak to no one about this."

"That includes your dog and sticks or any other . . . ."

Ki'ti broke in, "I will obey unequivocally."

"I will not punish you this time. I want you to realize that I could have because you knew what you did was wrong. I'm getting to understand you at this point. You now have a burden. By not punishing you, I have given you no outlet for what you did wrong. You are not freed from it. Do you understand?"

Ki'ti tried very hard to understand what the Wise One had said. She would get the fringes of it and then it would dissolve in lack of understanding.

"No."

"Let me say this. If I punish you, then you have made sacrifice for your disobedience. You understand that?"

"Yes."

"If I fail to punish you, you have not made sacrifice for your disobedience."

"You mean there is no way to get away free without sacrifice?"

"That is exactly what I mean. It means you have yet to give me the sacrifice for which your disobedience obligated you."

"Oh, that is not good."

"I want you to feel that. I want you to understand that. I want you to live with that. I want you to reason it."

"So many people, when they get away with wrongdoing, are sure they have gotten away free of punishment. Children call it getting away free," Ki'ti said, still struggling with what her few years of life had shown her.

"They have done nothing but lie to themselves. It's bad enough to lie, but to believe your own lie is nothing but irretrievably tangled mind web. Ki'ti," he continued, "why would you seek answers from the words of children?"

Ki'ti was tired. She had believed that some lucky people got off free of punishment when they did things wrong. Now she was told that they had believed a lie. Such freedom was not true. The wrongdoing stuck to you if you were not punished. She had begged for mercy. That meant she had to carry her own wrongdoing forever? Was that mercy? Was there such a thing as mercy? Did mercy mean unpunished but obligated? She wanted to sleep. She had to deal with the idea that getting by with something was a lie that led to irretrievably tangled mind web. She had so much to learn. She felt foolish, having sought answers from the words of children. Now she had an obligation to the Wise One. She wondered whether there was any way to remove the obligation.

Emaea had listened. She knew what Wamumur was saying but he would take small points and talk to her about them as if she were older than her years. She realized that Ki'ti was picking up wisdom fast, but sometimes she felt that Wamumur went too fast. Then she had a horrible thought. She wondered whether he felt his years were coming to a close. She realized she must guard herself in what she said or whether she might interfere. She wondered why Wamumur did not hand her the owl long enough for her to verify what Ki'ti said, and then she realized that he probably already was convinced that she had the story straight. She had named his place of origin and apparently she was correct. There was something else. And then she had a spark of enlightenment. Was it the huge man-like ape? Why wouldn't People talk about it?

Accompanied by Emaea, Ki'ti returned to the cave and her stories. She needed to submerge herself in her work so she didn't think too much about what had taken place. There would be time to sort it all out in the days to come. The season of cold days was here and she had to be prepared.

Wamumur paced the rock walk. He was troubled about something that was in his mind web and he seemed incapable of pulling it up. When Ki'ti said Onesto, he had a memory that he could not retrieve. And embedded in the memory was a visual memory of a huge man-like ape. Instead of fear, what he felt for the creature was overwhelming sympathy. What was his mind web telling him? Ki'ti's story made it seem that the Mol were frightened by the creature. But nothing in the story said the man-like ape did anything to them. Even when Chamul-na and Nanichak-na saw the one they saw, it was not threatening, but they were frightened. Why? Just because it was larger than they were? Wamumur continued pacing. The People gave him great space when he paced like this. He was Wise One and he was thinking. He stopped and touched the rock wall. His fingers traced a small fracture. He strained his mind web.

Wamumur wondered whether he needed to go where the man-like ape had been seen. He really didn't want to make that trip, but he could not bring the old into focus. He returned to the cave.

"Little Girl," he called.

Ki'ti came to the Wise One quickly. Ahriku trotted behind her like a shadow. She wondered whether the Wise One had changed his mind.

"Come walk with me."

She took his hand and they walked outside.

Finally he said, "What else can you tell me about the man-like ape?"

"I don't know, Wise One."

"Hold my owl and think into the story. When you get to the man-like ape, look at the images in your mind web and tell me what you see."

They sat on the rock walk ledge. Ki'ti held the buzzing owl and shut her eyes. She began to go through the story. When she saw the man-like ape, she studied.

"Are you there?" he asked.

"Yes," she replied.

"Then look carefully and tell me what are the surroundings of the man-like ape."

"He is in a forest of bamboo. He eats bamboo with the black and white bears. They get along well. He also eats other plants. He does not eat meat like we do. Oh, sometimes they might eat little animals."

"Are there many of them?"

"No, Wise One. People fear them so they try to kill them off. There were few when Torkiz lived here. There are fewer now."

Wamumur had his answer. His memory that he had not been able to see was clear. He could hear the shouting. He could see the slaughter. His Band of the Owl had killed a man-like ape. It was female. It had a baby. The baby cried just like People cried when someone died. The Band of the Owl killed the baby. They ate the meat from both animals. He had felt it was so wrong. The ape was not something they killed for food. It had not harmed them. He felt that his People had done something very wrong. He ate the meat and then, feeling guilty, he had vomited it up. He retched for hours. When he spoke to his parents about it, he was punished severely for his thoughts. It was just before he had been taken. Being punished for what he thought was right had made it easier to learn to love the People who took him away from the killing. The Band of the Owl had been killing the large man-like apes trying to get rid of all of them. As big as they were, the apes had not fought back.

"Did the Mol kill the man-like apes?" he asked.

"No, they just feared them. Once they saw the creatures, the Mol came over on the bridge to live on this side of the big river. One of the apes walked out on the bridge one day and the Mol got so frightened that they cut one of the sides of the bridge. The creature on the bridge fell into the river. No more of the creatures tried to cross the bridge, but the Mol decided to leave the area and move west. The People knew the Mol and they left with them partly because of the creatures and partly because the Others were killing People."

She wiggled to find a more comfortable place. Ahriku stood, walked around in a single circle, and curled into a ball next to her leg, tucking his tail around his legs.

Wamumur was in a spiral of time and fear and space. The People, the Mol, the Others, and the man-like ape could not all live in the same place. They would kill to avoid it. They would flee to avoid it. Why? Wamumur was no closer to an answer than when he was a child himself. That the apes did not compete with his People for food was something he either never knew or it didn't get stored in his mind web. But here in this place, all four had found that they could not co-exist. Then it appeared that all fled and they had come into a place where only they and some man-like apes lived separated by a big river at great distance. Wisdom must have it right, barriers are there for a purpose and to build bridges might not be wise. There must be a story in there somewhere, but what was the story?

Wamumur sat there for a very long time. Ki'ti didn't know what to do so she began to review the stories and remove her mind web from the things of the past. The man-like ape did not frighten her because it was not a predator and it did not seem warlike. She tried to understand the emphasis on the man-like ape but she could find nothing on which to base understanding. She began to feel that all this talk about what Chamul-na and Nanichak-na found at the big river was getting far more attention than it deserved.

Wamumur was overpowered by thoughts of how small the world seemed to be. He had not thought of his original People for a very, very long time. Now suddenly he was confronted with yellow owls that he remembered, someone named Torkiz who carved the yellow owls, the name of his People, the huge man-like ape, the people of the man with the green bag called the Mol, and how impossible it seemed for various humans to live together. He had traveled many miles and came right back to where he'd been as a child figuratively, not in space. Somehow, he still felt protective of the man-like apes. He decided that he would try to prevent his People from approaching the big river. He would not make a story of the man-like apes because that would simply draw his People with curiosity to confront the creatures and that could lead to fear and bloodshed.

Wamumur then began to think of his own behavior earlier that day. He reasoned that he was a poor parent. What had he done? Here he was, having been so sure that he was right in having sympathy for the man-like ape. He'd been severely punished for it. Then when Ki'ti did the same thing with the man with the green bag, she was severely punished. What manner of terrible spiral was he in? He was as awful a parent as his father had been. Had he become what his father was? He had to put an end to that now. He told Ki'ti to bring Emaea. The girl ran to do his bidding with Ahriku right on her heels.

Emaea came and the three of them walked to the north end of the rock walk where they sat.

"I want to apologize to Ki'ti, Emaea, but I want to do it in front of you. I have been poor at parenting. I have demanded much of her while demanding little of myself. I have not as great a sensitivity to ways of knowing as she has. I have tried to tie her into a pouch so that I can control what she learns. I cannot be prepared for her ways of knowing because she is more sensitive than I am. Wisdom seems to have poured a lot of ways of knowing into her. Who would have thought that a yellow owl would sing a story? I have put fear into her so that she does not come when she should to discuss what has occurred. I have made her feel guilty for doing what she sees as perfectly normal to do."

"Many years ago, my People killed a man-like ape and her baby. They ate them. I felt wretched so I vomited. I told my parents of my sympathy for the man-like ape and that I didn't think we should kill them. I was punished severely. Ki'ti felt sympathy for the man with the green bag and his family. She was punished severely. I am the worst of my first father. I feel much failure. I ask, should we return her to her first parents?"

Ki'ti turned to the Wise One and kneeled beside him, not waiting for Emaea to speak. She put her hand on his chest "Wise One, you have taught me so much. You may not be the best parent ever, but you are not a bad parent. I know that you love me and more than that, you love the People. I know that you are trying to build me to be as good a Wise One as you are, so the People have a good Wise One in the future. My first parents told me they have no understanding of how to raise a Wise One. So of all the People here, you and Emaea are the best."

"I hoped you'd be better than I, Little Girl."

"Wise One, Wisdom made me and you of dirt. Wisdom didn't make People perfect, or there would be no need for Wisdom."

Emaea laughed a light lovely laugh. It came out before she could catch it. A little girl had taken what Emaea knew to Wamumur was an enormous issue and trimmed it down to the right size. She had done it so that Wamumur never lost authority. Truly, Ki'ti's days as a child had passed.

"Little Girl, I forgive you for earlier. To forgive doesn't get you away free from what we discussed, but it means I no longer hold it against you. I do still insist that any communication that you have that is nor normal People-to-People communication, you tell me or Emaea about immediately. Is that clear? I may not have as wide a range of ways of knowing as you have, but I have more Wisdom than you."

"Yes. I promise, Wise One. I promise unequivocally."

"I wish I had greater understanding how to be a parent, but I will ask Wisdom to guide me and I will check things with Emaea before I confront you, Little Girl. I don't want to hurt you, but your sensitivity leaves you open to abuse from the spiritual world. That is something I do understand. That would be worse than abuse from anyone."

"I will try to be more careful, Wise One. Please, Wise One, can we protect the man-like apes?"

"I have already decided we will protect them by keeping silent about them. If we speak of them, the curiosity that lives within will cause People to go there and if they go, I can assure you that because of fear the man-like apes will die. So we will look at the path as leading to a dead end, a broken bridge."

"I see," she replied and she did.

Emaea was feeling a sense of relief that she had not felt before. She also felt complimented in a strange way in that she would now be considered as co-parent to Ki'ti. Wamumur had been overbearing in his approach, shoving her aside, and she had sat back. She would do so no longer.

Ki'ti got a hand up from Wamumur and took it. She stood and threw her arms open wide. She hugged the man. Wamumur was warmed. He had been harder on himself than at any other time in his life. He picked up the child and hugged her. She wrapped her arms around his neck.

"I love you to the bottom of my belly, my father and Wise One," Ki'ti said, and meant it. With her arms around his neck she could not do a palm strike. She knew he knew how sincere she was. Emaea felt that the world had come into balance. Things were good, very good.

In the cave, Kai continued on with his toolmaking. He was becoming better as time passed. Ermol-na spent time with him teaching him some of the finer points and showing him how the man with the green bag achieved a certain edge. Kai listened carefully and was a good learner. He was determined not to let his time of inactivity go for nothing. He would contribute in the ways he could.

During the cold season confinement, Meeka became woman and joined with Lamul. Alu and Guy-na had a baby boy named Minal and Inst had a baby girl named Walu. Alu and Guy-na had lost their first baby on the trek to Cave Sumbrel, so this child was cherished as a great gift. The cave was alive with children. Totamu was so pleased. She had been very concerned for a while that the People were shrinking. They started at seventeen at the time of Baambas and had grown to fifty-one through mergers and births. That was a great size for the People. It was big enough for defense and large enough to have numbers of hunters to provide for the needs of the large group. It also was large enough that the amount of meat hunted had to be significant. Either a large number of small animals was needed or a large one. Procurement of meat was excellent at the present. For the future, during the season of cold days some of the women worked diligently on making thin rope from which fish nets would be constructed. Fish would be a welcome addition to their diet.

The season of new leaves arrived and the women began to find excitement in watching vines grow that had real strength to them. They were excited about the raft building and adding to their stores by fishing. *By early in the season of warm nights,* they thought, *they would be able to begin working on the rafts.* They dreamed of the season of warm nights.

During the season of cold days, there was a time when short days began to grow longer. People guessed at the day of the change, having no tools to guide them but having a general sense of the position of the sun and length of days. When the longer days were established, the People set age. If a child had been born before the last short day of the year, then the child was a year old. If the child were born after the days began to lengthen, the child's age was nothing until the next season of cold days was completed. They judged age at the completion of a year, not the beginning.

Totamu turned sixty-five. That age was unheard of but she was amazingly well for her age. Her cough was still present and she became short of breath when walking uphill, but she managed with the new leaves. Wamumur was pressing right behind her at sixty-two and Emaea at sixty. Wamumur had some pain in his legs but when the weather warmed usually that improved significantly. He did better when he could move about. Emaea was surprisingly free of aches and pains or debilitating conditions. Ermol-na at thirty-nine still had black hair without a single strand of white. The only other person over thirty who had color in his hair was Wamumur who still had his brown streak at the left temple, a short streak, but a streak nevertheless. Even Grypchon-na and Hahami-na were white headed.

The People had resumed the grooming habits they had before leaving for Cave Kwa. The Others who had joined them had picked up the habits of the People and they kept their hair combed, nails cleaned, and teeth picked. Clothing was washed off when it became too soiled for good hygiene. They were careful to keep the cave swept and the bedding shaken out and rolled during the day. Food was given to the dogs or removed to the refuse pile after meals, unless there was further use for it. After eating the marrow, no bones were permitted to be tossed carelessly on the cave floor. Small ones were tossed into the fire, larger ones were given to the dogs for food or stored outside by the refuse pile for burning as fuel or for conversion to tools or other necessities when needed. The People were altogether healthy except for the residuals from the ashfall.

The season of new leaves turned to the season of warm nights and the women continued looking for vines. They would bring samples and Totamu would determine the vines weren't ready yet. Likichi was beginning to wonder whether they could catch fish in the season of colorful leaves. She thought it would take that long before Totamu would be finally satisfied with the proffered vines.

But the day came when Meeka brought in a vine from near the field where the men would run the beasts over the ledge. Totamu held up the vine and showed the women. "This is what we are looking for! Find many of these and we will be ready to build rafts," she said encouragingly. The women examined the vine. The next day they planned to hunt for comparable vines.

The following day was stormy. The rain left the air clean and fragrant but put a damper on their vine hunting. The day after that was lovely and the women who were not minding the children left early in various directions in pairs to vine hunt. By high sun, they had baskets brimming full of vines. Some women repeatedly wrapped vines over their heads to keep them from tangling and wore them back to the cave.

The men agreed to build temporary tents in the lowland by the lake so that the raft builders could be closer to their work. A few people would remain at the caves and the majority would go to the lake to tend to the raft building and net making. Domur and Manak, Alu and Guy-na, and Lai, Olintak and Slamika would remain at the cave since they had infants. Fish baskets were already made with lids so fish couldn't jump out, and leather strap handles made it easier to carry fish filled baskets.

Kai's leg had mended but Totamu insisted he take it easy for a while. He and Mitrak and Ketra would go to the lake but he would not be running back and forth. His leg had mended amazingly well. He was weak from disuse of the leg, but there was no significant limp. *He had been lucky,* the People thought. He had become proficient in tool making so he planned to carry a number of broken pieces to repair while at the lake.

Men began to carry the bamboo logs to the lake and set up tents. It was an exciting time. Most of the People had little if any memory of the bamboo rafts. It would be a time to learn. Finally, those who were going to the lake began to walk through the forest and down the hill to the water. Mothers planned to teach the children to swim so they'd be safe. A few adults didn't know how to swim so they were urged not to go out on the rafts or into the water until they learned.

The men laid the poles at the water's edge while Totamu officiously oversaw the laying of every pole. The poles had a diameter a little longer than the hand of the men from heel of the hand to the longest finger. They laid them out so that the widest part was nearest the water and the top of the pole was higher on land. That would make getting the rafts into water easier. The women took the vines and wrapped the large end of one pole to the next pole until seven poles had been tied together about two arms length from the base of the raft following Totamu's directions. Then they took a short pole and wrapped it horizontally, making a crosspiece to the long poles about a half a body length from the end of the wrapped poles. Totamu demonstrated how to do it and watched to be sure the wrapping was done right. They made an additional wrapping of the long poles about midway on the raft and placed a crosspiece near that wrapping. Finally, the narrowest part of the long poles was wrapped with the vines about an arm's length from the end and another crosspiece was added.

Before they completed another raft, the People tested the first one. Kai had been busy making the long poles they would use to propel the rafts. Grypchon-na and Likichi had been feverishly finishing nets.

The raft was dragged into the water. It took eight men to get it launched. Pechki waded out into the water once the raft was afloat and stepped onto it. Totamu wanted to go but didn't want to get wet. She saw that the raft was very good. Water did come over the woman's feet but that was normal for bamboo rafts. It wouldn't sink, just bow somewhat where the weight was. Pechki gave Ghanya a hand and he stepped aboard with a grin from ear to ear. He'd never seen a bamboo raft and he was fascinated. To him, it was the best creation of all time. He was about to give Minagle a hand up when he was offered a hand to get off so the raft could be brought to shore. They didn't want to do anything at that moment but be certain the raft was working properly. The children had been watching wide eyed.

The People quickly completed the remaining four rafts with Totamu looking over their shoulders, and each raft was tested. All the rafts were good. They decided to have a trial of the rafts. Pechki took a long pole and stood toward the large end of a raft. Ghanya got on with Minagle. They sat on a crosspiece in the middle of the raft.

Likichi, Amey, Flayk, and Chamul-na each took a long pole. They boarded and were joined by others who were eager to know what floating on a raft was like. Hahami-na and Blanagah got on Flayk's raft; Kai and Mitrak boarded Amey's raft; Liho and Lamk climbed aboard Chamul-na's raft and he told them to sit carefully on the middle crosspiece, wondering whether they really knew how to swim. Likichi took Emaea and Ki'ti. Slowly, the rafts headed into the lake in different directions. Chamul-na kept near the shore because he was concerned about his passengers' swimming ability. The day was bright, sunny, and calm. Only the lightest breeze blew from the west.

Liho said in a loud voice, "Look down there!" She could see several large fish with yellow tails, a yellowish cast to their bodies, and gray on top. "They look like the sun!" Chamul-na had spotted the golden line fish but had no idea what kind of fish they were. He'd never seen one. He'd been observing them from his vantage point of standing on the raft. He was definitely encouraged by the presence of fish that were the right size for eating.

Ki'ti was so tense as she sat with Emaea that Emaea asked her, "You do know how to swim, Little Girl?"

"Oh, yes," Ki'ti replied.

Likichi spoke out, "She is a very good swimmer, Emaea. Why do you ask?"

"Just because of her tension. She's as tight as a runner's leg."

Ki'ti said in her own defense, "I am just so excited. This is wonderful! We can't walk on water, but look at Likichi. She can stand on it!"

Likichi leaned her head back and laughed and laughed. Emaea joined her. It was a good day, a very good day.

The rafts returned to the shore and baskets made for fishing were placed on the rafts. Kai had made fish nets attached to a pole to which a green branch had been looped. The fish net was made from plant fibers to form rope, which had been tied into small squares by knotting. The nets were secured to the looped branch by rope fibers beginning at the pole and threaded through the holes in the net and over the loop and back through the net in a continuous sequence until they were tied back at the pole. Minnows could get through but large fish would be trapped. This time, Pechki took a basket and placed it where the passengers had sat and she pushed off. She headed for the area where their creek emptied into the lake. She held the net to see if she could catch a fish in it if she saw one. She spotted two fish that were slender and silver, but she thought them too small. She waited patiently.

Chamul-na put his pole and fish net on the raft, climbed aboard, and started to push off with the pole for the area where they'd seen the yellow fish.

Ghanya came running splashing into the deeper water. Chamul-na had forgotten the fish basket! The two men exchanged a smile and Chamul-na left, pushing off with hardly a droplet of water falling from his pole.

The other rafts headed out.

Men began to construct a fire pit surrounded by cooking sticks. They had always put the fish on sticks with the meat facing the fire to cook them. The fish looked like sentinels surrounding the fire pit once they were stuck on the sticks and the sticks were set in the ground. Most of the people on shore were scurrying about hunting for rocks to surround the fire pit, or gathering wood, or selecting sticks that would hold the fish. A few ravens in the trees were making their raven-talk noises as they watched the people below.

Ermi and Kai were teaching the children who could walk how to swim. When they would get cold in the water, he'd send them to shore and those who had warmed up would come to the water. Smig was the first to learn how to float. He thought watching the sky was great and having water in his ears did not bother him. Tita was a natural for swimming. She automatically placed her face fully in the water and opened her eyes. She propelled herself instantly because of something she wanted to see. In fact, Kai lifted her out of the water because she failed to lift her head to breathe. After that, she took time to make herself poke her head up to breathe and down she'd go again, as if the world of water was her own personal place. Kai had to pull her out when her lips began to turn blue from the chill. She did not want to have to sit wrapped in skins while her shivers stopped. She loved the new water world. Arkan-na spoke sharply to her about going near the water unless an adult supervised. She did not like it, but she promised to stay on shore unless someone watched her. She had seen fish down there and really wanted to know where their homes were.

While Smig loved the water, his twin, Ekoy, did not share his opinion. It was hard to get him to enter the water and even harder to get him to get his face wet. Ekuktu and Wamumal had to take him aside and let him know there was no choice in the matter—he needed to straighten up and act like a strong boy so all could approve of him. When he realized approval entered in, he decided that he would have to do it, so his refusal and irritable behavior stopped, although his fear didn't. Kai and Ermi were firm with him and he learned.

Chamul-na had reservations about Liho and Lamk's swimming ability. Kai and Ermi took a break from the little ones and called Lamk, Liho, and Ki'ti. They came quickly. Ermi told all three of them to swim out to where Kai stood in the water, to touch him, and then to return to shore. Kai was out in the water at a good distance. First, Ki'ti entered the water. She swam strongly to Kai, touched him, turned and swam back to shore. Then Lamk entered the water. He was not a strong swimmer but managed to make it to Kai, although he was tired. Kai held him briefly and talked to him about swimming. Then Kai tossed him back into the water giving him a headstart. Lamk made it back. Then Liho entered the water. She made it halfway to Kai when she began to lose strength. Kai dived into the water and rescued her. She had technically been able to swim, but not competently enough for her to be considered water safe. For that matter, neither was Lamk. A new swim class was set up for Lamk and Liho. By the end of the season of warm nights all of the children would be proficient at swimming. It was a requirement for survival. Cold water or not, each member of the People had to be able to swim.

Chamul-na headed back to shore first. His basket was filled with snout trout (dark on top with white underbellies), gold line barbels (dark on top with yellow sides, darker yellow tail, and fins), ray finned fish (dark on top with light underbellies), and bullhead (catfish with mottled coloration). He had gathered about thirty fish. Likichi had thirty-five fish, mostly bullhead and snout trout. Pechki had twenty-five fish but her net had come apart. She had mostly gold line barbels. Amey had twenty snout trout. Flayk had thirty-seven bullheads and two gold line barbels. They not only had enough fish for the group at the lake but they could send some up to the cave. Ghanya volunteered and took a basket of fish to the people at the cave. They were just getting ready to cook and were delighted with the fish that had been brought cleaned and ready for cooking.

At the lake, the fire was crackling and the fish were cleaned fairly quickly, speared, and set to cook. The initial remains were taken into the lake and dropped off. Before the remains had been taken to the lake, the ravens each had stolen a piece and headed down shore a good distance away.

Parents were given the fish for their children first, because they needed to be deboned. The young children had no idea where the bones were, and parents didn't want them to swallow bones. Deboned fish remains were tossed aside while bold ravens would come swooping down to raid the refuse before it was taken out to the lake and dumped.

Children played while the parents ate. Frakja came running with something pinched between his fingers. At the water's edge, he'd found a little freshwater shrimp. He had pinched it too tightly. Grypchon-na explained that they didn't eat those and the child needed to leave them alone. Frakja was taught that he needed to pick up living things carefully so that they didn't die in the process. Grypchon-na showed him where he'd pinched too tightly. For the future Frankja was permitted to play with shrimp in his open hand and then admonished to let them go back to the water. Grypchon-na explained that the shrimp were a little like dogs. They ate the foods that drifted down from the dead fish and from what People ate that night. It kept the bottom of lakes from being garbage heaps, like the dogs ate the meat off bones on land so they kept the living areas from becoming a rotten meat heap. Frakja was fascinated and listened carefully. He would be gentle with his hands in the future.

"Will they eat this one since it's dead?" he asked.

"I think so," his father answered. "Throw it far out."

All of the adults wanted to know how the different fish tasted. There was much trading during the meal. Most people favored the snout trout and the catfish. Totamu favored the ray finned fish. She thought the others were too picky about bones.

The men relaxed that evening and discussed setting up drying racks the next day. Some were restless and wanted to return to hunting, but they wanted the women to have everything they needed for the care and preservation of fish before they returned to their hunting. They still had a number of bamboo poles. That evening they would transport the remaining poles to the lake while others found pole racks to set them on. The women could string rope between the poles and have enough room to dry the fish for the whole season of warm nights. All the adults were content with a day that had gone well. Kai was the only one who was concerned. One of his nets, the one Pechki used, had fallen apart and he wanted to fix it, but more than that he wanted to know why it came apart. He also realized that he probably should make spare nets for each raft. He knew that Ekuktu was talented in woodworking, so he decided to talk to him about the nets.

The sandy shoreline extended for a long distance. Ghanya asked Minagle if she'd like to run. They had been running for quite a while and enjoyed it. They walked to the shore and then began to run. Ki'ti watched them knowing she could not have kept up the speed. She was awed. She watched the whole run and the dip in the lake afterward. She dreamed some day of having someone with whom to join who would be as good a match as Ghanya and Minagle or Domur and Manak.

Babies were settled in the tents and adults watched as Wisdom sucked the color from the land making brilliant sunsets of the post-Baambas sky. The sky above was aglow with vivid reds and purples and yellows. They watched it reflect on the water of the lake. There was such peace.

Ki'ti leaned against Wamumur and whispered, "It wasn't always this peaceful here."

He smiled. "You are right. It wasn't. Aren't we blessed of Wisdom?"

"Yes, Father, we are blessed of Wisdom."

Emaea smiled. In all her life she had never thought she could be so happy. She leaned against the aurochs skin that had been propped against the hillside. She felt a warmth for the People. This, she mused, must be how Wisdom had planned for them to live. She would treasure the day and the evening and the night as something to savor from time to time from her mind web. And, oh, how good that trout was! She burped.

"That fish still sending up little bubbles?" Ki'ti laughed, joined by Emaea and Wamumur.

Wamumur shoved Ki'ti so she fell into the sand. Then he tickled her. She was so shocked that she almost lost her breath laughing. Wamumur had definitely changed as a parent. She was glad he found out that he was being like his father. It turned him into someone kinder and gentler and sometimes really funny. The difference was not lost on Totamu. She had no idea what caused the difference, but she was finally at ease about how Ki'ti was being raised.

By the end of the season of warm nights they had a huge supply of meat, both animal and fish; they had lots of plants that had been dried and placed in baskets, safe for use from the present until the following season of warm nights. They had skins to make into garments and all were prepared for the upcoming cave time.

By the end of the season, all the children ages three and above knew how to swim well enough to survive in water. Women had learned how to row a raft. Even Domur, Alu, Inst, and Olintak, who had been at the caves all season of warm nights, were brought down to learn raft rowing for several days. The break had been a delight and provided something to talk about during the hours of nursing. They knew even if no one else did the wonderful value of having a cave of about fifty inhabitants. The variety was great. It made life more interesting and People could do what they were good at. They had endless activities to keep them alive in life, activities that would have been denied them if they had been a People of only eight. The People were healthy physically and in the way they treated each other. Life was very good.

Chapter 8

The seasons of cold days were warmer and the vivid colors in the sunsets had dimmed. It had been five years since the rafts had been put on the lake. Fishing had become totally integrated into meat acquisition. Hunters still checked the outlying lands for signs of life. The People noticed that at the edges of the ashfall, plants were spearing their way through. They had no desire to go there but were heartened that the place was springing back to life and color would return to the ash-covered land. Chamul-na and Nanichak-na made one more trip to the rope bridge and discovered that as hard as they searched, they did not see a single man-like ape. They listened and failed to hear anything that sounded like one. They had taken each of three of the well-concealed but still viable paths to the north that led off from the larger ancient path. The paths went into the high mountains, many of which were like Notempa and Baambas, covered with what they knew now was white rain. They had found one encampment, probably Mol, possibly only a year old, but no people. Other hunters had scoured the areas to the northeast, east, and southeast but found nothing. There had been some earthquake activity that was very strong recently. It was thought to have originated in the west but there was no way for them to be sure and Ki'ti's ways of knowing didn't tell her.

Nanichak-na and Chamul-na had gathered their hunting gear and planned again to check the paths that led west to see if they could find answers to the earthquake activity. If it seemed that earthquakes were getting closer to their area, they wanted to know. They left quietly one morning and headed to the ancient path. They walked briskly and listened to the forest that they had come to know well. All sounded normal.

Meanwhile, Neamu-na, Mootmu-na, and Ermol-na had taken younger men with them to patrol again the northeast, east, and southeast. Grypchon-na and Manak went south to take another look at the ashfall landscapes.

About five days into the scouting, Manak said, "Father, what is that?"

Grypchon-na looked where Manak pointed. He squinted and could barely make out a few dots that appeared to be moving on the ashfall. They chose places to sit on the mountainside to watch the moving dots. Both took the time to eat and water themselves.

"I think that might be People," Manak said with wonder.

"Anybody crossing all that ashfall would have to be crazy. Nobody would know where to go."

"That's true."

They continued to watch as the sun went from overhead to the west. Manak took the water bags to the closest creek and filled all of them. He returned with a question on his face.

"They are people, Son. There are four of them."

"Four people out on the ashfall. What are they thinking?"

"They seem to be following our old path," Grypchon-na said.

"How could they have found that?" Manak asked.

"Could they have already known where the path was?"

"You mean Abiedelai-na's people, the Others?" Manak was shocked at the idea. "Why would they want to come this way?"

"That is a very good question." Grypchon-na was not happy with the prospect of seeing them again. Their way of life was not like the People's; they were argumentative and did not think first about the welfare of the People. He loved Arkan-na's family, but then they had embraced the way of life of the People and were welcome. No one thought of them as Others but rather as People.

They continued to watch the arrival of the travelers from concealment at the edge of the forest. When the travelers reached the grassland, the four fell to the ground and touched the grass very much like they themselves had years ago.

Manak observed, "They are Others, Father. There is no question."

"You can see better than I. Are they ones we know?"

"I cannot be sure. I need them to get a little closer."

"Let's hope they move this way before Wisdom sucks the color from the land," Grypchon-na said while straining to see.

The four travelers got up and continued walking.

"One of them, the one that appears to be the leader, has something wrong with his arm. Something is really wrong with his arm!"

As time passed, Manak tried to see the face of the man with the odd arm. Leaping to his feet, he said, "Father that is Cue-na."

Grypchon-na and Manak rushed to meet the Others. They had had their differences in the past but it seemed the travelers had a real need and the two people were obliged to help. The Others grouped together, when they saw the two men approaching. It appeared that two men tried to protect two women.

Manak called out, "Cue-na!"

The oldest man looked up with tears forming in his eyes. He lifted one arm and fell to his knees.

Grypchon-na was the first to arrive and he took Cue-na's good hand to help him to stand. Grypchon-na was repulsed at Cue-na's bad arm. It stank.

"What happened to you?" he asked.

"War injury. I had to get the young people out to safety."

"Where are the Others?" Manak asked.

"Dead, all dead," Sum answered. "My wife, Keptu, and Aryna, and my father are all that are left."

Grypchon-na could see that they were dehydrated.

He offered a water bag. "Drink very slowly and not too much at one time. You will have plenty of water. Manak, go to camp and get a stretcher. Run with the wind."

Manak ran with everything in him. He was not a fast runner but he gave it what he had. It took two days to reach the camp. Lai and Guy-na were there. They took a stretcher and ran to meet the Others, making the run in a day.

Guy-na could not believe what had happened to his relatives. While they had been slaughtered, his family had grown and flourished in a land with People who were peace loving. The Winds of Change were strange and it seemed they were blowing again.

They loaded Cue-na on the stretcher. His fever was very high and he sweated profusely. They kept the water bags full at every chance because Cue-na's need was so great. Sum, Keptu, and Aryna were strangely silent. They only spoke when absolutely necessary. They seemed cowed and terrified.

By the time they reached the caves, the women had set up sleeping places for the Others and had made a specially soft spot for Cue-na. Totamu had heard about Cue-na's injury from Manak and she had little hope of his recovery. When a wound stank like Manak described, short of cutting off the limb and searing it with fire, she had no idea what to do. Caring for injury meant doing something immediately, not waiting for days and days and days.

She had a cup of blueberry tea while she considered what, if anything, she could do. While she waited, she gathered maggots to eat the decayed flesh on the wound.

It took four days for the group to reach the caves. On the third day, Cue-na died. The three young people were distraught. Except for Aryna, they did not remember the People well, and they were not sure they wanted to go to caves at all. They would have to speak the language of the People and that did not please them much. They felt their lives had literally fallen apart and there would be no way to resume a life. They felt lost and abandoned.

While the stretcher bearers carried Cue-na's body, Grypchon-na left the group to prepare the People to dig a grave in the area they had reserved for burials. He thought it ironic that their real first burial, discounting the one that was done quietly for Amey's dead baby, would be for one of the Others who had chosen to leave them after the ashfall sojourn. And Cue-na had been one of the most vocal about leaving. Life could deliver strange twists and turns, he knew.

When he arrived back home, the women set about rearranging the bedding and removing all trace of the place they had made for Cue-na. Minagle, Domur, Meeka, and Liho were excited to see Aryna and Keptu. They didn't know Sum or Keptu very well, but they had spent much time with Aryna. Aryna was the only one of the Others who looked back when they left.

When the stretcher arrived, the men took Cue-na's body straight to the burial ground. All the members of the group who were home went to the site and they solemnly had a funeral for the man who lived to be forty-five years old. The People remembered him so they had their say in as positive manner as they could. For what he had done, he definitely deserved to be buried as Cue-na. The three young people spoke in tears remembering particularly how he had taken them through the ashfall to find the People so they would be safe.

With the burial over, the People returned to the cave. The three Others sat on their bedding until Totamu suggested they unroll the bedding and stretch out for a little while to rest from the trip and the sadness they'd just been through.

Meeka came over and looked into the eyes of Aryna. "Do you remember me?" she asked.

Aryna looked, "Meeka," she sobbed. They threw their arms around each other.

"Oh, Aryna, when you looked back, I wanted to run to you and bring you with us."

"I know. I wanted to stay."

"You're here now. I am so glad that you're here."

"I am too."

Keptu looked at Meeka. She looked around. Someone else was coming, then another. Minagle and Domur arrived with children. Then Liho with a child. The Others didn't recognize them until they said their names and then the old memories came rushing back. Everyone hugged Aryna and Keptu, welcoming them.

Lamk went to Sum and told him his name. Sum remembered. Lamk told him that the People were terribly saddened by their losses. He welcomed his old friend.

"We thought you might shame us by telling us that you told us we'd have trouble, but when Cue-na said that, I couldn't understand. I didn't remember your telling us we'd have trouble. I remember that the men wished us well."

"They would have done nothing but wish you well. We did not have the same customs. Things we do your people would not have done. What we don't do, you would have done. We are always focused on the health and strength of our People; we do not compete; we help all who need help; we welcome strangers who are traveling. We are a peaceful People."

"It looks like you found a wonderful place to be."

"We have. We watch for other humans, but we have seen none. We have fields that give us good meat and a lake that gives us good fish. We survive the cold times well. It is good."

Sum looked long at Lamk. "We met warlike people from the beginning. They fought us and we fought them and both sides had bad injuries. Lately, they started ambushing us when we'd be separated from one another. They killed women and children. Anyone they could find in groups of three or two or one." He said the numbers and signed them. "Mostly we didn't go alone anywhere. Toward the end of the last battle, Cue-na managed to get us together and told us to follow him. He led us through the woods while the battle continued. He already knew the battle was lost due to the injuries he'd seen. He had us run swiftly through the forest. His arm flapped as he ran and tried to hold it, while carrying his weapons that he wouldn't have been able to use with one arm. We ran and ran into the ashfall and he seemed to follow the path we'd taken from your cave. He kept going, hardly talking, just progressing. Then he turned onto your path. We'd stop and get meat from the caches and in some were water bags. That saved our lives. We kept going until you found us."

"Who were these people?"

"They were us."

"Your people, the Minguat, fought other Minguat? How can that be?"

"Lamk, you may remember that we fought among ourselves. We were like that. I, for one, have learned that the end of such custom is death."

Lamk reached out and hugged Sum. "I am so glad you survived, my friend. I am so glad!"

The evening meal was served, and the travelers couldn't believe their good fortune. The food was wonderful and none of them had to keep looking for Others to attack. The People did decide to keep watch for a while on the ash-fall land to be certain no one followed the survivors.

After the evening meal, the young people were shown to the creek and they bathed, though that was not something they did customarily. Liho explained that the People bathed regularly. In warm weather, bathing was in the creek and in cold seasons it was in the lower part of the cave. They kept clean so they did not have lice and because it kept them healthy. Males and females bathed together. The People had learned from the Others that they didn't do that, but they had learned to become one with the People and now thought nothing of it. Quickly, Sum, Keptu, and Aryna bathed modestly keeping their eyes to themselves.

After bathing, they gathered the sleeping mats and covers and shook them outside because they had gotten ash all over them. They didn't realize the women had already swept out the ash they brought into the cave.

The next day, Lamk and Manak took the three newcomers to the lake and showed them the rafts. The women came down ready to take the rafts out. Likichi took Sum and Keptu out while Pechki took Aryna. They didn't go far out because they didn't know if the young people could swim. After the rafting, Ermol-na and Lamul tested the young people for swimming and found they needed to learn. They spent the next few days teaching swimming to the three Others. Keptu was really good at it. Sum and Aryna took longer but cast on the People as they were, they knew they had to learn so they worked assiduously at it, wondering whether it was a condition of being able to live there. Likichi realized what they thought and did nothing whatever to change their thinking. In addition, the remaining adults of the home cave, who didn't know how, learned to swim.

It was five days later when Hahami-na announced that he'd seen Chamul-na and Nanichak-na returning. They were accompanied by three very tall men. They were not People or Others and these men were only wearing a strip of leather secured by a band at the waist.

The People tried to prepare but had no idea what to do. They all grouped to the south end of the rock walk to meet these new arrivals. Ki'ti had figured out these people must be the Mol, and she was correct. She and Emaea were fascinated finally to see them. They looked much like the Others—or more like a combination of the People and the Others. They were very tall.

The Mol spoke their language poorly, but they did speak it. They learned from the People who had lived in the caves of the animal paintings very long ago. As they entered the home cave, the Mol had to bend down to go through the vestibule. Once in the cave they could stand with ease.

Nanichak-na noticed the addition of the three Others and pointed it out to Chamul-na. They did not approach the newcomers because they were occupied with three of their own. It was near time for the evening meal and most people had assembled already in the large gathering area where they normally ate. The newcomers were given mats for seating, and making themselves comfortable, they thanked the People.

Ki'ti and one of the Mol could not stop looking at each other. Ki'ti didn't feel threatened, she felt a communication she couldn't quite understand emanating from the Mol who stared at her. It was neither bad nor good but inquisitive, and felt kind at the same time. Somehow, she felt as if the young man knew a lot about her already. She lowered her eyes.

The men talked into the night while the women cleaned up from dinner and prepared the sleeping mats and covers. Some women gathered outside to gossip about the Mol. Ki'ti and Emaea had walked far down the rock walk.

"The Mol named Untuk kept staring at me. I was drawn to him also. Mother, what is the significance?" Ki'ti asked Emaea.

"I do not know. I realized the two of you were drawn to each other but I don't understand why. You are so very different. He is much taller than you."

"I almost feel that he knows me."

"Chamul-na and Nanichak-na may have said something about our storytellers. That might be it."

"Well is it bad manners to stare at someone else?"

"I don't think this was bad manners, Little Girl, but rather another of your ways of knowing that I don't understand. I think there is a drawing because there is some information the two of you need to share. Did you notice the bag around his neck? The other two don't have them."

"You are right. I didn't notice but I can bring up the image in my mind web. Do you think there is a yellow owl in there?"

"I cannot know. There should not be another unless it is broken or unless he came from Wamumur's People. He doesn't look like Wamumur."

"That's true, and clearly he is not People. So I wonder what is in that bag."

"I expect that you will find out." Emaea looked at Ki'ti and wondered. There had been no one among the People for Ki'ti to join when she became woman. Ki'ti didn't talk of it often but there was a yearning. She understood that well.

Emaea wondered why Chamul-na and Nanichak-na had brought the Mol to their cave. To her it made no sense. But she knew that the men were not thoughtless, they had no doubt reasoned every angle they could. She could not wait to whisper with Wamumur in bed. Ah! It would not be necessary to wait; she could see her husband approaching from the cave.

"Why did you leave?" he asked.

"The women were leaving and it appeared to be a conversation for men. We left to talk. Why are the Mol here?"

"In a word, wives," Wamumur said.

"Not me!" Ki'ti said firmly.

"Then, with whom will you join?" he asked.

"Not them. They are too tall."

"Well, you cannot join with Frakja and you'll have to wait," he flashed eight, "years for Trokug or Smig or Ekoy. What did you have in mind?"

"Wise One, I have no plan."

"Then don't be too rash in judging the Mol by height. Height is a small factor in the choice of joining."

"But he wears funny clothes."

Wamumur looked at her. He had noticed the staring between her and Untuk.

"Oh, so you've already chosen Untuk?"

"Wise One, I . . . ."

Wamumur interrupted, "I noticed the staring between the two of you. I heard that as soon as he heard of you from Chamul-na and Nanichak-na, he has wanted to meet you. He is not a Wise One, but I think there was a Wise One in his ancestry. There is some reason he really wants to meet you."

"After the staring I feel uncomfortable."

"That is not discomfort from the staring, I am persuaded, but rather your meeting someone about whom you know nothing. At times like that it's always awkward. The best way to solve the awkwardness is to communicate. They will be here a while. They do understand if they join with a woman here they have to stay here. Returning to the Mol with one of our women is not something we will permit. Visiting briefly is acceptable for any other woman than you, but not living there."

Ki'ti stood. She wondered where the Mol were. Emaea and Wamumur accompanied her back to the cave. The girl's curiosity was going wild, but her actions were self protective. She wanted to know about the strangers, particularly the one who stared at her, but she hesitated to find out. She thought she might just be a novelty because she was a storyteller. She didn't want to be a novelty.

It was dark and she headed to the privy. She remembered that she had no one with her so she turned back to the cave and ran headlong into Untuk.

"I'm sorry," she said apologetically.

"I'm not. I would love to talk to you."

"Well, right now I'm headed to the privy and I have to have accompaniment. I had forgotten for the moment so I have to get someone."

"I would be glad to accompany you."

Ki'ti looked at his eyes. She was totally unprepared for the offer but didn't want to be rude. "Will you turn away while I use the privy?" she asked.

"Of course," he said softly.

"Then that will be fine," she said, having no idea at all how to avoid this encounter.

They walked to the privy in silence. She used it and then he did. They turned back to the cave.

"I have wanted to meet you for days," Untuk said. "I heard about your storytelling. I heard about your taking the green bag to the dead man of the Mol and how you suffered for doing it. I heard about your travel to the place where giants played. I heard about your finding the animal images that I've never seen until we traveled here. We stopped to look at them. I heard about you over and over. I have been so eager to meet you."

Ki'ti was totally embarrassed that Chamul-na and Nanichak-na had been so liberal in spreading her story. Some of it she would gladly have forgotten, but could not. She would gladly have dropped through a hole in the earth but she was confronting a stranger who knew of her.

"In some ways I see you as a hero," he said.

"Well, believe me, I am no hero. My former impulsive behavior has been curbed, because I took that bag to the cave in strict disobedience to my father."

"You did and I understand you suffered greatly. You gave my people a gift. You brought them together. I passed by them today and knew their joy."

"We believe that when you die and are buried Wisdom brings you to himself through the ground to the place where we were made. You aren't where you are buried."

"You did notice that my people are not buried."

"Oh," was all that Ki'ti could say. She wondered whether the man with the green bag could communicate with her because he wasn't buried. She knew Wamumur thought that rather than the man himself, it could be evil spirits that lurked around the bodies that communicated rather than the dead themselves. She found it confusing.

"Will you sit with me?" he asked.

She agreed and the two sat a little way down the rock walk. They looked at the starry sky as Ahriku hobbled over to sit by Ki'ti. "Poor Ahriku," she said.

Untuk got to his feet quickly looking at the wolf. He hadn't seen the dogs but heard them when they arrived. They had been hushed so quickly that he had forgotten.

"You can sit. Ahriku is my special dog, and he will not hurt you. He is very old."

Untuk sat back down eyeing the dog which really looked like a wolf to him. He put his arm around Ki'ti's shoulders. She seemed as special to him as he thought she might. He loved her big blue eyes and long eyelashes. Her fine brown hair blew in the wind and he watched it curve around her face. When he put his arm around her shoulders, she stiffened and then relaxed. Ki'ti's People's custom was that the gesture meant something between a man and a woman. In his customs she realized the gesture might mean nothing.

"What do you have in the bag at your neck?" she asked.

He was surprised but said, "It is a little yellow owl that was broken. It belonged to my ancestor from long ago when my people lived near here. They had to run from here and when they did this little owl broke. I still keep it as a token of my family from long ago."

"Look what I have in my bag," she offered.

His eyes dilated when he saw the intact owl.

"It was owned by someone named Ilea who loved a stone worker named Torkiz. It was left in the cave of the animals. Torkiz made the images you saw."

Untuk was shocked. He could not retain the words but let them tumble out. "Ilea was Mol. Torkiz was People. They did not join but they copulated in his cave for years. They were in love and joined as well as any people ever joined, but not in a pronouncement as his People required. When they fled from the man-like apes and the Others, Ilea and Torkiz were separated for the rest of their lives. My father came from that union down the ancestry line. Their son had the owl when it broke. My family has handed it to the eldest boy ever since. It has been uncountable generations."

"Why didn't they throw away a broken owl?"

"Because it was a symbol for the broken union of two lovers."

"I see," Ki'ti said wistfully.

"How did you know the names Ilea and Torkiz?"

She looked at him expecting him to laugh scornfully. "The owl sang the story to me."

"What?" he said. *What did she mean?* he wondered.

"I had the owl that belonged to Torkiz. The one I found in the cave belonged to Ilea. The owl sang the names to me. Somehow Wamumur's and mine got mixed up in the beginning. Maybe it was when the pouch was made for mine. I was supposed to have Ilea's owl. I discovered when I'd prepare to sleep that Torkiz's owl would sing. Wamumur cannot hear it. All he hears is buzzing. Wamumur made me give him the owl that belonged to Torkiz and he gave me the one that belonged to Ilea. Hers doesn't sing. At least not yet."

Without asking, Untuk pulled her to his lap and leaned down and kissed her. She was shocked and tried to push him—then discovered to her surprise that she didn't wish to push him away, embracing him with warmth. Slowly he touched her in ways no one had ever touched her, and she felt like her belly had turned to water. She felt that this should not happen, but she didn't want it to stop. She responded to his every advance. She wondered whether this was love. Untuk was definitely in love. He had waited so long for the right woman and when he heard her story, he knew he'd found her, even though he had not seen her. He could not resist her when he met her, and she was responsive.

Wamumur came to the cave entrance to find her. He noticed what was happening, smiled, and called again. The two separated and Untuk helped her up to go to Wamumur. They looked at each other again as she went to the Wise One. He escorted her into the cave to their sleeping mats. She dutifully went to kiss and hug Emaea and then repeated the gestures with Wamumur.

"He isn't so bad, is he?" Wamumur asked.

"No, he is very special," she admitted.

"That is good," Emaea said.

"The Winds of Change are blowing," Ki'ti said, feeling overwhelmed.

Emaea smiled. She reached out a hand and took Ki'ti's. Her smile brought one from Ki'ti.

The next day dawned bright and cloudless. Ki'ti asked Wamumur if she could take Untuk to the lake. He said that he would gather several people to take the three visitors to the lake. It might look a bit ungracious if only two went to the lake. Some of the women planned to fish and it would be good to share their manner of fishing.

Ki'ti prepared for the lake. She was careful to pick her teeth and comb her hair which now was below shoulder length. It waved slightly and curved around her face. Where the sun hit it for days at the lake, there were streaks of gold highlights running down the hair. In the sunlight it shone gold streaks like Liho's hair did all over. She took good care of it and bathed daily to avoid lice. She didn't want her hair cut again.

Ki'ti asked Emaea whether she shouldn't have a longer tunic.

"Whatever for?" came the reply.

How, she wondered, could Ki'ti tell her that she felt virtually naked in front of Untuk, so she said just that, despite her awkward feeling.

Emaea laughed quietly, holding Ki'ti's hands. "It wouldn't matter if the tunic came to the ground, Little Girl," she said, "men can see what's underneath."

"What do you mean?"

Emaea smiled directly at her with her mouth and eyes, "Haven't you already discovered the answer to that?"

"Oh, Emaea, am I so transparent?"

"My Dear One, you are woman and so am I."

"I see," Ki'ti said, but didn't really.

The fishing group headed for the lake. Ki'ti and Untuk walked together. Ahriku trotted behind dutifully. It appeared that there was no limit to what they could devise for conversation. He found it extremely hard to keep his hands off her. She did not seem to have the same trouble. She was happy just holding hands.

When they reached the lake shore, Pechki called to Ki'ti and Untuk. She asked Untuk whether he could swim. He replied he could swim some, but didn't consider himself a swimmer. She explained he must take lessons starting that day, but to board the raft for now and sit in the middle with Ki'ti. He was delighted. Pechki took them out onto the lake and showed them fish in the crystal clear water below and let them enjoy time on the water. Then she noticed the two other Mol visitors were finishing with their swim lessons, so she returned the raft to shore and informed Kai and Guy-na, the swim instructors of the day, that they had another student. The men already discovered that Mihalee and Tongip needed lessons.

Ki'ti went to the place where Emaea had put down an aurochs skin and together they watched the young men learn to swim. It would take days and days and days. The star of the swim lessons was Untuk. He wanted to get this requirement behind him as quickly as possible.

When Untuk emerged from the water before Mihalee and Tongip, Wamumur walked to meet him. "Come walk with me," he requested.

Untuk went with him with a quick glance at Ki'ti, who looked as mystified as he.

"You find Ki'ti attractive?" Wamumur asked.

"That is putting it mildly," Untuk replied.

"Are you thinking to join with her?" Wamumur persisted.

"If that were possible it would fill my largest dreams."

"What do you find appealing about her?"

"First, the way she looks. No one among the Mol keeps themselves clean and groomed like she does. She even smells good. And her eyes. I get lost in them. She is very bright. And there is something between us. A spark. Some kind of feeling draws us together."

"Those things come and go. You do know that she is our storyteller. She will become the Wise One of the People when Emaea and I are gone to Wisdom. Do you understand what that means?"

"Not fully, Wise One," the young man said truthfully.

"If you join with her, it means this: she doesn't belong to you, she belongs to the People. She must be protected at all costs. It is her primary job to tell the stories we have heard for years during the cold season confinement. It is our security. After she tells them, she will be exhausted, because Wisdom speaks through her and each word must not vary from what was from the beginning of time, and then you must make her sleep. She won't want to sleep. When she lets Wisdom speak through her, it saps energy like a long run. But it makes her feel as if she could run forever. When she uses alternate ways of knowing, a kind of knowing that you and sometimes I don't understand, she has the same need for sleep. And she won't want it. Do you understand?"

"Yes, Wise One."

"You must keep her from evil spirits. Do you understand that?"

"I have no idea what that means. I can protect her from assaults from Others and that involves evil spirits sometimes, but other than that, I don't know."

"Then, if you join, I will have to teach you."

"If we can join, you would find me an eager and obedient learner. I already love and cherish her. I would do whatever is necessary to protect and care for her. I have no preconceived ideas what a Wise One is or should be. I will be obedient to you and to Emaea."

"Now here's your greatest challenge," Wamumur said. "She is wiser and smarter than you'll ever be. Don't think you can outsmart her. It won't work. What you need to do is to look after her needs. Not her wants. Her needs. You don't want her to tire significantly—ever. That is the worst thing that can happen to her because it puts her off balance. She makes poor judgments when she is fatigued."

"How do you know when she's tired?"

"Her shoulders will droop. She will become slow in movement. She will stare off into space without batting her eyes for a long time. She will not respond appropriately when you talk to her. You have to understand she uses energy differently from you. She uses spiritual energy and that takes more out of you than physical energy does. That seems strange but it's true."

"So while she watches over the People, it would be my job to watch over her."

"Yes. Then this is also challenging. You have to make her obey you. You are not as smart or knowledgeable, but you have to make her obey you. Do you understand?"

"That could be difficult."

"Are you man enough for the responsibility?"

"Wise One, all I can say is that I long for it. I will need to learn from you. When you see me do something wrong, I would need you to correct me. I will be obedient as I've said before."

"You will need that. You will need to learn very quickly. It will be critical. If you join with Ki'ti, in some way the fate and health of our People will be in your hands."

"Wise One, you don't know me well. All I can say for myself is I am a serious person. I do not take responsibility lightly. Never have. I would love her and cherish her, but I would never let it out of my sight that my responsibility to her would be responsibility to the People and their future. I can understand and appreciate that. Life would be a lot easier without that, but the sacrifice would be not having the most wonderful woman I ever met."

"You really think after all that that Ki'ti is the most wonderful woman you ever met?"

"Yes, I do."

"Then what would you do if she were drawn to do something in the future like delivering the green bag and you knew it was all wrong and had told her not to do it. When she did that, Wisdom had begun to suck the color from the land and trackers had to follow her with great difficulty."

"First, I would try to keep my eyes on her especially after telling her 'No,' because from what I've heard that can get lost in her mind web when she travels another. I am wise enough to know I cannot keep my eyes on her all day every day. I, like you, would depend on the People to know where she was and whether she went off alone. I have heard your threats to her. I would reiterate those threats. She cannot be permitted to go off into situations that are dangerous either for herself or for me or for the People. I would hold her.

My size makes that possible. I would punish her, if that were necessary. I think if I absolutely had to, I could disable her so that she could not wander off. I would not want to do that ever," he said shivering.

"My Son," Wamumur said, "You have my permission should you want it to join with my daughter. You will become my Son and I shall teach you."

The two men embraced very briefly. The heart of Untuk was soaring. He walked quickly to Ki'ti.

"Will you walk the shore with me?" he asked her.

In response, she arose and took his hand as they walked along the shore line. She gave Ahriku a signal to remain with Wamumur. They walked a great distance before a word was said.

"What did Wamumur want to talk to you about?" she asked, wondering whether she wanted to hear the answer.

"He talked to me about you and me. He wanted to know what I would be like as a husband to you."

Ki'ti experienced a watery feeling in her belly again. She didn't like the feeling. It made her feel weak.

Untuk found a place to sit on a log that was hidden by holly bushes from the view of the People at the lake. He pulled Ki'ti to his lap and kissed her deeply and with great feeling. Her mind web was aswirl with feeling. She could grasp no reason, only great overwhelming feelings for this young man she'd just met. He touched her and held her, and her world, she felt, would never be the same. She tried to grasp what the Winds of Change were doing to her and all she could feel was being swept along.

Untuk wanted her desperately but felt after talking to Wamumur that they should join before he took her fully. So he tried to cool down the warmth they had generated. He was convinced she was his. The manly odor of his clean sweat was overpowering to her. She swam in him.

He told her, "Your father has given permission for us to join." There, it was out. "Will you be my wife?" he asked, staring into her big blue eyes.

"What can I say but yes?" she asked.

"Well, do you say yes?" he asked.

"Yes, Untuk, I say yes."

He forgot the attempt to quell the warmth and kissed her forcefully, trying to let her know his joy. She understood, for hers was the same. After all the years of wondering whether she'd ever have someone with whom to join, she had one who was attractive, kind, and who loved her.

"We will walk some more," he said.

"When will we join?" she asked.

"When can we join?" he asked in return.

"We can join when the pronouncement is made. If we want to do it tonight, then the pronouncement has to be made tonight."

"Who has to approve?"

"Wamumur. I will ask him if you want to do it tonight. We would have to prepare our cave if that's the case."

"You mean you go to a separate cave on the first night?"

"Yes, or however many nights you feel are necessary."

"Ah, many, many nights, I think," he said, and they laughed.

They returned to the People at the lake hand in hand. They walked up to Wamumur who was at the water's edge.

Ki'ti waited for Wamumur to recognize her. Untuk paid attention to the encounter.

"Yes, Little Girl?" he asked.

"Would you please pronounce Untuk and me joined tonight?"

Wamumur looked at her and then Untuk. It was good, he was convinced. "I will," he said, "and you had better get busy readying your cave. Wisdom sucks color from the land early in the mountains."

The two headed up the hill hand in hand followed by Ahriku. Both were virtually trembling with excitement. Each felt as if they were the most special person on earth. While they made their way to the caves, Ki'ti carefully explained what would be necessary to prepare.

When they got there and Ki'ti reached for a broom, Totamu waddled over. She was becoming weaker and weaker and had some difficulty walking.

"You are joining?"

"Yes, Izumo. Wise One will make the pronouncement tonight."

"Young man, do you have any idea what responsibility you are taking on?"

"Yes, the Wise One made it very clear. He will also teach me what I need to know, and I will apply myself to learning."

"Little Girl," Totamu said sharply, "you know you will have to obey him."

"Yes, Izumo, I shall obey him as if he were Wamumur."

"Then it is good. It is good." Bent over from age, she headed for tea.

Ki'ti took the broom and headed for the cave next to the one where the man of the Mol was found years ago. She swept the ceiling and the walls while Untuk gathered rocks and made a hearth and brought wood for fire. She and he both went to the cave for sleeping mats and coverings. Totamu stopped them holding her arm outstretched as if to block them.

"I have something for you," she said. They followed her to her part of the cave. She handed them the largest aurochs skin they'd ever seen. It had been softened and the hair was left on. "I made this for you when I learned you were to be Wise One. It should keep you both very comfortable."

The two were stupefied at the gift. Normally gifts were not given when People joined. Ki'ti went to the old woman and hugged her. She seemed unwilling to let go, so the old woman gently pushed her away. "Save that for later," she said making both Ki'ti and Untuk blush.

They took the skin and carried it to their temporary cave. They were ready for Wisdom to suck all color from the land and the day's events in the home cave to end.

The fishers and visitors returned from the lake. They had gathered and set to dry a number of fish. Since not all rafts had been on the lake, the number of fish was fewer than a five raft run. Still it was good. Three men remained to guard the drying fish from bears, ravens, or any other scavengers.

While Ki'ti and Untuk had come together, Tongip had found his interest in Aryna was returned only slightly. When he understood the reason for her coolness, he felt compassion and began to get her to talk about the difficult experiences since they left the Others. She had never shared her mental burdens, and found doing so brought many tears in front of this kind young man who was so very tall. Meanwhile, Mihalee was becoming homesick.

The evening meal was called and the People came together for a feast. There were roasts and fish and vegetables. Everyone ate well and enjoyed the food. When Wamumur arose at the end of the meal to make his pronouncement, most of the People were shocked to hear Ki'ti and Untuk would join considering the short time the two had known each other. Chamul-na and Totamu went about after dinner assuring People their concerns were unnecessary. This joining was special. The People believed them.

Ermol-na played the drum. Ghanya had made a flute-like instrument from a waterfowl bone and the tones he produced pierced the evening's music joyfully. The new couple danced obligatorily and then left the home cave for First Night.

Outside, when the young people headed for their cave, Untuk picked up Ki'ti and carried her down the rock walk to the cave. Ahriku followed along limping slightly.

"Put me down, Untuk. I feel silly," Ki'ti insisted.

"Never, my wife," he responded.

"What will people think?" she said, obviously uncomfortable.

"From this time on, they can think what they will. I will follow the Wise One in his advice. He said I must make you obey me. That is why I do not put you down. You must learn you have to obey me. Do you understand?"

"I do. I admit I don't like it. Yes, I do understand. Wisdom knows I don't want to understand!"

"Forget that I carry you. Just let go of all the burdens you carry and relax for this evening," he said as he laid her on the soft skin. He kissed her and then pulled himself away to make the fire. He had an ember and got the fire going quickly. He had gathered much wood and the cave glowed. Ki'ti was surprised to see that Untuk had taken an armful of moss and put it in a spot in the cave near the fire. He had laid a piece of leather on the moss. He picked up Ahriku who was lying by the entrance and laid him on the little bed. Ki'ti was deeply touched. Ahriku looked at Untuk and put his head down to sleep with contentment.

Then he came to her and lay beside her for a long time. He reached over and they kissed. They touched and murmured to each other for a long time in play. Finally, Untuk could stand it no longer and he began to present himself for penetration. As he began, Ki'ti inhaled sharply at the initial discomfort. As he rocked, she began to feel something of a filling unlike any way of knowing she'd ever had. She could see into the very belly of Untuk and knew he would be true to his words. He would care for her, even when she wouldn't want him to. He would protect her. He would keep her Wise One. And he would love her until one of them died, as would she love him.

The first time was a gentle rocking which she loved. The next time they joined that night it was feverish and at the edges of rough. She loved it too. *How many ways of expressing this love were there?* she wondered. They would try to discover that night.

At the cave, gossip was running rampant. Finally, Wamumur rose and cleared his throat. The cave instantly became quiet.

"Today I talked to Untuk. Before he met Ki'ti he knew her story from Chamul-na and Nanichak-na. They left out nothing. I asked Untuk questions that you would find difficult to answer. The two of them are devoted to each other even though little time has passed. I have not lost the proper function of my mind web. I suggest that you have better things to discuss than the two young people or the state of my mind web. Watch and you will see that this joining was designed in the belly of Wisdom. That is all I have to say." He finished with a palm strike.

The gossip immediately stopped. The cave calmed down and the People went to sleep shortly afterward. The Winds of Change had come again and wasted no time at all.

When Wisdom brought the sun's first glow to fade the darkness, Ki'ti and Untuk were still undressed and awake.

"I need to bathe," Ki'ti said.

"So then do I," Untuk said. They joined hands and went down the steps farther north from the ones by the home cave. They bathed quickly downstream from the main bathing area and returned to the cave, started to dress, spontaneously changed the direction of their mind webs, and began again to make love. They could not seem to become satiated.

They did not leave the cave until high sun. People in the cave were shocked, but having been admonished by Wamumur, they kept their thoughts to themselves. When the couple emerged, it was to go to the privy and stop at the cave to eat. Then they retreated to the cave and slept. They awakened when the evening meal was called. Ki'ti took the time to comb their hair. They dressed and went to the evening meal. As soon as it was over, they returned to their cave.

Ki'ti was ready for more lovemaking, but Untuk slowed her down by asking, "What does 'ways of knowing' mean?"

She hadn't really thought much about that. She had to rove her mind web and then she told him, "Some you know, like the conversation we are having now, or looking at a person's smile or frown; you have probably felt watched. Sometimes you know from hand signals."

He nodded.

"Sometimes you know things by feeling something like the little yellow owl."

He shook his head. He did not understand.

"Sometimes you just hear something or see something or feel something. Sometimes you dream it when you sleep or when you're awake. Sometimes like with me and the owl—you hear it sing to you. Sometimes you know what will happen in the future or what happened in the past as clear as if the sun's light shined on it. And you find out you're right."

Untuk looked at her amazed. She spoke of a world he didn't know at all.

"Sometimes you get the visual form of internal feelings, thoughts, or intentions of others. For example, I can sometimes see from looking at the edges of a person if they hurt or lie or are filled with vitality."

Untuk realized that his wife had dimensions he never dreamed of. He could see why Wamumur wanted her protected.

"Sometimes when a person touches you they communicate things they would never say to your face. For someone to take my hand is not wise for anyone who wants to lie to the People. I know it instantly through touch.

"Sometimes Wisdom simply tells People something. Wisdom told Wamumur to get the People to the north because Baambas was going to destroy the land. We barely escaped. With the stories, I don't have to memorize the stories perfectly because Wisdom puts them in my mind web so I cannot forget. Does that answer your questions, my husband?"

"Probably more than answers it. You have all that information and feelings going on inside while you look like a perfectly normal young woman?"

"Yes. Only, it seems normal to me now. For a while I fought against it. Oh, how I fought! I didn't want the responsibility or the protection or the constant watching."

"But you were chosen."

"Yes. Wisdom leaves no options. I learned that the hard way because I thought I had a choice."

"I see," he said and he did. "I wonder whether I'm up to all this."

"You are. I learned that when you picked me up. Your touch told me. When you filled me with yourself, I knew that you loved me and the People equally. That is why I must obey you like Wamumur unequivocally. And do you think I want to?"

"I suspect sometimes you'd like to run away from it all."

"Yes. Wamumur has made that impossible. He told me if I ever did run off again he'd hit my foot with a rock so I would be crippled and couldn't run ever again. I don't want that to happen."

"You do know that I have had to promise him the same thing."

"Yes. I knew when you picked me up. Your touch communicated your promises to my father."

"That is completely frightening," he said, running his fingers through the aurochs fur.

"Not at all. It's just another way of knowing. Well, you asked."

"I did, and I thank you for sharing. I need to understand as quickly as I can. You can help me."

"I'm not sure I want to," she laughed because he had begun tickling her. "Don't do that!" she gasped. "I hate being tickled."

He didn't stop but tickled her more gently. She began to return the tickling but he could hold her at arms length to tickle her and she couldn't reach him. Somehow that felt unfair. When she was almost breathless, he stopped and kissed her. Her emotions were all over the place. *Who was this man? He could get her to talk and then shake her emotionally from top to bottom. Did all women feel this?* she wondered.

He loved to see her naked, so he lifted her tunic over her head. Her tunic was very short and she needed a new one. He still wore his leather. He traced her body with his fingertips lingering here and there. She felt vulnerable but didn't understand to what. All these new thoughts and feelings. It was good that newly joined people had time in a cave to themselves. She thought she'd have stayed blood red if she'd participated in all this joining play in the cave. She'd never seen anyone in the dark of night do half the things they were doing. *Is that what couples did when they wandered off?* she wondered. Yet she could hardly wait to experience more. As if he heard her wish, they began again. And she found there was more.

Wamumur had seen Ki'ti and talked with her. He realized that the two young people were well matched from an attraction to sexual fulfillment. He was delighted and shared with Emaea. He also laughed that they might hold the record for the longest stay in the other cave. They joked about how long it would be. At the end of seven days, it was already longer than what any other pair had spent in the cave. They still did not return.

Minagle asked Ki'ti when they'd return and she smiled and said they weren't ready yet. Minagle was amazed. But she had a good feeling about what Ki'ti was experiencing and was content. She shared that with Manak who had also been wondering but would never have asked. He was relieved.

Aryna and Tongip were becoming closer and closer. He had caused her to share with him in ways that she'd never shared with anyone. Their relationship had moved to one that was physical, but that was going slowly. One evening they walked to the beach and watched the sky while Wisdom sucked the color from the land. Tongip had his arm around her shoulders and he leaned down to kiss her. She responded, then fought, and then responded with warmth. He touched her and she touched him. They pulled off their clothing and copulated in fury on the shore out of sight of the place where rafts were launched. They repeated joining several times. Aryna went from weeping to expressing joy and to weeping again. Tongip did not understand the emotional reversals, but he enjoyed their copulating, and she had agreed each time. He lay on the damp sand, exhausted. She looked down at him.

"What is the meaning of all this, Tongip?"

He smiled, "I thought it would mean we'd join," he said.

"You want to join with me?" she asked timidly, totally unsure of herself.

"To have a wife such as you, beautiful, copulating with such intensity, spending time as we have—who could ask for more? Don't you realize that I love you?"

"I didn't think anyone would ever love me," she said while tears fell from her eyes to his chest.

"Why not, Aryna, you are lovely."

"I've always been told that I was nothing. That I was ugly. That I was lazy. All bad things. Nobody ever looked at me. I have been treated well by the People, but still nobody ever told me I was lovely."

"Look at your people. The Minguat, they were called?"

She nodded.

"They argued all the time and didn't make people feel good or work for the benefit of all. They were probably so self centered they never saw what your feelings were. Toward the end, they were at war and thinking of survival. My Dear One, *I* care about your feelings. *I* want to see that you have good feelings for the rest of your life."

"I just feel so unworthy."

"I wish I could wash away your feelings of unworthiness. All I can tell you is that you have been caused to believe a lie. You are as worthy as anyone ever born. Don't ever let anyone tell you otherwise."

He pulled her up and shook out her tunic and helped her into it. He surrounded her with his arms and held her tight to his chest. Her head came to his shoulder, unlike Ki'ti's whose head came to the mid-chest level of Untuk. Aryna's belly called to her. She had the same watery feeling that Ki'ti had experienced. She too wondered whether this was love. She would find Ki'ti and talk to her.

The two walked up the path back to the cave. Midway, he stopped her. He kissed her passionately.

He said, "Will you join me?"

She looked at him unsure, but she replied, "Yes."

"Will you talk to Wamumur or should I?"

"I think you should," she said, not at all sure that this was a good idea but it seemed better than anything she had considered.

They reached the cave and he found Wamumur right away. He suggested they would really have to hurry to prepare a cave and it had to be at least three caves from the other couple. Totamu told Aryna to sweep their chosen cave and Tongip to prepare the hearth. She told them to gather their sleeping things and carry them down to their cave after it was prepared. This had to be done before the evening meal. They got busy fast. Aryna had no time to think. She just did what she thought was best for her to do.

The evening meal was called and afterward Wamumur pronounced Aryna and Tongip joined. They left the cave as soon as they could after dancing and headed for their cave which was not quite as far down the rock walk as Ki'ti and Untuk's. Tongip lit the fire quickly and came to her. He was extremely gentle and seduced her with great care. The two spent the rest of the night learning each other and how to please the other. Aryna felt awakened from a deep sleep. She was finally coming of age. Her body had been there for a while, but her emotions had been tangled and twisted to the point that only someone like Tongip would have been able to help her make them straight.

At the end of fourteen days, Wamumur and Emaea talked of Ki'ti's stay in their cave. Surely by now was her time of bleeding. They would not need to be in their cave then. But little did they know that the Mol did not perceive a need to refrain from copulating when a female bled. They simply went to wash afterward. They had used the lower part of the stream for bathing but that hadn't slowed them down. Wamumur and Emaea didn't know whether to speak to the young people or leave it alone. So, they decided that Ki'ti was joined and this was not an area they needed to speak to them about. They did feel it odd that the two did not return to the cave.

Totamu felt that Wamumur and Emaea should tell the young people to return, but they told Totamu that it was none of their business. The young people would return when they returned. All knew that when first joined, couples would do and try things they wouldn't do in the main cave. The cave had a controlling atmosphere. For someone like Ki'ti, Wamumur reasoned the exploration and trial phase might require longer.

Little would Wamumur have guessed that his daughter was kneeling at that moment lowering herself onto the erect member of her husband while her large naked breasts swung a bit—to her husband's delight. In his entire life, Wamumur had never conceived of doing such a thing and he would have found it scandalous. Emaea would have been shocked. They might, too, have interfered. Totamu might have considered banishing the young people, though she didn't have that power. It was definitely something that wouldn't take place in the home cave, though some of the People would have to admit to participating in the practice in the woods or fields or anywhere they could be alone, to do what might draw attention in communal cave. What would have really horrified Wamumur and Emaea was Untuk's taking her from the back as dogs do. Ki'ti didn't like it at all, so it only happened a few times.

Aryna was participating in the same things. The Mol were not repressed at all when it came to sexual activity. Aryna, unlike Ki'ti, had no knowledge at all. The Others expected females to comply with whatever a male wanted. Women were subservient. She took it for granted that all of the activity involving copulating was normal and should evoke pleasure for the man. She was hesitant to voice her feelings about any of it for fear of not being approved. Finally, Tongip had to open the gates of communication by telling her that he was certain she had some likes and dislikes, and he wanted to know what they were. She was so shocked at his question that she answered directly and truthfully. He listened. He wanted to please her, not just himself. That brought a new dimension to their lovemaking and caused their time in the cave to increase substantially. Aryna could not believe the turn her life was taking. She hoped that Ki'ti's was equally as good.

Finally, the day arrived that Aryna and Tongip returned to the home cave. The People were delighted. The couple set up their sleeping place and were part of the People. Still, Ki'ti and Untuk had not returned. It was a total enigma. People were careful not to discuss it, but it was in their minds. Aryna and Tongip understood but they were not about to enlighten the People.

Emaea found Ki'ti and took her aside. She asked her directly why they had not returned to the home cave. Ki'ti told her truthfully that they were enjoying each other tremendously and that they had not reached a point of wanting to do only what was approved for the communal cave. She told Emaea truthfully that the two had considered remaining in their cave for the season of the cold days. She told Emaea that the two were so amazingly suited to each other for copulating that it was enormous joy for them and sometimes they would even let it out loud. They knew the People in the main cave would not approve.

Emaea sat back on her heels. She was Wise One to her former group. She knew things. She had anticipated that there would come a time when the other caves would become used for a variety of reasons. She hadn't anticipated that her daughter might be the first. She would talk to Wamumur.

Ki'ti did not feel wrong about their length of time in their small cave. She inwardly wanted to have the rest of her life with Untuk in their cave. She loved the freedom. Untuk, however, was beginning to feel the pressure to return to the home cave. He had already learned that the times for more ardent lovemaking took place away from the home cave in stolen moments. He was unsure what to do. He loved his wife and he loved the People. He knew that Ki'ti had great responsibility to the People. He thought some of that responsibility might mean an end to their personal cave. The same day Emaea had talked to Ki'ti, Untuk did the same thing. To his amazement, Ki'ti wept.

"I'm sorry, my husband. I have been selfish and self centered. I could stay in that cave of ours for the rest of my days and be totally happy."

"I understand, but your responsibility is to the People as well as to me. You are ignoring your People."

"That means we have to slip off?"

"That's exactly what it means."

"How do we do that in the season of cold days?" she asked.

"I'd have to say carefully," he replied.

"Can you find out where others go?"

"I will try. I will also try to find a place I can fix for us that is away from the main cave life but not a far distance, so we can walk there in the season of cold days."

"Then I suppose we must return. Not tonight, my husband. Not tonight."

"Then tomorrow morning we carry back our sleeping mats and covers, my wife. It is time."

They went to their sleeping cave and stayed there not sleeping all night. Ahriku slept on his bed by the fire.

The next morning, Untuk met Mihalee. He was returning home. He was terribly homesick. He had hoped to find a wife, but there were no more single women available. So he would return and wait for his cousin to become woman. That did not please him but it would be no longer than a year. And he would remain at home, not far away having to speak a different language. These People had been very hospitable but he was well ready for home. The two talked briefly and then hugged. They would miss each other.

Nanichak-na and Chamul-na agreed to accompany the young man to the hunting spot where they'd met him and the other two Mol. It was not far and they decided it was safer for travel through the forest for the young man to have company. Mihalee wished they would go to his family caves, but they didn't want to travel that far. The men set off on a lovely day. When they eventually reached the place where the hunters had gathered, they were surprised to find other Mol there. Mihalee explained his absence and that Untuk and Tongip had found wives and had remained behind. He explained that he was returning home to wait for his cousin, Elma, to become woman. The men of the Mol laughed. Elma was woman. Mihalee's sadness was replaced with excitement.

The season of cold days came on. As her husband insisted, Ki'ti and he returned to the main cave. They were very repressed in their joining under the skins by night by the numbers of People surrounding them. Untuk learned of a number of places available for couples away from the main cave, and the signs used to indicate they were occupied, since fires would not be lit at any of them. He and Ki'ti would share these caves many times. It almost made up for the lack of their own private cave. Totamu, Wamumur, and Emaea never knew of the alternate caves. There was no need to enlighten them!

Wamumur began to teach Untuk what he needed to know to husband his wife. It was far more an in depth training than most young men would have been given. It involved how to keep her impetuousness controlled and not break her spirit. There had to be balance. He called on Emaea and Manak for help.

Untuk was a very serious and responsible young man. When he learned that Ki'ti made cracks for herself to hide in so she didn't have to obey, he found the idea hilarious. It sounded so incongruous to anything he had ever entertained intellectually. He'd never dreamed of such an outlandish but clever idea. Manak assured him it was anything but hilarious. He urged the young man to secure promises from her that she would obey each demand unequivocally. It would save a lot of grief for both him and her. Wamumur assured the young man that if Ki'ti's actions needed to be corrected and he failed, Wamumur would attend to it more severely. That absolutely got Untuk's attention. The Wise One definitely had that power, even though Ki'ti was Untuk's wife. He had control over her becoming Wise One. That control was total. Wamumur told Untuk that if he and his wife disagreed and she was becoming too assertive, he was to start calling her Little Girl. That, he assured him, would remind her of her responsibility. He had reluctant thoughts about having to call his wife, Little Girl, but he promised Wamumur that if it became necessary, he would. Wamumur talked about the humility that lay as the foundation for success of the People and the way that pride was destruc-tive. He informed the young man that his wife's worst fault was pride. He said she expressed it in ways that didn't look like pride—like finding cracks to hide in to avoid obeying. He tried to teach his new son as much as possible all at once. Finally, Wamumur realized it might have to come through time and experience with Ki'ti.

One day when it was cold and the People had gathered inside to do various work, Ki'ti pressed Untuk to take time to visit one of the special caves. He told her that was impractical at the time. She continued to press. Finally, perturbed, he took her wrist and pulled her from the cave without season-of-cold-days clothing. He took her to the food cave which was nearby, leaned down, and swatted her on the rump once hard.

"What has gotten into you, my husband?" she asked with tears falling from her eyes.

"You asked a question. I answered you. You must obey, my wife."

"Or?" Ki'ti said with her hands on her hips.

"Or you will have a lot more than I just gave you. Look at me! Don't you remember what you learned when you disobeyed as a child? How much worse to disobey your husband? Don't do that to me. If I fail to discipline you, your father will discipline you worse than I would have." He had her by the shoulders, his hands strong, fingers pressing hard into her skin. "I do this for you, for us, and for the People. You must obey. I can force you, but you should do it for love of me, of us, and of the People."

She wept, completely chastised. "Forgive me, my husband," she whispered.

He wrapped his arms about her and forgave her. Then, abruptly, he took her by the wrist and they returned to the cave. "You have stories to work on," he said and let her go. She lowered her head to him. Wamumur saw the whole episode and had noted her headstrong behavior. He knew. When he saw Untuk return with her and saw the difference in her attitude, he exchanged a look of approval with Untuk. Untuk was taking on well the additional responsibility that came with Ki'ti.

Chapter 9

"I was just lucky. Minagle was available and she *is* partly one of us. You couldn't really know that she wasn't one of us. Nothing weird about her head and she is slender of body," Ghanya said, leaning against the rock wall while standing below the rock path by the big tree.

"What would you have done if you'd had to join with one of them?" Sum asked.

"I wouldn't have chosen to join with anyone," Ghanya boasted. "I'd have waited until I found one of us. You and Keptu arrived with Aryna. That added more of us Minguat."

"Yes, well she chose a Mol."

"She might not have. She knows we are superior!" Ghanya said.

"You might have reason to reevaluate your estimation of the Minguat if you'd been through the war we just had. I don't think we are so superior." Sum wondered how his cousin could believe such silly ideas about superiority, after having experienced war for no apparent reason where almost the entire group of Minguat on both sides had lost their lives.

"What are you talking about? We're smarter than they are. They probably couldn't defend themselves if our people made war on them. They're soft. They'd just run."

"If we hadn't run, we'd be dead," Sum said flatly. Ghanya's arrogance was irritating Sum. "Both groups of Minguat are almost totally gone from this earth. That is *not* smart! You lived with them for years and you're alive and well. I don't get your point, Ghanya. I think you have overrated the Minguat. We aren't smarter than they are. You should be able to see how fortunate you are. As for smart, I'm not so young that I don't remember that girl who told the stories. You think we have memories like that?"

"But that's what they depend on. Memories. We think forward. We figure out things."

"You're puffing like Baambas, Ghanya. I saw what we do. We kill each other. Is that smart? I guess my wife still agrees with you. She thinks we are superior because for generations uncountable we've told ourselves we are superior. You don't become something just because you tell yourself you are. I think we are fools to do that. And thinking forward? Who saw to it that we had food through that season of cold days during the ashfall?"

"I'm sorry you feel that way," Ghanya said. "You should have seen them when we took a dead body to the cave in the hills. The Wise Ones and Ki'ti were acting like they were with people who weren't there. Totally lost their ways in their mind webs. Monkeys to me—just monkeys!"

"Does Minagle know how you feel?" Sum asked.

"I doubt it. Why would I share that with her? She's just a woman."

Wamumur had heard enough. He had been standing on the rock wall leaning against the big tree, branches of which shaded the rock path. He heard every word. He used the silent hunter's walk and went to find Guy-na. He waved to Guy-na and asked him to find Arkan-na and meet him at the end of the rock walk. The three came together and Arkan-na asked, "Wise One, what is the nature of this meeting?"

"I just overheard a conversation that chilled me to the bone. Ghanya was speaking to Sum about the superiority of the Others over the People. Until now, I didn't know how he felt. I had some thoughts, but nothing I could put my finger on. I am appalled and I am not sure what to do."

"What makes you think he thinks we think we are superior?" Guy-na asked.

"He said that you have been taught that for generations and generations. He views us as soft, incapable of defending ourselves against Others. He finds our People unattractive. Frankly, feeling as he does, I don't know why he is still among us." Wamumur was obviously troubled by the incident—more than they at first assumed.

"We live here by the grace of the People," Arkan-na said. "I was raised to think we were superior. When we were confined with the People during the cold season of the ashfall, I saw the lie we had been given to believe. I saw a People who were taught to reason and not to think more of themselves than they should. It was a huge enlightenment. That is why we are here. Your way is the better way. Look at what happened to my people who left. Three are alive!"

"I cannot let this go on ignored. Ghanya's view of the People is like a fruit rotten to the core. Place it with other fruit and it destroys the lot."

Arkan-na was concerned about his son for two reasons: the first was that he didn't know his son had such biased feelings and felt so superior, and second he feared for Ghanya in the little cave community. What would become of him? Basically, he'd been called a rotten fruit. It was true.

"Who was with him when he said these things?" Arkan-na asked.

"Sum," Wamumur responded. "Sum disagreed with him, but he did say that his wife agrees with Ghanya."

"That's interesting," Guy-na said, "It was Gurkma, Sum's father, who was the greatest bigot of our old people. He used to urge us to eradicate the People. Nobody much listened to him. It looks like the tables got turned on him. Sum must have seen through it."

Arkan-na said, "If he didn't figure out Gurkma's nonsense for himself, the war should have made it clear. At any rate it is Ghanya who is the problem and possibly, if I get this right, Wamumur, Keptu is another."

"Yes, Sum indicated his wife held the beliefs that Ghanya has."

"Let Guy-na and me take Sum and Ghanya to the lake and confront them," Arkan-na said. "I expect them to be honest about what they said. Let us have People hidden in the vegetation so they hear the whole thing. Then we will discuss what to do about this problem."

"I agree," Wamumur said. "Give me to high sun to get two of my men hidden by the log near the shore. You have the young men sit on the log and you stand with your backs to the water. We will hide in the bushes. Unless they are expert hunters they will not know we are there. You question them and then you will show them that we have heard all. Then we will discuss what to do."

It was arranged. Wamumur first went to the women to make sure they would watch the route to the lake and keep people away. Then he got Nanichak-na and Grypchon-na, Minagle's father, to go with him and hide in the bushes to listen to what the young men would say.

Wamumur wondered all morning what should be done if the arrogance was severe. He knew that could not last as part of the People. The young man was a danger and Wamumur was deeply concerned. He would have Emaea discover what Minagle thought of him as a husband before the meeting.

Minagle thought it odd that Emaea asked her about Ghanya. Her husband was a good husband, she thought, but they didn't have what Ki'ti and Untuk had—but then who did? And maybe what they had was just newly joined love. The conversation was light and Minagle didn't think overlong about it.

Nanichak-na, Grypchon-na, and Wamumur went down the hill to the lake while no one was out in the open field. They skirted around the usual approach to the lake and took the steep way down where there was only an animal trail that had been made and used for years. That would not give away their presence on the main path. In fact, when Arkan-na and Guy-na took the two young men to the lake, they wondered whether the older People were actually there. They scanned the woods after telling the young men to sit on the log. They saw nothing. They detected no man scent. They just assumed, knowing the People, that they were in place. Their disguise amazed Arkan-na. His visual search almost made Wamumur laugh. The Others could not see the People in hiding.

Arkan-na began. "You both were talking this morning." Arkan-na's words were not a question.

The two young men nodded.

"Ghanya, it seems you think the Minguat are superior to the People who took us in when we were starving, saved our lives, and who have given you a peaceful place to live for the years since Baambas."

Ghanya fidgeted but he admitted that they had been told for years that they were superior. He mentioned how Gurkma constantly talked about how the People should be exterminated and it would be a better world.

"And you didn't learn anything from our cold season confinement with the People?"

"What was I supposed to learn?" Ghanya asked sarcastically. "They took us in and kept us alive. Knowing what we believed, they should have made war on us then. We could not have defended ourselves. They'd have been free of us."

"Let me understand, Ghanya. You actually think that if these People were smart, you'd be dead?"

"Ummmm. I guess that's what I mean."

"My son," Arkan-na said, "I never taught you such rubbish."

"You didn't have to. It was all around us. Look at the Chief. He and his wife joked about the People all the time. He made fun of their heads and their stocky build. He called them stupid inferiors. Well, not at first. But toward the end when we knew we'd leave for the east, he joked about them all the time. He said they ran like sloths. Alak also made fun of them even while we were confined during the cold season. He thought they were stupid not to have killed us when they could. They said so in the cave in our language. The -na hunters and the ones who weren't -na hunters joked about the title. It meant nothing unless you were hungry."

"Are you trying to imply that what you said is legitimized by the fact that others in the cave did the same thing? Did it ever occur to you that some of us learned a lot from the People? We learned that our way was *not* good! Did that ever occur to you?"

"Why should it? We *are* superior."

"Then, Ghanya, if you really think that, why are you here?" Guy-na asked his brother.

"I don't know why any of us is here. If we'd gone east, isn't it possible that we'd have won the war?"

"Oh, my Son, your thinking is badly twisted. If we'd gone east, we'd be dead."

"Well," Ghanya boasted, "I can fight. I'm strong."

Sum had had about all he could take. "Ghanya, they had better weapons. You would be dead. It was the warriors who were boastful they picked off first."

"How can that be?" Ghanya was shocked at the news.

"Oh, my son. Your mind web is as torn as if a bat tried to fly through it. Boastful people are not smart and they fail often because they neglect thinking. They say they are so strong, but no strength backs them up. They call themselves winners, but no wins are credited to them. All their superiority is in their imaginations, not in fact. They are puffed up like birds when it's really cold. They look big but the substance is totally lacking." Arkan-na was appalled at this person he thought he knew.

"Look behind you," Arkan-na told the young men.

They did.

Sum asked, "What are we looking for?"

"Just look," Arkan-na insisted. He still tried to see the People in the forest. Knowing they were there and not being able to see them impressed Arkan-na even more.

"Father, there is nothing there," Ghanya said with irritation.

Arkan-na and Guy-na waved to the unseen audience. Wamumur and Nanichak-na and Grypchon-na stood and came out of the bushes. The two young men were startled speechless. Any one of the three men could easily have killed Ghanya and Sum and probably the others.

"Were you superior enough to detect three men behind you?" Arkan-na asked Ghanya.

"No," he admitted.

The men had smeared mud on their bodies in deceptive camouflage. Mud removed their odor and made them exceptionally difficult to see in a natural setting.

"They concealed themselves so well that even though we looked, knowing they were there, we could not see them," Guy-na said with admiration.

"What do you of the Minguat do with members who think they are superior?" Wamumur asked, wasting no time getting to the point.

"When I lived among the Minguat," Guy-na said, "There was much boastful posturing. It was worthless arrogance. I think it was done to make some feel good about our kind. We actually ignored it."

"Did it work to make you feel better about yourselves?" Wamumur asked.

"Of course not, or we wouldn't have had to keep doing it."

"So you did nothing when your members talked of exterminating us?"

"Truthfully, nobody paid real attention to it, except, apparently, my son."

"Well, we see this behavior as rotten fruit. A piece of rotten fruit can ruin a whole basket if permitted to lie with other good fruit. We remove rotten fruit and throw it as far away as possible." Wamumur had his hands on his hips. "Loose talk like this can disrupt function of the mind web and cause aberrant behavior that is harmful to the person who has the problem—and to the others around him. Ghanya, you need to realize that any group of people rises to the level of competence required by the environment in which they live, or they die. Just because people differ from you does not mean they are intellectually inferior."

Ghanya was becoming very uncomfortable, while Sum was fascinated. He could not get over their art of concealment, and the idea that people rose to the level of competence that was environmentally required fascinated him.

"Ghanya, what you think is not something we can control. What I will tell you is if you ever speak of these things again, it will cease to be thought. You will then have acted on your own rotten ideas by speaking them so that others can hear the evil thoughts. We will not tolerate rotten ideas shared here and will remove you from the People. You may think we are soft. You may discover at your peril how soft we are not. Choosing to live peacefully is just that—choice. We can rely on each other because we *don't* try to be better than each other. When we lived near the sea and one of the People became arrogant and worthless, we simply traded him to seafarers as a slave. Here, we are too far from the sea. In Cave Kwa just before you arrived, a member became violent and threatening to Minagle. That person—how shall I put it?—met with an accident. You have seen our Wise One of the future. When she disobeyed, she was punished severely. Do not mistake our hospitality. We do not make a a large issue of it. We do not prolong agony. We act and we act decisively for the health and well being of the People. Sum, you need to correct Keptu. We do not make a difference between males and females in discipline, as you have heard. We will have no rotten fruit among our People!" He punctuated his words with a firm palm strike which was followed by palm strikes of the People, Arkan-na, and Guy-na.

Wamumur paused, signaling with his hands that he wasn't through.

"I have decided that our People have made a mistake that I will correct tonight. We have been a mix of three peoples: the People, the Others, the Mol. Tonight, we all become the People. Anyone choosing to refrain can pack his or her things and leave. You, Ghanya, have until tonight to think and get your mind web straight. If you choose to leave, you cannot take Minagle and the children with you. That is all I have to say."

"Son," Arkan-na said, "I am disappointed in you. If Wamumur had ordered me to spear you, I would have done it without question. He is right. Your ideas are like rotten fruit."

"I have something to ask," Grypchon-na said. "Minagle is my daughter. Do you love her?"

Ghanya thought a moment and said, "I do love her. I started to love her by pretending she was one of us. But I love her for who she is. I really do love her. I don't know what I'd do without her."

Ghanya was frightened. His father's words were the harshest words he'd ever heard in his life. He needed to think and decide what he would do that evening. Could he even consider leaving? If he stayed and made one mention of the Minguat and being superior, he might meet with an accident. Ghanya didn't miss the meaning. It meant they'd kill him. Did that mean they killed the person who had scared Minagle so badly? They killed him for what he did? Bad fruit. Yes, what the guy did was like bad fruit. But his own thoughts were that he *was* superior. Wasn't he? Obviously his father didn't think so. Sum didn't think so. Had he, as he was accused of doing, believed a lie? Was he inferior to *these* People? They were really good at camouflage. He was so confused.

Wamumur looked at Ghanya. "Get out of my sight until tonight."

Ghanya got up and sprinted up the hill. He didn't look back. He raced to the field where they made the animals fall over the cliff, running all the way to the dropoff and stepping down to the ledge. He crawled into the tiny little cave and sat there looking out on the land below. He watched some monkeys in the trees as they fought among themselves over a piece of fruit. Ghanya shivered. Was he thinking he was so smart that he might get himself killed?

He no longer considered the People soft. He wasn't sure how he thought of them comparatively, but he didn't think they were soft anymore! If they would kill one of their own for misconduct with a girl, what might they do to him for making fun of them? He wondered how they killed the man.

Sum went to find Keptu. How was he supposed to deal with his wife? He found her and asked her to walk with him. She joined him, wondering what he had to discuss. He told her of the morning's conversation. He told her about the meeting at the lake with Arkan-na and Guy-na. He told her about Wamumur, Grypchon-na, and Nanichak-na who had been hidden in the bushes and had left no sign on the trail and how they were completely invisible until they were called out. He told of the idea of rotten fruit and what the people did with rotten fruit. He told her they did not discriminate where males and females were concerned when it came to discipline. When he finished, she was shaking.

"They are not soft, are they?"

"No, my wife, and if you hold onto your ideas of them as inferior, bad things will happen and I won't be able to stop them, and furthermore, I won't want to."

"You are turning from me?"

"I am no longer willing to live with someone who hates someone else for no reason. They are right. It is like rotten fruit."

"But that's what we were taught."

"We were taught wrong. These are very intelligent people. To keep thinking wrong thoughts confuses your mind web. You can correct your errors. When you know what you were taught is wrong, why would you hang onto it?"

"I am frightened," she said and wept.

"Do you really think it is right to move to a place where People offer you great hospitality and then you make fun of them?"

"I'm sorry, my husband. I didn't see it that way. I saw it the way I was taught. We are not taught to think for ourselves!" she said defensively.

"Tonight you will have to choose to stay here or leave. This is not a decision that is lightly taken. You can be killed for making fun of them if you stay and do it later."

"You are staying aren't you?"

"Of course. I like the People. I recognize that they saved our lives—twice. They have much to teach me."

"I cannot leave you. I love you."

"Then you had better find out how to get rid of your feelings of superiority and never again consider these People inferior. In fact, if you remain you have to consider yourself one of the People."

She lowered her head and wept. She had never been told what and how to think except by the Minguat. She wondered how well she would do or whether she'd be killed if she stayed. She was certain that if she left she would die.

The evening meal in the cave was perfectly normal. Most people had no idea what had occurred that morning. When the meal was finished and the clean up had taken place, Wamumur stood and cleared his throat. "I wish to speak to all," he said.

Everyone gathered in the central area. They sat and prepared to listen carefully. Wamumur loomed large. The shadows he cast on the wall were huge and ominous.

"I have watched this group grow. We have the People, the Others, and the Mol living here. Tonight that all changes. It is clear that we tend to see ourselves as three peoples, not one. That is not good. Tonight we make decisions. Anyone living here at the end of the meeting lives here as one of the People. No longer will there be Others or Mol. Just People. We are all the same. We may have different colored hair, or eyes, or skin, or different shaped heads or eyes, or height, or feet," he added, thinking of the little one with six toes. The last comment made people laugh. "All of that is irrelevant. We are all of us the People. We work to the good of the People. We are kind, not puffed up and self serving; filled with humility, not arrogance; known for hospitality; peaceful, not warlike. And because of that we are strong, not weak. Being the People does not mean we share physical characteristics but rather we live a certain way with Wisdom as our Guide. Some of you may not want to be People. That is fine. You are free to leave. Anyone who remains is People. If anyone is joined with People and chooses to leave, he or she cannot take his People husband or wife. But, if the husband or wife who is People chooses to leave, that person can never return to live among the People, for they know the People already and have rejected what is good for them. Once Wisdom fades this night's darkness, all inhabitants will be People. That is all I have to say. Are there questions?"

There was dead silence. As with some of the situations in the cave, only a few knew why this was happening. Most felt this had already happened. Most of those who arrived at the cave felt part of the People. Now they would all truly be equal. They did not sense that there was a problem with bigotry that motivated the meeting. Some thought it a nice gesture.

Ki'ti put her arm around Untuk. She looked up into his eyes, "Are you pleased to call yourself People?" she asked. Ahriku was curled up next to her sleeping.

Untuk grinned from ear to ear. "I thought I already became People when we joined."

"I guess it wasn't made clear in the past."

"I'm Other and you are Mol. Now we are People?" Aryna asked Tongip.

"It is good," he smiled. He held her hand and looked into her eyes. She echoed his words.

Wamumur watched the People. He wondered whether he'd ever be as wise as he felt he should be. Apparently, there had been more significance with respect to origin than he had thought. It was good for it to come out. He'd never guessed rotten fruit was in their midst.

Grypchon-na noticed that Ghanya was standing near Keptu. He hoped the young man was not up to no good, but he wondered. Time would make all things clear. He worried for his daughter.

The cave settled for the night. Wamumur could not sleep. He was greatly concerned. He had shared with Emaea and Ki'ti what had caused the meeting, but the rest of the People never knew the whole story.

When Wisdom dissipated the darkness with rays of light from the sun, Totamu did not rise from her bed. She was alive but too tired to get up. Pechki was ripping loose at the belly. Her mother was her most special person. She could not bear it if she became ill. She refused to let herself think farther than that. The alarm for Totamu's condition was so significant that no one seemed to notice that two people were missing from the cave. Wamumur knew. He had watched them leave.

It was not until Minagle went to Grypchon-na and asked whether he'd seen Ghanya that any attention was drawn to the event of the night before. It seemed that Ghanya was missing. Sum missed his wife also. Keptu had waked before he did; he wondered where she had been for so long. Then, he became concerned and looked for Ghanya.

Ermol-na who was the entrance guard during the first part of the night told Wamumur that Ghanya and Keptu had left the cave together in the middle of the night. He thought they might have decided to leave and the People had agreed not to stop anyone who was leaving. Each took weapons and some skins. That was all he could see was missing. They might also have taken some dried meat. Wamumur nodded. He told Ermol-na that he, too, had watched them leave. In a matter of hours, it was clear to all. Ghanya and Keptu had left. Hunters tracked the couple to the river that headed east. It would take them to the sea if they followed it all the way.

As soon as the hunters knew the direction the pair had gone, they returned. The two would probably die in the next few days, they considered.

Sum grieved but was not terribly surprised. He had certainly loved his wife, but he had found that he had much to learn and that pulled him to the People. He worried about what might happen to the two in their flight. Minagle was torn apart. On the one hand, her Izumo was in bed during the day, and, on the other, husband had left the cave with someone else! He didn't want to be People? She was horrified. Now she had no husband and two children. She did not think Ghanya would return. *He had an awful lot of pride,* she thought. She had no idea why he chose not to be People. She wondered whether she'd done something wrong.

Considering that she might think she'd done something wrong, Grypchon-na found his daughter and explained briefly what had happened. It wasn't her. Ghanya felt superior to People and didn't want to be one. Neither did Keptu. Both had believed the lie that was taught to the Others that they were superior to People. Minagle was stupefied! She'd lived for years with a man she didn't know. How could that be? They had been intimate. He had been so kind and thoughtful where she was concerned. How could this be? Her belly ached with sorrow.

The cave was busy preparing for the evening meal when a shout from Lamk outside brought hunters quickly to the rock wall. Keptu was crawling through some brush at the top of the hill across from the cave. She was bloody and apparently in pain. A stretcher was taken to her immediately and she was brought to the cave. She barely managed to tell of their flight and then running into a bear in the dark. The bear hit her first and when Ghanya tried to help her, the bear killed him and began to eat him. Her mind web flew away then, and it didn't return. Sometime after a solemn evening meal was finished, her last breath exhaled. *Would she walk with Wisdom?* some wondered. The People buried her in their grave site next to Cue-na.

Wamumur asked Arkan-na and Ey whether they wanted hunters to find the body of Ghanya. Arkan-na assured them that he did not. It was too risky to take a body from a bear that decided to eat it. He felt his son had shamed him. He wanted to have nothing to do with retrieving the body. His son was Other. He was People. That was all he had to say. Ey stood beside him grief stricken. She understood why he spoke as he did, but he was talking about his son. Ghanya had seemed such a happy person and now he was dead. It was hard for her to take in. Ghanya had been a year older than she. She never understood the superiority that the Others felt and had mostly ignored it. She said nothing.

Wamumur assured Arkan-na that People did not take shame that was not theirs to own. Ghanya shamed himself, not his father. Arkan-na showed gratitude for the comment by lowering his head. He would try not to carry shame and feelings of guilt that were not his to carry.

Minagle felt sorry for Sum. The young man had been in war for many seasons. His young body was scarred. He'd made a frightful trek to find the People. Then her own husband had run off with his wife. And she died before his eyes. Sum knew she was experiencing the same pain as he was. The two tried to comfort each other. Both were brokenhearted. She wavered emotionally between grief and anger. Sum thought of Minagle as woman before she ever saw him as man. To her, he was a young one who had been injured by her husband. To him, she had been injured by her husband, but didn't know the depth of it. He would not enlighten her.

As the season-of-new-leaves days passed and the two continued to try for mutual support, they drew together. Sum and Minagle walked down the path by the stream and up to the top of the hill while they talked. Although he was younger than she, he was taller and they fit well together while walking. After she made a complimentary comment to him, he put his arms around her and hugged her. She began to push him away and changed her mind. Without prior consideration and for many emotional reasons, they joined without pronouncement. They didn't discuss joining, but the time spent outside or in one of the secret caves filled them with a sense of wellbeing and of being loved. Neither was ready to trust another for permanence but each found immediate solace together. Between Likichi and Domur, Minagle's children did not lack. Minagle did manage to remember to feed Song. At age two, she still nursed from time to time. Meeluf at five was doing well with the other children. From time to time, Sum taught Meeluf hunter's knowledge in the field so he would understand what he saw when he was allowed to go to watch a hunt. He would draw pictures in the dirt with a stick to show him where to aim for a kill on specific animals. It would be a while before the boy had the hand-eye coordination to be routinely successful even with a slingshot, but he was gaining valuable knowledge.

Totamu's continuous coughing was unproductive. She was fatigued and found she was sleeping more than she was awake. She sensed her time to walk with Wisdom was near. She talked to Pechki about the herbs and medicinals that she had accumulated over the years. She was confident that Pechki knew enough to attend to the People's basic needs. She wondered about the others. Ki'ti had been the one she chose to teach, but then Wisdom snatched her away. She thought Ki'ti could still search her mind web for creating some of the remedies that would be needed, even if she hadn't learned all the details. Totamu looked back over her life. She had lived seventy years. She loved every one of them. Some were admittedly better than others, but she was happy with her life. If her days were ending, she was ready.

In a matter of a few days, Totamu began the return to Wisdom. The cave was in uproar, but quiet was maintained. There was weeping such as they had never seen—tears flowed profusely as quietly as possible. Totamu had been seen as virtually immortal. No one could imagine life without her. The People planned to bury Totamu higher than the site they'd chosen for their other burials. She would overlook the graves in death as she overlooked the cave administration in life. It seemed fitting to all. She would be buried in the same manner as Enut years ago, except that the young girls gathered flowers by the armloads to place around her and over her in the place where she'd lie in the ground. When Totamu was laid on the dirt floor of the excavated hole, she wore the long dress Pechki had made for her. It still had the three places where the shells had been sewed on. One was missing—the one that was buried with Enut. Flowers covered the woman from head to toe and all around. Nanichak-na took a sharp stone and a wooden comb and placed them atop the flowers. Ki'ti told the story of the creation of the people. She barely maintained her composure. Wamumur had his belly ripped so badly he found standing there for the story time very hard. He also wondered how long it would be before he would go to meet her. He was only three years younger than she, and Emaea was five years younger than Totamu.

The men gathered more meat by coaxing animals to go over the ledge or spearing them. The women fished. Children, who were safe swimmers, played by the lake shore until the season of warm nights came to an end. One day, when a large flock of geese landed on the lake on their journey south, the women used four-string throws to capture about ten of the large geese, and they had a feast of goose roasted over a fire on a turning spit. The People were delighted with the different meat. Leaves fell and the world began to turn bleak for the season of cold days. Sum and Minagle finally joined. They used a private cave for a single night. Minagle became wife to one much younger than she. Sum became husband and father overnight. Meeluf loved his new father. His new father seemed to approve of him where his old father rarely approved. It made him feel good.

Even though the People were all equal as adults, there would always be leaders. Totamu had been the administrative leader of the cave. Her busy little body was everywhere at once, pushing People when they needed pushing, slowing them down when that was necessary. She had a mental inventory of all the food that was stored, as well as pelts by type and quantity. She knew who needed clothing and who needed tools. She knew when a joined couple was having difficulty and when help was needed to raise a child. Cave life functioned well; the People were clean and healthy because Totamu took it upon herself to see to it that what needed doing was done. She was a second mother to everyone in the cave and she had relished it. There was nobody who was willing to jump into her shoes. Finally, it became clear that Totamu's successor would be Likichi. Everyone had expected Pechki to do it, but Likichi had the same drive Totamu had to be sure all was functioning well and contingency plans were available. Likichi didn't take over through self-proclamation. It was more a function of People going to her when they had questions or needed help. Little by little, her leadership was clear and Pechki, Veymun, Amey, and Flayk made it clear that it was to Likichi that People needed to go, each breathing a sigh of relief it wasn't to them. Totamu's job was huge and all-consuming.

When Wisdom brought the sun's first glow to fade the darkness, Ki'ti went to find Ahriku and discovered that her little dog had breathed his last. She had seen him weaken over the last year. His muzzle, ears, and the top of his head were grizzled. She had loved that dog who went through the ashfall with her, saved Manak from a serpent, strengthened her through her learning to become Wise One, took the trip with her to the place where the giants played, guarded the First Night cave when she spent so much time there with Untuk. Ahriku had been with her through every major event in her life. She kneeled down and laid her head on his back and circled her arms around his body. He was part of her. How could she turn loose? Her belly ripped apart. She lost tears but was so choked up she could not utter a sound. He had asked for nothing but to be by her. She had totally taken him for granted. He was so special. And she hadn't been with him when his life slipped away. In fact she had paid little attention to him lately. But that didn't mean she loved him less. She just took his being there for granted in the same way she took Totamu's being there for granted. In the same way with Wise One's being there and Emaea's. *Was she about to lose them, too?* she wondered in horror. *She didn't want that. She didn't want that at all.*

Untuk found her on the floor on her knees, doubled over to her chest. Her hair was all over the place and her position was not very dignified. Then he saw what had happened. He tried to pull her up but she did not want to let go. "Please, go dig the hole," was all she could get out.

Untuk wondered about the People momentarily. Did they bury dogs? He had never known anyone to do that. To humor Ki'ti, he'd be glad to do it. He mentioned it to Wamumur. Wamumur let others know. Soon, children gathered flowers for the dog. Some of them had managed to overcome their fear and get close to Ahriku. Others had just known he was special to Ki'ti. They made as big a flower gathering for the dog as the adults had for Totamu. Untuk was shocked, and found the practice fascinating. He went to tell Ki'ti that the hole in the earth was ready. The one he dug was overlooking the area where the dogs lived. It was midway up the hill. To Untuk's utter surprise, the entire cave turned out for the dog. What he'd seen was Ahriku's last days, not his life.

Ki'ti carried Ahriku from the cave and laid the dog on his side in the grave. His eyes were shut. Then the children formed a line and started covering the dog with flowers. Ki'ti wept for her loss and also with love for the children who made this gesture for Ahriku. Had he been a person, he would have been so pleased, she thought. Ki'ti sat at the side of the grave after it had been filled. Untuk left her there to mourn. When she didn't want to come after he called the third time, he told her if she didn't come now, he'd carry her down. She stood and waved weakly to the place in the ground and followed Untuk down to the cave. It was time for the evening meal. She ate little, but she was there. As if on cue from Wisdom or some other source unknown, as Ki'ti thought to get the sleeping mats laid out, a wobbly little recently weaned pup crawled into her lap. She looked for someone who might have put the dog there, but no one was around. A smiling Nanichak-na said from the entrance, "He just walked in here all by himself. I let him because I wanted to know where he'd go. I should have known."

The little dog looked into her eyes just like Ahriku had years ago. "I don't think I can do this right now," she said to the dog with a sob. He didn't understand, curling up comfortably with his head on her leg. She silently dropped tears onto the pup, grieving for her lost dog. She looked around feeling that she was being watched. Had Wisdom sent her another dog? "If that's you, Wisdom, thank you," she whispered. "You are Panriku, Little Wolf." She stroked him.

When Untuk returned to her after filling Ahriku's grave, he found her sitting on the ground with the pup in her lap. She had stopped crying. "Another dog?" he asked.

"Yes. He came to me exactly like Ahriku did. His name is Panriku."

"Little Wolf?" he asked.

"Exactly," she smiled.

"Let's get these sleeping mats unrolled. I'm really tired," he said.

Ki'ti automatically unrolled the first mat and then the second. She placed the softer pads on the sleeping mats and laid the covers over the top. Untuk slid into the bedding and shut his eyes. Ki'ti reached over and hugged him. She was so accustomed to a hug and kiss for Emaea and Wamumur that it was automatic. He held her tight and then released her. "I really am tired," he said.

She lay down and covered herself. The little dog poked his nose under the covers and came to lie down right beside her. She felt as if she were reliving part of her life. She wondered whether Ahriku had been the father of this little dog. She cried for warmth of the new pup. She cried for the loss of her first dog, her loyal friend. She cried for Totamu. She cried for impermanence of those she loved. She cried that she and others had to continue on when they were bereft. Her belly ached. Her sinuses were clogged. She fell asleep.

Ki'ti awakened because her face was being licked. She looked at the face of Panriku and laughed.

"What is the matter with you?" she asked.

She got up and noticed Untuk was still sleeping. She wondered briefly whether he felt well. She let him sleep. She went to the entrance and took the pup to the steps so he would go relieve himself. As if he'd been trained, he scampered off. She saw Chamul-na at the entrance and asked him to guard while she went to the privy. Even as an adult, she was protected. He agreed and she left the cold rock walk and went down the steps. Walking to the end of the open area to where the stream turned, she went to the privy and relieved herself. Her feet were cold. She should have put on her boots, but she hadn't noticed it was cold. Returning to the cave, she put on her warm pants and boots and jacket. When her hands warmed, she felt Untuk. He was normal in temperature. She hoped he was well, but still didn't want to wake him up. Panriku returned to her.

There was a huge earthquake, the biggest they'd had. It shook for what felt like a very long time and knocked some of the ceiling and walls loose. If Totamu had been sleeping where she normally slept, a rock would have hit her. It might have killed her. It was alarming, but they had experienced earthquakes before. It wasn't new. The quake was followed by numerous aftershocks. They were smaller, but equally as disquieting. When one of the aftershocks hit, there was an enormous crashing sound north of them. It was deafening. Chamul-na and Nanichak-na took Kai, Lamul, and Manak and followed the trail to the north. They wanted to see whether they could determine what caused the huge crash. They followed the path north. When they got to the turnoff for the caves of the animals, they decided to check the caves for damage. Want they saw astounded them. It was as if someone had taken the cave and cut it off and set the top of the cave on the hearth level. All the wonderful animal images were gone, they thought. They did check around a little and found a small hole they could crawl through to enter the cave. Manak crawled in and found some of the images were still there, but many had been covered. Chamul-na called to him to get out before they had another quake. He did.

Nanichak-na wondered whether the Winds of Change were starting to blow again. This was a big earthquake. They looked for more damage but found nothing more. Chamul-na wondered whether their cave was safe from collapsing like that one had. What made him feel better is even though this one caved in, the roof did not go down all the way to the floor. If People had been there, many would have lived. They returned to their home cave satisfied they had seen the major damage from the quake. By the time Wisdom sucked the color from the land, the aftershocks had stopped.

After the men returned, Chamul-na and Nanichak-na gathered Neamu-na, Gruid-na, Mootmu-na, Ermol-na and Hahami-na, together with Wamumur and Emaea. The hunters felt it was time to make Kai, Ekuktu, Lamul, Lai, and Manak -na hunters. All agreed. Wamumur said he also thought that Slamika should be included. The hunters looked at themselves. They were embarrassed. They should have included him. They hadn't. Of course, they agreed, he definitely should become one. That same night, Gruid-na would make the pronouncement.

Wind blew in the tree tops on the hill sending away colorful leaves that had served their purpose. The day seemed too lovely. Crystal blue skies were in evidence in the last year, making the People think the haze from Baambas had cleared. It was chilly. Even children wore boots and jackets. They had finished bringing wood to the cave and were getting ready for Wisdom to suck color from the land, when Wamumur called the cave to order. People wondered what was happening now.

Wamumur said that he had some information to share. Gruid-na would make the pronouncement. Gruid-na called Manak, Lai, Kai, Ekuktu, and Lamul to the front. Chamul-na waved at Gruid-na, until he remembered to call Slamika. The six men stood there wondering what was about to happen.

Gruid-na announced to the People the time had come that all these men were now -na hunters. The men were very surprised. This was not how pronouncements had been done in the past. But they were delighted to receive the honor.

Gruid-na walked down the line saying their new name and putting his hands on their shoulders as he did. He put his hands on the shoulders of Manak saying "Manak-na," then Lai saying "Lai-na," then Slamika saying "Slamika-na," then Lamul saying "Lamul-na," then Kai saying, "Kai-na," and finally Ekuktu saying "Ekuktu-na." As each hunter's name was called, he lowered his head.

Knowing that this event was about to take place, Ki'ti had already explained to Untuk what was happening and what it meant and how it was to be received. The Mol had nothing like this and Untuk was intrigued. He hoped someday to have the -na designation. He wondered whether he ever would since his main job was to safeguard Ki'ti, not bring home food. He could and did hunt but it was secondary, not primary in his set of responsibilities.

Emaea had paid attention to Gruid-na. His mind web was usually as well ordered as a slingshot hitting the center of a circle in practice, but recently he had begun to forget things like Slamika at the ceremony. That struck her as the slingshot missing the practice target altogether. She discussed it with Wamumur who had noticed the same problem. He thought it had gone on longer than she had. It was something to watch. Hunters needed every faculty to be keenly sharp if they were to survive. The death of Ghanya was one of those incidents that still struck Emaea as totally unnecessary. He left in the middle of the night, but hunters sometimes did walk at night. However, Ghanya was emotionally shaken when he left, Emaea had no doubt. That would be enough to throw the balance of life in favor of the hunter, not the hunted, and Ghanya had become the hunted. Emaea didn't miss the fact that Ghanya had given his life for another.

The season of warm nights had seemed warmer. At a discussion of significances with Wamumur and Emaea, Ki'ti asked whether the warmer seasons of cold days were because time had passed since the ashfall from Baambas. They discussed it for some time. They concluded either it had or they were getting used to the cold. They also reasoned they had been this far north for several periods of seasons. They really couldn't compare with where they lived prior to Baambas. They were convinced the air must be clearing more and more each season. They thought it would be interesting to see when the temperature leveled out for several years so they would have a better knowledge of the real climate of the region.

Wamumur asked Emaea and Ki'ti whether it wouldn't be a good idea to include Untuk in the discussions they had. It would help him understand the People and the Wise Ones. They agreed it would be good, so Ki'ti went to find Untuk. He gladly returned with her to the meeting. The discussions lasted all day. Many topics were addressed, including what they thought of the progress of the three groups becoming the People. Their discussions became so involved they had to continue after the evening meal. Untuk had much to add that was of value, and the three were glad they had asked him to join them. All the while, Panriku lay at Ki'ti's feet. The tiny size of the pup often brought tears to her eyes because she found him as faithful as the dog she'd lost.

By the season of warm nights, Likichi had begun to make Untuk's season-of-the-cold-days garments. His leather wouldn't get him through the cold. She had never made such a huge garment. It was a challenge but she loved a challenge. His foot size made her smile. She had made him a tunic when he joined with Ki'ti. She just about had the season-of-cold-days garments finished. She wondered where Untuk might be found, and realized he was meeting with the Wise Ones. She would have to wait. At the evening meal she asked him to try on a few items to make sure they fit comfortably. He went with her and she did the fitting quickly so he could return to the meeting.

The meeting continued. Wamumur had been speaking, and then he took a long pause. "I have thought long and carefully about what I am going to do now." He touched Ki'ti's shoulder. "Emaea and I have agreed on this. We think it wise. Beginning tomorrow, both of us step down from the roles we have had for so long. You are young, we will be available in advisory capacity only. You, my dear, will be Wise One to these People. You are ready."

Ki'ti recoiled. "Father, please, it is too soon! How can you think I am ready?" she asked.

"Little Girl," he said and paused, "you are more ready than I was when I began," he assured her. He did a palm strike.

"And the same is true for me," Emaea told her, and followed with a palm strike.

Wamumur continued. "The hunters will come to you with their questions. You will answer them to the best of your ability. Do not put them off. Go through your mind web, reason, and ask for Wisdom's guidance and then answer them. If absolutely necessary, you may discuss with us, but I don't want to have you coming to us for every little question—only the things that you cannot possibly reason out. Talk to Untuk first. He knows the hunter's world. Don't be uncomfortable asking the hunters questions. I have asked them as many as they've asked me."

"Little Girl," Emaea began, "You know the world of Wisdom and you know what it is to be People. We have come a long way together. You need to keep the People together. Do not let little differences become wide breaks. The first resposibilty you have is to be certain that the People learn to think things through and that they are supportive of each other. As long as those two things occur, you will be a good Wise One. Use the men's council at night. Listen to them. You will learn a world of information that way. Keep it in your mind web. It will come in handy sometime in the future."

"You know," Wamumur said, "we cannot live much longer. By doing what we do now, when we go to be with Wisdom, you will be experienced and have things well in hand. Little Girl, do not be weak. There are times when you must be forceful. Those who were Others will look for weakness. You already have respect that is given you by Wisdom's choice of you. You must from tomorrow morning go forth and gain the respect of the People on your own. Be confident. Be strong. Treat all equally. Stay true to the stories, and always look for the next Wise One. Do what you do because it is right, not so People will like you." He followed his words with a forceful palm strike.

"I have listened, my father," she assured him. She affirmed the palm strike with one equally firm. "Will you make the pronouncement?"

"Yes. Now." And he was good to his word.

Wamumur cleared his throat and the People turned toward him. He said very clearly and slowly so there would be no questions, "Tonight Emaea and I turn over the responsibility of Wise One to Ki'ti. When you awaken tomorrow as Wisdom restores color to the land, you will have one Wise One. No longer do you come to Emaea or me with questions. You go to her. My seat at the men's council after the evening meal will now be hers. Wisdom has clearly chosen her. Do not argue with Wisdom or me or Emaea. She is not immature in these matters. She is more mature than I was when I became Wise One. I have taught her everything she needs to know. There is nothing else I can teach her. She will go with you as Wise One from this time onwards. Go with Wisdom. That is all I have to say." He did a forceful palm strike.

The response of the People went from sharp inhalation and surprise to a sense of finality of Wamumur's decision and dead silence. No one was prepared for the change, but they all accepted it as coming from Wisdom. The People followed him with forceful palm strikes. In time, some would talk about the age of the new Wise One, but none would say aloud they questioned Wamumur's judgment.

"This changes things," Untuk told her after the pronouncement.

"It surely does," she replied.

"No, I mean something different from what you mean."

"What do you mean?" she asked.

"We can no longer go slipping off to the caves whenever we get a spare moment. You are going to have to be available."

"Untuk, I cannot live without occasionally going to the caves!" She was deflated. She had not considered having to be available constantly. It was one of the things she certainly knew, but knowing and reality were two different things. Her hair had fallen across part of her face, and Untuk reached out and smoothed it back. He put his arm around her and held her to him. "Come," he said. It was not totally dark outside and he took her to one of the adult caves beyond the hillside across from the home cave. There they unleashed their passion briefly and fiercely, and then returned to the home cave and slept. Little did they know their sign that a cave was in use had doubled. Now it would also be a little dog named Panriku waiting outside along with a standing log used traditionally by the People. Not only did Ki'ti have a new role cut out for herself, but Untuk also had to keep her as Wise One as well as satisfied wife. With some People, that might not have been considered much of a responsibility. For Untuk with Ki'ti it was an enormous responsibility.

At the morning meal, Ki'ti discovered that her place in the line of being served food had changed. She now was the last of the men. That made her want to laugh, but she dared not. She rose to the occasion, and took her food with her head lowered to the food servers. She and Untuk sat together in the greater gathering space and ate. Ki'ti realized that initially everything she did would set precedent. She was concerned that she be seen as Wise One to every member of the People. She forced herself to smile and recognize, eye to eye, every person she came in contact with. No longer would she allow herself to look down to keep her personal space. She was available to all, and she would keep an eye on all. She began to see herself as mother to the People. She smiled. Perhaps, after all, she could do this. *Wisdom*, she cried out silently, *be with me. I can do this only with You.*

Song toddled over. The two-year-old daughter of Minagle was adorable. She had straight black hair like her parents, Minagle and Ghanya, and deep blue eyes. She had a piece of meat on a bone in her hand and she climbed onto Ki'ti's lap without asking permission. Ki'ti smiled despite the grease smear on her tunic. Surely, she would be mother to the People, and Song had figured it out right away. Minagle called to Song, afraid she might be a bother to Ki'ti, but Ki'ti waved Minagle back and smiled. She put her hands on Song's head and smiled broadly at her. Song leaned against her and smiled back. Untuk wondered whether they'd have children and when. He considered it. He didn't think they were ready. He knew that Wisdom would be the judge, not he or Ki'ti.

As the day wore on, Ki'ti found Nanichak-na. He was the oldest of the hunters and one of her favorites. She asked whether he knew of the location of other caves to the north. He was surprised, but assured her that other than the one that fell in the earthquake, he wasn't aware of others. He wanted to know why.

"I have often wondered about the earthquakes we get in this area. I was deeply troubled that the animal cave collapsed. I think that if we have another large earthquake, we should consider moving the People elsewhere. That is why I wondered."

"I have had similar concerns," he admitted. "I didn't discuss it because I didn't want to alarm anyone."

Ki'ti stood straight and firm, reminding him of Totamu in her younger days. "I look at this place. It is perfect. Sometimes I wonder if it is too perfect. Could it be that earthquakes hit the same area over and over? If we went north, I wonder, could we avoid the worst of the shaking?"

"You do know why we don't go very far north from here?"

"Yes. It is fear of the man-like apes."

"The last time we checked, we could not find any."

"Well, Nanichak-na, I am not suggesting we make any rash moves. I do think it is something we should be considering and devise a plan, so that if it becomes necessary, we know where we will go. I remember when Baambas started smoking, Wamumur and you hunters had a plan for a place for us to go to be safe. Cave Kwa wasn't the most perfect place, but it saved our lives. I want to have a place that will be our sanctuary if this one seems to be failing. Sometimes, I look at the walls above us and sense that someday they, too, will flatten out against the floor here. It is unsettling when this place is so perfect with the fields where animals graze, and the dropoff, and the lake. Do you ever think about it's being too perfect?"

"Many times, Wise One, many times."

Ki'ti lowered her head the moment he called her *Wise One*. He had bestowed on her a great compliment, it helped her gain her assurance quickly.

Nanichak-na reached out his hand and took hers. "I worried about your leadership. I worry no longer. You are truly ready to be Wise One. I respect you, Wise One."

She could not curb her impetuous nature and threw her arms around the old man. "I need you, Great Hunter," she said. She had borrowed her sister's epithet for Nanichak-na. It was fitting.

"I am yours," he said, pulling away a little shocked at what had just happened, but recognizing it was the Little Girl growing into Wise One. He realized he should not have been surprised, and returned the hug with warmth.

"I will speak with some hunters. We can make a sweep of the area to see what we can find to the north. We can discuss it further tonight at the men's council."

She lowered her head to him and thanked him.

Her brother, Frakja, came to her. He lowered his head.

"What is it, my brother?" she asked.

"Are you still my sister?" he asked.

Ki'ti touched his shoulder. "Of course, my brother. I just got a responsibility, not removed from you. You will always be my brother."

"I wanted to be certain. It scared me a little last night. You got taken away once. I wanted to be sure that you are still there."

"Always, my brother. Now, work to be a great hunter so I may approve."

"I will Wise One. I promise I will."

She watched him go, and smiled wistfully. Yesterday he would not have responded in the same way. *What a difference a day and responsibility could make*, she thought.

As Untuk approached her from the back, he wistfully recognized that he could no longer use the hunter's walk to go behind her and sweep her off her feet. She had to maintain a certain dignity now. He must do the same.

"How's it going, Dear One?" he asked.

"It is going well, my husband. Very well."

"That is good," he said, on his way to the creek to help some of the hunters move a fallen tree.

"Wise One," Pechki said, "I am having trouble deciding which kind of plant this is from the ones that came in from the gathering. Would you please look at it? I asked Likichi and she can't remember either."

Ki'ti felt very strange when her grandmother addressed her as Wise One. She immediately followed Pechki to the place where herbs were dried and stored.

"This is the one," Pechki said, holding up the yellow flowered plant.

"That one, yes. Totamu told me about that one. Wait a moment." Ki'ti searched her mind web. "For fevers. Use the whole plant dried and broken into many pieces. A pinch into tea is sufficient. If not, you can use more."

"Thank you, Wise One," Pechki said. She was comfortable that Ki'ti had remembered correctly. She had been confident that what she didn't know, Likichi might, and Ki'ti would. She'd been right.

Ki'ti went through the day making sure to contact in some way or another every one of the People, if for no other reason than to ask if they were well. She treated all the People as equally valuable members. She truly loved them all. She wondered whether Wamumur had. This was the first time, she realized, that she was able truly to see through his eyes. She was making a pattern for her days. She realized she needed to be well grounded in her People, and in what their living circumstances were. She needed to care for their safety now and in the future. This day, she had learned more than in some years in the past. It was good. She also realized that it was good that Wamumur had done what he had done. She would have to remember to turn over her role as Wise One some day, before she lost it in death. It made things easier for the person who was new to the job.

At the men's council after the evening meal, the hunters gathered. Nanichak-na showed her where to sit. She took Wamumur's seat in council. She was more comfortable than she expected to be. Panriku came to sit beside her. The hunters raised eyebrows but no one said anything. Nanichak-na opened the discussion with the idea he and Ki'ti had dealt with earlier in the day. There was no need to consider a move right away, but they needed to consider the earthquakes and the damage that had occurred at the animal cave and plan for a move north if the earthquake activity continued. Discussion began.

"Does anyone know of caves to the north?" Chamul-na asked. He had considered that with the addition of the Mol, they might know of some.

Ermol-na mentioned that he'd never seen any when they went northeast in their sweep of the area. Manak-na said that in all the travels he'd made south and east he'd seen none. Grypchon-na said there might be some beyond the place where the land flattened and the lake was, off the ancient path, but he'd never seen any.

Tongip had never spoken at the men's council. He squirmed and shifted and finally said, "I have talked to Aryna about making a visit to the Mol. It would have to be soon, because I would not want us to be traveling during the season of cold days. I personally do not know of any other caves north of here, but the Mol might. I used to live in caves with them to the west. I am willing to ask whether their mind webs hold information that could be helpful." That was the most public speaking Tongip had ever done, and he felt drained.

Ki'ti wondered whether Aryna wanted to make the trip. She didn't want to ask, because she felt the information was personal. Aryna's history was Other and the Mol feared Others. Chamul-na asked the question.

"I wanted to have her meet my parents and grandparents, and for all of them to meet her," he said. "You have seen that Untuk and I speak the words of the People as well as our words. The Mol know your words from long ago. The Mol sometimes travel and talk with People to the east. We know the words of several languages. Visiting will be simple knowing the words."

Chamul-na asked, "If you make the trip, would you let me join you? I have wanted to explore that area many times."

"Of course," Tongip offered, glad to have another hunter along.

"When will you go?" Chamul-na asked. Light from the fire flickered on the walls behind him. Shadows moved around the wall and played in the fire.

"We planned to prepare tonight or tomorrow night at the latest, and leave the next morning. Could you be ready to go tomorrow morning?"

"Anytime you're ready, I am. One of my favorite ways to spend a day is in traveling and exploring," he replied.

Nanichak-na said, "I would like to go to see whether we can repair the bridge well enough to cross over and explore the other side of the river to the north."

Chamul-na looked up. "Not without me!" he said with feeling.

Manak-na said to Chamul-na, "Domur and I could go with Tongip, if you'd rather take this time to go to the bridge."

Mootmu-na punched Chamul-na in the shoulder. "Now, look what you've done," he said.

Ermol-na said, "If Chamul-na and Nanichak-na go to the bridge, I will go with them."

Lamul-na joined the discussion, "I think I should go. If there is a need for a younger person to attempt to cross the part of the bridge that is standing, I am better able."

When the discussion ended, Manak-na, Domur, and their children would leave with Tongip and Aryna the next morning to visit his relatives. Chamul-na, Nanichak-na, Lamul-na, and Kai-na would go to the bridge at the same time. Both groups would try to keep the time of their absence to a minimum.

When the meeting adjourned, the hunters were not displeased with their new Wise One. In fact, it pleased them that she was forward looking for their safety. "It was good," they felt, and said so.

Ki'ti was relieved as her first day ended. She silently thanked Wisdom for sucking color from the land to give sleep and rest to the People. She was as tired as if they had trekked all day. Wamumur and Emaea breathed a sigh of relief and enjoyed a new sense of freedom they hadn't known since they left childhood.

Chapter 10

Wisdom returned color to the land with a gray sky, reminding Nanichak-na of the days of ashfall. In his mind, gray skies were ominous and warranted caution, but then most people told him he viewed things too darkly. The cave came to life and the morning meal was prepared, and a few of the people were getting ready to leave. Nanichak-na, Chamul-na, Lamul-na, and Kai-na were ready for departure to the broken bridge. They did not wait for the women to provide food, but took some dried meat to eat on the way, gathered their materials, and left. They took no dogs, just the meager things that hunters on hunter trek carried. They could hardly wait to reach their destination, and take a good careful look at the area and possibilities for future residency should the need arrive.

Ki'ti met them on the rock walk. She walked up to Nanichak-na and placed her hands on his shoulders, "Go with Wisdom," she said. Then she placed her hands on Chamul-na's shoulders and said, "Go with Wisdom." Then Lamul-na, and then Kai-na. The hunters were a little surprised, but they liked it. Ki'ti watched them leave.

They took the gentle slope upwards to the mountains and the open field at the base of the cave of the man with the green bag. They were invigorated. Each in his own way loved to explore and problem solve. They walked briskly and reached the ancient pathway quickly.

Back at the cave, Tongip and Aryna, along with Manak-na and Domur with their children, Tuma and Mhank, were leaving surrounded by well wishers. They finally separated themselves from their relatives and friends and followed the same gentle slope upwards that the hunters had taken earlier. Before they left, Ki'ti did the same with each of the adults and then put her hands on one shoulder of each child while stooping down and looking at them. "Obey your parents," she said to each, "Obey your parents." The children were amazed and listened carefully to her words—she was Wise One, and she had words for them! Ki'ti placed her hands on the two dogs' heads and patted them. She did not say anything aloud to them, but in her thoughts asked Wisdom to bless them. Ki'ti had just created a new custom. No one would want to leave without her touching farewell. This little group of travelers, too, reached the ancient path and began to follow it.

The creation of a new custom was not missed by Wamumur and Emaea. They looked at each other and smiled. Ki'ti was definitely Wisdom's child.

Tongip and Manak-na led with Aryna and Domur and the children following. The walk was a good one and an edge of coolness made it possible for them to trek in comfort. Manak-na pointed out the cave of the man with the green bag to Tongip. He had seen it before from a distance. He excused himself for a moment and climbed up the steep path and stood there singing something that the people on the ground level could not really hear. Then he came down and they walked off as if no detour had occurred.

They stayed overnight at a place where they found a rock overhang. The children had never trekked and they could not forget Ki'ti's words. They were very careful to do exactly what they were told. Domur had a fire made quickly with Aryna's help, and they cooked some rhino meat they'd carried with them. They had some tubers to add to the boiling bag. Domur fed the dogs and showed them where to stay. They ate and quickly slept while the men shared the watch. When Wisdom returned color to the land, they were up. They had dried meat to eat for quick meals when trekking. The women packed up and Domur combed her hair and then the children's hair. She handed the comb to Manak-na. Aryna had been given a comb, but she misplaced it. She asked if she might borrow Domur's comb and when Manak-na finished, he handed it to her. Domur would remember to ask Ekuktu-na to make another for this family. Aryna combed Tongip's hair and then her own. Both had snarls. The children were delighted to be able to walk and eat food at the same time. In the cave, it was custom to sit quietly and eat and then get up. Walking and eating at the same time was not permitted in the cave.

When they neared the panda bamboo forest, the children were told to look for them. They spent hours searching for the big bears, but it took a very long time before they spotted one. Tongip saw the first far up a hill moving ponderously in the bamboo, and he carefully pointed it out.

"That big bear eats bamboo," Tongip told the children.

"How does that fill him up? If I only ate greens I'd be hungry," Tuma said. "They eat *lots* of bamboo," he said, laughing.

They turned west from the main trail at a place Tongip recognized easily. Even for Manak-na, it was hard to see the turnoff. They traveled for days on what was a path, but you had to know it to see it well. Tongip led the way each day, walking as fast as the children could go. The children traveled well always wondering what was over the next hill. To Domur, the next hill looked just like the one before it. She was able to trek on and on like the People but she noticed that Aryna was tiring.

One evening, Tongip showed them the tiny hearth where they met the People. They used it for their evening meal. They would continue on until they reached the overhang where the Mol camped in this area. By the time the stars were out in profusion, Tongip showed them the huge overhang. They unrolled their sleeping mats and bedded down the children. Tongip set two other tiny fires. Manak-na was fascinated. Tongip explained that the two little fires arranged that way would identify those in the cave as Mol. The little group bedded down for the night.

When Wisdom returned color to the land, the dogs began to bark. Domur quieted them quickly. Tongip jumped up and headed off alone. He met his people and there was much hugging and whooping. After their initial excitement, they walked to the overhang.

Tongip introduced everyone. The Mol seemed pleased to meet everyone but Tongip's wife, Aryna, and the dogs. They had problems with Others, those called the Minguat. Aryna was clearly Other. And the wolves? They did not see them as something People could use safely. They tried desperately to be hospitable, but were frightened at the same time. They wondered whether Aryna was a spy and whether the wolves would attack.

Tongip tried to explain to Lifu, the chief Mol hunter, his father, that Aryna came from the southwest in the lowland on the other side of the mountains, not the east. It didn't seem to matter to him. They had to move because of the Others long ago, but not so long that it wasn't a fresh memory. He felt that Tongip should have remembered. Tongip assured him he did remember, but that Aryna was a peaceful person and he loved her. He also tried to explain that regardless of how they, including himself, looked—they were all People. He asked whether he and his wife were welcome. Lifu begrudgingly assured him they were. He knew Tongip would turn around and they'd never see him again if they rebuffed his wife and friends. He was also having difficulty with his son's having said he was People, not mentioning Mol.

Their reception was mixed, with older people drawn back and younger ones surrounding the visitors. Lifu quickly made the rounds and encouraged the older ones to receive Tongip's wife. They did it as Lifu, with reserve but not hostility. The children of the Mol eagerly encouraged the children of the People to play. There was no inherent fear of the People.

Gnomuth gathered the hunters, along with Tongip and Manak-na. As Chief, he had to keep things calm and pleasant. It was difficult with the Other and the dogs. The women met with Aryna and Domur to talk about their trip.

Gnomuth said, "We welcome Tongip and Manak-na of the People. May they live long. They grace our hearth with their presence. They have brought a day that is free of cloud and warm from sun. That is good. They have also brought wolves they have trained to carry things for them. That is interesting and we should talk of this in the future. We extend to these guests and their wives and family our caves for their comfort, our food that they may be filled, and our water that they may not thirst. We will ask why they have come after the morning meal. We extend our welcome."

The morning meal was served. They gathered in much the same manner as the People. They also did not walk around while eating. They gathered in small groups and chatted quietly. Children had to remain with their parents. When they finished eating, they carried their bowls to a large leather bag of water where they rinsed each bowl clean. They turned the bowls upside down on a long piece of wood. Women would check the bowls later to assure that they had been cleaned well.

Domur finished and walked to the edge of the cave entrance. She could see mountains everywhere. The Mol had picked a place in the foothills to live. It was a lovely place. May joined her at the cave entrance.

"You are looking far over there at our river?" May asked.

"Yes. What is it?"

"It is a big river that goes from here to the big salt sea to the far east. Where we live it can be crossed. We used to have our people living on both sides of the river near the ancient path that you used. There was a bridge across the river on the ancient path once. This is the first place between here and there that you can cross the river easily. We think of it as Mol River."

"It is lovely. Is it safe for your children?" Domur asked.

"We take children to the lake to teach them to swim. They are not allowed near the river until they are grown. Their water world is the lake. We insist now that they become very good swimmers, both boys and girls. We didn't make swimming required until recently. Some of our adults cannot swim."

"We do the same, but all of us now swim, including those who were Mol," Domur said as she spotted Aryna. "Aryna, come, this is May."

May started to step back, but stopped herself. Aryna had done nothing to cause fear except be an Other. "Welcome to our cave, Aryna," May said.

"Thank you. The Mol are very nice people. You can tell I think so, since I joined with one." She smiled an open, bright smile, showing teeth that were white and formed in a perfect bite.

May smiled, "Tongip is one of our very special young men. He is an excellent hunter and he can track exceptionally well. Ah, but is he a good lover?"

Aryna was shocked at the question and blushed, but then she grinned at May and whispered, "Outstanding!"

May smiled. In their group, young men were taught how to be lovers and May had taught Tongip. May would not share that with Aryna!

"And how is Untuk?" May asked, looking at Aryna.

"He is fine. He joined with our Wise One. They are very happy together. Unfortunately, he cannot travel unless he leaves her alone, because our Wise Ones do not normally travel unless we are moving to another place. He won't want to leave her alone, because part of his responsibility is seeing that she's safe."

"Really? Is that because your Wise One is some kind of treasure?"

"You could say that. Our Wise One has all our stories from the beginning of time in her mind web. If she met with an accident, we'd lose our stories," Domur responded.

"What's so important about your stories?" May asked.

"Our stories tell of our beginning and all our history. By knowing the stories, we have understanding of things that can and do happen. The stories impart Wisdom. The ashfall from the volcano is an example. We knew that it could cause us to have cold weather as an aftermath. It did get cold for many, many seasons following the ashfall. We knew to prepare warm clothing that we'd never had to wear before to survive the cold. Otherwise, we'd have been late to keep ourselves warm."

"I see," May responded, but she really didn't. She was too busy entertaining other thoughts.

"Another thing is that our stories tell us how to be. One of our requirements is that we take in and treat well those who travel past us."

"We have that same rule, but for us it's a rule. We don't get it from a story," May said.

"It's interesting you have the same requirement for behavior. My Minguat did not have anything like that. They were interested in what they could get from others, not what they could give," Aryna said. "This is much the better way."

Domur looked up. "If you have rules, what is the basis for the rules, May? We have our stories as the basis but where did your rule come from?"

May looked really surprised. "I have no idea," she responded. "I guess they came from old council meetings, but I am not sure at all. You are making me wonder. What's the basis of your stories?"

Domur lowered her head. Then she said quietly, "We consider that, even though they mostly come from experiences, they are inspired by Wisdom." May remained silent briefly. Then, she directed the women to move to the area of the overhang.

The Mol's cave had a huge covered area overhung by an enormous flat rock. It was a loggia of sorts that provided pre-cave shelter. In good weather, most people spent time in the loggia.

Gnomuth took two pieces of wood that had been carved in intricate designs, each about an arm's length long. He tapped them together in a rhythmic manner while he chanted something that the People could not understand. All the men followed him through the cave entrance to the loggia where they turned east to the traditional meeting place for men. Then Gnomuth welcomed the visitors again.

"We would know the purpose of your visit," he said solemnly.

Tongip extended his hand. Gnomuth passed another stick to him. This one was thinner and looked like a miniature walking stick. It was carved intricately with a bearded male face at the top. Tongip held the staff and began to speak.

"We came first so that my family could meet my wife, and a few of my new People could meet my family." The comment drew murmurs and approving nods all around.

"Then we came because we must soon find another place to live. The earthquake has destroyed the cave where Torkiz lived with Ilea. The top of the cave fell as one piece down to the floor of the cave. Only through a tiny hole can one crawl to see some of the master's animal images. We live in the cave of the People from long ago. We are concerned about the earthquake activity and if it continues, we must find a new home. We came to know whether you know of other cave groups north of the bridge."

There was much murmuring and jostling as the men in council spoke among themselves.

Gnomuth held out his hand. Tongip handed him the staff.

"Tongip, you should remember that the Gar live north of the bridge. That is why we live here. Yes, there are other good caves there, but the Gar may live in them. It is dangerous."

Manak-na held his silence while wondering who the Gar were.

Tongip held out his hand. Gnomuth passed the staff to him.

"People have been to the bridge and seen no Gar. As we speak, there are others heading to the bridge to determine whether any are there. It is possible that we may find safer earth for our dwelling north of here. The People came from ashfall from a volcano to the south. There are Others to the east. The plan is to look to the north."

Gnomuth extended his hand for the staff and Tongip passed it.

"Why don't you and several of us take the trek down to the bridge on the north side of the river? You would soon learn what you want to know. If you take Gukmor, he can show you the caves I mentioned. He has been there. They are several days trek from the bridge." Gukmor nodded. Tongip smiled. He loved Gukmor.

"You can smell them two days before you get there!" Putan, a Mol hunter added, and the Mol hunters burst out laughing. To the Mol, the Gar stank. Manak-na had no idea why the hunters were laughing. He chose not to ask.

Tongip looked at Manak-na silently asking about the trek. Manak-na nodded.

Tongip held out his hand for the staff. "We would very much like to make such a trek, if Gukmor is willing."

Gukmor nodded his willingness.

"When could we leave?" Tongip asked.

Gukmor held out his hand for the staff.

"First, can this man, Manak-na, keep up with us?" Gukmor asked and Tongip nodded affirmative. Then Gukmor said, "I can have some hunters ready to leave after high sun."

Tongip nodded. Manak-na found it hard to believe how quickly the Mol responded to the request.

Gnomuth held out his hand. Gukmor passed the staff.

"We shall enjoy meeting your family while you trek to the caves. We will treat them as special guests. If the Gar are still in the bamboo forest, do not disturb them but turn around and come home. If they are gone we would like to know."

Tongip held out his hand for the staff. Gnomuth passed it to him.

"I thank the Mol for their hospitality and for helping us on our quest for knowledge. It is greatly appreciated. We show our gratitude with these gifts." He laid out a bag of dried fish and a net for catching lake fish. He explained about the bamboo rafts and catching fish in the nets. "There is a place at the lake where one could stand to net fish. It would not be as efficient as if the Mol had bamboo rafts, but it would provide some fish for you." He explained that the hunters could see how the handle and rim worked, and, if they wanted to make others, Domur knew how to knot the nets. They would share their knowledge.

There were nods of approval all around and many glances one to another as the net was passed around.

Gnomuth extended his hand for the staff.

"You and your People are kind," he said. He felt odd referring to Tongip as People, but continued on. "We would like to learn of this net and also of the bamboo rafts. Fish will be a good supplement to the food we enjoy now and in the future. We will ask Domur for her help to teach us while you are gone. When you return, we will ask to send two hunters to see these rafts."

Tongip nodded to each of the council members. The meeting broke up. Tongip smiled with Manak-na. It was good to have something special to share when visiting. The bamboo rafts and fishing had added much to their lives. It should do the same for the Mol.

The men went off to gather their trekking gear. Along with Tongip, Manak-na, and Gukmor, Mungum and Ghoman of the Mol joined the trek.

Meanwhile, Nanichak-na, Chamul-na, Lamul-na, and Kai-na had reached the bridge on the south side of the river. They stood there surveying the bridge and the opposite side of the chasm. The rope still hung securely from one side to the other. It was thick rope that made the two sides of the bridge when it was serviceable. From the thick rope they could see that thinner rope had made loops from one side of the thick rope to the other back and forth. The broken thick rope hung from the loops. The thinner ropes swayed lightly in the breeze. The thinner loops had been woven in such a way as to make a footpath. The weaving was not very thick, so the walking was something one would have had to do carefully. Nanichak-na wondered whether the dogs could have made it across. The two sides of thick rope were tied to huge boulders on both sides of the river. The rope appeared to be deteriorating. To rebuild the bridge would require starting over. They could use the season of cold days to make rope if they gathered needed supplies quickly. They listened very carefully but could hear nothing on the other side but birds and the occasional small animal scurrying in the understory. They decided to melt into the brush and wait for a good while to see what might appear on the other side. They waited until time for the evening meal. Nothing had passed the area on foot taller than a man's half arm. Wisdom began to suck the color from the land.

The hunters chose to eat dried meat that night, forgoing fire and a warm meal. They considered that the man-like apes might be nocturnal and they would take turns keeping watch through the night. When Wisdom returned color to the land, it was clear there did not appear to be anything large on the other side of the river, let alone anything hostile.

Lamul-na stretched. He was ready for the reason he had come on this trek. "I will crawl across to the other side to see what I can find there."

The others wondered how safe that might be. Kai-na was concerned about his younger brother, but his relative youth and good athletic ability were needed. Kai-na nodded to his brother, approving and showing concern.

Lamul-na went to the rope and followed it to the gap. He put his left arm and leg over the rope and head first began his crossing. His heart was pounding in his chest. The depth of the chasm wasn't terribly bad, maybe four or more men tall, but the rocks that would meet anyone who fell would provide death or a wishing for it, most likely the former since the rocks were jagged and large. He took his time, concentrating on the place where he was, not the far side. Instead of dangling his legs, he used his feet to help propel him forward. Slowly, ever so slowly, he moved across the rope. The rope danced with the activity, which was somewhat unsettling to the young man. Finally, he reached the other side. He carefully, and even more slowly, pulled himself to land. He stood and began to survey his surroundings.

"Wait!" Kai-na called to him. "I'm going to join you!" Kai-na wondered at his own outburst. He was terrified at the thought of crossing the river on a rope, but it was his younger brother on the other side. He could not leave him to explore alone.

Nanichak-na and Chamul-na both nodded approval, and Kai-na used the same technique his brother had, arriving on the other side without incident. The two agreed they would take some time to scout out the area and would meet the others back in time for the evening meal. Nanichak-na threw them some dried meat in a pouch and Lamul-na had a water skin. Silently, they disappeared into the forest following the continuation of the hard packed path. It was more overgrown, but still quite clear.

The two younger men were surprised at the lack of wildlife in the area. They followed the path over hills and eventually it led them to a stream that appeared to drain into the river. It was northeast of the bridge and opened out into a sheltered valley. There did not appear to be any caves that might provide habitation. The young men did agree that they might not be far enough north to avoid earthquake activity. They looked for other paths that might head west or east along the main path. There was nothing they could see. They kept their ears alert to the least sound, hearing nothing but birds and an occasional small deer. They encountered a barking deer and found the meeting so funny that the two laughed uproariously, releasing tension that had been kept held tightly in case of need for flight or fight. The idea of the man-like apes had not been far from their thoughts. They had not seen any game trails through the underbrush. It was as if the whole area were abandoned. What they did notice is the stands of bamboo that were supposed to support the man-like apes appeared to be dying off. The plants had brown leaves and looked unhealthy. Lamul-na and Kai-na could find no insects on the plants, and they did not appear to have fungal attachments. They assumed the problem was lack of sunlight. The bamboo grew here with other plants, many of which were tall hardwoods, which might be blocking sunlight from the bamboo.

Lamul-na stopped to check the sunlight. "I think we should return now to report what we know. I think we may want to take several days, or whatever it would take, to follow this path as far as it goes. For now, we need to return."

Kai-na had turned to listen to his brother. "I agree but I really want to keep going. Let's suggest it this evening," he said with a palm strike.

"Yes, let's," Lamul-na seconded the palm strike. The two were grinning like boys. They made the trip back much quicker, sniffing the air for information and enjoying the day. They still had the wariness hunters needed in strange places, but they were enjoying what they had already seen from the back side now. They had gained some familiarity with the north side of the river and the forests.

When they reached the bridge, they carefully crawled across the large rope and settled down to share the day's exploration with Nanichak-na and Chamul-na, who both were wishing they could have traded places with the younger men. Nanichak-na had speared a small deer and had it roasting by the time Lamul-na and Kai-na returned. The delicious smell had met them long before they had arrived at the bridge. They sat around the campfire late in the darkness going over every detail of the day's trek and their desire to continue on.

"You cannot make the kind of trip you want now. The season of cold days is arriving quickly. You could be stranded in a heavy white rain without shelter. It's too much to risk. The season of new leaves is the time for such a trip," Chamul-na asserted.

"But what if the earthquakes continue through the cold? Isn't there a chance we could be killed in the cave during the season of cold days?"

"There is always that possibility," Nanichak-na contributed, "but the danger is losing two of our prized young men. We cannot travel in the seasons of cold days. We have to wait until the season of new leaves. So it is wiser for us to wait."

"We could make a shelter outside the cave, just in case?" Lamul-na mused.

"Now, that would be a great use of time," Nanichak-na said. "Do you know how to make large shelters?"

"I don't," Lamul-na replied. "I'm thinking that there are some among us who have made shelters of some size. Do you know?" He looked at the older men.

"We made shelters when we lived by the river," Chamul-na said. "Then the Mol may have ways of making shelters, or those who became People from the Others."

Nobody mentioned that the Mol among them were People, not Mol.

Nanichak-na said, "At the men's council meeting, we can discuss this on our return. As for now, we need to sleep and then return home when Wisdom fades the darkness."

"I'll take the first watch," Kai-na volunteered. He had been so impressed with his younger brother that day. It was the first time that Kai-na had seen the thinking side of his brother. On hunts, most of the time Lamul-na took directions from the older hunters. He had been seen as a quiet member of the People until this day.

The hunters settled down and soon slept.

On the north side of the river, Tongip, Manak-na, Gukmor, Mungum, and Ghoman had just roasted a young boar for their meal. They sat around a small hearth eating the meat which was hot and savory. They were hungry, and between their hunger and the temperature of the meat, they were laughing and enjoying themselves. Stars began twinkling in the sky and the sliver of moon cast little light. The fire seemed all the brighter.

"We made very good time today," Mungum observed.

"And it seems we'll have no clouds for tomorrow," Gukmor contributed.

"How can you tell?" Manak-na asked.

"See the clear sky to the west?" Mungum asked.

"Yes," Manak-na replied.

"Most of our clouds come from the west. If it is clear, we can expect a good day. That doesn't always hold true, but mostly it does," Gukmor said.

"We need to stop at our storage place tomorrow to pick up some grains," Tongip said.

Ghoman shoved him in the shoulder, "Tongip, once you say you're People and now you're Mol again?"

"Forgive me," the young man said, laughing, "I need to remember that I am a visitor here."

"You'll always be Mol to me, but I can also accept that you are now People," Gukmor said.

"Thanks!"

Manak-na had finished eating and was lying on his back on the ground. He stared up into the starry sky and looked at the patterns he'd known for a lifetime. It was very bright and the moon was out. Part of his mind web was always alert to sounds when on the trail. There had been nothing new to observe. He wondered where the wildlife was. There had been birds certainly, but it was very quiet compared to forests he'd trekked through in his hunting experience. Even now, despite the noise from Tongip and the Mol, it was eerily quiet to the young man. The nocturnal animals should be making noise now. It was way too quiet.

Ghoman asked, "Who'll take the first watch?"

Before anyone could speak, Manak-na asked about the manner in which the watch changed. The Mol explained their practice and then Manak-na volunteered to take first watch. That surprised the Mol, but they were happy to be able to sleep. Tongip would take second watch.

Manak-na's watch began. It was still extremely quiet for a forest that was healthy. He added a bit more fuel to the fire as it died down. A rodent scurried through the bushes nearby. One owl hooted at a distance. Otherwise it was all silent, even for insects.

Manak-na knew the sky contained two sets of stars that looked like snares for small mammals. One was larger than the other. He knew that the tip of the string where the small snare would be tied was the star that never moves. Wisdom put it there for many reasons. It showed travelers where they were, and it helped hunters time their night watches. Two stars on the big snare aligned with the star that never moves. Those stars and the star that never moves, if connected, made a straight line. That straight line revolves around the star that never moves like a rope revolves around a stick in the ground to draw a circle. The tail of the big snare then would point either to the right or left or up or down. Location depended on the time of year. Manak-na knew that when the tail on the big snare pointed down this night, his watch would be finished. He'd then touch Tongip's shoulder to waken him. Tongip would take over and Manak-na would sleep.

When Wisdom restored color to the land, they resumed moving north of the river, east to the location of their storage area. Inside the rock structure, Mungum pulled out a hard skin, shaped like a tube, filled with grains. He took half the grains and left the other half. He put the cap back on the tube. It was a very tight fit. He put the grains into a soft leather pouch, pulling the sides up and tying it with a strip of leather. Meanwhile, Gukmor had descended to the river to get water. The men started a small fire in the hearth and made a cooked cereal out of the grains and a tea from some leaves. While the cereal cooked, they added dried fruits. They ate using the small wooden bowls they carried. Then they extinguished the fire and continued on the path.

Manak-na was having a strange experience. He had been viewed as tall by the People and the Others, but as the only one of the People by birth among the Mol, he was extremely short. The stride of the Mol was significantly longer than his. He had to step more times than they to cover the same distance. It made him wonder how women felt when they trekked. Did they tire faster because they had to take more steps than a man? He'd never entertained such thoughts. He wasn't really tiring but he had to concentrate to keep up.

The Mol were as fascinated as Manak-na at the lack of animal life. As they neared the bridge, they began to notice the bamboo leaves were turning yellow and brown. They wondered why, and when they examined the plants they could find no sign of disease, just the poor color. They had not used the area for many, many, many passings of seasons, so they had not been there frequently except to scout for possible threats. In that time, the hardwoods had grown tall and were blocking sunshine from the bamboo.

When they reached the bridge, they could tell that the area had just been occupied by the smell and the deer remains on the other side of the river. They turned up the same path that Lamul-na and Kai-na had traveled the day before. Instead of traveling a half day as the People had, they traveled for many days. The path followed the river after going over a hill. From there, they trekked until they arrived at another river which came from the north. The path followed alongside the river to the north. When they reached the source of that river, they descended to a valley. The path followed the edge of the valley northeast until it met another river that flowed from the north. At that point, the path continued on the east side of the river across another rope bridge that was in disrepair but had both sides holding.

While they ate dinner at the end of the trail, Manak-na said, "I cannot help but wonder who made this path and who built these bridges."

Ghoman said, "Our ancients built them. We don't have stories like you do, but our history, little as it is, tells of giants in ancient times. Those giants were our ancients. They moved from the north to the south and back, claiming all this land: far north to the huge lake, south to the salt sea, east to the salt sea, and west into these mountains. They built the bridges so they could trade with people in all regions. They were not like us. They didn't live in caves but spent most of their time traveling from place to place wherever the wildlife went or wherever the climate was most favorable. But they always had the north-south travel on the pathway. Some were fairly sedentary and some were just traders or travelers all the time."

"Giants?" Manak-na asked. He was already feeling that the Mol were giants.

"Well, all we know is that we think we are a lot shorter than they were. When we say giant, it probably means something to one of us and another to someone else. We never really analyzed it," Ghoman continued, "But they were a lot bigger than we are now. In our language, giant implies great height. We think of the Gar as giants."

"What else do you know about them?"

Ghoman frowned. "They were giants, traveled and traded, and, oh, they let their hair grow long. I'm not sure whether they wore clothing. It was warmer then. There were many of them. Some had flocks of animals, something we stopped doing because it was too hard to tend them when we can just hunt."

Mungum said, "They did not like the Gar. The Gar are man-like apes that eat bamboo."

"So the Mol have interacted with the Gar for a long time?"

"Yes," Gukmor said flatly. "The Gar usually are placid, but when they feel threatened, they can become quite fierce. That's why we fled the area many, many generations ago. They felt threatened by us and the People, so they began to threaten back. We have wondered whether the Gar actually overthrew the ancients or whether our ancients just left for elsewhere. They could be anywhere, since they were so mobile, but I think they are gone. I'm thinking they were pretty much the same size as the Gar. We don't know that part of our history."

"That is fascinating," Manak-na admitted. His mind web was running fast. The ancient Mol built the path. The man-like apes were called Gar by the Mol.

"Oh, and the Gar really stink!" Mungum said.

Manak-na finally understood why the Mol laughed back at the cave about stinking. He was getting an education. So much to learn. The Mol had much information but it wasn't organized and ready like the stories made the information of the People. It seemed that it just began to fall to the front of their mind webs when they talked about it. Manak-na could not understand what he thought of their disregard for their own knowledge. He had learned something of geography from their ramblings. To the north was a huge lake. He wondered whether that might not be a good destination.

He looked up and said, "The huge lake you mentioned that is to the north. Does the pathway lead to the lake?"

Ghoman looked surprised that Manak-na would want to know that, but he answered, "It goes there and then borders the east side of the lake—not at the lake's edge but rather through the high lands. That's as far as I've been on the path, so I don't know more than that."

"And it is fresh water?" Manak-na asked.

Ghoman laughed. "That's what a lake is."

"Can you see across the lake?" Manak-na asked.

Ghoman smiled. "In some places. It's surrounded by mountains. Climb them to get a view. And I'll tell you that if you were to walk the east side of the lake in a hunter party, it would take you longer than a moon."

Manak-na was shocked. Even Tongip was hit hard. He'd never heard that information.

"Longer than a moon! How can that be, Ghoman. Are you teasing?" Tongip was amazed.

"No, on my life. It is true. I did that when I was young and kept wondering when the lake would end."

"One more question, Ghoman," Manak-na said, "How long would it take to trek from here to this lake?"

Ghoman rested his head on his hand. He was silent for a while, his face reflecting thought. Finally, he said, "I think you are looking for a new land. The lake would be wonderful, Manak-na. But you need to know that for a large number of people to travel there with children and old people, it would take the better part of a set of seasons—maybe longer. Perhaps, if you took it in stages it would work. I don't know. It is not an easy trek, but the path goes there, so you could find it. You also need to know that the further north you travel, the colder the seasons of cold days and the shorter the seasons of warm nights. It is colder now than it has been for a long time. Up there it could be bitterly cold."

Manak-na thanked Ghoman. He gazed into the sky and wondered at all he'd heard. Still, there was silence in the forest. He drifted in his mind web and considered the Mol. They had rules, but they didn't know the basis for them. Their information was disorganized in their mind webs. It tumbled out when they spoke. But they were filled with information. Smoke from the fire was blowing into his eyes, so he got up and moved.

During this time, Domur had shown the Mol how to use the nets and how to make them. They had fished enough to have some for an appetizer for one meal. The Mol were definitely ready to make fish part of their diet.

While sitting in the sunshine working on nets, Domur asked, "Do you know the way to give a green color to skins?"

"Have you ever seen a green skin?" Kamal, Putan's wife, asked.

"Yes, the Mol who was found at the caves. He had a green bag. It was still with him."

"That's right. Mihalee told us about him and that you had moved his body to be with his family," Yukich said. Yukich was the wife of Gnomuth, the Chief of the Mol.

Domur was happy to hear her voice. It was sweet and melodious. It differed some way from the Mol speech, but Domur couldn't understand what the difference was. It was a very slight difference. Domur smiled thinking about the green bag and then the man's being moved to the cave.

"We are grateful to the People for uniting the family of Mol," Baway, Lifu's wife, added. Her white hair shone in the sun. "That was a kind thing."

"For some reason our young Wise One seemed to know right where his family was. It was unusual for the knowledge of Wisdom to be shed like that," Domur said.

"You sound like wisdom is a person," Yukich said. Yukich made it a point to try to stay informed and be able to avoid or reduce problems by knowing how the Mol were doing in much the same way as Totamu had in years gone by.

"To us, yes, Wisdom is a person." Domur felt she was on shaky ground.

"To us wisdom is another word for smart."

"To us Wisdom is the Creator of all that is and ever will be. Wisdom leads us in all our life activities," Domur continued.

"You worship wisdom?" Baway asked.

"You could say that," Domur said quietly. "Our stories tell us of what Wisdom has taught us through the years."

"Was wisdom like our ancients, the giant ones of old?" Kamal was trying to understand.

"I don't know about your ancients," Domur said.

"Our ancients built the road. They ranged from the big lake to the north many, many seasons from here to the salt sea in the south and to the salt sea to the east. Nobody much lives to the west. Our ancients were giants, huge men that would have made us look very small. They were at least as large as the man-like apes that live north of the bridge." Yukich looked to see whether Domur had understood what she said. They spoke the words of the People, but it was not their first words.

"Wisdom was not one of us but rather lives somewhere that holds all that is. Wisdom is greater than one of our ancestors, because Wisdom created all that is." Domur was choosing her words carefully. She had not been called on to speak of Wisdom and this was uncharted territory for her. Domur could see that the Mol were losing interest, so she said, "The coloring of the green bag? I still wonder how that color was achieved."

Belu looked up. She was Mungum's wife, and did a lot of work with skins. "I would guess, since I've never seen the bag, that it was done with algae from a lake. We don't color skins, so I have no real idea what was used, but that would be my guess. I learned that boiled algae will make a green color bath for skins. The longer you leave it in the color bath the darker it gets. Once it's colored, you bathe it in salt water—I think."

"That's interesting. Thank you," Domur said.

"I need your help here," Elaha, Gukmor's wife, said. "I think I lost what I was doing."

Domur sat beside her and took the knotted net and looked at it. "Here it is," she remarked. "It needs to be undone to here and then redone. If you'll undo it, I'll be glad to start it again."

"Thank you, Domur. After tasting the fish the other night, believe me, I want more."

There was a smattering of light laughter. Everyone agreed that fish would be a welcome change.

When the men north of the river awakened, they prepared to trek quickly and continued north.

Manak-na caught the drift of something on the wind. It was an odor that he found unfamiliar. He noticed it was coming from the north. As they continued, the scent became stronger. It was not pleasant.

Finally, unable to contain his curiosity any longer, Manak-na asked, "What is that odor?"

"We wondered when you'd ask. That's Gar," Ghoman said.

They continued on. The odor became more and more pungent. Then they could see the caves.

"There," Gukmor pointed, "Those are the caves of the Gar. And there is no movement around here." He was curious.

As the men approached, they could tell that the caves seemed to have been abandoned. The odor of Gar was overwhelming. Manak-na agreed that they could not live there. The path did continue on and he knew that if they chose to move, they'd have to pass by these caves, which looked fairly good.

"You wouldn't want to live here," Gukmor shouted.

"What have you found?" Ghoman shouted back.

"The walls of these caves have fractured. Look at this." Gukmor showed the men the fractures and the crumbling rock all over the floor. "This may be why they left."

Manak-na noticed that the caves lacked hearths. "Did they not use fire?" he asked.

"I don't think they knew how," Tongip answered. "They were really hairy and their coats of hair may have done a good job of protecting them. Look, over here there is a pile of leaves and grasses. That may have been their bedding."

"Or their garbage heap," Ghoman chuckled and was met with laughter from the others.

Tongip said, "I need to get out of here or I may vomit. The odor is really revolting."

"We need to start the trip home," Ghoman said. "This has been a great diversion as trips like these always are, but it is time to return home. Manak-na, have you found what you wanted to know?"

"I have. If we need to relocate, this path may take us where we need to go, and it's safe. The caves are out of the question, though."

Everyone laughed heartily and began to move away from the caves and the odor.

When at last all had returned to the Mol caves, there was a great feast while the hunters told of their findings. When Wisdom returned color to the land, the People left to return to their home accompanied by the two Mol hunters, Gukmor and Alme, who would examine the bamboo rafts.

The trip was uneventful until they reached the grassy land below the cave of the man with the green bag. Gukmor stopped them and ascended the path that was so well concealed from below. He knelt out of sight and spent quite some time there.

"Tongip, what is he doing?" Aryna asked softly.

With his arm around the shoulders of his wife, Tongip explained, "He is checking to see if what I suspected is right. I think the man with the green bag is descended from Torkiz and Ilea. Domur asked about the green bag. Torkiz had a green bag. Nobody has found it since he died. His last son left the Mol and went to search out Torkiz. Since Torkiz is our hero, if this is his son, we want to know. If he is, Gukmor will want to know. Gukmor is descended from Torkiz and Ilea. The man with the green bag would be a relative."

"So that's why people seemed so interested when I asked about the green bag? You do know that he had a yellow owl?" Domur added quietly.

"Where is it?" Alme inquired.

"Our Wise One has it. Wamumur has one and so does our Wise One. The man named Torkiz came from the group of people where Wamumur was born. They are of the same Band of the Owl that lived far west from here."

"Does this Wamumur also draw?" Alme asked.

"No. He has seen the work of Torkiz at the cave that collapsed in the last big earthquake," Tongip said and added, "He knows Torkiz was of his original ancestors."

"How does he know that?" Gukmor asked, hearing the discussion after descending the path to the cave.

"Our Wise One told him. The owl sang the message," Tongip replied, knowing the response that would bring from the Mol.

Gukmor laughed out loud.

"Do not laugh, my dearest uncle. It is true. When you meet our Wise One, you will see a tiny female who has more knowledge and wisdom in her than anyone I have ever known. She sees what we cannot. She knows a lie the moment it is concocted. She can see and hear through time. I've never known anyone like her."

Gukmor and Alme looked at Tongip, then at each other, then at Tongip, then at the People. They did not know what to believe from Tongip's words. "Have you been bewitched?" Gukmor asked quite seriously.

"Wait until you meet her and judge for yourself. You are in for a surprise. What are you doing with the green bag?" Tongip asked.

"I brought the green bag to carry home to show the Chief that it is the green bag that we've had described to us through the years. He may wish to move the bodies to our burial ground where we can revere the place where they are without having to make such a trek."

"I ask you, Gukmor, to put the bag back and pick it up on your return. I think it would be good to keep it away from our Wise One." Manak-na hoped he didn't need to explain further.

Gukmor looked hard at Manak-na. "The bag could not hurt anyone," he said flatly.

Manak-na looked hard back at Gukmor. He respected the man's skepticism, but he also knew that bag should stay where it was at least until the Mol left.

"Gukmor," Manak-na said not quite testily, "That bag speaks to our Wise One. It was she who went against our prior Wise One, Wamumur, her father, and took the bag to the cave. She knew that was the mission of the Mol who died in the cave here. For that she was severely punished. But she was off in a mind web of very, very, very long ago. Until then she'd had no experience with mind webs of long ago."

Gukmor turned the bag over and over. "See here, this is the mark of Torkiz." The green bag did, in fact, bear a black squiggle. "If you looked at the drawings in the cave, each one had this mark on it."

"We never noticed," Manak-na said. "Then the body is likely the son of Torkiz, since he has the green bag with the mark of Torkiz on it. That is all the more reason to keep the bag away from our Wise One."

"I will put it back. But on our way home, we will pick it up."

"Of course," Manak-na said. He would be glad to be rid of the green bag and the bodies. Every time they passed that place there were memories that he saw as not good.

They arrived at the caves and the People flowed out in greeting. A feast was prepared and the hunters who had been to the south side of the bridge were very eager to share their experiences with those who had been to the north side.

When Ki'ti saw Gukmor, she walked directly to him, followed by Untuk. Tongip said, "Gukmor, this is . . . ."

Untuk was with her, but when he saw Gukmor, he threw his arms around the man in childish delight and he threw his arms around Gukmor. "How good to see you again!"

Since Tongip had begun the introduction, Untuk stood back.

Tongip continued, "Gukmor, this is our Wise One."

Ki'ti came forward and offered her hand to the older man.

Gukmor placed one knee on the ground and bent the other to come to eye level of this tiny person. "I have heard much about you. Can it be true?"

Ki'ti spoke almost in a whisper. "I see that you have some disquieted feelings about what you have heard. Gukmor of the Mol, I am just a simple person who is used by Wisdom. To quiet your concerns, I will tell you that I know that you are descended of Torkiz, that the man with the green bag is his son, that you will move the bodies to your caves that overlook the river. My father and you are very distant relatives because of Torkiz. Therefore, there must be peace among us and we welcome you to our caves. We will talk more at the men's council tonight. It is good to meet you. Where is the other Mol?" she asked.

Tongip put his hand on Alme's back and introduced the younger Mol. Gukmor was dumbfounded. This tiny person knew things that she could not have known. What he'd been told might just be true. *If Wisdom was their God, why did he pick such a tiny and unassuming person to be his speaker?* he wondered. And Untuk and she were joined. This was a shock to him, but he handled it as well as he could with an open mind and yet skepticism too.

Ki'ti said to Untuk, "Please, show the visitors to the places we have prepared for them and make them comfortable. The food is almost ready. Please, show them where the privy and bathing areas are. Thank you, Dear One."

While showing the visitors the bathing area, Gukmor asked Untuk, "Is she really as unique as I hear? She looks like someone you'd never see in a crowd. I expected height or beauty. She has neither."

"Gukmor, true beauty comes from within. You know that. Being a Wise One is not a popularity issue. It is a choice made by Wisdom. The person chosen doesn't get the opportunity to decline. It is a heavy role and few could accept it. We of the Mol had nothing like this. Only the People do. The Others certainly don't! By choosing someone who isn't very tall or beautiful, Wisdom shows who Wisdom is."

"Untuk, you have grown in understanding yourself. Perhaps, this is good. I will wait to see."

Meanwhile, Domur sought out Ekuktu-na and asked him to make Aryna a comb. He gave her one for Aryna from the small stash he kept in case of need. Domur took it directly to Aryna and cautioned her to keep it safeguarded because it took a long time to make them. Aryna understood.

They all gathered in the largest cave for eating. The Mol were offered food first, then the -na hunters and Wise One, and then the women and children. Along with the main meat, there was smoked fish of three kinds so the Mol could enjoy that as well. There were greens and tubers and fruit. The People had prepared a feast.

Finally, they moved to the end of the cave for the men's council.

"I call the men's council together," Ki'ti said. "We recognize Gukmor and Alme as guests and welcome them. We have much to discuss. I have invited Wamumur and Emaea to join us. First, we will hear from Nanichak-na, Chamul-na, Lamul-na, and Kai-na about their travel to the south of the bridge. Then, we will hear from Tongip, Manak-na, and Gukmor about their travel to the north of the bridge. Then we will hear from our guests and learn if we can help them and how. So that we keep order, I will nod to the next speaker. When that speaker has finished, he will look around. Make eye contact with him if you wish to speak, and if he nods to you then you are free to speak."

Gukmor was amazed again. Here was this little girl. She couldn't have lived even close to twenty years. Yet she handled the men's council with ease. He also noticed she had a wolf pup curled up beside her. He continued to watch as the girl nodded to Nanichak-na.

Nanichak-na said, "We traveled to the bridge and the trip was uneventful. At the bridge, Lamul-na climbed across the rope and then

Kai-na did the same. They trekked into the forest after the morning meal until well beyond high sun. The forest was very quiet. The largest fur bearing animal there was a barking deer. The bamboo is turning yellow and brown. It does not look healthy at all. We could see no disease on the plants." He stopped speaking.

Tongip got eye contact with Nanichak-na. Nanichak-na nodded to him.

Tongip began, "We took the little trail north of the river that is across from where the Mol live in caves. We trekked to the bridge and arrived there after Nanichak-na, Chamul-na, Kai-na, and Lamul-na had gone. They must have had a great deer feast." He smiled and the People he named grinned back.

Tongip continued, "We trekked for" he signed seven "days. We, too, found the bamboo troubled. We arrived at the cave of the Gar. The Gar are men-like apes that smell sickeningly bad. They are taller than the Mol. They have left the area. We wondered whether their caves might be a refuge for you if you fled earthquakes, but the odor would be impossible to live with. The caves, also, have fracture marks in the rocks that look fresh. They might be dangerous even if the odor were tolerable. We talked about land we know that is very, very, very far north. It borders a wonderful lake that is surrounded by mountains. The lake is huge. Since the cold has come, it may be too cold there in the season of cold days now, but it used to be wonderful. For hunters, it would take many moons to trek there. For a People with children and old ones, it would take about a a full cycle of seasons or more. Travel there could be done in stages. The path does go from here to the lake. The Mol call it the path of the dragon. Dragon is the four-legged, winged serpent that breathes fire. You remember the dragon on the wall in the cave?"

The men nodded.

"Our ancients said the dragon helped them build the path. We think that's a silly story." Tongip cleared his throat and continued, "Having the path for travel may make it sound too easy. Such a trek would be extremely difficult." Tongip looked around.

Manak-na looked at the floor. Tongip had been People for a short while. He had managed to take the material he needed to present, and he had organized it well. Manak-na realized that the Mol had the information and could organize it, but for some reason they did not. Tongip realized he needed to do it for the People. Manak-na was impressed. At the same time Manak-na didn't quite know what to think of the dragon path story. Since it didn't seem as organized, Manak-na thought Tongip might have just added it spontaneously.

Grypchon-na made eye contact with Tongip. Tongip nodded to him.

"I want to know whether the bridge is something we could fix in a short time. If not, how would we get to the north part of the pathway?" Gukmor made eye contact. Grypchon-na nodded to him.

"We would permit you to trek through our land and cross where we did. To build the bridge would be very hard and take a long, long time. Some People might lose their lives doing it. It would make sense to trek through our land and cross that way." Wamumur made eye contact with Gukmor. Gukmor nodded.

"Can you assure us that the offer would be valid in the season of new leaves?" Gukmor made eye contact, and Wamumur nodded.

"I have the word of our Chief that you may cross there whenever you choose. His word is his life." Ki'ti made eye contact with Gukmor. He nodded to her.

"We have received much good information from both groups. I want to thank the Mol for taking our People to the caves of the Gar. I hope that you will carry our thanks to your Chief. We will spend time until Wisdom fades the darkness of the coming night considering which way to cross the river, for cross it I fear we must. Then we will discuss that further."

The People who did not attend the men's council were not oblivious. The council was a meeting where the issues discussed were done so in front of the entire cave. Anyone who chose to listen could. This night it was very quiet in the cave.

"Now, we would like to hear from our guests. Is there something we can do for you?" Ki'ti looked at Gukmor, but it was Alme who sought eye contact. Ki'ti nodded to him.

Alme said haltingly, because he didn't have the skill with the language that Gukmor did, "We would like to learn to build rafts to fish our lake. We used the nets and the fish is good to add to our meat. It would be kind of you to show us how to build rafts so we can go out on the lake."

Ki'ti smiled at him. She sought eye contact. After some time, Alme remembered about the eye contact and nodded to her, his face reddening.

Ki'ti raised her voice and said, "Would those in the cave willing to introduce these visitors to fishing with rafts and raft building please stand." Pechki and Likichi stood and so did Neamu-na and Chamul-na. Ki'ti continued, "After we eat the morning meal when Wisdom has returned the color to the land after the coming night, go with these People and they will show you how to fish on the rafts, and then the men will take you to the forest to show you how to harvest the bamboo for drying. Now, I ask, is there anything else that must be considered this night?"

No one made eye contact, so the group dispersed.

In the morning, Pechki, Likichi, Chamul-na, and Neamu-na went with the visitors to the lake. The Mol were fascinated with the rafts. Both Gukmor and Alme knew how to swim, so the women could teach the techniques of fishing with ease. Pechki took Gukmor out, and Likichi took Alme on her raft. Neamu-na poled Pechki's raft and Chamul-na poled Likichi's.

Pechki caught a ray finned fish, and she thought of Totamu with a gulp. For a moment she almost burst into tears, but then she regained her composure. How she missed her mother. She showed Gukmor how to take the net and transfer the fish to the basket. Then she handed him the net. He would catch and transfer the next fish. He caught a snout trout. He managed to transfer the fish without incident. He watched carefully when she fished. He remembered.

Likichi netted a golden line barbel, and Alme smiled at the beautiful fish unlike any he'd ever seen. He watched her as she netted the fish and transferred it to the basket. Then she handed the net to Alme. He netted another barbel, and successfully made the transfer to the basket. They fished until high sun. At that point, they had enough fish to contribute to the night meal. They went up to the caves and the men thanked the People for the fishing lessons.

After getting something to eat, the men trekked back to the bamboo forest where Neamu-na and Chamlu-na taught the the two Mol how to harvest the bamboo and get it to the proper length. They impressed on them that they had to make a hole first in the section where they would burn the bamboo to prevent an explosion of the segment they were burning. They agreed it would be hard work, but they also knew the value of making the rafts. They were filled with great enthusiasm. They wondered about the vines connecting the pieces of the rafts. Likichi said she'd ask Domur to give them some samples of the vines, the next day she would show them how to vine the rafts. The Mol were grateful for the shared information for fishing. Each worked hard to keep the information in memory. They had two bamboo stalks to carry home in addition to the sample vines so their people could use the appropriate ones for holding the rafts together.

At the men's council that night, there was a discussion of building a structure in which they could live that would not be inside the cave. Structures were not something new to the People. They had built homes from what the land provided. At the river where most remembered living, the People had built homes of trees and grasses, but the temperature was so much milder there. The thought was to practice ideas and they could do that in the little valley outside the caves. All agreed this would be wise.

Hahami-na got the nod. "I think," he began slowly for him, "that we might also consider making a permanent structure here where we could live outside the caves. The caves could be used for a storage area, and that way we would not have to move the entire group to a place that might have some hardships we have not even considered. Here we have the lake, the dropoff, a good water supply, and the caves. If we built strong structures that would not fall on us in an earthquake, we could remain here."

There were affirmative murmurs all around. Nobody really wanted to leave this special place.

Hahami-na nodded to Gruid-na, who said, "We cannot build as large as our cave. We will have to make individual home structures for smaller groups. Then we can make a larger one for cooking and eating and gathering. It will not be the same. The cave is good. All members are looked out for in the cave. That is all I have to say."

There was more murmuring.

Wamumur got the nod from Gruid-na. "I think that making a variety of structures will give us a better idea of what we want to do. I remember in my old land homes that were huge. They were made from live trees. The men would climb the birches and tie them together at the top. That made an arch at the top." He used his hands to show his meaning. "The building was a very long one. The hearths were placed along the center. Smoke holes above the hearths kept the air fresh. The roof and sides were made from attaching slender trees, and then connecting strong grasses and mosses and mud. Over all that were bundles of grasses starting low and overhanging them with more bundles of grasses. It shed rain well. We could try that."

More murmuring continued.

Wamumur nodded to Ki'ti and she added, "This is good. We should try these structures while the season of colorful leaves remains. We have choices as to whether we go or stay. It will be very good to see what we develop in the time before the season of cold days comes. If we can remain here, it will be good. Wisdom has blessed us with this place. Wisdom has also blessed us with the knowledge that this cave could collapse, and Wisdom would approve of our discussion tonight. It is good."

Never in his wildest dreams would Wamumur ever have issued a statement of approval of his People, even if he wholeheartedly approved. This was Ki'ti true and simple. It was good. He nodded in her direction, communicating his approval of her actions. She raised an eyebrow with an almost imperceptible smile. She understood the message. She glanced at Emaea. Emaea was beaming.

The Mol were fascinated. Each knew their Chief made decisions. They had input before the decisions were made—even the lowest hunter did. But, once the decision was made, that was it. They had to support the decision of the Chief. This was an amazing difference. It seemed that the Wise One had known they had to leave the caves. That seemed to imply a need to travel to a land where there were no earthquakes, or at least a lower hazard from them. And then at a council meeting, the idea they might be able to remain in different structures gave a different dimension, and the Wise One approved. Not to mention the Wise One was virtually a little girl. She managed her People in a positive way, pulling from them the best they had to give. Gukmor had been troubled that Tongip and Untuk were so eager to become People—now, he was beginning to understand why Tongip and Untuk were so attracted to the People. There was something special here, something different. Gukmor wondered whether that difference centered around the word, "Wisdom."

The cave quieted for the night. Outside, the sky was clear and all was peaceful. Untuk put his arm around Ki'ti and pulled her toward their sleeping place, Panriku at her heels.

"Can we not go to our favorite spot first?" she asked.

"My Dear One, I see you clearly. Tonight, Wisdom was in you. You need sleep now. It may be that some time soon we can have our time, but not now."

Ki'ti bristled with stubbornness. Untuk picked her up in front of everyone. Wamumur knew in his heart exactly what had happened. He smiled. He approved of Untuk. Untuk carried her quickly to their sleeping place, and *told* her to make the bed quickly and walked away. He usually *asked* her to do things like that, but she knew when he *told* her to do something *he* would enforce it. Yet, she didn't feel tired! The bed was quickly done, and she sat on it grumpily with Panriku snuggling against her leg. Untuk returned with a piece of dried fish.

"Here, eat this," he said.

"Where's yours?" she asked.

"I was not just filled with Wisdom, Dear One. Now, eat the softer part and I'll take care of the tough part."

Ki'ti ate the dried fish and handed the tough edge to Untuk who handed it to Panriku. Panriku looked with adoring eyes at Untuk as he happily gulped the treat.

"I feel a conspiracy," Ki'ti wryly said.

"Ah, you are wise and we are uncovered," Untuk said with a chuckle.

The two slid in between the skins and snuggled together. Untuk held her tightly to him and she began to relax. He could feel the vibrancy of the coming together with Wisdom draining from her.

"I guess I really am tired, Untuk. I love you." She fell asleep.

After Wisdom returned color to the land, Likichi took the Mol to the lake and began to show them the details of the vining.

"Whether we are here next season of warm nights or gone, the rafts will be here. If you forget or want refreshing, you can come here to check the vining," Likichi reminded them.

"I appreciate your help from the bottom of my belly," Gukmor assured her. He really liked this woman who saw to the functioning of the cave. He was impressed by the women of the People and how bright and efficient they seemed to be. Their way of thinking included all members of the group and they all seemed equal. Sometimes women even attended the men's council. That was interesting to him. Whatever the cause, he found these women delightful and extremely helpful.

"It is nothing," Likichi assured him with a guileless smile, and she meant it.

The men had learned all they came to learn. They had come to understand a great deal about these People who were neighbors, and they were impressed. They would return to their home the next day with enough stories to keep the Mol listening for a long time. He hoped the People would remain. They were good neighbors.

The Mol put one long and one short bamboo stick outside the cave. The two sticks would be the guide for their raft making. That evening, Untuk and Ki'ti came to them with a pouch of dried fish, a gift to the Mol. They also brought another pouch with a large rhino roast that had been smoked in their caves, and another with a roast of aurochs. They could transport the pouches and their packs by suspending them from the poles.

Gukmor sniffed the roasts and salivated immediately. "That smells like it came from the mountains of the Gods," he exclaimed.

"It is nothing but a few spices our People use," Ki'ti said.

"Wise One," Gukmor said, "will you tell me your age?"

Untuk was horrified he'd ask.

"Gukmor of the Mol, my years on this earth are—Untuk, how do you say?"

Untuk said, "She is fourteen," he said in the language of the Mol.

"But my years on earth do not account for what Wisdom has done with me. I am not a child and have not been a child for" she showed five fingers "years."

"You are clearly not a child, but you *look* like a little girl."

"I am no longer a little girl," she said quietly looking at the ground.

"I am so sorry if I offended you," Gukmor said.

"You did not offend me. When I lose sight of myself and Wisdom's role, when I get filled with pride and leave off the humility that our People require, then Wamumur and Emaea and Untuk are permitted to call me 'Little Girl,' and it stings."

"I see," Gukmor said, not sure that he did. "Please take no offense. I was not referring to you as a little girl except for the way you look on the outside. Once you open your mouth to speak, it is clear you are no child."

"I am not offended, Gukmor. I am, however, reminded that I am to express humility at all times. Your words are to my benefit." She smiled a smile that stole his heart. Untuk put his hand on her shoulder.

"I have met a true Wise One. I am grateful that I had the experience."

"And I am grateful to have met Gukmor of the Mol," she returned.

"Untuk," Gukmor said, "you have found a true treasure. Guard her with your life."

"I shall, Gukmor. I am glad you can see who she truly is."

"I shall never meet another half as deceptively awesome. This has been an incredible mind web stretching for me."

"You will be leaving early?" she asked.

"Yes. Probably before the cave awakens. We have far to go."

"Then, Gukmor and Alme of the Mol, go with Wisdom," she said with her bright smile.

"We shall, Wise One," Gukmor said, while Alme was still reeling from the strange conversation.

They parted and Untuk took her by the hand to the tiny cave near the grave of Ahriku to remind her she was woman. They placed an upright log beside the opening, and Panriku curled up outside the doorway knowing he had time for a short nap.

Chapter 11

By the time the cave was awakening, the Mol hunters had departed. The day was bright with a mild breeze. They stopped at the cave of the man with the green bag, picked up the green bag, and continued for their home. They left much heavier laden than they arrived.

Wamumur was invigorated. He had not had a project for quite some time and the idea of re-creating a bent tree structure large enough to contain the People appealed to him. Again, he had purpose. Lamul-na and Slamika-na, Lai-na and Kai-na, along with Sum and Tongip had all mentioned a desire to work on this structure. Wamumur had discussed it with Emaea, and she planned to get together with some of the women to cut long strips of leather for ties for the tops of trees.

Wamumur had thought long and hard, and had just the place in his mind web—and a plan. In the valley by the caves was a forested area where there were plenty of birch trees of a good height. They were slender because there were so many of them growing close together. The ground was level. As soon as he finished eating, Wamumur strode over to the forested area and began to survey the trees. There were enough to make his design. He took a pouch of mud to the selected area and painted mud on the trunks of the trees he wanted to keep. Ten unmarked trees would have to be removed, which would provide them with space for a very long and wide structure. There were thirty trees that formed a line on one side, and twenty-eight trees on the other side that formed an almost parallel line. In the center, there were three strong trees that would remain for supports. His plan was to take strips of leather and tie the opposing tree tops together. The base of each tree on the outside would make the foundation edge for the exterior walls of the structure; its arched top would form the roof.

Wamumur began by having the unnecessary trees removed. Stone hand axes took considerable time to fell trees, but these trunks were not overly large. The greatest challenge was removing the stumps. They set fire to the stumps and watched them through day and night so the fire would not spread. Little by little they were able to get rid of the stumps.

Once the stumps were removed, the climbers began with the center tree to form the first arch. Lai-na and Lamul-na climbed the trees that would form the opposing outside walls into an arch. Lamul-na carried his length of leather strip coiled around his neck. Lai-na had his wrapped around his forearm. Each climbed the slender trees quickly. As the tree tops began to bend, they came nearer and nearer the center tree. The branches at the top became tangled. They descended to get hand axes and climbed again, eliminating lower branches while leaving stubs for future hangers. They chopped off the tangling limbs of the trees. When they climbed high enough, they were able to tie the arched tops together. This time, the tree bending worked. The first arch was tied with the leather strips and the height of the structure as seen from what would be the floor was very high. From time to time, the People came to see the fascinating structure begin to form.

The plan provided for many arched trees. Only three mid-structure center trees had strong supported arches. There would be two hearths, each located between the strong center trees that supported the middle arches. They would leave openings at the top of the structure for smoke to exit. The People functioned as a unit at this point. They worked diligently because nobody really wanted to leave this area. If this structure was successful, they knew, they could continue to stay here in this place they considered home. Motivation was high.

When the uneven floor became a problem, it was Emaea who organized the children to take baskets to the lake shore to gather sandy soil. They brought the sand up and periodically they were permitted to dump sand in areas that would become floor. The children felt honored to participate.

Finally, all the arches were completed. The men made certain that the roof line was as level as they could get it. At that point, they began to attach long, slender, limbed birch trunks as crosspieces to the walls and then to the roof itself. Emaea had a number of women working to cut leather strips. As soon as a huge quantity of leather strips was taken to the site, it seemed they were used up and another supply was needed. Emaea smiled as she realized that the pieces tied on were likely to remain in place even in great wind or earthquake. They were definitely tied to stay.

When the crosspieces were tied to the top, Lamul-na and Lai-na were teased about becoming monkeys. They had learned to climb at the heights that frightened some of the others. The way they moved from place to place did remind some of monkeys. At each location in the roof between the central support trees, the young men formed squares attached to the roof line that would become smoke holes.

Wamumur discussed with Likichi the need for making two smoke hole covers. He asked her to gather women to assemble two cubes of bamboo to which a strong, thick rhino hide would be stretched and secured across the top. The side of the bamboo cube opposite the leather would be the base. The base would attach to the roof over the smoke hole. Smoke would escape and rain would stay out. Wamumur asked Lamul-na and Lai-na to mud the arched ceiling over the center support trees to prevent stray cinders from setting fire to the ceiling.

Ki'ti was never so happy. Her People were working together on a huge project that could make this residence one they'd keep for a long time. Oddly, those who had begun alternative projects abandoned them to participate on Wamumur's long tree home. She saw that the People were happy. *This was very good*, she thought.

When the long tree home frame was completed and it was a frame that was probably more framed than was absolutely necessary, the men began to harvest grass bundles. The bundles were tied with leather strips and carried to the structure to be tied to the frame. The base of each bundle was tied with the tips of the grasses deliberately pointing to the ground. This process was repeated from the lower level up. Then the second level began and there was a significant overlap of the new bundles of grasses with the first level that had been attached. The People continued this addition of the bundles of grasses until the structure was covered. There was, however, no finished covering at the top of the arches where the bundles met. It was Ekuktu-na who solved the problem of what to do at the top. He had considered the fish. Overlapping scales gave him the idea that overlapping sheets of birch bark from felled trees would provide a solution for finishing the roof top. He suggested they harvest birch bark and tie it across the top so that rain would drain off the birch bark to the grasses where it would drip down. The builders understood at once and immediately began to harvest the bark from trees they had already cut down. They carefully took the widest pieces to minimize the tracking of water through the birch bark openings. They were sewed to the top so that wind would not blow them off. The birch bark pieces overlapped on the south side.

The smoke hole covers had been done with excellence and were tied securely to the structure at the top. They extended about an arm's length beyond the edges of the smoke hole and rose about the distance from a man's elbow to his finger tips above the smoke hole. They had been tried and found to function well.

At the far back of the structure, crosspieces of birch had been placed from side to side making a making a room with birch log sides and a birch log ceiling, where things could be stored or hung. It was Manak-na who concluded that along the sides of the parallel walls of the long tree home inside there should be shelves made for storing personal items on the ground level.

Manak-na set up bench/sleeping place makers and before long the inside of the building began to look like a very special home. Between the bench/sleeping places, there was a niche where spears and tall items could be stored. In some places the beds were double and triple decked for children or for items that one might wish to store above the floor level to keep them out of the hands of little children. Adult bench/sleeping places had added poles from which leathers could be hung for a bit of privacy.

Arkan-na and Untuk went to the end of the rock walk and gathered large stones for the hearth surrounds. They had the two hearths formed in one afternoon. The entrance was viewed as a problem until Chamul-na came up with the idea of an extension on the front that would open not straight out but through a side of the extension. Doing that would prevent direct wind from any direction from blowing to the interior. They could store things that were used outside in the front extension and not have to have them in the living space in much the same way they had kept the booted gaments near the cave entry way back in the ashfall. It kept the living space neater. Chamul-na directed the extension using two trees on either side outside the main structure's entrance. He made the ceiling height about nine feet tall, unlike the towering height of the main structure. The main structure paralleled the caves like a long millipede. Chamul-na made the new opening to the side away from the caves in case there was an earthquake that sent rock toward them.

Veymun sought out Ki'ti. She asked her, "Have you seen Gruid-na?"

Ki'ti looked at her carefully. She seemed far more distraught than she appeared. "No, I have not seen him. Where was he when you last saw him?"

"This afternoon, he was sitting on the stone walk and was watching the building. I went to find him and I have looked everywhere. I just cannot find him."

Ki'ti called to Likichi. If anyone would know where Gruid-na was, it would be Likichi. Likichi came to them. Ki'ti nodded to Veymun.

Veymun said, "I cannot find Gruid-na. He was sitting on the stone walk watching the building and now he has disappeared. I've been everywhere looking for him, and I cannot find him. Do you know where he is?" Veymun was clearly shaken.

Likichi put her arm around Veymun. "I haven't seen him. Maybe he just went for a walk?" Likichi looked for Domur. Finally, she saw her daughter. She said, "Wait here a moment, Veymun. I'll get Domur to start searching."

Likichi went to Domur to ask her to start a group of people looking for Gruid-na. She explained he was old and like some old people, his mind was not well; he might have wandered off. If he got confused, it could be dangerous for him. Likichi went back to Veymun. She explained while Domur and the young people looked for him, they would wait and have some tea. They talked about what they as a People could do to help watch over Gruid-na.

Domur asked Alu, Mitrak, Shmyukuk, Wamumal, Meeka, Liho, and Minagle to help search for Gruid-na. They briefly discussed who would search where, and then they went off in all directions. They searched diligently every nook and cranny where he might be. They had gone into the depths of the caves and checked every known cave of seclusion; they had asked everyone whose paths they crossed; they had walked the paths that were near the caves. Nothing. They were unable to find him. The search party grew larger as there was growing concern for Gruid-na. It was known he seemed to be having memory problems. At one time, he would be present and then he lapsed to a time unknown to most of the People. He spoke of another time. Unlike Ki'ti's getting lost in someone else's time from long ago, Gruid-na got lost in his own time of long ago.

On a hunch, Ki'ti and Untuk went to the lake. They hoped to find the man there. But he wasn't there. Manak-na and Arkan-na went to the overhang to check the ledge and the drop. He was not there. Ermol-na and Nanichak-na went to the cave of the man with the green bag. There, sitting among the dead was Gruid-na.

"Gruid-na, *what are you doing here?*" Ermol-na asked with irritation, as if Gruid-na were perfectly normal doing something absurd.

Gruid-na looked at them as if they were strangers. He realized someone had asked a question. He answered, "It is my time to die, so I came to be with the dead."

Ermol-na and Nanichak-na looked at each other. They had known he was having memory problems, but not that his mind web was this disordered.

"Gruid-na, it is not your time yet. You need to come home with us," Nanichak-na said.

313

"My friend, is that you?" Gruid-na asked.

"Yes, it is, Gruid-na. Come with me now. The evening meal will be ready soon."

Gruid-na stood. It would be difficult getting him down the path. Both wondered how he'd gotten up there. They struggled to help him and finally got him down.

The old man was still coming and going in his mind web "Where is my friend?" Gruid-na asked.

"I'm right here, Gruid-na," Nanichak-na said, with a hand on the old man's shoulder. "Right here."

"I mean the other one. Limush-na. Where is Limush-na?"

"Gruid-na, Limush-na died many, many years ago." Nanichak-na tried to reason with the old man.

"It isn't nice to tease me. I need to finish something with Limush-na. We were just chatting."

Nanichak-na and Ermol-na looked at each other—confused.

Ermol-na said, "Gruid-na, let's go home. The evening meal is almost ready. You can talk to Limush-na there."

"Who are you?" Gruid-na asked, bewildered.

"I am Ermol-na, husband of your daughter, Flayk," he answered mechanically.

"I have no daughter. I just had a son. His name is Mootmu. He is strong."

They continued ushering Gruid-na to the home cave.

"What do you think we'll have for the evening meal?" Ermol-na asked in frustration.

"If Totamu has anything to do with it, it'll be fin fish. I hate fin fish," Gruid-na grumbled. The men realized he was in the time before Baambas when they lived near the lake and slow moving river.

When they reached level ground, Nanichak-na suggested Ermol-na go quickly to prepare the People. He was delighted to fly away from the old man whom he could not understand.

Veymun was distraught. Likichi had the situation as well under control as she could. She went to her herbs to get a combination that she knew would calm people who were agitated. She hoped it would work with Gruid-na.

When Gruid-na arrived, Nanichak-na seated him by Veymun. He recognized her and was delighted to see her. She handed him a cup of the tea Likichi had made, which he drank all at once. Likichi went to the food serving area for two bowls of food for Gruid-na and Veymun. The cave was quiet. *They might as well eat in peace*, she thought.

As he ate, Gruid-na did seem calmer, but he continued to ask for Limush-na. Veymun told him Limush-na had taken a trip to a far away place. Gruid-na seemed to accept that. After he ate, Gruid-na became sleepy, so Veymun prepared his sleeping place for him. He wondered why she didn't join him. She explained she had a few things to do and would be there soon. He went to sleep and began to snore softly.

Veymun, Likichi, Pechki, Ki'ti, Emaea, and Wamumur gathered together after the evening meal. They talked of Gruid-na and how best to take care of someone like this.

They decided the best thing to do would be to have every member of the People understand that Gruid-na was sick in his mind web. All needed to work together to assure that he was safe. If Gruid-na began to wander off, they needed to notify Veymun, Likichi, Emaea, or Wamumur and at least one hunter. From what the older People remembered, old ones like this could come and go in the present and past. They needed to be treated well, but they also needed to be cared for gently, since their drifting to another time could be dangerous for them.

For several days after that, Gruid-na became belligerent and more agitated. Then one high sun, when he was arguing with Nanichak-na about returning to the cave on the hill, he slumped. The man seemed unable to speak and he was drooling. Later he seemed to return partially to his mind web, but he could not stand, and his speech was slurred. He looked so helpless. The hunters took him to his sleeping place. He did not look well. He would try to speak, making only sounds that made no sense. Gruid-na was very upset over his speech. Veymun sat with him trying to soothe him. For days, this continued. The old man could not get up, he could barely use his right arm, and his left was lifeless. Likichi and Pechki thought he had died on his left side, and the right side was was dying—too soon he'd walk with Wisdom.

At one point, the old man opened his eyes very wide. He said, "Limush-na, sorry." Veymun had no clue what he meant. She repeated it to Nanichak-na, who told her about Gruid-na's concern to find Limush-na the day they'd found him at the cave.

"I have an idea," Nanichak-na said. He leaned down close to Gruid-na's face, and said, "Gruid-na, Limush-na knows you're sorry. He said it was long ago, and his feeling for you is good."

Veymun and Nanichak-na waited. The frustration faded from the old man's face. He half smiled with tears flowing from his eyes. He seemed at peace. When Wisdom returned color to the land, Gruid-na had gone to walk with Wisdom. The People had a burial service for Gruid-na. The flowers were about gone but there were some yellow ones atop the second hill and a few hunters took children to gather them. Ki'ti told the story and then they returned to the cave and their responsibilities.

The service would be repeated two days later for Veymun, whose broken heart just stopped, and she went to walk with Wisdom. She would lie next to Gruid-na in death as she had in life.

The structure that would become their home was almost finished. It was nice and in some ways more comfortable than the cave. It was dark inside, but since they had used oil lamps in the cave, they could use them in their new home. Some light came in the smoke hole, but not enough for a structure as large as this. They were all looking forward to the move.

"Wise One, may I have a moment?" Nanichak-na asked.

"Any time," Ki'ti assured him. She loved him dearly.

"I feel that I may have caused Gruid-na's death," he said, "and it makes me feel guilty."

"What do you mean?" His face expressed the emotional pain he felt. She ached for him.

"He was trying to tell somebody named Limush-na that he was sorry for something. I don't know what he was sorry about, but I could tell it bothered him a lot. It bothered him when he was in the cave of the man with the green bag. So I told him that Limush-na knew he was sorry, and he was forgiven. I thought that might ease his troubles. He finally seemed at peace, and then he went to Wisdom."

Ki'ti was surprised that Nanichak-na would dissemble, but she could understand his desire to ease Gruid-na's feelings. She went through her mind web. She could find nothing that addressed this issue. There was much that addressed the issue of lying.

"Nanichak-na, Dear Hunter, ease yourself. You did not cause the death of Gruid-na. The elders of the People have told me of other deaths where People had Gruid-na's signs. We have no way to cure that. It seems to follow mind web confusion as where they are in time. Nanichak-na, he would have gone to Wisdom anyway. You eased his mind web and gave him comfort. It might have been better to say *you felt* Limush-na knew he was sorry and forgave him, but the lie did not cause harm. In no way did you end Gruid-na's life. I would entreat you not to lie again." Ki'ti put one hand on Nanichak-na's forearm, and the other on his shoulder. She looked directly into his eyes.

Nanichak-na felt compassion from her. He lowered his head. "I will not lie again!" he said, and did a strong and loud palm strike.

She repeated his palm strike.

Nanichak-na left feeling clean for the first time since he lied.

The structure that would be home for the People was finally finished. At high sun they began the move of personal items from the cave to their new home with great excitement. The younger hunters' benches/sleeping places were located just inside the entryway. So they could respond quickly to any emergency. The older hunters who were still active came next. The older people who did not actively hunt were located further back into the structure. The arrangement was similar to the cave arrangement. The hearths would be tended by the same People who tended them in the cave and their benches/sleeping places were convenient to the hearths. It turned out everyone was pleased with their spaces. The benches/sleeping places were a real surprise; the bedding would be much more comfortable off the ground. The children who were given elevated sleeping places were delighted. Ki'ti and Untuk's sleeping place was located near the very back of the structure. Because it was so far from a hearth, bear skins were hung as curtains to keep what warmth they generated inside their enclosure. Ki'ti and Untuk were delighted with the privacy the skins afforded. Manak-na had built benches for them at the farthest inside center pole so they could survey the entire structure at a glance. That bench had soft skins laid on it for comfort.

The People had provided safety exits through the grasses at certain spots along the structure wall. From inside, the grasses could be pushed out, moving on leather ties, unlike the other parts of the lower grass levels which were tied to be inflexible. The exits were marked with mud smeared all over the grasses and were between bench/sleeping places. They were not to be touched for exit unless needed for fire or attack. The dwelling was snug, and the People were happy that they would not have to move to distant lands.

Ki'ti felt a horrible ripping pain in her abdomen. She kept from crying out, but asked Untuk to get Likichi quickly. Likichi ran to find Ki'ti doubled up in pain. She asked several questions, and from the signs said to Ki'ti, "It looks like you are pregnant and the baby is coming too soon."

"How could I be pregnant?" Ki'ti asked.

"My Dear, when two adults, male and female . . ."

"I didn't mean that. I felt no signs of pregnancy," Ki'ti said petulantly, through the pain.

"Then you must be losing it early," Likichi said. "I'm so sorry."

The thought *if this were early, how on earth could a woman pass a baby at full term,* wandered through Ki'ti's mind web. Finally it was over, and Likichi showed her the tiny little thing that might have become one of the People. Ki'ti looked at the odd shape. She'd seen incompletely formed babies before. It was sad, but she felt disassociated from the shape she saw, as opposed to how she's feel at the appearance of a full term baby that had life.

"Can you tell what it was: boy or girl?"

"Not positively," Likichi said.

Ki'ti composed herself. Some women's wraps and absorbent material had been brought quietly by Minagle. Ki'ti went to the lower part of the cave to wash. She dressed. She felt empty and very tired. Untuk came for her and picked her up, carrying her to the upper level where he helped her stand. They walked hand in hand to their new home. Going directly to their room, he helped her lie down. He gently covered her with the bear skin.

"Sleep a while," he said. He lowered the bear skin curtain making the little room nearly dark. She closed her eyes and was asleep in minutes.

People were settling in their new spaces. Hearths were already in use for the evening meal. There would be a feast for this first night. Ki'ti slept through it all. Wamumur held the men's council for her. He blessed the new structure asking for Wisdom to heal Ki'ti quickly. Ki'ti entered into a prophetic Wisdom dream in which she was part of a time to come. She clearly saw herself with two children, leading her People along a trail that descended to an immense valley. They would cross the valley on the trail, but she saw no trail. She stood staff in hand, with her hair blowing in the wind, gazing at the land below. She felt as if she'd done this at another time, as if she were seeing what had been, not what was to come, yet in her dream she knew it was to come. She looked into the valley and could see a bright white light floating beckoning her on.

"Come, come, this way, come," it seemed to say.

"Who are you?" Ki'ti demanded.

"I come from Wisdom. I am a messenger sent to show you the way. Come."

Ki'ti hesitated. She was unsure this light was really from Wisdom. She'd never experienced anything like this.

"Do not be afraid. Follow me! I am from Wisdom."

"How do I know where you are from?" she demanded again.

"Because I am Wisdom's messenger to the People. I am Kimseaka, the Guiding Light. I showed Maknu-na and Rimlad where to go. I spoke to Wamumur telling him to leave the old home land. I now guide you."

Ki'ti sighed resignedly. She beckoned to her resting People to follow her, and they did. She followed the light. She didn't realize that her People did not see the light.

When Wisdom returned color to the land, she awoke. She struggled to understand where she was. She was not trekking. There was no guiding light or valley or cave for that matter. She was confused but soon remembered the new long tree home and the loss of what might have been a child now gone.

Ki'ti spoke to the People she saw on the way to the privy, but felt part of something else, not part of this happy group. Untuk noticed something different about her, and hurried to her side. He stayed while she made water, then walked her back to their seating place in their new home.

"Are you well?" he asked.

"I am well, Untuk, but I feel disconnected somehow. I'm sure it will pass as the day goes on," but she had unvoiced doubts.

He pulled her toward him. Looking into her eyes he said, "I'm sorry we lost a baby."

Tears flooded her eyes. She could see genuine pain in his face, and realized he hurt not only for her but also he grieved for the loss of their child who would never be. It was enlightening for her to realize a man who never carried a baby internally could care as much for it as a woman who had. "I'm sorry too, my husband. I didn't know I had a child in my belly. I never felt it move."

"Maybe that's why we lost it. Maybe Wisdom never gave it life."

She looked at him, amazed. "My husband, you understand much about Wisdom."

"My Dear One, I could not love you, join you, and live with you, and not learn about Wisdom. I try to learn new things daily."

"Thank you, Wisdom," Ki'ti softly said looking up, "for giving me this wonderful man."

Untuk hugged her tightly. He loved her with great passion.

No one in the long tree home that day would know their Wise One had any problem. She appeared the same to all. Ki'ti had seen what was to come and, though it was not now, she knew it was inevitable they would eventually leave. She did not know why. She grieved for her unborn child, and for the eventual move. She, too, loved this place and would be sad to move. She wanted to speak to Wamumur and Emaea. She asked Untuk to find them.

They arrived together. Wamumur said, "Good morning, Little Girl, I'm saddened to hear about your loss."

"Thank you," she said quietly, thoughtfully smiling in recognition that a once harsh name had become a term of endearment.

Emaea put her arm around Ki'ti's shoulders, saying nothing.

"I've had a dream," Ki'ti admitted wearily. "I can't talk to any but you about this. It's another time. I'm so confused and tired. In the dream I'm leading the People from here. I don't know why we had to leave. We did not seem saddened or frightened during the trek. At the top of a great hill, I saw a great white light. The light insisted we follow. It proclaimed it was the same light that led Maknu-na and Rimlad. It said it was the same light that led you, Wamumur, from the old land. The light said its name was Kimseaka."

"If you ever see that light, Little Girl, follow it. It *is* of Wisdom," Wamumur said.

"Wise One, in this . . ."

"Stop!" Wamumur said firmly. "Little Girl, you do not call me Wise One any longer for any reason! There is only one Wise One—*it is you*. Don't ever do that again," he admonished.

"Wamumur and Emaea, please listen, in this dream I had two children. The boy was about" she flashed ten fingers "and the girl" she flashed seven and then eight with a facial reflection of uncertainty as to which number would be accurate.

Emaea smiled and brushed her hand over Ki'ti's hair. "You are now Wise One. You will have dreams. Information to guide the People will be given to you in various ways. You know how to protect yourself. The dream you describe tells *what will be* and *when*," Emaea said. "The dream will not come to pass until the time you have those children and they have reached that age. I think the dream is lovely, for it means you will have children, who will live. You will be blessed, Dear One."

Wamumur added, "Little Girl, you are Wise One. You have been given permission from Wisdom now to receive these dreams and use the information for the People. You may come to us at any time you choose, as long as we are in this world."

"Thank you both. I wonder if we can go back a moment, Emaea, with another concern. After the pain of yesterday, I cannot imagine passing a fully live baby through my body."

"Little Girl!" Emaea said, "what a thing to say! Don't be afraid. At that time, the body makes changes that make it possible."

"That is good," Ki'ti said, sounding unsure.

"One thing is certain," Wamumur said, "When the time comes to have a baby, you will have it."

The three of them along with Untuk laughed. Some of Ki'ti's tension drained away. They hadn't laughed at her dream. In fact, they had told how to use the dream for guidance in the future. And if she ever saw this light called Kimseaka, it was not to be feared.

Wamumur cleared his throat and said, "Many years ago, I fear you may have seen something you should not have seen. We were trekking to the cave called Kwa. I had my back to the trekking line and I was angry."

"I saw," Ki'ti responded. "I turned away for fear of seeing something I shouldn't have seen."

"I let you think I'd never blasphemed Wisdom," he admitted. "I did blaspheme that day. I was angry that we were forced to move. People were struggling almost beyond endurance. Wisdom had the power to stop the volcano."

Emaea was shocked but covered well. Ki'ti remained silent, feeling privileged to hear his admission.

"That was terrible sin toward Wisdom," Wamumur continued. "I know in the deepest part of my belly that Wisdom ALWAYS blesses us even though sometimes the blessings may look to us like curses. We must always take the time to learn why the difficult times are blessings. What I see is that we have found a wonderful place to live in peace. We have thrived here and yet we are going to have to move again. I think for us we will always be on the move. Still, I don't know why it must be so. The move here was more than ashfall."

Ki'ti eyed him carefully. Finally, she knew what she'd seen all those years ago.

Wamumur continued, "Why I want you to know this truth is so you will continue to search for the reason we had to leave the place to the south. There has to be more to it than simply avoiding a volcano. Wisdom works all things for purposes. So, my Wise One, I leave you with the charge of continuing to search for why Wisdom caused us to move. It's another story."

Ki'ti was dumbstruck! After spending time thinking, she responded, "I will accept this responsibility, and when it becomes clear—whether in my life or the next Wise One's life or after that—it deserves a story. A story so others will not be tempted to sin against Wisdom through misunderstandings."

"Thank you, Little Girl. You have made me proud to be your father and proud to have been part of training you to be the Wise One. You have excelled in what you do. I fully approve you."

Emaea interjected, "I agree fully. You *are* approved by all, Little Girl."

The long tree home of the People resonated with joy. It was warm enough in seasons of cold days and cool in seasons of warm nights. The smoke hole covers at the top permitted the smoke to exit while blocking white rain and snow. The People remained healthy. Their relationship with the Mol was infrequent but good. The Mol had claimed the remains of the man with the green bag and his family. The Mol were certain it was the son of Torkiz and his family. They were surprised at his clothing, for it was not Mol.

Earthquakes continued, and sometimes large pieces of the caves would drop to the cave floor. That was especially true in the part of the cave where they had lived, so the move prevented some probable deaths. Although it was unusual for the People, their population increased. The long tree home did require enlarging. The front entrance was moved and the home extended. It seemed a real blessing to have to add on.

Within ten years, Wamumur and Emaea were still living. In fact, none of the older People had died since Gruid-na and Veymun. Panriku had died and his place had been taken by Achiriku (Pretty Wolf) a female pup who at this time was old herself. Their population of the People had expanded to about 100. Ki'ti had become pregnant and gave birth to a boy. They named him Yomuk, which meant a stone that was very hard to break. He had the physical characteristics of the Mol and a loving spirit. When Ki'ti became pregnant with the second child, she knew it would be a girl. Wamumur and Emaea were beside themselves with joy, but both remembered as did Ki'ti, that this was prophetic. They were amazed when Ki'ti had another boy at a seemingly early time. The baby was fully formed but tiny. He survived only a few days. Ki'ti found herself pregnant again immediately after the loss of their little son. This one, she knew, would live. It would be female. The timing of age was right. When the girl was born, they called the baby Elemaea.

Ki'ti thought of the passing of time in terms of the ages of her children. When Yomuk was five years old, Chamul-na went to Wisdom quietly in his sleep. A sadness passed over the People, and his grave was heavily laden with flowers. When Yomuk was in his sixth year, Pechki and Neamu-na had gone fishing at the lake when a storm arose. The raft was found, but the bodies were never located. Ki'ti made a memorial grave where they would have been buried. It contained some of their personal things, and a large part of Ki'ti's heart. Her grandparents were so special, and not having a proper burial for them grieved her. She was confident that Wisdom found them even under-water, but it was outside the realm of normal.

When Yomuk was eight years old, Ki'ti remembered hearing a scream. She wondered where it originated, until she realized she was the source. She had been walking with Emaea, who was eighty-three and Wamumur who was two years older. They were at the north end of the caves on the rock walk. It was a walk the three shared since they moved to these caves. They walked there just to talk and reminisce about the growth of the People. As they stood at the end of the walk, an earthquake hit. Emaea fell over the edge and in his attempt to catch her, Wamumur joined her. The position of their bodies made it clear to Ki'ti that both had gone to walk with Wisdom. Untuk came running when he heard her scream. So did most of the hunters. No one could have imagined such a death for the former Wise Ones.

Quickly, hunters ran to the rocky ground where the bodies lay. Neither retained any life. It was the saddest day the People had known. Untuk carried Ki'ti to their little curtained bed in the long tree home. She had ceased screaming and simply sobbed quietly. Untuk held her, cupping the back of her head in his left hand. He felt the little rise in the back of her head that was a characteristic of the real People. Wamumur and Emaea both had it. Minagle did not. He knew Minagle was Likichi's daughter, but she didn't look like it. She wasn't adopted. Untuk smiled, and distractedly remembered his first thoughts that the bump was the place where their phenomenal memories were stored.

Likichi brought a gourd containing tea. Ki'ti drank the tea, thinking as she sipped it that it had a vile taste. Moments after she returned the cup, she was asleep.

The next day, she had to rise and preside over the burial of her adoptive parents. No one would be standing nearby to be sure she told the story correctly. No one else would be able to share with her spiritual things that taught her of Wisdom. She alone had full responsibility for the spiritual well being of the People. She was truly overwhelmed.

Somehow, she got through the grave side service. She noticed that the shared grave was half filled with flowers of every color imaginable. It was so filled with flowers the bodies were totally covered. For that Ki'ti was grateful. She could not see that the bodies were covered with red ocher, a gift of the Mol, a gift with preservative qualities. She did notice Wamumur's neck bag with the yellow owl hanging around Untuk's neck. He whispered he'd been given it in trust for the next Wise One.

Pain ripped her belly. She returned to her sleeping place and slept for three risings of the sun, when Untuk shook her arm and woke her. Achiriku lay on the sand floor just outside Ki'ti's sleeping place, keeping watch.

"You have slept long enough," he said. "You have important responsibilities."

Ki'ti knew he spoke the truth. She steeled herself and rose to resume the role Wisdom had given her. The People were relieved to see her return. Somehow they knew that life would continue on.

Within a month, Achiriku died in her sleep and she was buried as the others had been with the People there to wish her well. And many flowers were brought to cover her body before burial.

As Ki'ti and Untuk's children grew, the People continued to grow in number, albeit they mixed with the Minguat and Mol. When Yomuk was nine, it was clear that something had to change. Winds were blowing, Winds of Change. It was the irresistible force making things shift whether from place to place, or ways of doing things, whatever Wisdom chose. The number of game animals required to feed the growing number of people was diminishing. That fact had been apparent for several years. The People would soon have to move to a place where they could find enough game to feed themselves. The time had come to plan the move. It would take a year of preparation for the move to begin. Ki'ti had not forgotten her dream. She knew what to do. The men's council had known of the dream for years. They were ready when the time came.

Ki'ti had passed thirty years. The People would plan what necessary supplies and food could be carried to follow their Wise One to a new land. Unlike the former trek where the Wise One was last in line, because of the dream, Ki'ti would lead with Manak-na and Untuk. Following the ancient path, the dragon path, they hoped to move to the large lake the Mol had described long ago. They trekked past the cave of the man with the green bag, past the fallen down cave filled with amazing animals, and then turning to follow the path to the land of the Mol. They feasted for three days with the Mol, and then continued. Two Mol couples asked to join them. They were told they had to become People to do that. They agreed. They understood the role of Wisdom, and wanted that guidance.

When the People crossed the river, they reached the bridge where they continued the ancient path. No one had been prepared for the Gar caves that still smelled foul after all those years. The trekkers found the footpath to the bridge north of the Gar caves to be in bad shape. Hunters would have to carry the dogs across. Extreme caution was necessary. Even young children were carried across.

After traveling for more than thirty days, the People arrived at a hill overlooking a huge valley. Ki'ti came to an abrupt halt. She had seen this once long ago. It was from her dream. And there below was the light. She had to deviate from the path as it could no longer be seen. A landslide had wiped it out. She would follow the light. She gazed out over the new land, her walking stick held in her right hand.

Ki'ti's eyes dilated. In an instant, she moved imperceptibly into the world of the spirit, where she would *know* of things to come. The People would continue to place their trust in Wisdom, and they would flourish by adding the Mol and Minguat until they became very different in appearance. Ki'ti had never asked Wamumur why he shook his fists in the direction of the volcano, but after many years he told her. Wisdom moved them for a reason, and she had discovered the reason. Often the reason could not be understood for many years. Sometimes the People might think that Wisdom was doing anything but looking out for their welfare. Such was never the case, but passing time was sometimes required to understand actions in outcomes. Their line had been suffering with low birth rates, and some children, and even their mothers, failed to survive birth. By merging with Others and the Mol, they would continue on, different but stronger. Ki'ti had seen the improved growth in their numbers. In those cases, where there was joining of People with Mol or People with Others, birth rates rose. It was even higher when the woman was not People.

Wisdom brought no evil, but instead a great blessing. She finally fully understood. Those for whom Ki'ti would be an ancestor would not die out, but rather would continue through the ages to come. The original People would be there in their descendants. Ki'ti could see the future in her own children. She had a moment of assurance—that certainty of knowing. She understood what Wisdom approved when Baambas caused their move long ago. Wisdom saved them from extinction, first, from the volcano by forcing the trek, and, second, from their own birth difficulties by providing the Others and the Mol with whom they would intermingle and thrive as long as the stars and moon shone by night and the sun by day. Wamumur, the Wise One, simply had had a momentary lapse in faith during the time of the volcano's explosion, when he shook his fists. Without awareness of the significance, later on he had unwittingly fully supported Wisdom's real blessing. The People, The Others, and the Mol—Wamumur said they were all People. As one, Ki'ti knew, they would continue. She hugged herself, wishing Wamumur was within her arms. How she wished he knew what she had come to understand, but in death and in Wisdom's company, perhaps he did.

Ki'ti looked up. "Wisdom," she said aloud but quietly. "I almost credited myself with reasoning out the mystery. I do recognize it is from you that my mind web gained the understanding—just as it was you who gave me the stories. From the bottom of my belly, I give you thanks."

Bibliography

Achilli, A., Perego, U.A., Bravi, C. M., Coble, M. D., Kong, Q.-P., Woodward, S. R., Salas, A., Terroni, A., Bandelt, H.-J., "The Phylogeny of the Four Pan-American MtDNA Haplogroups: Implications for Evolutionary and disease Studies," *PLoS ONE*, 3(3) e1764.

Adovasio, J.M., Page, J., *The First Americans: In Pursuit of Archaeology's Greatest Mystery*, Modern Library, Imprint of Random House, 2003.

Ao, H., Deng, C, Dekkers, M. J., Sun, Y., Liu, Q., Zhu, R., "Pleistocene environmental evolution in the Nihewan Basin and implications for early human colonization of North China," *Quaternary International*, 2010.

Bae, C., "The late Middle Pleistocene hominin fossil record of eastern Asia: Synthesis and review," *American Journal of Physical Anthropology*, supplement yearbook, 143(51), 2010.

Bae, K., "Origin and patterns of the Upper Paleolithic industries in the Korean Peninsula and movement of modern humans in East Asia," *Quaternary International*, 211(1-2), 2010.

Bailey, S., "A Closer Look at Neanderthal Postcanine Dental Morphology: The Mandibular Dentition," *The Anatomical Record*, 269, 2002.

Bailey, S. E., Wu, L., "A comparative dental metrical and morphological analysis of a Middle Pleistocene hominin maxilla from Chaoxian (Chaohu), China," *Quaternary International*, 211(1-2), 2010.

Bailliet, G., Rothhammer, F., Garnese, F. R., Bravi,C.M., and Bianchi, N. O., "Founder Mitochondrial Haplotypes in Amerindian Populations," *The Journal of Human Genetics*, 54, 1994.

Balter, M., "Child Burial Provides Rare Glimpse of Early Americans," *ScienceNOW*, Feb 2011.

Banks, W., D'Errico, F., Dibble, H., Krishtalka, L., West, D., Olszewski, D., Peterson, A., Anderson, D., Gillam, J., Montet-White, A., Crucifix, M., Marean, C., Sánchez-Goñi, M., Wohlfarth, B., Vanhaeran, M., "Eco-Cultural Niche Modeling: New Tools for Reconstructing the Geography and Ecology of Past Human Populations," *PaleoAnthropology*, 2006.

Bannai, M., Ohashi, J., Harihara, S., Takahashi, Y., Juji, T., Omoto, K., Tokunaga, K., "Analysis of HLA genes and haplotypes in Ainu (from Hokkaido, northern Japan) supports the premise that they descent from Upper Paleolithic populations of East Asia," *Tissue Antigens*, 55, 2000.

Bengston, John D., *In Hot Pursuit of Language in Prehistory*, John Benjamin Publishing Co., The Netherlands, 2008.

Benson, L., Lund, S., Smoot, J., Rhode, D., Spencer, R., Verosub, K., Louderback, L., Johnson, C., "The rise and fall of Lake Bonneville between 45 and 10.5 ka," *Quaternary International*, 235(1-2), 2009.

Boeskorov, G. G., "The North of Eastern Siberia: Refuge of Mammoth Fauna in the Holocene," *Gondwana Research*, 7(2) 2004, available in English in ScienceDirect, November 2005

Bogoras, W., *The Jesup North Pacific Expedition, Memoir of the American Museum of Natural History, Volume VII, The Chukchee*, Leiden, E. J. Brill,

Ltd., Printers and Publishers, 1975 (reprint of the 1904-1909 edition). This publication is routinely referred to as *The Chukchee*.

Bolnick, D. A., Shook, B. A, Campbell, L, Goddard, I, "Problematic Use of Greenberg's Linguistic Classification of the Americas in Studies of Native American Genetic Variation," *American Journal of Human Genetics,* 75(3): 2004.

Bonnichsen, R. Lepper, B., Stanford, D., Waters, M., *Paleoamerican Origins: Beyond Clovis,* Center for the Study of the First Americans, Department of Anthropology, Texas A&M University, 2005.

Borrell, B., "Bon Voyage, Caveman," *Archaeology,* 63(3), May/June 2010. (possibility of seafaring by *Homo erectus* at 130,000 ya)

Bower, B., "Asian Trek," *Science News,* 171(14), 4/7/2007.

Bower, B., "Ancient hominids may have been seafarers," *Science News,* 177(3), 2010.

Brantingham, P., Gao, X., Madsen, D., Bettinger, R., Elston, r., " The initial Upper Paleolithic at Shuidonggou, Northwestern China," in *The Early Upper Paleolithic beyond Western Europe,* Ed. By Brantingham, P, Juhn, S., and Kerry, K., 2004.

Cannon, M. D., "Explaining variability in Early Paleoindian foraging," *Quaternary International,* 191(1), 2008.

Catto, N., "Quaternary floral and faunal asssemblages: Ecological and taphonomical investigations," *Quaternary International,* 233(2), 2011.

Catto, N., "Quaternary landscape evolution: Interplay of climate, tectonics, geomorphology, and natural hazards," *Quaternary International,* 233(1), 2011.

Chauhan, P. R., "Large mammal fossil occurrences and associated archaeological evidence in Pleistocene contexts of peninsular India and Sri Lanka," *Quaternary International,* 192(1), 2008.

Chen, C., An, J, Chen, H., "Analysis of the Xionanhai lithic assemblage, excavated in 1978," *Quaternary International,* 211(1-2), 2010.

Chen, X-Y., Cui, G-H., Yang, J-X., "Threatened fishes of the world: *Pseudobagrus medianalis* (Regan) 1904 (Bagridae), *Environmental Biology of Fishes,* 81(3), 2008.

Chlachula, J., Drozdov, N., Ovodov, N., "Last Interglacial peopling of Siberia: the Middle Palaeolithic site Ust'-Izhul', the upper Yenisei area," *Boreas,* 32, 2003.

Ciochon, R., Bettis III, A., "Asian *Homo erectus* converges in time," *Nature,* 458, March 2009

Cione, A., Tonni, E., Soibelzon, L., "The Broken Zig-Zag: Late Cenozoic large mammal and tortoise extinction in South America," *Rev. Mus. Argentino Cienc. Nat.,* n.s., 5(1), 2003.

Coppens, Y., Tseveendorj, D., Demeter, F., Turbat, T., and Giscard, P., "Discovery of an archaic *Homo sapiens* skullcap in Northeast Mongolia," *Comptes Rendus Palevol,* 7(1), Feb 2008. Note: The findings are that the skullcap shows similarities with Neanderthals, Chinese Homo erectus, and West/Far East archaic Homo sapiens. Dating is possible late Pleistocene.

Corvinus, G., "*Homo erectus* in East and Southeast Asia, and the questions of the age of the species and its association with stone artifacts, with special attention to handaxe-like tools," *Quaternary International,* 117, 2004.

Coxe, W., *The Russian Discoveries Between Asia and America,* Readex Microprint Corp., 1966, copy of Coxe's document from 1780.

Cremo, M., Thompson, R., *Forbidden Archaeology: The Hidden History of the Human Race,* Unlimited Resources, 1996-2011.

Delluc, B., Delluc, G., "Art Paléolithique, saisons et climats," *Comptes Rendus Palevol,* 5, 2006.

Demske, D., Heumann, G., Granoszewski, W., Nita, M., Mamakowa, K., Tarasov, P., Oberhänsli, H., "Late glacial and Holocene vegetation and regional climate variability evidenced in high-resolution pollen records from Lake Baikal," *Global and Planetary Change,* 46, 2005.

Derbeneva, O. A., Sukernik, R. I., Volodko, N.V., Hosseini, s. H., Lott, M. T., and Wallace, D. C., "Analysis of Mitochondrial DNA Diversity in the Aleuts of the Commander Islands and Its Implications for the Genetic History of Beringia," *The American Journal of Human Genetics*, 71(2): 2002.

Derenko, M., Malyarchuk, B., Grzybowski, T., Denisove, G., Dambueva, I., Perkova, M., Dorzhu, C., Luzina, F., Lee, H. K., Vanecek, T., Villems, R., and Zakharov, I., "Phylogeographic analysis of Mitochondrial DNA in Northern Asian Populations," *The American Journal of Human Genetics*, 81, November 2007.

Dillehay, T. D., *The Settlement of the Americas: A New Prehistory*, Basic Books of the Perseus Books Group, 2000.

Dixon, E. J. and G. S. Smith, "Broken canines from Alaskan cave deposits: re-evaluating evidence for domesticated dog and early humans in Alaska." *American Antiquity*, 51(2): 1986.

Doelman, T., "Flexibility and Creativity in Microblade Core Manufacture in Southern Primorye, Far East Russia," *Asian Perspectives*, 47(2), 2009.

Elliott, D.K., *Dynamics of Extinction*, John Wiley & Sons, New York, 1986.

Erlandson, J., Moss, M., Des Lauriers, M., "Life on the edge: early maritime cultures of the Pacific coast of North America, *Quaternary Science Reviews*, 27, 2008.

Etler, D., "The Fossil Evidence for Human Evolution in Asia," *Annual Review of Anthropology*, 25, 1996.

Etler, D., "*Homo erectus* in East Asia: Human Ancestor or Evolutionary Dead-End?" *Athena Review*, 4(1) [Cannot locate year. The author is from Department of Anthropology, Cabrillio college, Aptos, California.]

Etler, D., Crummett, T., Wolpoff, M., "Longgupo: Early Homo Colonizer or Late Pliocene Lufengpithecus Survivor in South China?" *Human Evolution*, 16(1-12), 2001.

Fell, B., *America B.C.,* Artisan Publishers, 2010.

Fiedel, Stuart J., "Older Than We Thought: Implications of Corrected Dates for Paleoindians," *American Antiquity,* 64(1), 1999.

Finlayson, Clive, *The HUMANS WHO WENT EXTINCT, Why Neanderthals died out and we survived.* Oxford University Press, 2009.

Fitzhugh, W., "Stone Shamans and Flying Deer of Northern Mongolia: Deer Goddess of Siberia or Chimera of the Steppe?" *Arctic Anthropology,* 46(1-2) 2009.

Flam, F.: "Red hair a part of the Neanderthal genetic profile" *The Philadelphia Inquirer,* October 26, 2007.

Flannery, T., *The Eternal Frontier,* Atlantic Monthly Press, New York, 2001.

Forster, P., Harding, R., Torroni, A., and Bandelt, H. J., "Origin and Evolution of Native American mtDNA Variation: A Reappraisal," *The American Journal of Human Genetics,* 59(4): 1996.

Froehle, A., Churchill, S., "Energetic Competition Between Neandertals and Anatomically Modern Humans," *PaleoAnthropology,* 2009.

Gilbert, M. T. P., Jenkins, D. L., Götherstrom, A., Naveran, N. Sanchez, J. J., Hofreiter, M., Thomsen, P. F., Binladen, J., Higham, T. F. G., Yohe, R. M., II, Parr, R. Cummings, L. S. Willerslev, E., "DNA from Pre-Clovis Human Coprolites in Oregon, North America," *Science Express,* April 2008.

Gilligan, I., "The Prehistoric Development of clothing: Archaeological Implications of a thermal Model," *Journal of Archaeological Method Theory,* 17, 2010.

Gladyshev, S., olsen, J., Tabarev, A., Kuzmin, Y., "Peleoenvironment. The Stone Age: Chronology and Periodization of Upper Paleolithic Sites in Mongolia." *Archaeology Ethnology & Anthropology of Eurasia,* 38(3), 2010.

Goebel, T., Waters, M., Dikova, M., "The Archaeology of Ushki Lake, Kamchatka, and the Pleistocene Peopling of the Americas," *Science,* 301(5632), 2003.

Goldberg, E., Chebykin, E., Zhuchenko, N., Vorobyeva, S., Stepanova, O., Khlystov, O., Ivanov, E., Weinberg, E, Gvozdkov, A., "Uranium isotopes as proxies of the Lake Baikal watershed (East Siberia) during the past 150 ka," *Palaeogeography, Palaeoclimatology, Palaeoecology,* 294(1-2) August 2010.

Golubenko, M. V., Stepanov, V. A., Gubina, M. A., Zhadanov, S. I., Ossipova, L. Pl, Damba, L., Voevoda, M. I., Dipierri, J. E., Villems, R., Malhi, R. S., Beringian "Standstill and Spread of Native American Founders," *PLoS ONE* 2(9): eB29. doi;10.1371/journal.pone.0000829.

Goodyear, Albert C., "Evidence for Pre-Clovis Sites in the Eastern United States," unpublished and undated manuscript, http://allendale-xpedition. net/publications/AL_ORIGN1.PDF

Grayson, D., Meltzer, D., "A requiem for North American overkill," *Journal of Archaeological Science,* 30(5), 2003.

Grove, C., "Ice-age child's remains discovered in Interior," *Anchorage Daily News,* 2/24/2011

Hall, R., "Cenozoic plate tectonic reconstruction of SE Asia," from Fraser, L., Matthews, S., Murphy, R., (Eds.), *Petroleum Geology of Southeast Asia,* Geological Society of London Special Publication 26, 1997.

Hapgood, C., *Maps of the Ancient Sea Kings,* Adventures Unlimited Press, 1966.

Hardaker, C., *The First American: the Suppressed Story of the People Who Discovered the New World,* New Page Books, 2007.

Haynes, C,. V., Jr., "Younger Dryas 'Black mats' and the Rancholabrean termination in North America," *National Academy of Sciences of the USA,* 2008. (See also: for photographs http://www.georgehoward.net/Vance%20 Haynes'%20Black%20Mat.htm)

Heaton, T. H., On Your Knees Cave, http://orgs.usd.edu'esci/alaska/oykc. html 2002.

Henry, A., Brooks, A., Piperno, D., "Microfossils in calculus demonstrate consumption of plants and cooked foods in Neanderthal diets," *Proceedings of the National Academy of Sciences,* 108(2), 2010.

Hoffecker, J. F., *A Prehistory of the North: Human Settlement of the Higher Latitudes,* Rutgers University Press, New Brunswick, New Jersey, 2005.

Honeychurch, W., Amartuvshin, C., "Hinterlands, Urban Centers, and Mobile Settings: The 'New' Old World Archaeology from the Eurasian Steppe," *Asian Perspectives,* 46(1) 2007.

Hopkins, D. M., Matthews, J. V, Jr., Schweger, C. E., Young, S. B., *Paleoecology of Beringia,* Academic Press, New York, 1982.

Huyghe, P., *Columbus Was Last: From 200,000 B.C. To 1492 A Heretical History of Who Was First,* Anomalist Books, 1992.

Igarashi, Y., Zharov, A., "Climate and vegetation change during the late Pleistocene and early Holocene in Sakhalin and Hokkaido, northeast Asia," *Quaternary International,* xxx (in process), 2011.

Inman, M.: "Neanderthals Had Same 'Language Gene' as Modern Humans," *National Geographic News,* October 18, 2007, http://news.nationalgeographic.com/news/2007/10/071018-neandertal-gene.html

Jackinsky, M., "Evidence of woolly mammoths on Peninsula grows," *Alaska Daily News,* 3/13/2011.

Jackson, Jr., L. E., Wilson, M. C., "The Ice-Free Corridor Revisited," *Geotimes,* Feb. 2004.

Jiang, Y-E., Chen, X-Y, Yang, J-X., "Threatened fishes of the world: Yunnanilus discoloris Zhou & He 1989 (Cobitidae)," *Environmental Biology of Fishes,* 86(1), 2009.

Jin, J. J. H., Shipman, P., "documenting natural wear on antlers: A first step in identifying use-wear on purported antler tools," *Quaternary International,* 211(1-2) 2010.

Johnson, John F. C., *Chugach Legends: Stories and Photographs of the Chugach Region*, Chugach Alaska Corporation, 1984.

Joling, D., "Warming brings unwelcome change to Alaska villages," *Anchorage Daily News*, 3/27/ 2011.

Joseph, F., *Discovering the Mysteries of Ancient America: Lost History and Legends, Unearthed and Explored*, New Page Books, 2006.

Khenzykhenova, F., "Paleoenvironments of Palaeolithic humans in the Baikal region," *Quaternary International*, 179(1), 2008.

Khenzykhenova, F., Sato, T., Lipnina, E., Medvedev, G., Kato, H., Kogai, S., Maximenko, K., Novosel'zeva, V., "Upper paleolithic mammal fauna of the Baikal region, east Siberia (new data)," *Quaternary International*, 231, 2011.

Kienast, F., Schirrmeister, L., Siegert, C., Tarasov, P., "Palaeobotanical evidence for warm summers in the East Siberian Arctic during the last cold stage," *Quaternary Research*, 63(3), 2005.

King, G., Bailey, G., "Tectonics and human evolution," *Antiquity*, 80, 2006.

Klein, H. S., Schiffner, D. C., "The Current Debate about the Origins of the Paleoindian of America," *Journal of Social History*, 37(2), Winter 2003.

Kolomiets, V. L., Gladyshev, S. A., Bezrukova, E. V., Rybin, E. P., Letunova, P. P., Abzaeva, A. A., "Paleoenvironment The Stone Age: Environment and human behavior in northern Mongolia during the Upper Pleistocene," *Archaeology, Ethnology, and Anthropology of Eurasia*, 37(1), 2009.

Komatsu, G., Olsen, J., Ormo, J., Di. Achille, G., Kring, D., Matsui T., "The Tsenkher structure in the Gobi-Altai, Mongolia: Geomorphological hints of an impact origin," *Geomorphology*, 74(1-4), March 2006.

Kornfeld, M., Larson, M. L., "Bonebeds and other myths: Paleoindian to Archaic transition on North American Great Plains and Rocky Mountains," *Quaternary International*, 191(1), 2008.

Krause, J., Orlando, L., Serre, D., Viola, B., Prüfer, K., Richards, M., Hublin, J., Hänni, C., Derevianko, A., Pääbo, S., "Neanderthals in central Asia and Siberia," *Nature LETTERS,* 449, 2007.

Kunz, Michael, M. Bever, C. Adkins, *The Mesa Site: Paleoindians above the Arctic Circle,* U. S. Department of the Interior, Bureau of Land Management, BLM-Alaska Open File Report 86, BLM/AK/ST-03/001+8100+020, April 2003.

Kurochkin, E., Kuzmin, Y., Antoshchenko-Olenev, I., Zabelin, V., Krivonogov, S., Nohrina, T., Lbova, L., Burr, G, and Cruz, R., "The timing of ostrich existence in Central Asia: AMS 14C age of eggshells from Mongolia and southern Siberia (a pilot study)," *Nuclear Instruments and Methods in Physics Research Section B: Beam Interactions with Materials and Atoms,* 268(7-8), April 2010.

Kuzmin, Y., Orlova, L., "Radiocarbon chronology and environment of woolly mammoth (*Mammuthus primigenius* Blum.) in northern Asia: results and perspectives," *Earth-Science Reviews,* 68, 2004.

Kuzmin, Y., Richards, M., Yoneda, M., "Paleodietary Patterning and Radiocarbon Dating of Neolithic Populations in the Primorye Province, Russian Far East," *Ancient Biomolecules,* 4(2), 2002.

Lam, Y. M., Brunson, K, Meadow, R., Yuan, J., "Integrating taphonomy into the practice of zooarchaeology in China," *Quaternary International,* 211(1-2), 2010.

Lee, H., "Paleoenvironment: The Stone Age. Projectile Points and Their Implications," *Archaeology Ethnology & Anthropology of Eurasia,* 38(3), 2010.

Lell, J. T., Sukernik, R. I., Starikovskaya, Y. B., Su, B., Jin, L., Schurr, T. G., Underhill, P. A., Wallace, D. C., "The Dual Origin and Siberian Affinities of Native American Y Chromosomes," *The American Journal of Human Genetics,* 70, 2002.

Lister, A., Bahn, P. G., *Mammoths: Giants of the Ice Age,* Richard Green Publisher, 1994.

Liu, W., Wu, X., Pei, S., Wu, Xiujie, Norton, C. J., "Huanglong Cave: A Late Pleistocene human fossil site in Hubei Province, China," *Quaternary International,* 211(1-2), 2010.

Lu, X., Xiong, D., Chen, C., "Threatened fishes of the world: *Sinocyclocheilus grahami* (Regan 1904) (Cyprinidae)," *Environmental Biology of Fishes,* 85(2), 2009.

Ma, S., Wang, Y., Xu, L., "Taxonomic and Phylogenetic Studies on the Genus Muntiacus," *Acta Theriologica Sinica* VI(3) 1986. (Translated by Will Downs, Dept of Geology, Bilby Research Cneter, Northern Arizona Univ., 1991)

Macé, F., "Human Rhythm and Divine Rhythm in Ainu Epics," *Diogenes,* 46(1), 1998.

Marwick, b., "Biogeography of Middle Pleistocene hominins in mainland Southeast Asia: A review of current evidence," *Quaternary International,* 202(1-2), 2009.

Mednikova, M., Dobrovolskaya, M., Buzhilova, A., Kandinov, M., "A Fossil Human Humerus from Khvalynsk: Morphology and Taxonomy," *Archaeology Ethnology & Anthropology of Eurasia,* 38(1), 2010.

Meltzer, D., *First Peoples in a New World: Colonizing Ice Age America,* University of California Press, 2009.

Merriwether, D. A., Hall, W. W., Vahine, A., and Ferrell, R. E., "mtDNA Variation Indicates Mongolia May Have Been the Source for the Founding Population for the New World," *The American Journal of Human Genetics,* 59, 1996.

Mol, D., de Vos, J., van der Plicht, J., "The presence and extinction of *Elephas antiquus* Falconer and Cautley, 1847, in Europe," *Quaternary International,* 169-170, 2007.

Moncel, M., "Oldest human expansions in Eurasia: Favouring and limiting factors," *Quaternary International,* 223-4, 2010.

Naske, C-M., Slotnick, H. E., *Alaska A History of the 49th State,* 2nd Ed., University of Oklahoma Press, Norman, 1979.

Neel, J. V., Biggar, R. J., Sukernik, R. I., "Virologic and genetic studies relate Amerind origins to the indigenous people of the Mongolia/Manchuria/

southeastern Siberia region," *Proceedings of the National Academy of Sciences, USA,* 91, 1994.

Nikolskiy, P. A., Basilyan, A. E., Sulerzhitsky, L. D., and Pitulko, V. V., "Prelude to the extinction: Revision of the Achchagyl-Allaikha and Berelyokh mass accumulations of mammoth," *Quaternary International,* 219(1-2), 2010.

Norton, C. J., "The nature of megafaunal extinctions during the MIS 3-2 transition in Japan," *Quaternary International,* 211(1-2), 2010.

Norton, C. J., Jin, J. J. H., "Hominin morphological and behavioral variation in eastern Asia and Australasia: current perspectives," *Quaternary International,* 211(1-2), 2010.

O'Neill, D., *The Last Giant of Beringia: The Mystery of the Bering Land Bridge,* Westview Press, Perseus Books Group, New York, 2004.

Oppenheimer, S., "The great arc of dispersal of modern humans: Africa to Australia," *Quaternary International,* 202(1-2), 2009.

Orlova, L. A., Kuzmin, Y. V., Stuart, A. J., Tikhonov, A. N., "Chronology and environment of woolly mammoth (Mammuthus primigenius Blumenbach) extinction in northern Asia," *The World of Elephants – International Congress,* Rome 2001.

Osipov, E., Khlystov, O., "Glaciers and meltwater flux to Lake Baikal during the Last Glacial Maximum," *Palaeogeography, Palaeoclimatology, Palaeoecology,* 294(1-2) 2010.

Palombo, M. R., "Quaternary mammal communities at a glance," *Quaternary International,* 212(2), 2010.

Park, S., "L'hominidé du Pléistocène supérieur en Corée, *L'anthropologie,* 110, 2006.

Pei, S., Gao, X., Feng, X., Chen, F., Dennell, R., "Lithic assemblage from the Jingshuiwan Paleolithic site of the early Late Pleistocene in the Three Gorges, China," *Quaternary International,* 211(1-2), January 2010.

Pietrusewsky, M., "A multivariate analysis of measurements recorded in early and more modern crania from East Asia and Southeast Asia," *Quaternary International*, 211(1-2), 2010.

Pimenoff, V., Comas, D., Palo, J., Vershubsky, G., Kozlov, A, Sajantila, A., "Northwest Siberian Khanty and Mansi in the junction of West and East Eurasian gene pools as revealed by uniparental markers," *European Journal of Human Genetics*, 16, 2008.

Pitulko, V., "The Berelekh Quest: A Review of Forty Years of Research in the Mammoth Graveyard in Northeast Siberia," *Geoarchaeology*, 26(1), 2011.

Ponce de León, M., Golovanova, L., Doronichev, V., Romanova, G., Akazaqa, T., Kondo, O., Ishida, H., Zollikofer, C., "Neanderthal brain size at birth provides insights into the evolution of human life history," *Proceedings of the National Academy of Sciences*, 105(37), Sept 2008.

Potter, B. A., Reuther, J. D., Bowers, P. M., and Relvin-Reymiller, C., "Little Delta Dune Site: A Late-Pleistocene Multicomponent Site in Central Alaska," *Archaeology: North America*, CRP 25, 2008.

Powell, E., "Mongolia," *Archaeology*, 59(1) Jan/Feb 2006.

Prokopenko, A., Kuzmin, M., Li, H., Woo, K., Catto, N., "Lake Hovsgol basin as a new study site for long continental paleoclimate records in continental interior Asia: General contest and current status," *Quaternary International*, 205, 2009.

Quade, J., Forester, R. M., Pratt, W. L., Carter, C., "Black Mats, Spring-Fed Streams, and Late-Glacial-Age Recharge in the Southern Great Basin," *Quaternary Research*, 49(2) 1998.

Ransom, J. E., "Derivation of the Word Alaska," *American Anthropologist*, 42, 1942.

Razjigaeva, N., Korotky, A., Grebennikova, T., Ganzey, L., Mokhova, L., Bazarova, V. Sulerzhitsky, L., Lutaenko, K., "Holocene climatic changes and environmental history of Iturup Island, Kurile Islands, northwestern Pacific," *The Holocene*, 12, 2002.

Rose, W. I., Chesner, C. A., "Dispersal of ash in the great Toba Eruption, 74 ka," *Geology,* 15, 1987.

Rudaya, N., Tarasov, P., Dorofeyuk, N., Solovieva, N., Kalugin, I., Andreev, Daryin, A., Diekmann, B., Riedel, F., Tserendash, N., Wagner, M., "Holocene environments and climate in the Mongolian Altai reconstructed from the Hoton-Nur pollen and diatom records: a step towards better understanding climate dynamics in Central Asia," *Quaternary Science Reviews,* 28(5-6) 2009.

Ruvinsky, J., "The Great American Extinction," *Discover,* 28(8) 2007.

Saillard, J., Forster, P., Lynnerup, N., Bandelt, H.-J., Nørby, S., "mtDNA Variation among Greenland Eskimos: The Edge of the Beringian Expansion," *The Journal of Human Genetics,* 2000 September; 67(3): 718-726.

Saleeby, B. M., "Out of Place Bones: beyond the study of prehistoric subsistence," Arctic Research of the United States, *U. S. National Science Foundation,* 2002.

Sattler, H. R., *The Earliest Americans,* Clarion Books, New York, 1993.

Schepartz, L. A., Miller-Antonio, S., "Taphonomy, Life History, and Human Exploitation of Rhinoceros sinensis at the Middle Pleistocene site of Panxian Dadong, Guizhou, China," *International Journal of Osteoarchaeology,* 2008.

Schrenk, F., Muller, S. *The Neanderthals,* Routledge, 2005.

Seong, C., "Tanged points, microblades and Late Palaeolithic hunting in Korea," *Antiquity,* 82, 2008.

Shen, G., Fang, Y., Bischoff, J. L., Feng, Y., and Zhao, J., "Mass spectrometric U-series dating of the Chaoxian hominin site at Yinshan, eastern China," *Quaternary International,* 211(1-2), 2010.

Sher, A., Weinstock, J., Baryshnikov, G., Davydov, S., Boeskorov, G., Zazhigin, V., Nikolskiy, P., "The first record of 'spelaeoid' bears in Arctic Siberia, *Quaternary Science Reviews,* 30, 2010.

Shichi, K., Takahara, H., Krivonogov, S., Bezrukova, E., Kashiwaya, K., Takehara, A., Nakamura, T., "Late Pleistocene and Holocene vegetation and climate records from Lake Kotokel, central Baikal region," *Quaternary International,* 205, 2009.

Smith, T., Toussaint, M., Reid, D., Olejniczak, A., Hublin, J., "Rapid dental development in a Middle Paleolithic Belgian Neanderthal," *Proceedings of the National Academy of Sciences,* 104(51), Dec. 2007.

Snodgrass, J., Leonard, W., "Neandertal Energetics Revisited: Insight Into Population Dynamics and Life History Evolution," *PaleoAnthropology,* 2009.

Starikovskaya, Y. B., Sukernik, R. I., Schurr, T. G., Kogelnik, A. M., and Wallace, D. C. "mtDNA diversity in Chukchi and Siberian Eskimos: Implications for the Genetic History of Ancient Beringia and the Peopling of the New World," *The American Journal of Human Genetics,* 63, 1998.

Stephan, A. E., *The First Athabascans of Alaska: Strawberries,* Dorrance Publishing Co, Inc., Pittsburg, 1996.

Stone, R., "A Surprising Survival Story in the Siberian Arctic," *Science,* 303(5642): 2004.

Stringer, C., Finlayson, J., Barton, R., Fernández-Jalvo, Y., Cáceres, I., Sabin, R., Rhodes, E., Currant, A., Rodriguez-Vidal, J., Giles-Pacheco, F., Riquelme-Cantal, J., "Neanderthal exploitation of marine mammals in Gibraltar," *Proceedings of the National Academy of Sciences,* 105(38) Sept. 2008.

Strong, S., "The Most Revered of Foxes: Knowledge of Animals and Animal Power in an Ainu *Kamui Yukar,*" *Asian Ethnology,* 68(1), 2009.

Sykes, B., *The Seven Daughters of Eve,* W.W. Norton & Company, New York, 2001.

Szathmary, E. J. E., "mtDNA and the Peopling of the Americas," *The Journal of Human Genetics,* 53, 1993.

Tamm, E., Kivisild, T., Reidla, M., Metspalu, M., Smith, D. G., Mulligan, C. J., Bravi, C. M., Rickards, O., Martinez-Labarga, C., Khusnutdinova, E. K., Fedorova, S. A., Torroni, A., Neel, J. V., Barrantes, R., Schurr, T. G., "Mitochondrial DNA 'clock' for the Amerinds and its implications for timing their entry into North America," *Proceedings of the National Academy of Sciences, USA,* 91, 1994.

Tarasov, P., Williams, J., Andreev, A., Nakagawa, T., Bezrukova, E., Herzschuh, U., Igarashi, Y., Müller, S., Werner, K., Zheng, Z., "Satellite- and polllen-based quantitative woody cover reconstructions for northern Asia: Verification and application to late-Quaternary pollen data," *Earth and Planetary Science Letters,* 264(1-2), 2007.

Tattersall, I., *Masters of the Planet, The Search for Our Human Origins,* Palgrace Macmillan, 2012

Than, K., "Neanderthals, Humans Interbred—First Solid DNA Evidence: Most of us have some Neanderthal genes, study finds," May 6, 2010 for *National Geographic News,* http://news.nationalgeographic.com/news/2010/05/100506-science-neanderthals-humans-mated-interbred-dna-gene/

Tianyuan, L., Etler, D., "New Middle Pleistocene hominid crania from Yunxian in China," *Nature,* 357, June 1992.

Tong, H., Moigne, A-M., "Quaternary Rhinoceros of China," in English, *Acta Anthropologica Sinica,* Supplement to Volume 19, 2000.

Torroni, A., Sukernik, R. I., Schurr, Tl G., Starikovskaya, Y. B., Cabell, M. F., Crawford, M. H., Comuzzie, A. G., Wallace, D. C., "mtDNA Variations of Aboriginal Siberians Reveals distinct Genetic Affinities with Native Americans," *The American Journal of Human Genetics,* 53, 1993.

Vasil'ev, S. A., Kuzmin, Y. V., Orlova, L. A., Dementiev, V. N., "Radiocarbon-Based Chronology of the Paleolithic in Siberia and Its Relevance to the Peopling of the New World," *Radiocarbon,* 44(2), 2002.

Vialet, A., Guipert, G., Jianing, H., Xiaobo, F., Zune, L., Youping, W., de Lumley, M.-A., de Lumley, H., "Homo erectus from the Yunxian and Nankin

Chinese sites: Anthropological insights using 3D virtual imaging techniques," *Comptes Rendus Palevol* 9(6-7), 2010.

Volodko, N. V., Starikovskaya, E. B., Mazunin, I. O., Eltsov, N. P., Naidenko, P. V., Wallace, D. C., and Sukernik, R. I., "Mitochondrial Genome Diversity in Arctic Siberians, with Particular Reference to the Evolutionary History of Beringia and Pleistocenic Peopling of the Americas," *American Journal of Human Genetics*, 82(5), 2008.

Wagner, D. P., McAvoy, J. M., "Pedoarchaeology of Cactus Hill, a sandy Paleoindian site in southeastern Virginia, U. S. A." *Geoarchaeology*, 19(4), 2004.

Waguespack, N. M., Surovell, T. A., "Clovis Hunting Strategies, or How to Make Out on Plentiful Resources," *American Antiquity*, 68(2), 2003.

Wang, J., "Late Paleozoic macrofloral assemblages from Weibel coalfield, with reference to vegetational change through the Late Paleozoic Ice-age in the North China Block," *International Journal of Coal Geology*, 83(2-3), 2010.

Waters-Rist, A., Bazaliiskii, V. I., Weber, A, Goriunova, O. I., Katzenberg, A., "Activity-induced dental modification in holocene Siberian hunter-fisher-gatherers," *American Journal of Physical Anthropology*, 143(2), 2010.

West, F. H., Ed., *AMERICAN BEGINNINGS: the Prehistory and Palaeoecology of Beringia*, The University of Chicago Press, Chicago, 1996.

Wiedmer, M., Montgomery, D., Gillespie, A., Greenberg, H., "Late Quaternary megafloods from Glaial Lake Atna, Ssouthcentral Alaska, U.S.A., *Quaternary Research*, 73, 2010.

Woodman, N., Athfield, N., "Post-Clovis survival of American Mastodon in the southern Great Lakes Region of North America," *Quaternary Research*, 72(3), 20009.

Wu, X., "Fossil Humankind and Other Anthropoid Primates of China," *International Journal of Primatology*, 25(5) 2004.

Wu, X., "On the origins of modern humans in China," *Quaternary International*, 117(1), 2004.

Wu, X., Schepartz, L. A., Norton, C. J., "Morphological and morphometric analysis of variation in the Zhoukoudian Homo erectus brain endocasts," *Quaternary International*, 211(1-2) 2010.

Wu, Y-S., Chen, Y-S., Xiao, J-Y., "A preliminary study on vegetation and climate changes in Dianchi Lake area in the last 40,000 years," partial in English, *Acta Botanica Sinica*, 33(5), 1991.

Wynn, T., coolidge, F. L., *How to Think like a Neanderthal*, Oxford University Press, 2012.

Xiao, J., Jin, C., Zhu, Y., "Age of the fossil Dali Man in north-central China deduced from chronostratigraphy of the loess-paleosol sequence," *Quaternary Science Reviews*, 21, 2002.

Xiangcan, J., "Lake Dianchi," *Experience and Lessons Learned Brief*, final version 2004.

Xu, J-X., Ferguson, D. K., Li, C-S., Wang, Y-F., "Late Miocene vegetation and the climate of the Lühe region in Yunnan, southwestern China," *Review of Palaeobotany and Palynology*, 148(1), 2008.

Yahner, R. H., "Barking in a primitive ungulate, *Muntiacus reevesi:* function and adaptiveness," *The American Naturalist*, 116(2), 1980.

Zang, W., Wang, Y., Zheng, S., Yang, X., Li, Y., Fu, X., Li, N., "Taxonomic investigations on permineralized conifer woods from the Late Paleozoic Angaran deposits of northeastern Inner Mongolia, China, and their palaeoclimatic significance," *Review of Palaeobotany and Palynology*, 144(3-4), May 2007.

Zhang, Y., Stiner, M, Dennell, R., Wang, C., Zhang, Sh, Gao, X., "Zooarchaeological perspectives on the Chinese Early and Late Paleolithic from the Ma'anshan site (Guizhou, South China)," *Journal of Archaeological Science*, 37(8), 2010.

Zhu, R., An, Z., Potts, R., Hoffman, K., "Magnetostratigraphic dating of early humans in China," *Earth-Science Reviews*, 61(3-4) June 2003.

Zorich, Z., "Did *Homo erectus* Coddle His Grandparents?" *Discover*, 27(1) Jan. 2006.

No author designated. "Bone fossil points to a mystery human species," *USA Today*, Mar 25, 2010. [Three types of humans lived within 60 miles of each other in southern Siberia.]

WEBSITES

America's Stone Age Explorers http://www.pbs.org/wgbh/nova/transcripts/3116_stoneage.html (8/23/2010)

Ancestral Human Skull Found in China (80,000 to 100,000 ya) http://news.nationalgeographic.com/news/2008/02/080220-china-fossil.html

Ancient bison bones supports theory about Ice Age seafarers being first in Americas http://www.thaindian.com/newsportal/world-news/ancient-bison-bones-supports-theory-abo... (9/5/2010)

Archaeology and landscape in the Altai Mountains of Mongolia http://montilianaltai.uoregon.edu/ (1/30/2011)

Archaeology of the Altai Republic http://eng.altai-republic.ru/modules.php?op=modload&name=Sections&file=index&req=viewarticle&artid=20... (1/30/2011)

Archaic Human Culture http://anthro.palomar.edu/homo2/mod_homo_3.htm (9/9/2010)

Asia Map http://www.lib.utexas.edu/maps/middle_east_and_asia/asia_ref_200.jpg (9/3/2010)

Bamboo http://earthnotes.tripod.com/bamboo.htm (9/13/2010)

Berelekh Map http://www.maplandia.com/russia/magadanskaya-oblast/susumanskiy-rayon/berelekh/ (8/31/2010)

Chinese Fossil Hominids http://www.chineseprehistory.com/table.htm (1/17/2011)

Chinese River Dolphin http://www.nmfs.noaa.gov/pr/species/mammals/cetaceans/chineseriverdolphin.htm

Chinamap http://en.wikipedia.org/wiki/File:China_100.78713E_35.63718N.jpg (8/20/2010)

Chukchee Society http://lucy.ukc.ac.uk/ethnoatlas/hmar/cult_dir/culture.7837 (4/5/2011)

Chukchi Directions of time and space http://www.cosmicelk.net/Chukchidirections.htm (4/5/2011)

Chukchi Language http://en.wikipedia.org/wiki/Chukchi_language (4/5/2011)

Cro-Magnon http://en.wikipedia.org/wiki/Cro-Magnon (8/12/2010)

Denisova Cave (Siberia) http://archaeology.about.com/od/dathroughde-terms/qt/denisova_cave.htm (8?31/2010)

Dover Bronze Age Boat http://indigenousboats.blogspot.com/2008/01/dover-bronze-age-boat.html

Earliest Humanlike Footprints Found in Kenya http://donsmaps.com/erectus.html (9/11/2010)

Early Man 200,000 to 35,001BC http://www.telusplante.net/dgarneau/euro2.htm (8/12/2010)

Expansion of Homo sapiens http://amnh.org/exhibitions/permanent/humanorigins/history/expansion.php (9/5/2010)

Face of a Neanderthal woman http://www.femininebeauty.info/neanderthal-woman (8/23/2010)

First Americans http://www.nmhcpl.org/First_American.html (8/23/2010)

Four-horned Antelope http://en.wikipedia.org/wiki/Four-horned_Antelope (9/15/2010)

Geographical variability of mammoths in the Late Pleistocene http://www.zin.ru/annrep/2000/14.html (8/31/2010)

Geography of China http://en.wikipedia.org/wiki/Geography_of_China (9/3/2010)

Historical earthquakes in China http://drgeorgepc.com/EarthquakesChina.html (9/24/2010)

Historical SuperVolcanoes and Archeology Indicate Nuclear Winter Climate Models Exaggerate Effects http://nextbigfuture.com/2010/04/historical-supervolcanoes-and.html (8/20/2010)

Hominid Tools http://www.handprint.com/LS/ANC/stones.html (8/23/2010)

Homo erectus http://humanorigins.si.edu/evidence/human-fossils/species/homo-erectus (8/12/2010)

Homo erectus http://en.wikipedia.org/wiki/Homo_erectus (8/12/2010)

Homo erectus http://www.archaeologyinfo.com/homoerectus.htm (9/5/2010)

Homo erectus Survival http://www.archaeology.org/9703/newsbriefs/h.erectus.html (9/5/2010)

Homo neanderthalensis http://humanorigins.si.edu/evidence/human-fossils/species/homo-neanderthalensis (8/12/2010)

Humans wore shoes 40,000 years ago, fossil suggests http://www.stonepages.com/news/archives/002825.html (8/27/2010)

Hydropotes inermis (Chinese water deer) http://www.ultimateungulate.com/ Artiodactyla/Hydropotes_inermis.html (9/8/2010)

Ice Age Climate Cycles http://earthguide.ucsd.edu/virtualmuseum/climatechange2/03_1.shtml (1/29/2011)

Images of Neanderthals http://www.talkorigins.org/faqs/homs/savage.html (8/23/2010)

La Ferrassie Neanderthal Reconstruction http://s1.zetaboards.com/ anthroscape/topic/2448167/1/ (8/23/2010)

Late Pleistocene, now-extinct fauna of the southwest http://www.saguarojuniper.com/i_and_i/history/megafauna.html (8/22/2010)

Mammoth Fauna Map (Asia) http://library.thinkquestlorg/27130/ eng/3_4_1.htm (8/31/2010)

Meet the Neanderthals http://news.bbc.co.uk/2/hi/science/nature/1469607. stm (8/23/2010)

Mini Survival Crash Course http://sharingsustainablesolutions.org/ mini-survival-crash-course/(8/31/2010)

Mousterian http://en.wikipedia.org/wiki/Mousterian

Muntjac (barking deer) http://www.itsnature.org/ground/mammals-land/ muntjac/ (9/8/2010)

Neanderthal http://www.crystalinks.com/neanderthal.html

Neanderthal head flesh reconstruction side view http://australianmuseum. net.au/image/Neanderthal-head-flesh-reconstruction-side-view (8/23/2010)

Neanderthals Had Same "Language Gene" as Modern Humans http://news. nationalgeographic.com/2007/10/071018-neanderthal-gene.html

Neanderthals, Humans Interbred—First Solid DNA Evidence http://news.nationalgeographic.com/news/2010/05/100506-science-neanderthals-humans-. . .

Neanderthals more intelligent than thought http://www.msnbc.msn.com/id/39324819/ns/technology_and_science-science (9/24/2010)

Neanderthals Ranged Much Farther East Than Thought, Kate Ravillious for National Geographic News Oct. 1, 2007 http://news.nationalgeographic.com/news/2007/10/070930-njeanderthals.html (8/20/2010)

Neanderthal reconstructions http://www.daynes.com/en/reconstructions/neanderthal-4.php (8/23/2010)

Neanderthal reconstruction (Devil's Tower Child) http://www.ifi.uzh.ch/staff/zolli/CAP/Gib2.htm (8/23/2010)

Oldest American? Footprints from the Past. http://www.mexicanfootprints.co.uk/

Origins of Paleoindians http://en.wikipedia.org/wiki/Origins_of_Paleoindians (8/22/2010)

Pompeii-Like Excavations Tell Us More About Toba Super-Eruption http://www.sciencedaily.com/releases/2010/02/100227170841.htm

Primitive Humans conquered Sea, Surprising Finds Suggest http://news.nationalgeographic.com/news/2010/02/100217-crete-primitive-humans-mariners ... (9/5/2010)

Quaternary Period http://www3.hi.is/~oi/quaternary_geology.htm (8/31/2010)

Red hair a part of Neanderthal genetic profile http://seattletimes.nwsource.com/html/nationworld/2003975496_neanderthal26.html (8/26/2010)

Russia's North, Siberia and the Steppe http://fccorn.people.wm.edu/russiasperiphery/9d2b1087f7aa548c7fc56355b8decc66.html (4/5/2011)

Sacred Bones, Fields of Stones, Dr. Francis Allard Earthwatch Journal, October 2002, www.earthwatch.org

Savoonga artist to explore traditional native tattoos, Anchorage Daily News http://www.adn.com/2011/04/02/1788951/savoonga-artist-to-explore-traditional.html (4/5/2011)

Sea Grant research makes connections with prehistory http://seagrant.oregonstate.edu (10/2004)

Shamanism in Siberia http://www.sacred-texts.com/sha/sis/sis04.htm (4/5/2011)

Shiraoi Ainu Village http://members.virtualtourist.com/m/tt/52254/

Signs of Neanderthals Mating With Humans http://www.nytimes.com/2010/05/07/science/07neanderthal.html?_r=1 (8/26/2010)

Simple techniques for production of dried meat http://www.fao.org/docrep/003/x6932e/X6932E02.htm (9/27/2010)

Solutrean http://en.wikipedia.org/wiki/Solutrean (8/23/2010)

Special Report: Ancient Seafarers http://www.archaeology.org/9703/etc/specialreport.html (9/5/2010)

Stone Age Columbus http://www.bbc.co.uk/science/horizon/2002/columbusqa.shtml (8/23/2010)

Stone Age Site Yields Evidence of Advanced Culture http://history.culturalchina.com/en/51History9459.html (9/5/2010)

Straight-tusked elephant http://en.wikipedia.org/wiki/Straight-tusked_Elephant (10/3/2010)

Synoptic table of the principal old world prehistoric cultures http://en.wikipedia.org/wiki/Synoptic_table_of_the_principal_old_world_prehistoric_cultures (9/8/2010)

Tracing Human History Through Genetic Mutations http://partners.nytimes.com/library/national/science/050200sci-genetics-evolution.1.GIF.ht... (8/20/2010)

Transmitting the Ainu wisdom http://www.town.shiraoi.hokkaido.jp/ainu-tradition/yamamaru/index.html

Umiaq skin boat http://en.wikipedia.org/wiki/File:Umiaq_skin_boat.jpg

Volcanic Ash http://geology.com/articles/volcanic-ash.shtml (8/20/2010)

Zhirendong puts the chin in china http://johnhawks.net/weblog/fossils/china/zhirendong-2010-liu-chin.html

Zhoukoudian Relics Museum hppt: www.china.org.cn/english/features/museums/129075.htm (9/5/2010)

Made in the USA
Charleston, SC
04 October 2012